THE COLLEGE OF SORCERERS TRILOGY

BOOK ONE

THADDEUS OF BEEWICKE

LOUIS SAUVAIN

Book 1: Thaddeus of Beewicke
The College of Sorcerers Trilogy
© 2022 Louis Sauvain.

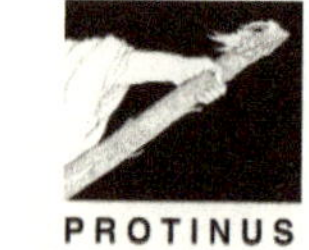

PROTINUS
Published by Protinus Press

Lingua Imperatoria translations: Laura Barnard, PhD
Development Editor: Barb Wilson, EditPartner.com
Editor/Proofreader: Barb Wilson; Peggie Ireland
Manuscript Editor: Janis Hunt Johnson, Ask Janis Editorial
Original Cover by Michael Yuen-Killick, Rainy Dog Studio,
Cover and Interior Design: Rebecca Finkel, F + P Graphic Design, FPGD.com
Maps and Illustrations: Sean Bodley, Mount Nittany Studio
Book Consultant: Judith Briles, TheBookShepherd.com

Books may be purchased in quantity by contacting the publisher
through the author's website: AuthorLouisSauvain@gmail.com

Library of Congress Control Number: 2022909388
ISBN trade paper KDP: 979-8-9859482-1-9
ISBN trade paper Ingram Spark: 979-8-9859482-2-6
ISBN eBook: 979-8-9859482-0-2
ISBN audiobook: 979-8-9859482-3-3

Fiction | Epic Fantasy | Teen & Young Adult | Sorcerers | Magic

First Edition
Printed in the USA

In memory of Joe W, who said:

Great literature is hard to do,

but most everybody likes a good yarn.

Contents

List of Illustrations

THE GREAT GLACIER
THE FROZEN SHALLOWS
THE WEST
ICE PORTS
THE IC
LAKE ILG
INFORN FOREST
ILGANZ
Somerset
GAGOELLE RIVER
ICCEN RIVER
N
NELDERN
NORDEN ROAD
Tarandon
NORDENNE ROAD
LAKE NILIN
THE NORZIL PLAINS
NORT RIVE
NORDENGELL
LUDIA
NORTHEAST
MIDINA ROA
PONTES PORT
LAKE NOREN
BEAST WOOD
TRAILIC ROAD
THE SEASIDE FOREST
TETHYS SEA
TOPE WOOD
THE HORN COAST
THE INNE SEA
LAPILL FOREST
MERNEN RIVER
TOPIAN
TECEN MOUNTAINS
Dorset Downs
TRESHWINN
PATI ROAD
PARI ROAD
SUT ROAD
COBBLY EKNOB
THE RED FOR
LEGEND
RIVER
ROAD
CITY/TOWN
MOUNTAINS
HILLS
FOREST
WETLANDS
BELT RIVER
WESTWALLIA
TUR
Glascoton
TURIAN RIVER
THE WALLIAN MARSHES
ADALANTINE OCEAN

LANDS
THE GREAT ICE WALL
IREZ
COLLEGIUM SORCERORUM
THE NORTHERN ROAD
NORTHIRST PEAKS
Walworth County
LANDS
ARX MONTIUM (MOUNTAINGAARD)
THE GREAT FLATSTONE RIVER
THE SOUTHERN CAVES
THE BARREN FLATS
BULCORAN FOREST
GAGDEN RIVER
BANNOCK
THE GREAT STRIUNN FOREST
MEF WOOD
LAKE CIRUM
THE GOLDEN RANGE
LAKE MARN
Copperville
LAKE GERNEM
THE
MERCEA
BAKEM ROAD
GREAT
MEKERN
MERNECA
NORTH
RIRGEV FOREST
ROAD
FREMOR ROAD
ARDENNIA PASS
THE GREAT BRAMILL FOREST
RIVER'S WOOD
MOORSTOWN
CITY ON THE PLAIN
BRAMILLEAN WETLANDS
BEEWICKE
MOORSLAND
LAKE THIAN
FOUNTAINDALE
CRICKLEWOOD
FRANTILLIA
IP WOOD
SCRALIA PASS
FRANTILLE ROAD
FRANTIL ROAD
THE GREAT FRANTILLEAN GRASS LANDS
THE GREAT FLATSTONE RIVER
BONEDELLUM SWAMPS
FROCEAN WOODS
FRANTILLA
Maritanius
VEXARE
BLACKCOVE
PORT STELLATUS
PORT OSTIA
FRANTILLAN SEA

Prologue

The Village of Beewicke, in the Farther Westlands

aughter filled the crisp autumn air as the young couple joined hands and ran up the gentle slope of the forest path. Reaching a small clearing, they fell into each other's arms at the foot of the ancient standing stone and embraced. The lush grass was soft under their weight. The old moon, *Luna Senex,* full this All Hallow's Eve, soared silently above. Gnarled trees surrounded them from the shadows, as if expectant. The youth and maiden shed their festive clothes and gazed lovingly at each other.

"Wife," the man said.

"Husband," said his bride.

They embraced again; each kiss more fervent than before. An azure glimmer from the sarsen reflected in their eyes. Warmth encompassed them as they coupled.

Once their lovemaking was completed, they lay asleep in each other's arms, blissful and spent in the shadow of the old standing stone. It towered above, pulsing with a faint blue light. The pulse reached out to them with a caress.

They were unaware of the circle of shining eyes from the surrounding tree line, watching quizzically, protectively.

~

Cedric wrung his hands as his wife cried out in pain. The village mid-wife had said it was going to be a difficult birthing.

The old woman chanted at the bed side of Hycynthya, and then pronounced, "The child is a storm coming and cannot wait to stir the first tempest."

Cedric clasped his wife's hand as if to sacrifice his own life for hers.

With a final cry from Hycynthya, a boy emerged. He came to join them on Mid-Summer's Eve. With a pleased smile, the wise woman informed them that this meant good luck.

Cedric's eyes flicked toward the ceiling, praying to the gods it would be so. After the baby's birth cord was tied and severed, he was gently wrapped and passed to his mother who gazed upon him with such wonder and love that Cedric felt, for an instant, a pang of jealousy—that is, until his wife turned her head and bestowed the same look on him.

"And what name will you give for the boy?" the old woman asked.

"Hycynthya and I have decided. We will call him Thaddeus," Cedric said.

"Very well." The old doula gave a solemn nod. "Then Thaddeus is the name I shall enter on the Village Tree. Yes, Thaddeus it shall be." The newborn seemed to acknowledge the old woman, still gazing upon him intently. "And there will be much work for this one."

Leaving Home I
Domo I

he weathered white-haired man reappeared from behind the sentinel elm and adjusted his garments. Tall and bony, his rugged frame suggested an austere life lived among the elements. His dusty robes fell to his knees, all gathered about with a wide, tooled leather belt. His sandals were laced in the knee-high, crossed-laced, Imperial fashion. And his eyes—should anyone take the trouble to notice—were of two different colors: one green and one brown.

Retrieving his staff from where it leaned against the trunk, he briefly surveyed the effects of the lingering drought of early summer, patted the tree, and smiled.

"There, now we are both refreshed."

Regaining the dusty road, Silvestrus shuffled over to his cart and affectionately rubbed the ears of his steadfast gray mule. "Asullus, my old friend, our goal lies but a short way over that hill, I trow, in the village of Beewicke. There you will get water, food, and a well-deserved rest. And I? Well, we shall see. So please lead us there with as much haste as you can manage; however, do not forget at least a degree of decorum."

The old man hefted himself onto the cart seat, jiggled the reins, and issued a command. The mule snorted and began moving at a plodding pace, resigned to further toil.

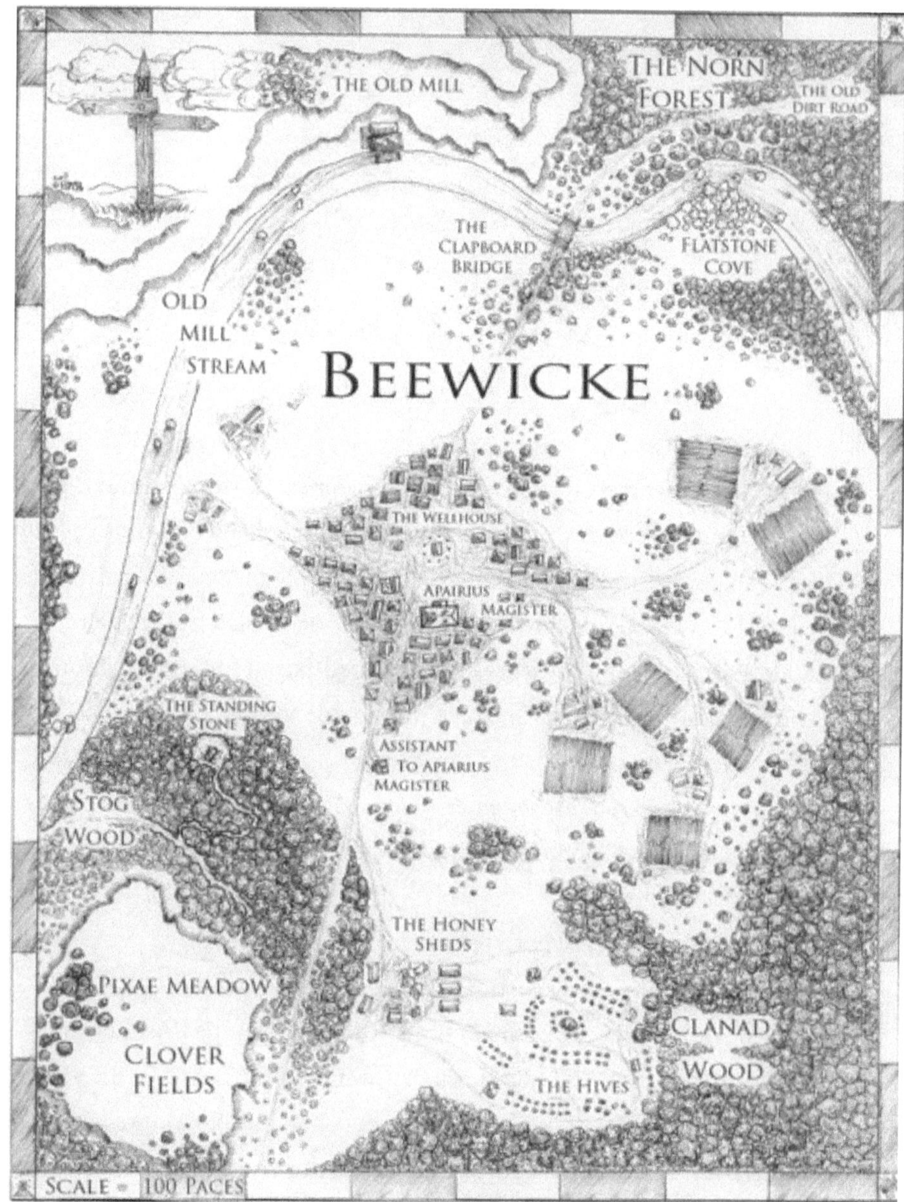
THE OLD MILL
THE NORN FOREST
THE OLD DIRT ROAD
THE CLAPBOARD BRIDGE
FLATSTONE COVE
OLD MILL STREAM
BEEWICKE
THE WELLHOUSE
APAIRIUS MAGISTER
THE STANDING STONE
ASSISTANT TO APIARIUS MAGISTER
STOG WOOD
THE HONEY SHEDS
PIXAE MEADOW
CLANAD WOOD
CLOVER FIELDS
THE HIVES
SCALE = 100 PACES

A splashing sound drew the traveler's attention. The old man pulled back on the reins and climbed down to investigate. "Wait here," he said. "I shall not be long."

The stream gurgled as it flowed over its rocky bed, forming small pools of backwater. The splashing sound came again, followed by the lilt of a whistled tune. The man made his way down the embankment and peered through the semi-darkness formed by a copse of overhanging willow tree branches. He beheld a boy holding a fishing pole, sitting on a large red rock lodged up against the bank. A nondescript hound sat at his side. The sun shone brighter on the embankment as a cloud passed.

Silvestrus nodded. He knew with certainty that this boy was one of those he sought. He pushed through the branches toward his quarry.

The old brown dog jerked his head, barking twice, and stood on guard. As Silvestrus approached, the hound sniffed the air twice, then quickly settled down with a whine.

"Ho, there, lad. How goes the fishing?"

The boy jumped to his feet as if confronted by an apparition. He stared hard, his eyes flicking warily. He calmed down when Silvestrus stepped out of the shade and into the light.

"Ah, fine, sir. I have two now." He patted a lumpy bag next to him. "And hopes for a third. They are of fair size, too, for trout."

Silvestrus moved closer to the stream's edge, surveyed the water, and then regarded the boy. He would be about fourteen or so and was sandy-haired and freckled. The old man thought the boy's eyes were green—green as river water—and his aspect was both earnest and curious.

"That sounds like success to me. Do you always have such luck with fish?"

"Why, yes, sir, ever since I can remember. My father has often remarked on this."

"Do you mind if I watch you, then? I would truly like to observe such a gift. Perhaps it might improve my own luck."

"If you wish it, sir."

The old man made his way over to a large rock opposite of the boy and settled down.

"Allow me to introduce myself. My name is Silvestrus, and I will share a secret with you. I am traveling toward Beewicke on a matter of some importance, though not of such import that I cannot take the time to learn something useful. What of you then, young *Magister Piscatorum?* What are your secrets?" The old man's glance sharpened.

"Secrets, sir? Of fishing? I mean, it's not just one thing. It's the weather and the season and the bait, and I cannot say exactly. I—" His voice trailed off as he caught the old one's gaze. "Well, it's not that hard, really. You just have to pay attention and be patient."

"I see. And your name, lad? If I may have it, that is."

"What? Oh. Thaddeus, sir. Cedric's son." He nodded toward the dog. "And this is Argus. He's my watchdog. My parents got him to look after me just after I was born."

"Very pleased to meet you, Thaddeus." The old man turned and nodded to the hound. "Enough eyes for your job, then, Argus?" The dog made no response. Silvestrus turned his attention back to the boy. "What is it that your father does, Thaddeus?"

"He's the assistant to *Apiarius Magister,* sir," the boy said with pride. "The Keeper of Bees in Beewicke."

"Are the hives good in Beewicke, then?"

"Oh, yes, sir. Beewicke is well-known for its bees and the quality of its honey. Have you never heard of it, sir? It's said our honey is very famous."

"Perhaps I have, now that I think on it. And do you favor the honey, then, Thaddeus?"

"Um, well, actually, sir, I think I've become rather tired of it, really. We have it quite a lot, and it seems the only thing folk from elsewhere know us for. But everyone says it's extraordinary, sir. My father has told me that the clover fields where the bees gather are blessed by the *Pixae,* and that's what makes our honey so good."

"Ah, yes, the *Pixae.* That would account for it, I suppose. So, tell me, Thaddeus, Cedric's son, do you believe the *Pixae* exist? Do you believe they are real?"

"Well, they must be, sir. I mean, if my father says they are. I've never seen one, myself, however. But everyone agrees our honey is the best, so it must be true."

Silvestrus noted Thaddeus appeared lost in thought for a moment, questions likely sparking inside him. Silvestrus was well aware he presented himself as if he knew things—things beyond the village—of the world. And to his eyes, Thaddeus seemed the curious type.

At last, it came.

"Sir, if you do not mind me asking, do you believe such things are real? Like the *Pixae*?"

The old man gave him a serious look and then gazed at the stream. He seemed to see something within it as if he found meaning in its depth. "Belief is a powerful thing, Thaddeus, perhaps a form of enchantment itself. So, do the *Pixae,* for example, exist only because some people believe in them? And do other things most folk do not see exist as well? Many people live in a world beyond just Beewicke, young Thaddeus. Who knows what may be found out there until one looks, eh? Now, as I have said, I do have a matter of importance to attend to. Perhaps you can do me a favor and tell me the direction to this Beewicke of yours. Is it far?"

"Oh, no, sir. You're practically there already. Just keep to the road and pass over the bridge. It's but a few moments further on."

"Thank you, Thaddeus. Are you fished out here—or is there another spot you favor?"

"Oh, I believe I'm quite finished, sir. I was sent to get dinner for my family. Besides, I don't think there are any more left as good as these." He indicated the two large bulges in his bag, one of them still quivering.

"Ah. Well, it is always good to feel certain of the future." Silvestrus glanced at the stream again. "Allow me to return your favor, however. You might wish to cast your line one more time. I suggest you try that eddy pool across the way, underneath the large willow there. Sometimes it is good to have an additional fish or two. You never know when you might be having an extra mouth for even tide. Fare thee well, lad."

"Yes, sir. I will, sir. And thank you."

Silvestrus rose to his feet and, with a wink for the dog, climbed carefully back up the embankment and strode to his cart. "Well, Asullus, I think the lad is not the only one to land his catch today. Let us make our way to this Beewicke and meet its good folk."

The old man clambered back onto the cart seat, checked the westward sun, and gave a short whistle as he flicked the reins. The old mule shook his head and began a trudge toward the bridge. From the river behind them, they heard a splash and a whoop of delighted surprise.

Silvestrus sat sipping a mug of honey-laced herbal tea in the sparse but cheery interior of Cedric's and Hycynthya's home. He gazed around the hut. Two pallets were laid out in one corner, a third in another. An open firepit lay at one end. Terra-cotta pots stood on the rough-hewn table, and a large kettle hung from a hook in the fireplace. Three clay lamps added only minimally to the room's meager light. The dirt floor of the hut was covered with clean rushes. One earthenware jar, larger than the rest, occupied a place of honor in the middle of the planked oaken table. Silvestrus knew it contained the local specialty.

The doorway darkened as Thaddeus skidded through the opening, animated and breathless. A moment later, the old hound rounded in, wheezing. He gave two warning barks for the visitor and shuffled over to the corner, circled twice, and settled down.

From the entranceway, Thaddeus called out, "Father! Mother! Look what I caught! I never saw a fish so big…and the others are large as well. And there's a traveler in the village! A Master Silvestrus. He's old and tall and—"

"Thaddeus," his father admonished. "We have a guest. Remember your manners!"

"I'm sorry, Father. I—" Catching sight of the old man, he turned toward him. "Sir, I am sorry. I meant no disrespect. I didn't know you were to be here."

The old man responded, "It is of no moment, my boy. I was able to reach your village due to your good directions and decided to seek out your parents to thank them for your excellent assistance."

Silvestrus sat forward and regarded the small family while he sipped his tea. He judged Thaddeus to be slightly taller than average, already the same height as Cedric, and not yet done with growing. He had a lithe frame that promised strength one day.

His father, on the other hand, ran to the stout. A stolid man, Cedric was dressed in the same type of tunic and jerkin as his son, but Cedric's hair and short beard were already showing signs of pepper-salt. His face was open and honest, like that of his son.

The boy's mother, Hycynthya, seemed a quiet, caring sort. Her hair was pulled back in an iron-gray bun held with twine. She was full-figured and dressed in the simple homespun smock that seemed to be favored by the ladies of Beewicke. Over it, she wore a patched and frayed apron. Cedric appeared to dote on her.

"And, I have come to ask a boon of them as well—a service, actually, that concerns you. If I may be so bold, it is something, I believe, that may have to do with your future. As I understand it, your parents are mindful of seeking an apprenticeship for you, yes?"

Startled, Thaddeus looked up. "I'm sorry, sir; you said a service that concerns me and my future—and an apprenticeship?"

"Why, yes, so I did. But first, as your village has no inn with an available room, your parents have graciously invited me to stay the night, along with my companion."

Thaddeus' eyebrows at once rose in question.

"I refer, of course, to my mule, Asullus. We have been together for many years, and for that, I name him companion. But we will discuss this matter of service later."

After an interval of pleasant conversation, they were interrupted by Hycynthya, who bade them come to the supper table.

Cedric cleared his throat. "Master Silvestrus, could I call upon you, if I might, to honor our humble home with a benediction for this even tide?"

"Of course. It is I who would be honored, Goodman Cedric."

The old man spoke briefly in a soft voice. He suspected the words were unfamiliar to them, though they appeared to listen to the invocation with reverence. Immediately following, Hycynthya served the meal.

The three freshly-caught fish, nestling in a bed of boiled onions, had been fire-cooked and garnished with herbs from the family garden. Accompanying the modest but succulent fare was a round of coarse dark bread, a modest wedge of white cheese, and a measure of honey from the gray crock. They washed it all down with thick, sweet purberry wine.

As the last of the juices were sopped up from the wooden trenchers, Silvestrus brought forth four large green apples from somewhere in his robes.

"Apples? In *Iunio*? That is a wonder indeed, Master Silvestrus," Hycynthya said, a note of awe in her voice. "How came you by them?"

"A simple matter of a preservation technique, my dear lady, that I was taught by my own Master when I was but a learner." He then produced a blue-bladed dagger with a worn leather handle from the same source and proceeded to core each apple in turn, passing them out to the delight of all.

After the dinner dishes were cleared, the old man turned to his hosts.

"Many thanks for an excellent dinner, Mistress Hycynthya." Silvestrus wiped his beard and hands with a frayed linen cloth and looked to Cedric. "But, to return to the service I mentioned earlier, Master Cedric, might I borrow your son for a time? It has somewhat to do with what you and I spoke of earlier. I have heard you have hereabouts a sarsen, one of the Old Guardians —what you would call a 'standing stone.' If it is not too far from here, I would ask, if perhaps, young Thaddeus could guide me to it? I realize it is late, but I understand sometimes these relics are best viewed by moonlight such as we have this evening. I have some torches in my cart, and we could use them to light our way."

Cedric glanced at his wife before replying. "Well, Master Silvestrus, Hycynthya and I know the stone you speak of—know it quite well, as it turns out." He paused and looked to his wife with fondness. "You might say Thaddeus and the stone are connected in a way." A small smile flickered across his face, then disappeared. "It's a bit of an odd request, but my son will not be a boy forever, and it is time he learned how it is to prove service to important folk. He will gladly direct you there."

Turning to his son, Cedric spoke. "Thaddeus, lead Master Silvestrus to the old stone he speaks of, then see he gets back safely. After that, to bed with you. The hour is late and the honey won't wait."

Thaddeus grimaced at the more-than-familiar phrase. His father did not seem to notice.

"Master Silvestrus, let me know soon enough if you need anything further," Cedric added.

"Thank you, but the lad and I will be fine. Please do not wait up for us, as we may be a while. Come, my boy, you can help me with the torches."

With a slight bow to Cedric and his wife, Silvestrus rose, gathered his cloak around him, took up his staff, and stepped across the home's threshold into the night. Thaddeus followed to find the old man rummaging through the supplies in his cart.

Silvestrus glanced at the boy. "You are quiet, lad. Is there something that troubles you?"

"I'm not sure, sir. I cannot understand what any of this means and what business you could possibly have with that stone…or with the likes of me."

Silvestrus found the torches and passed them to the boy. "Here, strike these, and we will have some light to brighten our journey. Now, Thaddeus of Beewicke, your father told me something earlier that was quite interesting. It turns out that your parents visited this very stone that we are going to see some fifteen years ago on a night quite similar to this one. In my travels, I have found that some of these stones have a certain *potestatem,* or power. Under the right circumstances, strange and unusual things can occur around them. I think this stone might be one of those."

Thaddeus handed a lighted torch to Silvestrus and kept the other one for himself. "Really, sir? Strange things? What would they have to do with me?"

"Well, it is said by the Wise that such power can often influence people and events for those who believe in that sort of thing. Some-times, if conditions are right, a portion of this power may even leech out of the stones into surrounding objects or people. Your parents were there at an auspicious time under special circumstances. That is why this may involve you. It is possible that this stone has influenced you in some way. And that is why I have come to Beewicke. I search for ones such as yourself. I want to know more about them."

Thaddeus looked mystified. Silvestrus expected his explanation sounded like some wonder tale the old men of his village were wont to tell when the boy was small.

The youngster spoke up. "But, sir, I know nothing of any of this. I would know if there was anything special about me, wouldn't I?"

"Perhaps so, perhaps not. How much does anyone really know about themselves—especially at the ripe old age of fourteen, eh?"

Thaddeus lowered his head and turned away.

"Now, lad, take no offense. I assure you none was intended. I only meant to say that we have a mystery here that may involve you. And such mysteries interest me mightily."

Silvestrus shifted the torch to his other hand. "All right, carry on, boy. The night is not getting any younger."

2

Leaving Home II
Domo II

With Silvestrus in tow, Thaddeus made his way South, past the offset area that circumscribed the beehives, reaching the end of the greensward and entering the meadow. Soon they reached the cleft in the forest wall that marked the beginning of a trail.

The tall boy halted to address the traveler. "Um, sir, once you look at the stone, will you be leaving in the morning, then?"

"As to that, if I am able to puzzle out some of this mystery tonight, and if it does involve you, I am of a mind to ask your father and mother about those plans of theirs for your apprenticeship. I may be able to offer you and your parents an interesting alternative."

"Um, an alternative, sir?" His head turned, shadows from the torchlight flickering across his face.

"Indeed. Perhaps you could accompany me, to your benefit, as my Apprentice. Should your parents agree, I could teach you about such mysteries as these and how to go about solving them. It would also allow me to learn more about whatever effect this stone may have had on you."

The boy stared at the old man with his mouth agape. "I'm to become your Apprentice? Here, sir?"

"Well, not here. At the school…where I teach. It is a place where other young fellows like yourself come to learn such things."

Thaddeus resumed his pace, peppering the traveler with questions. "You teach at a school? What is it like? Is it far from here? In Bostle? Or as far as Fountaindale?"

"My goodness, what a lot of questions. No, it is neither at Bostle nor Fountaindale. It is a bit farther away than that, actually. But it is a place where the mystery I have spoken of may be addressed and many questions answered. That is, if this mystery contains any substance. I believe it does, and I wonder now if you believe it as well?"

Thaddeus felt a pang of worry in his chest. He was surprised by the unfamiliar feeling. He considered the prospect of remaining the same as everyone else in Beewicke versus the chance of something beyond, as all very confusing. Different and opposing feelings tugged on him simultaneously. He hoped there was some truth to what the old man had said about the Guardian Stone—that it might shed light on the matter. And a part of him acknowledged this hope.

As Thaddeus opened his mouth to frame a further question, Silvestrus halted and peered into the gloom ahead. "Well now, this would be the place, would it not? Thank you for your guidance, Thaddeus. I believe I can go on alone from this point. Abide here. It will not be long."

Thaddeus felt a stab of disappointment and wondered why Silvestrus would simply leave him to wait. Despite his father's cautions, he had visited the stone dozens of times. But the careworn megalith had never seemed special to him. So why had this old man told him to stay behind? What did he expect to see that Thaddeus had never seen before?

Abruptly he looked up, but the wayfarer was gone—dissolved into the forest with nothing but the rapid dimming of a bobbing light to show the traveler's retreat.

Thaddeus decided he should follow along anyway. It was not as if he would get lost. He had a minor reputation in the village as a competent woodsman. He knew how to track his way about the village and the surrounding forest. He doubted this Silvestrus would detect him. Besides, if this business was something that truly involved him, did he not have a right—no, an obligation—to know all he could about it?

Overcoming his apprehension, he extinguished his torch. Stealthily he made his way up the path, easily following the old man's trace from the meadow through the trees and lingering at the opening to the small clearing that claimed the stone. Toward the back of a grassy knoll stood the well-worn megalith of giant's height. It was so black in the night that it seemed to absorb every drop of moonlight shining down upon it. Even the light from the old traveler's torch now seemed somehow diminished.

Perhaps because of a trick of light and shadow, the old stone now appeared to be outlined in a faint bluish haze to Thaddeus. He blinked, but the effect remained. He had never seen it as it appeared this night. It seemed to pulse.

How odd....

Thaddeus observed as the traveler, without hesitation, walked up to the stone and placed his left hand on it, murmuring several words in the same strange language he had used for the blessing of the meal. Suddenly, a ring on the old man's forefinger began to glow a brilliant blue—the same color as the haze that now surrounded the stone—but more intense.

The scene before Thaddeus seemed somehow familiar, though he would swear he had never seen anything like it before. After a moment, Silvestrus withdrew his hand, and the glow from his ring abruptly vanished. Still facing the sarsen, the old man suddenly spoke.

"All right, lad, I believe I have found what I came for. It is getting late. Do you not think we had better return to your home before your parents begin to worry?"

Thaddeus was chagrined. How clumsy must he have become to be so easily detected—but, more importantly, what did this all mean? Why had Master Silvestrus' ring and the stone both become blue? And then return to normal?

The old man turned, smiled at the young boy, and walked across the clearing to join his escort. Sheepishly, Thaddeus stood aside, allowing Silvestrus to lead them back to the *Pixae* meadows, where he retrieved, then relit, his torch. From there, the pair made their way back to the rough-hewn wood hut where his parents were anxiously awaiting them.

Despite his host's protestations, Silvestrus declined one of the sleeping pallets for his evening repose in favor of sleeping on his own bedroll near the banked firepit. He was soon asleep.

Thaddeus, restless under his covers, tossed onto his side. He stared blankly into the darkness.

What was that blue light? And how might it be connected to him? Did this stranger really mean to take him as an Apprentice to his school? Would his father allow this?

Thaddeus did not see how this was possible. He needed to know more.

The early sunlight was beginning to brighten the home's small space when Thaddeus became aware of voices. He eavesdropped unashamedly.

"...so you see, Master Silvestrus, his mother and I are getting on. And it is time—past time really, for Thaddeus to begin his apprenticeship with *Apiarius Magister.* We made the arrangements many years ago, you see, and it is expected. There is no finer work for the lad—your own craft excepted, I am sure—and it will give him a certain position in the village as well as a means to keep body and soul together. He'll be finding his own lass soon enough and wanting a family in due time. Of course, they will stay here with us. It will not be too crowded."

Thaddeus' brow furrowed, and he listened more closely as the discussion continued.

"And when the time comes, why, they can see us out and have the place to themselves and their children. That is the way things have always been done in these parts. Hycynthya and I have given it much thought, and that is what we see for him."

Thaddeus was well acquainted with this plan, having heard it regularly for most of the years of his youth—though more often recently. It had not particularly troubled him before. But now, with the arrival of the stranger and the blue light—whatever that may have been—this plan now seemed somehow confining. Something had changed, but he could not say what exactly.

He swallowed hard and continued to attend to the adults' conversation.

"Of course, good Cedric, that is clearly a well-thought-out aspiration with the best interest of the boy at heart." Silvestrus paused and, from the slurping sounds, it was clear he was sipping his morning tea. "I say, this honey is really quite excellent. However, from what you have said and from my own observations, there is a bit of a mystery about the boy. And it is a mystery that I am not likely to solve here, as I am sure you can understand. Though I have known you for only a short time, it is obvious that you and your wife have loved and cared well for young Thaddeus and want only the best for him. At the *Collegium*, he would be well trained and prepared for a profession of hard work, honest thought, and unstinting reward. And he will be at a place where such questions as those I have already alluded to can be delved into and their answers uncovered. I will also give you my guarantee as to his safety as well as his eventual success in the learning of a useful craft."

Shocked, Thaddeus' heart leaped. The old man meant to take him on as an apprentice!

His stomach clenched. He had never been away from home before —away from his mother, his father, from his good old dog, Argus— away from his friends, the village, from all he knew….

But his father would never consent to this. He felt an odd pang of disappointment at the thought. Thaddeus drew his blanket more tightly about him, anticipating his father's response.

Cedric spoke up immediately.

"Begging your pardon, Master Silvestrus, but we feel it is not right for the boy to fall prey to such strangeness. As I have said, his future is to play out here. Not in some type of far-off school. Not to be unfriendly, but we cannot abide this. I do not mean to be rude nor disrespectful, sir. You seem a goodly-schooled man and a decent sort, but this is near to foolishness. No, sir, this cannot be. Our boy must remain here and follow his path. It is our way."

Sensing the tension rising in his small home, Thaddeus shifted uneasily under his covers. A mixture of feelings churned inside him like an overstocked stew. Unlike the certainty of his father, he was now divided, with one leg in his old familiar home and another already on a dream road leading beyond the village and all that he knew.

Thaddeus' eyes peeped open to see a blue light suffusing the room, originating from the ring on the old man's finger. He was fascinated that the azure light was making a second appearance. It grew more intense the longer he gazed.

Silvestrus cleared his throat. "Goodman Cedric and Mistress Hycynthya, I know his absence could lead to hardship, so please allow me to leave with you a small amount to reimburse you for the expense of finding a replacement Apprentice. And to compensate you for a helper's position to manage the lad's chores during his absence."

To his astonishment, Thaddeus heard the clink of a sackful of coins. But how could this be? The man was only a traveler, a stranger—perhaps not much more than a vagabond.

His father gasped. "Master Silvestrus, we cannot take this! It's—"

"No more than you deserve to give up your son—your only child—at this important time. I assure you, good sir, I proffer it as a gesture of good faith and to ease your loss. Take it, please. I, ah, I see the boy is awake. No doubt he is also concerned about his future."

Shrugging off his thin blanket, Thaddeus sat up and faced the trio, convinced a scolding was surely to follow.

"Son," his father said, turning to face him. "Master Silvestrus feels you would make him a good Apprentice at his school and wishes to take you with him when he leaves. I am inclined to allow this. What do you say, lad?"

Thaddeus' heart hammered. Had his father not just said no? "I—I would like that, Father. But to be away, especially now with the collecting season coming on—"

"No worries on that account for you, my boy. We will make out, as we always have."

The first exhilaration of freedom thrummed through Thaddeus' veins. Then, unbidden, doubt crept into his awareness. Could he merely be trading one master for another?

He looked up to find the old man regarding him closely.

"Young Thaddeus, if you are to accompany me, it is needful that we depart this day—this morning, in fact. I will go and see to Asullus. Why not gather those things you will require for our journey and say your goodbyes? When you are ready, join me outside. But do not tarry. We have a long way to go, and the day is getting on."

Silvestrus turned to address his hosts. "Goodman Cedric. Goodwife Hycynthya. I thank you for the bounty and hospitality you have shared with a stranger, though I am, hopefully, a stranger no more." With a nod, the old man rose from his chair and went out to make his preparations.

An awkward silence followed. Finally, Thaddeus' father spoke. "Well, lad, it seems you will be leaving us now to start a new life. I never dreamed it would happen so. But the Gods sow as they will, and men reap as they may. Now, remember all the things your mother and I have taught you. Be wary of strangers and keep the family name proud. Come back to us when you can, perhaps during the summer. I—" He was overcome. "You know that we both love you," he whispered.

"Oh, my boy!" his mother cried and rushed to Thaddeus, crushing him to her ample bosom.

Thaddeus, throat constricting and eyes watering, was having difficulty saying, or seeing, anything.

"Goodbye, Mother. Goodbye, Father. I—I love you, too. I will make you proud of me."

"Yes. Well, come, Hycynthya. The boy has to get ready. You heard Master Silvestrus; he wants a quick starting."

Hycynthya nodded briskly, wiping her eyes on the hem of her apron.

Somewhat confused, Thaddeus glanced around the small house. He did not have that much to take: his knife, his walking stick—carved for him two summers ago by his father from the limb of an old forest oak— and his fishing gear, as well as a small bundle of clothes. That was all. He rolled them into a pack.

Cedric met him at the door. "Here, lad, you will be wanting to take these." He pressed three coins into his son's hand.

Thaddeus glanced down and gasped. "Father, I can't take these! This gold is for *Apiarius Magister!*"

"Never you mind, my boy. He'll not be missing it any." His father squeezed his son's fist shut around the coins.

Thaddeus was astounded. He had never possessed gold of his own before and had only seen it once, perhaps twice, in his entire life.

His mother came to him, holding a carefully wrapped package. "Here, my Taddy, I have fixed a small food poke for your journey. You are likely to be hungry. But be sure to share it with your Master, giving him the larger portion, as needs be."

"Yes, Mother, I will."

She embraced him fiercely and dabbed at her eyes again, then went to join her husband, who was waiting outdoors.

Thaddeus took a last lingering look around his home, then walked outside, shutting the door behind him.

Shading his eyes from the glare of the late spring sun, he found Master Silvestrus hoisting several bundles into the light dray as the mule waited patiently. Thaddeus walked to the cart and peered curiously at its contents. Wedged protectively in one corner was a large, slightly sticky stone crock with a lead seal.

The boy turned and knelt by his old dog, who had followed him outside. He rubbed the hound's neck, then hugged him close. "Goodbye, Argus. You've been the best watchdog ever. Now you must take care of Mother and Father." For his trouble, he received a face wash before the old dog lay down and closed his eyes.

Thaddeus' parents stood off to one side, his father's arm protectively around his mother's waist as if bracing them both for what was to come.

Silvestrus nodded. "Well, Thaddeus, are you ready?"

"Yes, Master Silvestrus. I believe I am."

"Good lad. Belief is the key, you see. It all begins with Belief."

"Begging your pardon, sir? Belief, sir?"

"More on that later, Thaddeus. There will be time."

He turned to the boy's parents. "Now, Cedric, Hycynthya, try not to worry. I know it will be hard, especially at first. I assure you, I will let no harm befall the boy. Thank you again for your hospitality and kindnesses. Fare thee well."

With that, Silvestrus shook hands all around, then climbed up to the cart seat and nodded to Thaddeus.

"Come, lad, let us be off."

"What? Oh, yes, sir." Thaddeus leaped up to sit beside the old man on the narrow bench.

He turned to face his parents. "Goodbye, Mother and Father. I will be back home soon as I may."

"*Prodi!*" his master commanded, and the mule, with a flick of his tail and toss of his head, set off down the path to the rough dirt road that led to the clapboard bridge over the Old Mill Stream.

Thaddeus looked back over his shoulder and waved until he could no longer make out the figures of his parents. He felt a growing sadness within him.

In Beewicke, at the home of the Assistant to *Apiarius Magister,* in a room no longer blue but now yellow with sunlight streaming, Cedric looked bleakly at his wife across a table upon which sat a half-empty pouch, surrounded by glittering coins spilling out from its throat.

"What went with our boy, Mother? Have we sold him off, then, for these little bits of shiny metal?" Cedric asked, tears coursing down the furrows of his dusty cheeks.

"No, my love," Hycynthya said, rising from her chair to move by her husband's side and placing her arm about his shoulder. "It was just his time to go, and he chose this way of his leaving, though he broke our hearts in the bargain."

"And so now, good wife?"

"So, now we must abide while our hearts heal, my husband."

3

Leaving Home III
Domo III

aster Silvestrus, his new Apprentice, and the old gray mule made their way through Beewicke's small collection of modest wood and stone dwellings and up over the bridge leading from town.

They turned east past the weathered, long-deserted mill and on out of the village, heading toward the Little Flatstone River. With time, the landscape gradually lost its familiarity. Thaddeus gazed back longingly, but at the same time, he felt a strange sense of certainty. He looked up to his new master.

"Please, sir, where is it we're going?"

"We will head east, then north, to the *Collegium*. Along the way, we will be joined by others, I think. But our route will take us first to Figberry, then Meadsville, Bostle, and finally, Fountaindale."

"All the way to Fountaindale, Master? That's at the end of the world!"

"Well, perhaps not quite so far as that, but far enough to begin with. We will pick up some supplies and other needful things there, strike out for Moorstown, and from that point head north, keeping an eye peeled for any…difficulties we may encounter as we journey."

"Difficulties, sir?" the lad queried.

"Ah, well. You are important, Thaddeus, as I have said before. That gives you a certain value, so to speak. There are always those who seek to interfere with that which is valuable. But, rest assured, while you are in my care, no harm shall come to you until we reach the *Collegium* itself."

Thaddeus nodded quickly as if he understood. One relieved concern, however, was immediately replaced by another.

"It seems a long way, Master," Thaddeus said.

"Yes, it is a long way. A very long way, actually." Silvestrus flicked the reins and nodded toward the gray mule. "Now Asullus here is not nearly so dull as he looks. He knows the way quite well. As I am indeed an old man, and I had a long night last eve, I find I require some rest. So, if you will be so kind as to take the reins, I will make a bed in the back and try to get some sleep. Thank you, lad."

He turned to the mule and spoke to it in that same strange language he had used in the benediction and at the old standing stone. The mule turned his head and uttered a word in reply.

Thaddeus, who had just taken the reins, sat frozen, his mouth open. The animal had spoken! Or had it? Perhaps he had misheard.

"Master Silvestrus—the mule! He…he just talked!"

"Did he now? Are you quite certain?"

"Why, yes. I mean, I believe so. I mean—"

"Well, lad, if that is what you believe, then it is likely so. Quite an interesting idea; do you agree?"

"Excuse me, Master?"

"Why, Belief, of course. Yes, quite interesting." The old man clambered into the back of the cart and settled down amid the bundles. He closed his eyes and, within moments, was snoring peacefully, despite the jouncing cart.

For a long time, Thaddeus stared at the gray mule's backside as it plodded along, its tail flicking the occasional fly. The animal seemed to have no trouble pulling the cart, baggage, and riders, though, despite his size. Thaddeus considered what he thought he had heard, trying to absorb the situation. Finally, there was nothing left for it but to ask.

"Excuse me, mule—I mean Asullus—but did you speak just now? I mean, can you speak, really?" His eyes fixed on the four-footed creature, Thaddeus was unsure he would receive a response.

Asullus looked back over his shoulder and regarded Thaddeus for a long moment. "Aye," he replied and turned back to the road.

Thaddeus fell back in his seat. "You—you *do* talk! How can that be? How is it possible? I mean, you shouldn't be able to, should you?" Words failed him.

The mule looked back at him once more. "Look ye, boy, I canno' watch the road an' talk at ye o'er me shoulder all at the same time. I might run into a tree or put me foot in a pothole. If ye wishes conversation, then get off yer hinder, come down here an' walk beside me. I do no' fancy a sprained fetlock on yer account."

At once, the boy scrambled down and strode forward until he was even with the mule's head.

"How do you…um, that is to say—"

"Ye boys do always ask the same questions. Ye'd think once in a while… Look ye, just ye listen an' donno' interrupt." The old mule snorted. "I was born toward the end o' the *Anno Cometae Magni*, the year o' the Great Comet, on a small farm in the Red Forest near the village of Cobbly Knob. No' so much o' a village it was, come to that. Smaller than Beewicke, anyways. An old witchin' woman there, Lady Lilith, she be the one as taught me to speak. So, after that, I always could, don' ye know, though she ha' told me often enough to be extra careful who it is I speak to.

"Then, oh, say ten years ago, Silvestrus, he shows up. 'Just travelin' through,' he says. An' he says he knows the Lady Lilith —tells me the two o' them go 'way back,' he did. They talks awhile, an' he comes o'er after, an' says 'Hullo' an' asks me how'd I like to come work fer him. So

I says, 'What's in it for me?' He says, 'Lots o' travel, lots o' interestin' people, an' lots o' oats.' I says, 'All right' an' came away wi' him, an' here I be, pulling a cart down this dusty road fer an old scarecrow an' some gawking hayseed.

"Anyway, 'fore I left, Lady Lilith, she warns me, 'Ye be cautious, Asullus,' she says, 'that Silvestrus is a Sorcerer, he is. Ye takes him in the wrong direction, an' ye're likely to end up yer days as a persimmon. But a good man he is, an' will treat you right…mostly.' An' that's how it is."

If Thaddeus was surprised before, now he was stunned. "A Sorcerer? Are you certain? I mean, with magicks and all? I thought—I mean, he seems so—"

"Aye, a Sorcerous one. An' one o' the most powerful as well. He's next in line fer *Princeps Academiae* at the *Collegium* if ye asks me. The College o' Sorcerers—that is where we're going, boy—'tis our final destination. Mayhap he told ye that already. 'Tis a nice enou' place an' all. Most o' the time, I'm in me stall there or lollygaggin' aboot the yard, grazin' the meadows, or blouzin' the ladies as come by. But ev'ry once in a while, he will come out to the tack room an' loads the old cart an' tells me, 'Well, Asullus, we need to go and get us some more likely lads. Are ye ready to go?' An' I says, 'Hell, no,' but I goes anyway. I think this is p'raps the seventh or eighth trip out fer me. Ye're the first one from 'round here, though. The Old Man's got some others to pick up on our way back, too, so he says."

"We're picking up others? Other boys?"

"Aye. Aye."

"Where are they? How does he know? Where does he find them?"

"That I donno' ken, boy. He just comes to the stable an' tells me, 'We're off!' an' off we are. The work's no' so hard, an' ye boys are no' so bad a lot as things go, though that one boy a few years back—a real pain in the ass he was, e'en if I does say so meself.

"Silvestrus dinno' always ha' a mule, though, ye know. He tells me he used to use one o' those centaurs, but that 'un dinno' like to be ridden much, an' they kept quibblin' aboot whether to go here or there, so the horse-man up an' quits. So here I be. I donno' argue so much, but I do eats summat.

"The Old Man, now, he ne'er complains. He's good company though he's always goin' on aboot how stubborn I be. But like I always says, people as live in glass houses should no' call the kettle black. I think we are s'posed to find the next boy in Meadsville, but I forgets the name. Ye lads are all pretty much the same—stupid, scared, an' pee in your beds at first. But ye all grows up pretty good. Most o' ye, anyways."

The trio traveled on in this manner, and keeping Shell Creek on the left, the small procession made its way down to the New Stone Bridge, which spanned the Little Flatstone River.

Once across, Asullus turned southeast, and the party headed into the Central Hills—usually a drier stretch of the country but greening up now. With Silvestrus at last awake from his nap, the troupe followed the *Via Prima* that led to Figberry.

Thaddeus had been to Figberry only once before. He had gone with his father to take a wagonload of 'Beewicke's Best' sent by *Apiarius Magister,* but he'd never been as far as Fountaindale. His mind was churning with new thoughts. After all, he was going to see the world!

"...so I says to her, I says, 'Well, sure, that stallion there might be a little higher off o' the ground, but if ye be talkin' aboot lanks an' shanks an' such, mind ye, then ye need look no further, Missy. I got all the—'"

Asullus' voice stopped abruptly, and he halted his pulling. His ears pricked as he cast his gaze back and forth among the nearby bushes and the low-lying hills. "Hold on, boy; there's summat not right here."

"What? What is it, Asullus?"

"Get ye behind me, boy! Master! In the bushes!"

Thaddeus, however, instinctively sprang to the cart for his quarterstaff. The next instant, sharp burning pains slammed into his left shoulder and right side, as an immense force knocked him over, leaving him crying out in agony.

Blinking back tears, he looked down to see two gray-feathered arrows protruding from his body.

Mother! Father! Thaddeus sobbed in surprise and pain.

Suddenly Asullus tossed his head in a peculiar manner and was free of his harness. He leaped off to the right, braying loudly. The mule's charge bowled over a man dressed in shabby clothing holding a bow. To Thaddeus' surprise, the old mule then reared up on his hindquarters and came down hard with his front hooves where the man's legs met. The man howled in pain, then vomited.

Asullus turned and galloped off, out of Thaddeus' line of sight.

Behind him, a deep and terrible voice intoned, *"Carlus, Illos Destrue!"*

Within the instant, a brilliant flash of light, accompanied by a great roaring sound, thundered in the glade.

From Thaddeus' left, a giant form dressed all in brown shambled into his line of vision. The figure stepped in front of him, facing toward two roughly dressed men who had just emerged from the brush, clad in forest green and armed with bows. The green-clad figures seemed initially surprised; still, they immediately began shooting their arrows at the larger figure.

Thaddeus stared at the big brown man—but this man was not like anyone he had ever seen before. The strange figure was tall and well-muscled, his brown color mottled like mud. His long arms dangled below his knees, each hand ending in razor-taloned fingers. He did not seem to be clothed. The head was squat and hairless, and he gave a guttural roar as he advanced on the hapless bandits.

The archer on the left dropped his bow and turned to run, but the creature reached out a long arm and snagged the sprinter's foot, sending him sprawling. The second man fired more arrows at the brown figure, but the brown creature backhanded him so that he rose in the air to land further on in a heap. The humanoid ambled over to the first thief, grabbed him around the neck, and dragged the struggling ambusher behind him.

As he advanced on the thief's fallen comrade, the second man desperately scrabbled backward from the huge figure. The creature, however, pinned him to the ground with one clawed foot, then squatted down. Casually inspecting the struggling man he held by the neck, he tore his arm off and began to eat.

Blinding pain now claimed Thaddeus, and he lost consciousness to the sound of the one-armed man's soul-piercing screams.

Through a fog, someone called Thaddeus' name, then once again. Slowly, he opened his eyes. Silvestrus stood over him, a look of concern on his face.

Thaddeus was no longer on the ground but in the back of the cart. His shoulder and side hurt, but less so than before. As he swam slowly out of the darkness surrounding him, he realized that his arm had been tied with a cloth that bulged and smelled oddly. His side had been bandaged as well. He found he did not wish to move. He was drowsy and, if not for the aching pain from his wounds, would have been content to stay exactly as he was.

"Thaddeus, lad, how fare you?"

"I'm all right, Master. There's only a little pain. What is it has happened, sir?"

"Ah, well. We are, I think, meant to believe that brigands attacked us—that is to say, highwaymen, common thieves. At least that is what one of them told me before he died from his—hmm—wounds. He said they had but recently taken to banditry, and we were to be their first catch of the day. He implied that they were not expecting much of a fight from a boy, an old man, and a mule pulling a cart—a cart possibly loaded with goods, and perhaps even treasure."

Here, Silvestrus paused, looked down, and scratched his beard. "But I am not certain that his tale is the truth. You see, I found these in the purse of the one whom I took to be their leader."

The old man reached into his robe and withdrew a leather purse. He opened it and held it so that Thaddeus could see its contents. There, sitting in his palm, lay seven bright golden coins of triangular shape. Thaddeus had never seen coins cut so. And, by the look of them, they were newly minted.

"Master Silvestrus, what are those pieces? I've never seen any shaped so, or so newly made."

"Ah, yes, Thaddeus. And that is because they are—how is it said— not from around here. Those are gold Centi-Dins from the Land of the Cin. They are triangular, as those folk are rumored to do most things in threes. And you are right, Thaddeus; they do appear to be newly minted. You have a good eye."

Thaddeus' brow furrowed. "The Land of the Cin? Where is that, Master?"

"Far to the East, my boy. Far, far to the East—quite beyond the Golden Range, actually."

"How, then, do they come to be here, Master?"

"Well, that is the question, is it not, my boy? That is the question. What are these coins, from such a distant place, doing in a supposed highwayman's purse on the road to the Central Hills? Hmm."

The old man stared down at the pieces in his hand, appearing lost in thought. Then he straightened abruptly, returned the coins to his purse, and looked at Thaddeus.

"As for you, you took two arrows—in your left shoulder and your right side—but the poultice and salve should help. As soon as you have rested a bit, we will be on our way to Figberry. I had planned to push on through to Meadsville by nightfall, but now I think it wiser that we dawdle, all things considered. I am going to have a look around. More of those fellows might be lurking about. Most likely not, but it is always best to be careful. No use having some unaccounted-for ragtag sneak up on you and open your neck while you are sleeping, eh? Now, try to get some rest, lad. Asullus here will stay with you."

"Thank you, Master. I feel sleepy, but I believe I'm well enough and have no wish to be a burden. I'm ready to leave whenever you wish." He began to doze off but regained his alertness with a start.

"Rest, Thaddeus. Be not troubled." The Sorcerer turned, spoke briefly to Asullus, and entered the nearby wood. Thaddeus' gaze followed the old man until he was lost among the trees. When he looked back, he sought for but could find no sign of the large brown man. Had it all been a nightmare?

"Well, laddie, how be ye farin'?" the old mule asked as he approached the wounded boy lying in the cart. "I saw those thorns they put in ye. Nasty business, but those lowlifes will no longer be troublin' decent folk in these parts—or any other parts, now that I thinks on it."

"I saw what you did, Asullus. You were very brave charging that man with the bow."

"Ah, think nothin' o' it, laddie. He got me peeved, was all. Imagine! Three people—well, two people an' a mule, that is— out on honest business, an' one o' 'em, a lad not yet shavin' regular. An' they goes an' wants to put slivers into us all. *Pfah!* What kind o' men would do such things? Well, they paid good fer their mistake, an' that's the certain o' it. Paid in a big way, I'm thinkin.'"

Thaddeus surveyed his bandages. They seemed to be rightly placed and tied, and he felt less pain than expected. He had once fallen into a prickle bush and made much more of a fuss over that than now. A vision of the seven golden triangular coins came to his mind. He was struck by how it had seemed to catch his master's attention.

"Asullus, the Master showed me gold coins he took from the purse of one of the robbers. They each had just three sides and seemed new. The Master said they were from the Land of the Cin."

The gray mule blinked several times. "Oh, did he now? From the Land o' the Cin, is it? Well, now, that be an interestin' bit o' news right there."

"Why would that be so, Asullus?" Thaddeus asked.

"'Tis more than an even bet no local brigand in these parts is to be havin' commerce with the likes o' the Cin. So, to account fer this, a body would ha' to say he either got those coins by robbin' a Cinnian just travelin' through the area—o' course, then, ye would ha' to ask, what was a Cinnian doin' visitin' in these parts—or ye might ha' to say these coins was gi'en to him."

"Why would anyone from Cin want to give coins to a highwayman?"

"Why, so the fellow'd do some task fer the giver, I say'd be likely."

"Oh? What kind of task, Asullus?"

"Hmm. Well, doin' away wi' a party o' three resemblin' us an' travelin' in this direction, comes to mind, immediate-like."

"Really? Who would want to get rid of us? We've harmed no one. Why would they do that?"

"I dinna know, to tell ye the truth. But I shall think on it now an', maybe, go ha' a chat wi' the Master. If we're to be dodgin' arrows an' such all the way to the East, then I'd like to be aware o' the process. Hmm. Interestin' that'd be."

"Asullus, may I ask you another question? About something else?"

"Ask away, laddie."

"You know, earlier today, when the robbers attacked, I thought I saw a sort of man. He was big and brown and ugly. And he looked like he was made of mud—or something like it. And he fought those bandits, but then I thought I saw him—"

"Ah, aye, I knows who you mean. But don' ye think on it, lad. Master Silvestrus says ye needs yer rest, no' summat else to stir ye all up."

"But, Asullus, please. I really do want to know. Who—or what—was it, and why did it do what it did?"

"Hmm. Well, I see ye'll no' be lettin' me go till I spills it, will ye? All right, but donno' be tellin' the Old Man where ye heard this. This is just 'tween ye, me, an' the fence post, aye?

"So, I told ye Master Silvestrus is a Sorcerer. Well, this do give him certain advantages in a scrap, don' ye know. This creature ye saw—an' make no mistake, 'twas no man, laddie— was a *Daemon Minor*, an' a mean 'un into the bargain. I always knows when he's aboot—smells bad an' makes me nose burn. I canno' pronounce his real name, though, so I just calls him Charles. Well, Charles's just like me—been working fer Silvestrus fer a time now. They two have some sort o' arrangement, I reckon. I think it's that he deals wi' the unpleasant folk, an', as a 'compense, gets to stay fer lunch if ye takes me meanin'—no' a pretty sight. Mostly, I donno' watch, but I ha' seen it a few times. I'll say this fer him, though; he's thorough. Also, ye know, the word gets around after a while. These days, anyone who's ever heard o' Master Silvestrus likely is aware o' Charles, too. Smart folk—meanin' those still livin'—knows as to avoid pesterin' the Old Man unless they wants to end up on the buffet. I think that's what surprised us today—these fellows was likely new at their work. Probably had no' gotten the word yet. Well, now they never will. Hope it was no' situation such as these men was starvin' an' could no' find work an' only took to robbin' 'cause they was desperate to feed their wee ones. I hate it as when that happens."

Silvestrus' abrupt return startled the pair.

"You will find, Thaddeus, that Asullus, here, is—beneath his leathery hide and in spite of his black heart—rather a sentimentalist. Sometimes it gets in the way, as he and I have had occasion to discuss from time to time. But there it is: stubborn."

The old mule snorted loudly.

"But, Thaddeus, I thought I told you to rest. Asullus, join me by that old stump a few paces yonder and let me look you over. An old mule with an untreated arrow wound somewhere would only slow us down."

The Sorcerer placed a gentle hand over the boy's eyes. "*Dormi.*"

Thaddeus knew nothing more.

4

Curls I
Cincinni I

hen Thaddeus next awakened, he felt much better and found, after testing himself gingerly, that he could sit up and then get up. Judging by the sun, it was late afternoon. With some effort, he carefully picked his way out of the back of the cart and slid down to stand, wobbly-legged at first, on the ground.

Silvestrus was sitting on an old tree stump a short distance from the cart, engrossed in conversation with Asullus. Neither had noticed him yet.

Thaddeus peered at the bushes where the bandits had hidden. Dark stains covered a wide swath of trampled grasses. He shivered as he realized what he was seeing. Just then, Silvestrus looked up and saw him. The Sorcerer rose and walked back to the cart.

"Ah, up at last. Good lad. How do you feel?"

"Well enough, Master. It hardly hurts at all. But shouldn't we somehow get word to my parents about what has happened?"

"Perhaps it would be better not to worry them over the matter at this time. But I am pleased you are feeling better. Well, there is not much more to be done here, so I suggest we pack up and head on to Figberry. We will stay with an acquaintance of mine there—a vintner with a large house. Exactly what we require."

The old man turned to the old mule. "Come, Asullus, time to be off."

Thaddeus rode in the back of the cart, one more bundle amidst all the other baggage, while Silvestrus sat on the cart seat, occasionally conversing with the gray mule and enjoying a pipe he had produced from somewhere in his robes.

Passing southeast, they left the last of the Central Hills and began descending the sloping terrain to Figberry. They turned from the grassland trail onto a country road, then followed it around the town to the north. The road eventually led to a large villa, beyond which were spread several hectares of neatly rowed grapevines.

With the setting of the sun, they pulled into a long, curving drive that wound its way to the villa's portico, and there came to a stop. Tall lattices outlining the entranceway were bending under the weight of cascading flowers in full bloom.

Gazing at the imposing manor, Thaddeus glimpsed the figure of a dark-haired young woman in an upper story window.

Ethne of Tarandon put down her curling stick and regarded herself in the mirror. She gave thought as to whether she should present as the lady of the manor or as Mistress. The pale young girl imagined what the other women would think if they but knew the truth. Perhaps some already suspected. She sighed.

There had not seemed to be much choice, she reflected. It was either die apace from coughing up bits of her lung or lose her life from childbirth. That was less certain, even though her mother had told her the old peddler woman had spoken with authority on this matter.

According to the peddler, a boy, handsome and tall, would someday come to her from the West, chaste and innocent. And at some point, the pair would unite their bodies and spirits together, later heralding the arrival of one who would change the world. Well, that was all quite non-specific, except that she was to "show him the way."

Show him *what* way?

That was always the trouble with prophecies. They could mean any of a hundred things at once—or nothing at all.

Ethne had held onto that saying over the years, though, through thick and thin, especially the thin. Oftentimes she wondered if her mother had seen her own loss in all this. She did not care to believe that. Nor did she care to think anyone knew what would happen once she was bequeathed to her uncle. Hah—he had not troubled himself long with her. No, not in the slightest. Summarily, she was sent off to the "special school."

It had been a school right enough and one where she had received quite the education—just not the kind a young girl would likely choose on her own.

Even so, the promise of the prophecy had sustained her until her emancipator—the vintner—had appeared. Ormerod was shrewd; she had to give him that, and sweet after a fashion; but otherwise, he was really just a client to her—or a mark, as Sister Cynthia would say.

Still, there had been something between them—at least to the extent that he was willing to bring her all the way from Fountaindale and establish her here in his home near Figberry, where she wanted for nothing. Nothing, that is, except love.

But she clung to the words: "a boy would come. And from him a gift; a gift that would change the world."

That would sound wonderful to anyone who had the time to wait, but she was in a race now—a race between time and her illness. And it was not certain which would prevail.

Turning her head, she coughed, yet again, into a red-flecked linen. Some days her ribs hurt so much she spent much of the day in tears. Verily, it was a race—and one she was not winning.

She fingered the glaze on the amulet hanging from the thin green brass chain around her neck. The white rose. Her mother said she had been given that to pass on to her daughter, but she never was specific about who had given it to her in the first place. She always felt comforted when she stroked it, though. Sometimes, on very bad days, she thought it gave off a scent she found soothing. And today—

Her hand sprang away from her throat. What had she just felt?

She collected her thoughts. Why, it felt as if it were a real rose! Soft petals…and there, the scent again, strong, very strong. That had never happened before. What might that mean?

A noise in the courtyard attracted her attention. It sounded like a horse and cart approaching. She rose and went to her window to look down at what she might find.

Her pale, slender arm moved slowly forward toward the gauzy, cream-colored fabric. The girl's graceful hand gently clasped the soft curtain and drew it slightly to one side. Her face, framed by dark curls, moved toward the window and gazed down to the courtyard, in time to see…yes, a cart, it was indeed —a dusty cart—and one drawn by an aging gray mule, not even by a horse.

The wagon pulled up and stopped near the manor's main entrance. The old driver, in robes as dusty as his cart, stepped down. In the back of the cart reclined a young man—several years younger than herself, if she was any judge. He appeared wounded, with bandages wrapping his left shoulder and right side.

Ah, they had been beset by bandits, she wagered. Ormerod often complained regarding them of late.

The boy was a comely youth, obviously country in origin, but in some distress. She would go to help him, of a certainty. But what an odd collection of travelers. An elderly cartman, a callow youth, and an old gray mule.

For the briefest moment, her eyes locked with those of the driver— an old man and a wise one, if she was any judge of humankind. And… was that a slight smile he gave to her so quickly?

Interesting.

At once, her mind flashed, and she started as if struck by lightning. The sweet smell of roses engulfed her senses.

Of course! *This is the boy.*

After all these years, it was the prophecy coming true. What else could account for this outlandish tableau?

But could it truly be this simple—and happening now?

She shivered. *So, it finally begins...*

All her life, she had been waiting for this moment. Well, she was ready. And, she knew what she must do, just as her mother —may her soul have rest—had told her, as the four old ladies had bidden her. She had always felt she had little choice in the matter, and so she became accustomed to the idea over time. But still, to see it happen now, after all she had been through. Well, it was all a bit of a shock.

Now, she must go and prepare. Yes, blue would be her theme today, and so, too, the room. She nodded at her decision as to how to proceed.

A frown of concentration replaced her smile as she turned back to her silvered looking-glass, underneath which paraded a line of jars, each containing a colorful powder.

Silvestrus clambered down from the cart, just as a fashionably dressed man in his middle years emerged from the building, shouting and waving his greeting.

"Master Silvestrus! Hail and welcome! How long has it been? How fare you? What on earth brings you to these parts? Can you stay with us for the Solstice? Where—"

"Peace, Ormerod. We were traveling from the West and were assaulted earlier today by bandits. One of our party is injured. I stopped here to beg succor."

"Oh, my goodness! Bandits, did you say? You know, I myself have had trouble of the same sort recently, with no few number of my own wagon shipments. I have sent several urgent missives to the Shire Reeve in Fountaindale requesting aid but have had no response, though I notice his tax agents appear always to be well-escorted. But here I am blathering on, and you have an injury."

"Not I, good Ormerod—my Apprentice. He is in the back of the cart. If one of the servants could perhaps aid us in getting him down and taking him to rest?"

"Of course! Of course! Annis! Gethin! To me! They will have him down jack-short and to bed. Ah, here they are. Boys, take the lad in the cart up to the green room—with care, mind you. He is injured. My, um, niece, who happens to be visiting at this time, has some skills in the healing arts. I will have her look in on the boy. But please come, please come…my, what a long time since our last visit. You know, it has been so dry this spring, not a drop from the clouds, and I am worried about my presses. You see…"

As Ormerod carried on, Silvestrus, on impulse, looked up to the villa's second story to behold a young woman with curled coal-black hair gazing down at him.

Now, who is this? he wondered. *Ah, interesting.*

Breaking his reverie, Silvestrus returned his attention to his host's complaints.

Noticing nothing beyond his own concerns, Ormerod escorted the older man into the villa, talking and gesticulating as he listed the misfortunes of the current growing season.

The two servants helped Thaddeus down from the cart and supported him through the columned courtyard and atrium, up a marble flight of stairs, down a richly carpeted hall, and into a large airy room filled with the deep reds of a waning sunset.

They placed Thaddeus atop a large pallet set on a raised platform, which they called a bed, despite his protestations that he could move under his own power. The elder of the two *tsk-tsk*ed over his clothes, then both left the room.

Thaddeus had never seen a room so large and splendid, nor any furnishings so ornate. Vases and amphorae filled with bright blue flowers were everywhere. Some things, however, puzzled him as to their purpose, like the large copper cauldron in one corner with a lidded box, about chair height, placed in the opposite nook.

Within moments, a middle-aged woman came in with a tray holding a moisture-beaded, gray pitcher with a matching cup. The woman placed the tray on a table by the bed. As the stern servant straightened, a younger maid, who Thaddeus guessed might be her daughter, entered with another tray, but this one held food—Thaddeus could tell from the aroma. She nodded to him.

"This is a meal plate, boy, but you are to wait on having at it," she instructed, setting the tray on the nearby table. "The Lady will be in shortly to see to this and your other needs." A slight frown of disapproval crossed her face but was gone in a trice.

The two women filed out quietly, and Thaddeus was left to his own devices. He wanted to explore the tray and see what lay beneath the bleached linen, but he hesitated. He was unused to being waited on and was unsure how to proceed.

A slight cough made him look up. A willowy young woman stood in the doorway.

All of a sudden, and without explanation, his face flushed; he was without breath and aware of a distinct thumping in his chest. As he had been trained to do, he stood up immediately.

He had never seen anyone so beautiful. The woman was slim and pale, with dark hair in ringlets that tumbled down over her shoulders to her waist. She had what appeared to be some type of paint on her face—red lips and cheeks, blue eyelids, and black lashes. And she was dressed in a gown of sky blue, the style and composition of which Thaddeus could not fathom. Around her slender neck was what appeared to be a white rose suspended in an oval frame, hanging from an old brass chain. It must have been well-crafted; it looked so real.

She glided toward Thaddeus with a grace that made his heart ache.

"Hello, boy. You are the old Sorcerer's Apprentice, are you not? I see the servants have brought you your food. When you eat, I advise that you do so sparingly. You have taken a great hurt today, as I understand it, and temperance is best for now."

Thaddeus could only stare stupidly.

"Do you speak?" she asked pointedly.

"I, um, yes ma'am. I mean, miss. I—uh… You are beautiful!" he blurted. Immediately, Thaddeus' visage matched the red of the setting sun.

The girl, who Thaddeus judged, when he was able to think again—to be only a few years older than himself—laughed a bright, silvery laugh. Her teeth were white, albeit uneven. But, no matter. It was a wondrous smile.

Thaddeus' heart melted.

"Why, thank you. And you are?"

"Oh. Thaddeus, miss. From Beewicke." Now, why had he said that—his flyspeck of a village, to this Imperial princess? *Cow's dung!*

She smiled. "Ah, 'tis where we have our honey from. It is very good. Do you enjoy it, Thaddeus?"

"Why, that is…well, everyone says so. I, uh—" Blood coursed hotly through his cheeks, but the girl spoke on.

"Ah. Well, Thaddeus, you may call me Ethne. Everyone does."

Everyone? Other boys? He would kill them all. Or the Daemon Charles could, and he would watch. He was surprised at the level of passion that flared inside him.

He swallowed. "That's a pretty name."

"Thank you again, Thaddeus. I am niece to Master Ormerod. He has sent me to tend to your hurts. I have some knowledge of the healing arts from my days in Fountaindale."

Fountaindale? That was where his master had said they were to go. The girl was from the end of the world! He wondered why she had come all the way out to this place.

"Now, Thaddeus, as it is needful that I see to your injuries, please put aside your clothes. They will be cleaned and returned to you after, or perhaps replaced. Yes. For now, remove your tunic, and I will examine your wounds."

Thaddeus sat stock still, unable to move. Was she serious? At last, he obliged, slipping the careworn and patched garment up over his shoulders and placing it carefully on a nearby chair.

"Come, Thaddeus, seat yourself on the bed here as you were. Now, just lie down on your back. This will not take long. And Thaddeus, your teeth are one of your good points, but they surely need scrubbing, and I do not need to see them always."

He instantly snapped his mouth shut and reddened further.

Thaddeus did all Ethne instructed, wondering just what she was about to subject him to, then decided she could do whatever she wished —remove his liver, for example. As she drew near him to begin her survey, he caught her scent and was again transported. She reached out her delicate hands and, after having him remove his trousers and short clothes as well, gently probed his body from head to foot.

After removing his bandages, she wiped clean the skin where the poultices had rested. Next, she withdrew several fresh leaves of a plant

Thaddeus could not identify from her belt pouch and placed them over his wounds, softly murmuring some words to herself. By the end of her ministrations, Thaddeus felt himself near the point of spontaneous combustion.

Ethne indicated a modest robe draped over the back of one of the chairs and signaled that he should put it on. He did so, then waited patiently.

"How strange. Those wounds seem but star points, nearly healed. Hmm. Not what I had expected from the old Sorcerer's report. I had less to do than I thought. Otherwise, you seem healthy as a young bull."

Thaddeus noticed she was thin—thinner than he had first thought—and really quite pale. Every so often, she removed a small linen from her pouch, turned her head, and coughed delicately into it. Once, after a particularly intense spell of coughing, she wiped away a drop of red spittle from the corner of her mouth. He became alarmed for her.

"Are you not well, Ethne?" he asked.

"It is the consuming sickness, I fear. I had it when I first met Master Ormerod. It was one of the reasons he brought me here. I think he felt the sun and breezes from the Central Hills would be felicitous for my health."

"When you first met him? I thought he was your uncle."

"Ah, Thaddeus, he is not my blood relation. Rather, we first met in Fountaindale, perhaps a year ago. He was there on business—a wine delivery, I believe. We spent some time together, and he offered to bring me here. He seems to care for me, treats me well, and provides for all my needs. It is customary for a girl such as I to refer to her benefactor as 'uncle.'"

Thaddeus nodded as if he understood what she meant.

Ethne looked down to her hands in her lap for a moment, then back up at Thaddeus as if judging something.

"Now, Thaddeus, you are from what we would call the backcountry. More importantly, you are now the Apprentice of a wise and powerful man. You would not wish, through a misdeed on your part, to embarrass him, would you?"

She did not wait for him to answer. "I thought not. Customs and manners differ widely, it is true, but you will be traveling in higher circles now and must need act in accordance. I am not required for a time, so let me teach you something of how to go about the business of creating a good impression when you are in society and, thus, bring credit to your Master."

The instruction proceeded for some time, with stops and starts for questions, demonstrations, and practice. Thaddeus' eagerness to please the young woman smothered the perplexity he might have felt under any other tutelage.

Yet he was also hungry and eyed the food tray with great interest. Seeing his gaze, his teacher smiled. The lessons, then, turned to the table.

"Here, Thaddeus, sit up now and let me see you eat. Begin with some of this broth." She stood back and removed the cloth from the food tray.

Thaddeus did as he was told, but his eyes never left her. Ethne took a seat nearby and observed his efforts patiently. Finishing the last mouthful, he belched appreciatively.

"Hmm," the girl responded.

The instruction then progressed to matters of hygiene, to attire and its use, and, finally, to social intercourse. By repose, his head was spinning. But he was an apt pupil and eager to excel.

At last, she turned to him. "You have done well, Thaddeus. If you practice what I have taught you, you run little risk of being turned out or receiving a cuff for your troubles. But I require rest now, and you need it as well. I will be by to see to your needs in the morning."

Heartbroken and yet buoyed by her promise, he watched her leave. As predicted, the serving women returned in minutes with two changes of clothes, retrieved his meal tray, and left the room. Thaddeus examined what they had left: quite the finest things he had ever seen. He put them carefully in the armoire for use in the morning.

With little else left to do, he doused all the candles in the room and climbed gratefully into the bed. The fresh scent and soft feel of his bedclothes were almost intoxicating. He closed his eyes but was, at first, sure the night would be unending.

Thoughts of home occupied him for a time, but soon enough, his feelings raced back to Ethne. *So beautiful.*

His concentration moved from a sense of loss to, inexplicably, those feelings which became rousing and troublesome…before exhaustion finally caught up to him and dragged him off to sleep.

5

Curls II
Cincinni II

Thaddeus eased awake with several blinks. His wounds seemed much better, though he felt a trifle guilty about lying abed so late in the morning—surely, many chores needed to be done. Again, it dawned upon him that he was indeed far from home. Sunlight falling on the fields outside the window gave him the time of day.

Stretching, he inhaled the fragrance of dozens of flowers the color of butter placed in various vases about his room. He ran his hand over the snowy linens, plump headrest—a "pillow," Ethne had called it—and filled with real goose feathers. At that moment, he felt himself an equal in luxury to any High King.

His mind wandered back to his beautiful visitor from the previous day. Ethne—so beautiful, so wonderful… If only he were a Sorcerer, he would wish her here in an instant.

A knock came at the door, which then slowly swung open. And there she was, the object of his heart. Coherent thought left him. Today she was dressed crown to heel in yellow.

"Thaddeus, I am returned as I promised. Fare you well this day?"

"Yes, miss—I mean, Ethne. I feel quite well. I hope you do as well."

"Yes, all things considered. Now I have come to continue your instruction. Have you finished your morning functions?"

ORMEROD'S VINEYARD

Thaddeus appeared disarmed by the question. "My functions?"

She raised an eyebrow. "Thaddeus—have you used your chamber pot? You will recall we spoke of this last night."

"Oh, yes, that. Uh, no. Not yet."

"Then will you please do so? I will wait outside the door for a few moments."

Thaddeus jumped up from the bed and hurried to the box-shaped chair in the corner. This was a new situation. He'd never before had to produce at someone's demand; he hoped he would be able to do well. After he finished, he used the cloths lying close by to cleanse himself as he had been taught and closed the lid. He put his robe back on and stood doubtfully in the middle of the room, waiting.

The door opened again, and Ethne entered, followed by the two women servants from the previous evening. One carried a tray of food, while the other had several folded towels and a variety of stoppered bottles in a wicker basket.

Lallie, the younger of Ethne's servants, placed the tray on the bedside table and stood waiting. The older servant, Morella, went to the chamber pot, pulled it away from the wall, and removed the bowl. She covered it with a towel and put a new one in its place. Opening one of the bottles, she sprinkled a portion of its contents on and around the chair. Leaving the remaining bottles by the commode, she gestured to her companion and left the room after a curt bow to Ethne.

Thaddeus eyed the covered tray eagerly. He looked to Ethne, however, for a cue on how to proceed. He did not want to put a clumsy foot forward with her now.

"Wait, Thaddeus. You will eat soon enough, but ablutions come first."

He was unsure of her meaning but began to get an idea as Ethne walked to the door and called down the stairs. Soon, the two housecarls from the courtyard, Annis and Gethin, trudged in with steaming buckets of water which they poured into the large copper kettle. Several trips were required before it was more than halfway full. Once the men had departed, Ethne retrieved two of the deep-blue stoppered bottles and poured their contents into the hot tub.

She looked at him critically. "Now, Thaddeus, it is time for you to bathe."

Thaddeus had certainly heard the term before, but it had always referred to a weekly command from his mother to go down to the river, plunge in, and roll over at least twice. Although it was usually pleasant, it was occasionally difficult to endure, especially in the months of dead winter.

This situation, however, was quite different.

"Uh, Ethne, how do I—?"

"Remove your clothing, Thaddeus, and step into the tub."

"Oh. All right." He blushed but did as he was bid, though he took the precaution of facing away from his Mistress of Instruction, gazing instead out the window at the workers toiling in the vineyards.

The water was hot and, settling in slowly, he soon felt like one of his mother's stew onions. It was a process that took time. Finally, he sat in the tub up to his neck with steam rising around him on all sides. However, the water proved soothing, the smells agreeable, and the bubbles pleasing. This new experience might not be too bad after all.

Suddenly a splash behind him and water sloshed over the edge of the tub.

He was no longer alone.

With a cry, he sprang up, then realized he should have stayed seated.

"Ethne! Wha—"

"Thaddeus. Sit down. You'll catch your death. There is no point in wasting hot water, and I need to bathe as much as you. Well, not quite as much, but still… Have you never taken a bath with a girl before? A sister, perhaps, or a village friend?"

"Well, yes…I mean, no. I have no sister. My mother used to take me to the river with her when I was young. And later, some of us would go with the other children while the mothers watched. But that was years ago. Now it's just me and my friends…or just me. But—"

"Would you prefer I leave?"

"No! Never! I mean, please don't leave on my account."

"All right, then. Now, Thaddeus, please turn around. It is awkward talking to your back, and I have some things to show you."

He accomplished the complex maneuver, managing to remain submerged from the neck down, though more water was lost over the side in the process. He was nervous about what he would see, but Ethne, too, was up to her chin in the cloudy water. However, his relief was followed by a stab of disappointment.

"Take your ease, Thaddeus. This will not be painful, I promise you. It is, after all, just another part of your education. Now, this is called a washing cloth, and you use it in this way…"

Finally, Ethne stood, then bent over, holding her long wet hair back with her hands, and brushed Thaddeus' cheek with her lips. "You are very sweet, Thaddeus. But now I must leave you. It will take me some time to dress this…" she said, gesturing at her mass of black curls.

"You may get out and dry yourself with the towels, then have some break-fast. Eat sparingly, though. We will have mid-day soon, and you will want to save room for that. Morella and Lallie will be back with some fresh clothes for you."

With that, she stepped out of the tub, wrapped herself in one of the large linens, retrieved her gown and other garments from where they lay on the floor, and moved to leave the room.

All bemused, Thaddeus remained in the tub for a time. Clearly, something had changed—exactly what he was not prepared to say. But now he knew of love. He had lately taken to wondering what such a state would be like, but these speculations, he realized, were as an ember to a forest in full conflagration.

Lazily he rose and stepped over the rim of the cauldron, picked up a linen, and strolled over to his pallet. Wrapping himself in the towel, he sat on the edge of the bed, pulled the table with the food tray toward him, and removed the cloth cover. Before him was a selection of fresh fruit—including purberries, of course—cheese, crusted bread, and a carafe of fresh goat's milk. He ate without hurry, occasionally pausing with food halfway to his mouth to relive certain moments of this glorious morning.

Toward the end of the meal, he was interrupted by the return of the serving women, one of whom removed his tray while the other laid out several garments for him. He had never before had such finery, although Morella referred to them dismissively as "cast-offs."

Recalling Ethne's gentle instruction from the night before, he brushed his teeth with salt, using a twig from the scrub bush, and chewed the mint leaf provided. Then, dressed in his new finery, he spent the intervening time until mid-day gazing out the window, drinking in the pastoral scene as if it were a mellow wine.

Eventually, a knock on the door revealed Annis, who called him for the mid-day meal, and whom he followed downstairs to the dining hall where he was greeted by Master Ormerod and Master Silvestrus—both of whom were solicitous concerning his health. He took the seat indicated by the older servant at the long table adorned by extravagant bouquets of lavender.

Within moments, Ethne made her entrance, stunning in a deep, purple gown—in honor of her uncle, Thaddeus assumed.

The meal was sumptuous by any standard—with venison, pickles, a light purberry vintage, mushrooms, and chicken. A rich pudding and a mixture of fresh vegetables completed the fare. It was all wonderful, even if some items were unfamiliar. However, he kept his gaze firmly fixed on Ethne, who shook her head ever so slightly when he picked up the wrong utensil and nodded when he chose correctly.

The only blemish on the day occurred when the cook came out from the kitchen with a large, polished tray which—with many *oohs* and *ahhs* from the other diners—she placed before Thaddeus. On the silver platter rested an ample round of white bread, a stone crock of fresh butter, and an entire honeycomb on porcelain.

Ormerod beamed as he announced to one and all, "I had it brought up from Beewicke this very morning, especially for our guest, young Thaddeus. There is nothing like a taste of home to aid in one's speedy recovery, as I always say."

Thaddeus smiled weakly as his fellow diners offered polite applause. Silvestrus, seated in the place of honor, covered his mouth and turned away as if to cough, but he could not disguise the twinkle in his eye.

As he was finishing his repast, Thaddeus took greater note of the people around him. Though Ethne had favored him with a wink or secret smile when no one was looking, it was to Ormerod that she gave the majority of her attention. The successful vintner, in turn, hardly took his eyes from her. Clearly, his "niece" was the light of his life, and Thaddeus was having trouble with his feelings about the situation.

On the one hand, Master Ormerod was his host and had thoughtfully provided him—a stranger and lowly Apprentice—with all manner of courtesy, care, and resource. And, certainly, the man had first claim to the feelings of loyalty and gratitude that the young woman bestowed upon him.

On the other hand, Thaddeus' chest was near to bursting with his own feelings of longing and adoration for the vintner's dark-haired beauty. He was also aware of intense jealousy and resentment at the attention Ethne showed the older man. Despite the respect for his elders his parents had instilled in him, reconciling this emotional dilemma was proving quite beyond him at the moment.

A *harrumph* from Silvestrus brought his awareness back to his immediate surroundings, and he stood with the others at the signal that the meal was ending. Silvestrus offered expressions of gratitude to Master Ormerod and a blessing on the house, on its members and lands, and particularly on the health and vitality of the current purberry vintage.

As the diners dispersed, Silvestrus bade Thaddeus follow him over to their host. The old man personally thanked the vintner for his hospitality, and Thaddeus gritted his teeth long enough to add the few lines of praise he could muster. Master Ormerod appeared pleased and bowed several times in acknowledgment.

Now that Ethne had declared Thaddeus fit to travel, Silvestrus made plans to resume their journey immediately. The vintner generously instructed his steward to provision the cart with what remained of the mid-day meal. Thaddeus was relieved to note that sufficient passes around the table had depleted the honeycomb to the point that not enough remained to be included in the parcel.

Leaving the dining hall, Thaddeus followed the Sorcerer out of the entranceway to where Asullus stood patiently, already hitched to the cart. He had been brushed and attended to assiduously, judging from how pleased with himself he seemed to be. Someone had even provided him with a garland of large white flowers that were draped around his neck—well, it was, after all, almost Mid-Summer.

The servants placed several additional bundles in the back of the cart as Thaddeus stood by, feeling useless. A wave of melancholy swept over him as he realized he would soon be separated from Ethne. He did not care for the feeling at all.

"Thaddeus." The whispered call came from the shadows of the villa's south wall next to the winery. He recognized the voice and immediately made his way to Ethne's side.

"Ethne, I—"

She pressed a finger to his lips. "Shhh. Dear Thaddeus, I know it will be hard for you for a time, but we must part now. I want—" She stopped abruptly, withdrew her linen from her belt, turned her head, and coughed several times. Drawing a shaky breath, she turned back to him.

"I want you to know I will think about you always, and I know you will, in time, become a wise and wonderful Sorcerer."

"Sorcerer? Why do you say I am to become a Sorcerer? Master Silvestrus is the Sorcerer, not I. He said only that he wished me to come with him to his school in order to study a mystery."

Ethne smiled, and the sun blazed forth more strongly than ever. "Thaddeus, Master Silvestrus takes boys to the *Collegium,* so he can teach them to become Sorcerers. And I know you will make a very good one. Well, it is time for you to go." She handed him a small packet. "Here, take this. It is to remind you of me if you wish it. When you tire of it, just cast it away."

"Never! I would never throw away anything you have given me."

She smiled again. "It is time now, Thaddeus. Be well always." She placed her small hand around the back of his neck, drew down his head, and kissed him full on the mouth.

His head swam.

"Farewell, my sweet Thaddeus."

The next thing he knew, the train of her purple gown was disappearing around the corner of the villa.

"Thaddeus! Are you ready, lad? We must go," Silvestrus called from the portico. Thaddeus tucked Ethne's parcel into his tunic and hurried back to his master, trying to compose himself on the way.

Ormerod glanced at Thaddeus, then looked away, his smile fading momentarily. "Ah, here is the boy now. Well, Master Silvestrus, good days to you. Please call upon me at any time I am able to offer a service. And, never fear: I shall keep a sharp eye out for any of those foreign coins you showed to me. And, if I find any, I will get word to you, soon as I may. Oh, and thank you, again, for your assistance with the press. It seems to be working fine now."

"Master Ormerod, my thanks to you. You have performed a greater service this day than you know, I believe. Thaddeus, lad, go around to Asullus and check his bridle fastening, will you not?"

The two men continued their pleasantries as Thaddeus walked up to the mule. "You look very pretty, Asullus, with that garland and all—matches your eyes, I think." He was immediately sorry to be so sharp with the beast. It was not Asullus' fault they were leaving.

"An' ye, laddie," the old mule replied softly, "might want to wipe yer mouth on the sleeve o' yer tunic sometime."

Startled, Thaddeus did so and was surprised at the red smear that decorated his sleeve. Chastened, the boy checked the hitching, found no fault, and returned to his master, who was concluding his goodbyes with the vintner.

The two men shook hands one final time, and Silvestrus shooed Thaddeus up onto the cart seat, following him closely. Settling down, he flicked the reins.

"All right, you lazy beast, show us a good pace if one like yourself can manage such a thing."

Asullus snorted and leaped forward, momentarily throwing his passengers off balance.

Thaddeus heard the old mule's colorful retort, but he was unsure what the beast said. Did Asullus really know such words? The last time he had heard that kind of language was from a teamster on one rainy and very muddy day on the road home from Figberry.

Thaddeus' eyes, however, were firmly fixed on the balcony of the villa, where he spotted a slim figure half-hidden by a window frame. A small hand waved briefly, and Thaddeus waved back. It was some time before he turned around.

This leaving business seemed to hurt a great deal more than it did in those tales of courage and adventure he had been told growing up.

The Imperial Palace, Cinoton
in the Land of the Cin, the Eastlands

The young ochre-skinned, black-haired boy made his way carefully down the dim and infrequently traveled corridor. Periodically, he stopped to look over his shoulder.

As the Cinnian Emperor's Most Favored Second Son, Soh-Nahk had nothing to fear from anyone in the palace. It was just that he was not fond of people knowing his business.

He was seeking a particular side passage that contained what he thought might be a wall with a hollow panel. At least, when he had discovered it last week, it had sounded hollow. And hollow panels could, possibly, have something interesting lying behind them.

Over the past year and a half, he had taken it upon himself to begin a methodical search of the palace, beginning with his own apartments and radiating out in quadrants. He had decided that if he was to find anything interesting, he needed to be both organized and thorough in his research. This resolve had led to his first discovery—that of his older brother's hidden collection of erotic parchments tucked away in a closet of his bedroom apartments.

His brother, Les-Nahk, was growing into quite the pig—wine and women in excess being the primary symptoms. He, himself, cared little for such things. He was a bit too young for such indulgences anyway, but his interests lay primarily in other areas.

Instead, he liked secrets. He liked knowing things others did not.

And, he liked having things that he had earned by his own merit. Last week, for example, he had found an ancient urn in which was concealed a long, slender poniard without a cross-guard. He considered this a lucky find and something that was sure to come in handy at some future point.

He knew his movements were always watched—and in two layers. First, there was the more obvious and easily detectable Watcher—probably a Junior Follower. Once most people noted the first, they assumed there were no others—and also, eluding that one meant eluding all observation.

Hah—he knew that to be a gross oversimplification of the situation.

People felt comfortable and self-congratulatory in such cases and, as a result, became careless. But he knew there was a second layer—a more subtle, probably more Senior Follower. It had not taken him long to piece out this puzzle. He fervently hoped it stopped there and that there was no third level. However, he tried to act as if additional Watchers laid in wait to follow him. *Vigilanti Semper* was his motto.

It became a game with him. He would go exploring, exposing himself enough so that the first Watcher would be satisfied. Then he would disappear for short periods but leave sufficient clues to put the second Watcher at ease. After that, he would again disappear, only to return just in time to prevent panic among his erstwhile Followers.

Today, he had already shed both his Watchers. He wanted to know more about that panel.

He padded down the little-used hallway, passing pastel vases and gem-bedecked urns of ancient dynasties of untold worth displayed on tall marble pedestals, then past murals of scenes of sinewy dragons in golden paint.

Curiously, there were no scenes of the dragons mating. Perhaps the artists had never witnessed such—at least those who had survived. Too bad; Les-Nahk would have enjoyed that. He shook his head.

Thank goodness for his little sister, Sim-Lea. She, at least, seemed above such seamy pastimes, so far, anyway. She was a sly one in her own right, though, having more in common with himself than others, he thought.

Finally, he reached the side corridor. Looking around once more, he ducked quickly down the darkened passageway, and then he counted: *one, two, three, four…*

Ah, here it was…

He rapped softly. Yes, hollow. Just as he remembered.

Now adjusted to the hallway's dimmer light, his gaze searched around the frame for hidden or less-prominent buttons, levers—anything that might trigger the panel to swing open, recess, or slide back—as he had found with similar designs on other various excursions.

Visually, he saw nothing obvious, so he ran his fingers gingerly around the teakwood panel's border. He was both methodical and careful. He still carried a scar from the needle point that had, once triggered from contact, sprung out from a frame he discovered to jab his thumb. Underneath had resided a picture of an old fat man chased by his concubines. Irritatingly, for all his wounding, there had been nothing of interest behind that portrait save an old papyrus prophylactic.

This time his gentle touch finally disclosed a small stud down and to the left, not present on the right-hand side of the panel. Carefully, he depressed what he felt sure was a release and waited.

His wait was not long. Almost at once, the entire two-paces-high, one-pace-wide panel fell forward. Instinctively, he jumped back, only to witness the entire wall piece slam to the floor with a loud crash.

Soh-Nahk cursed and waited, holding his breath, straining to hear anything that would suggest the noise had attracted his Watchers.

Time passed, and he detected no sign of discovery. Breathing a sigh of relief, he then took himself to task for being such a clumsy fool. The palace was a place of few second chances, he reminded himself. The inept, at all levels, regularly disappeared after a time, never to be seen again.

Slowly, bending down, he picked up the panel and stood it carefully against the wall. He would have to be quick. The leaning panel and the opening behind it would be obvious to anyone walking down this passageway, and he did not think it wise to attempt to replace it once he was through the opening. How could he know if it would allow him to open it back up again from the inside?

Once the panel rested lightly against the wall, he cautiously stuck his head into the opening. Dim shapes were outlined in the dancing dust motes his intrusion had disturbed. He would do well to have a candle or lantern with him on the next visit.

Cautiously, he stepped over the threshold.

Yes, furniture, chairs, sofas, rolled-up rugs, desks, and knickknacks of all descriptions greeted him. He was awash in pleasure. This find would take weeks, perhaps even months, to fully explore. *Excellent!*

Now, however, it was time to leave. He had eluded his Watchers for at least an hour, and that absence would attract unwanted attention. *I will return*, he promised the room, and soon.

He turned, poked his head partway out into the dim passageway, and looked both ways, as well as up and down, for good measure. He saw nothing. Stepping over the threshold, he slipped back into the hallway, then turned and replaced the panel with painstaking care.

Now to retrace his steps—erasing his footprints as he went—then show himself to any who might care and resume his public pose. There was a definite advantage to being the second-born in a family—no one ever expected anything of importance in him. He looked back one last time at the panel after he had wiped it clean, along with the other three that preceded it.

This was going to be fun.

6

Butterflies
Papiliones

"I said, Thaddeus—you seem to be *millibus*," the old Sorcerer observed.

"What? Oh. I am sorry, Master, I was just—"

"Thinking of a pretty young girl who has stolen your heart and from whom you are now separated with the experience of much pain and regret?"

"Yes, Master."

"Ah, *amores*. Believe it or not, I know exactly how you feel if that helps in any way. Probably not. Usually, time is the only remedy. Notice I did not say cure."

"Master, may I ask a question?"

"Of course, lad. The man who is ignorant but ignores the opportunity to rectify it when an opportunity presents itself is twice the fool."

"Sorcerers have great powers, do they not?"

"Well, yes. Some do."

"Have they the power to heal hurts, to restore health?"

"Yes, some more than others."

"Well, then—"

"Is it possible for the young maiden, Ethne, to be cured of her sickness through the use of Sorcery, and, if so, can I do it? And, finally, will I? Are those your questions, Thaddeus?"

"Yes, Master." He looked up hopefully. "Can you? Will you?"

"It would be possible, under the right circumstances, but I choose not to. It may be hard for you to understand and harder to accept." Silvestrus gave Thaddeus a considering look. "There will come a day, however, when I will explain it to you."

Thaddeus was stunned. How could this miraculous old man refuse to save his Ethne? It was her death warrant. Feelings of betrayal welled up inside him, and anger began to build like a billowing fire.

He managed to respond, "My parents used to say that a lot." The tension grew to be palpable.

"The lad ha' asked a fair question, Master Silvestrus."

Both started at the gray mule's interruption.

Twitching his long ears, Asullus continued, "An' a fair answer is warranted, I'm guessin'."

"And you, Asullus? Do you now think to put your two coppers' worth into our discussion? And on what basis, might I ask?"

"On the basis, Master, that just as it ha' fallen to ye to save me bacon on occasion, so it has fallen to me, sometime, to achieve the reverse. It is summat that gives me the right, I reckon. Aside from that, as any can see, she is a sweet lass, in spite o' her earlier callin', an' our Thaddeus here is clearly taken wi' her. Besides which, it was she who wove me this very garland wi' her own lovely hands, an' I am grateful to her on that account, as well as some others."

"I see. Well, fair enough. All right, I will give my reasons. I warn you, though, they are selfish in nature. I was intending to offer you a gradual instruction, Thaddeus, and not begin until all our company is assembled, but perhaps it would be better to make a start now. I will not attempt an explanation, however. That must wait for time to pass, and effort will be expended before understanding appears. Knowledge comes, but wisdom lingers, you see."

"I have heard that from my parents as well, Master." It was only his feelings that were making him so bold. The resentment in his voice was clear.

"*Harumph!* Very well, then. I will be direct. A Sorcerer is born with a certain talent. Once manhood begins to unfold—or womanhood, for that matter—that talent can, under the right circumstances and with the right training, flourish—and result in the ability to practice Sorcery. However, there is a price. A Sorcerer often lives to a great age—illness and accident notwithstanding—on occasion, even several times the life span of a normal man. With each use of the Art, however, that span is diminished by a certain amount. If the use is small, the loss is usually small. If great, however, the loss is likewise of similar magnitude. These deductions accumulate over time."

Silvestrus paused a moment as a bright blue butterfly fluttered quickly across his path.

"Thaddeus, I must tell you, Ethne is gravely ill. And the illness she carries she has passed to her master. I believe Ormerod may not be far behind her. To rid her of this contagion this far into its course would be tantamount to attempting to bring a dead spirit back to life. Few things take a greater toll from a Sorcerer than that, and the effort is not uncommonly fatal. It is a price I am unwilling to pay. Not for her, sweet though she is, and in love with her as you might be. It is possible you will come to understand and accept this in the season of things."

Thaddeus struggled with himself. It was the first time he had felt genuine wrath. Still, he realized he should not dare to feel this way toward the man who was now his master. Exercising every bit of control he could muster, he spoke with teeth-gritted fury.

"Ethne said I will become a Sorcerer someday. And that's the reason why you came for me and told my parents all those things about a 'mystery.' Well, I will become a Sorcerer; a great and powerful one. Then I will go to her and save her. You'll not have to trouble yourself,

Master! I don't care what the cost is! I will save her!" Blood pounded through his veins.

"All right, Thaddeus. It is your right and your choice. I would only —well, you have spoken. Perhaps, it is best to leave it at that for now."

For the greater portion of the day, Thaddeus looked out upon a countryside turned bleak. He had no words for his master.

Silvestrus was silent as well, smoking his pipe but seemingly thoughtful and concerned. The creaking of the cart, the groaning of the wheels, and the thudding *clip-clop* of Asullus' hooves were the only accompaniment.

The party reached Meadsville as the sun was setting. Silvestrus bade them set up camp in a wooded area west of the city.

Thaddeus, sullen and sulky, did as he was told, and only that, without speaking. He was lost in his sorrow, anger, frustration, and petulance. Once, while clearing the campsite, Silvestrus passed him muttering something about a "distraction." Asullus appeared sympathetic but let him be. Thaddeus had, in a short time, grown fond of the old mule and was grateful for his earlier intervention even though the mule must have known it would cost him.

After a trip to a nearby stream for water, Thaddeus was returning to camp when he came upon his master sitting on a log whittling on a branch amidst a great cloud of brilliant blue butterflies that hovered around him. He appeared to be listening to something but shook his head before nodding in Thaddeus' direction and returning to his task.

Within moments, the butterflies deserted Silvestrus and flew toward Thaddeus. They were soon flitting around him thick enough to obscure his vision. He was dazzled by their radiant color, and his spirits began to lift. However, their activity seemed particularly frenetic, and he had no idea what to make of it.

The butterflies, larger than those he was used to seeing at home, behaved peculiarly. They would fly pell-mell around his head as if to get his attention, then fly off as a group to the northeast of the camp near the forest edge where they lingered. As he stared at them, they flew back to him, again surrounded him with their frenzied fluttering, then raced for the forest edge once more. This behavior was repeated three more times before it occurred to Thaddeus to follow them.

The next time they rose and flew off, Thaddeus shrugged, set down the water buckets, and followed.

When he reached the floating mass, they flew down a path into the thickest part of the forest. Thaddeus looked back at the campsite. Silvestrus had disappeared, and Asullus lay napping. He shrugged and followed the fluttering host as it led him deeper into the underbrush, where the forest quickly darkened.

Just to the left of the path, the blue butterflies stopped and resumed their mad flurry. As Thaddeus neared the mass, it parted to reveal a huge, glistening spiderweb stretched between two tall birch trees.

Thaddeus approached the web, which was vibrating from the frantic efforts of its captive to free itself. Now he could see that near the center of the web was a singular blue butterfly, larger than the others. The creature struggled, caught in the sticky silk, barely able to move.

Now, Thaddeus understood the reason he had been summoned. The larger butterfly bore some important relationship to the others and required his help. Though he somehow understood, it was certainly a behavior he had never seen before.

How odd.

Gently, he held the beautiful creature, which quieted at his touch, and carefully pulled it clear of the web, thread by thread, till at last, it was free. The butterfly sat in the palm of his hand, wings slowly fanning before it flew up to circle his head three times, joining the blur of blue wings. Then suddenly, the larger butterfly shot straight up and away, its entourage raggedly following until all were lost to sight.

As he watched the last of them disappear, Thaddeus was aware of a growing sense of serenity. His emotional storm had subsided, and he was at peace.

Returning to camp, he found Silvestrus and Asullus animatedly conversing. The Sorcerer looked up and caught sight of his wandering charge.

"Ah, Thaddeus, are you all right? We were a bit concerned."

"Yes, Master Silvestrus. I was just walking in the woods for a space, following some beautiful butterflies. I rescued a big blue one from a spiderweb."

"Good lad. Glad you are safe. Perhaps next time before you go off on a jaunt, however, you will let one of us know."

"Of course, Master. I'm sorry. I promise I'll do better." The remainder of the weight that had been pressing down on him disappeared. He could not say why precisely, but he was feeling considerably more at peace, and he was no longer angry. Things seemed much as they had before—before Figberry. He picked up the water buckets from where he had left them and set them by the other campsite's provisions.

"Thaddeus, if you would, take Asullus with you and gather some firewood. It will be dark soon."

The boy nodded dutifully and trudged off with the old gray mule to the forest edge and began securing a night's supply of kindling and branches which he placed in the panniers Asullus carried on his back. As they walked, Asullus addressed the boy.

"Worried aboot ye, I was—though the Old Man did no' seem to be so much. An' ye're out chasing butterflies!" He snorted. "This be me last trip, that's fer certain. I'm back to Cobbly Knob after this, an' I'll be lettin' the lovely Lady Lilith tend to me wants 'stead of traipsin' all o'er yonder concerned wi' some young calf-struck, moon-eyed, wet-behind-the-scruntchian doe head, who can't seem to make up his mind whether to pick his nose or scratch at his behinder!"

"I said I was sorry, Asullus. It's just that they were so fair. And I—say, where is your garland? Did you lose it?"

"Nay, I slipped it off me neck an' put it inna cart. Dinno' want it to get all crushed or dirty, don' ye know. Well, lad, are ye feeling better aboot things now? Ye've seemed a bit put out lately—no' to say ye've no' a good reason."

"Hmm? No, I am fine, Asullus. I feel better, actually. I just wish you could have seen those blue butterflies. And that big one was so beautiful. It was just over there and, well, so beautiful. Oh, I said that already, didn't I?

It was almost dusk by the time they returned. Thaddeus built a fire, and soon they were enjoying the remnants of Master Ormerod's mid-day bounty. Following the even-tide meal, Silvestrus sat sipping purberry wine from his flask and gazing steadily into the fire, eyes half-lidded.

Suddenly, he straightened, alert.

"Right. Now, Thaddeus, Asullus, I am going into town tonight. I must meet with some people."

"Do you wish me to go with you, Master?"

Silvestrus looked thoughtfully at his Apprentice. "Perhaps it would be better if you stayed here, Thaddeus. You have had, all in all, a fairly demanding day or two. However, I will trust the pair of you to maintain the camp and keep out of trouble. If all goes well, I will return later in the day tomorrow." With that, he stood, took up his walking staff, and set off on a trail leading east.

"Aye, well, there he goes, the old ghost—an' leaving us wi' the dishes to do. Quite a surprise there, eh? Sorcerers! Well, come on, lad. Hop to. Ye're the one wi' the opposable thumbs. Me, I'll go scout around a bit. Maybe I'll see me some blue butterflies, too. *Pfah!*"

Later that evening, Thaddeus bedded down for the night while Asullus lay nearby. The old mule was of the opinion that the camp was not likely to be bothered during Silvestrus' absence.

"Did somethin', he did. Always does when we camp, an' he has to be away. It'd take a troll or some such to get through to us, mind ye. But then, I'd just run away. I'm fast as needs be if properly motivated. Ye—well, there be limits to everyone's luck, laddie. I'd keep ye in me memories, though, I would."

"Why, thank you, Asullus. How good it is to have a true friend in times of trouble," Thaddeus replied dryly.

"Aye, right ye are, me boy. 'Tis indeed. Now try to get some sleep. I expect tomorrow'll be an interestin' day. I'm a bit restless, so donno' mind me. Somethin' in the air, maybe."

Thaddeus lay on his back on his bedroll, watching the night sky. He mused for some time regarding the number of stars there might be in the night's sky before turning on his side. It was then he felt the lump in his tunic. Reaching in, he pulled out the packet Ethne had given him, a small square of canvas folded over and tied with a leather thong. Inside was a linen cloth wrapped in a bit of bright yarn.

Thaddeus opened it and recognized her scent immediately. He carefully laid back the kerchief to reveal a heavy swatch of dark curls tied with a sky-blue ribbon. He held it to his face.

Oh, so soft…and her smell. Feelings rushed back to him as if from a dream, and damp drops fell on the cloth that she had touched.

Eventually, slumber overtook him.

Thaddeus gradually became aware it was getting lighter. Slowly, he opened his eyes a crack. It was lighter, but not with moonlight, nor yet with sunlight. The light was blue—a bright, brilliant blue. He opened his eyes further. The sense of peace he felt earlier returned.

He sat up slowly, rubbed his eyes, and looked toward the source of the light. At first, it was painful, but as his vision adjusted, he could see more clearly.

Something, a figure perhaps only a pace-and-a-half tall, a girl's—no, a small, delicate woman's—figure stood there. A cascade of blue hair fell down her back. She had large, luminous eyes of a deeper blue and fragile features except for full lips and prominent cheekbones. She wore only a pale, filmy covering. This tiny woman stood before him, but seemed to be not really a woman—she was more ethereal. Her gaze was steady, her manner regal. She smiled.

Calm and peace, like a gradually rising tide, continued to wash up inside him. He felt better. Suddenly a realization swept over him. It was like he had felt this afternoon in the spiderweb with the blue butterflies.

The creature addressed him.

"Thaddeus of Beewicke, I am Caerulea, *Regina Papilionium*, and I have come to speak with you—to thank you, that is. It was I whom you saved from certain death earlier today in the spiderweb. I had foolishly sampled too much of my Lord's nectar, and it went to my head. It always seems to affect my judgment—also my reflexes. My mother, Queen before me, often said, 'If you do drink, then do not fly.' In any event, that is how I came to be in my predicament.

"I sensed your party nearby and sent my courtiers to fetch one of you. I gather that the older one, Silvestrus, was disinclined or, for some reason, thought you better suited to rescue me. Then you came and freed me. My Lord Spadix, *Rex Blattarum*, is away this night—in fact, most nights—so I have come for you to show you a Queen's gratitude. While you are young yet, I sense a great power lying latent within you. It reminds me of the sun, and I am attracted to light such as that. Come."

The blue butterfly Queen moved forward and took his hand. Thaddeus found himself powerless to deny her. Suddenly, great blue wings unfurled behind her, and Thaddeus was lifted up and borne swiftly over the treetops. As they flew, hundreds of butterflies joined them in a dance of bright blue light. Though all in her court appeared fair, Caerulea was the fairest of them all.

"There." She indicated a small patch in the forest. "My home. You will be my guest tonight. You will find the gratitude of the Queen of the Butterflies is not insignificant."

Once his feet regained the earth, he looked around the clearing, noting the house-sized leaves and massive tree trunks —which could have been twigs but for their girth—and mushrooms the size of horses. His senses had been clouded since he had first seen Caerulea, so it took some time for him to realize what had happened.

The Queen approached him, proffering one goblet of the two she held.

"Here, dear Thaddeus, drink with me of this potion of thanks." The boy accepted the cup. The dark blue liquid—*was everything here to be blue?*—swirled around in his goblet on its own. He put the measure to his lips and sipped. Nectar, he knew immediately...or, at least, a kind of nectar. This was a special brew certainly.

He quaffed the cup's mix, noting that Caerulea did so as well. She held out her hand to receive his now-empty goblet, which he readily gave up. Then it seemed the vessels were no longer there.

Indeed, I am with Faerrae, he mused.

"Now, my young beekeeper, let us partake of the entertainments of the Fey," she said, taking his arm and guiding over to a pair of toadstools set 'round a ring of morel. The Queen clapped once, and dancers and musicians appeared. They were quite good, he judged, aside from being unlike any other beings he had ever seen before.

Caerulea inclined closer to him. "Ah, Thaddeus, you saved my life. So, I will now return a favor. May any future pain you suffer be diminished by this measure." She leaned forward and made an odd gesture with her hand.

For the briefest instant, he felt confused, but these sensations vanished in a moment. *How odd*, he thought...how odd, indeed. His astonishment, however, was as muted as was everything else that followed that night.

The embers of the fire slowly died. Asullus' head rested on his crossed front legs. His eyes flicked over to the empty bedroll.

"Ah, laddie, I hopes ye knows what ye're aboot this night. I canno' follow ye there… Butterflies! *Pfah!*"

On the ground to one side, on a smudged piece of cloth that had once been white, lay a handful of dark curls with a sky-blue ribbon, undone.

7

Friends
Amici

Thaddeus lay near the encampment in a bed of grass. Consciousness slowly returned to him, and at the same time, the awareness that he was terribly ill. His head felt like it had been bashed with a stone cudgel, and his eyes burned fiercely, especially at the back of his head. Covered with dew and shivering, he ached all over. He struggled to pry open his lids, as they seemed as heavy as millstones. He could not remember ever having felt so awful—not even with the fevers he had occasionally endured as a child.

A rasping baritone broke into his misery.

"Well, laddie, top o' the mornin' to ye! How fare ye, me fine brawny one? Now, what would ye ha' fer break-fast? Would a slab o' cold, greasy bacon be to yer tastin'? Or, p'rhaps, some o' that renowned Beewicke honey? I ha' saved some extra special just fer ye! Or I can toss some o' that yellow-churned, congealed cowcurd that we ha' up in the air an' we can see if butter-fly! Haw! Haw! Haw! Or, if you're no' in the mood fer a heavy meal o' grease an' lard, how aboot some light entertainment? Ye may not know this, but as a youth, I was champion o' me herd at braying wi' a special award fer 'volume-at-a-distance.' Permit me to gi' ye a wee bit o' demonstration."

Thaddeus lurched to his feet and unsteadily wove his way down to the stream where he vomited. He thrust his head under the chilling surface of the water, which gave him only slight relief.

After, he managed to drag himself back to camp and wrapped a blanket around himself as he sat cross-legged, shivering next to the morning fire. Balefully glaring at his semi-equine companion, he tried to get warm.

Asullus, meanwhile, was preening himself, polishing his hooves on a clump of coarse grass and grinning from long ear to long ear.

"I thought you were my friend, Asullus."

"Oh, laddie, but I am. I mean, what are friends fer but to wait up the entire night till just before the dawn, no' knowin' where yer bucko boy might be nor what kind o' trouble he may be in, an' me no' able to be there to lend a hoof or two? An' then, from out o' the sky, pretty as ye will, he comes floatin' down, airy as all, in the arms o' an itty-bitty, nekid blue lass wi' giant wings. An' him bein' bare-buff as a jaybird, himself, full up to his scuppers on some kind o' *Faerrae* nectar, three sheets to the wind an' drunk as a skunk into the bargain. Also, singin'— off-key, mind ye—at the top o' his lungs, happy as a hamster who's found his hidey-hole, playin' at some kind o' lepidopterist, wi' no word or 'hello, how be ye?' An' his own heart broke into a million pieces no' six hours past, but somehow now forgettin' it all fer some new *Faerrae* lass. What's no' to be happy aboot?"

Asullus had gone from a grin to a grimace during his diatribe—a point not lost on Thaddeus.

"I'm sorry, Asullus," he said, his remorse evident.

The old mule sighed. "Ah, laddie, I'll no' be blamin' ye—well, no' entirely, anyways. Was beguiled, ye was, as happens now an' then. When ye mix wi' the *Faerrae,* ye must be verra cautious. Ha' their own purposes, they do, an' all yer wishes an' wants mean no more to 'em than a puff of air in the wind. I saw ye off, I did, but ye was too far gone 'fore I could do much, so I just stood watch, hopin' ye'd come back to us in one piece, don' ye know, an' way before the Old Man got back. He'd no' be happy 'bout such goin's-on, mark me. And so, praise love, ye did."

"You're right, Asullus. It was my own decision, and I didn't resist it. It was so strange. I hardly remember any of it. Although, there was one part. Caerulea—she's the Queen, and she said she wanted to thank me for saving her life from the spider. So, she told me she had given me a mark and that I was now *Amicus Faerrarum*, a Friend of the *Faerrae*. She said it would bring me good luck, make me welcome in certain circles, and provide some protection against evils of one kind or another."

"Well, now, that'd be no small gift, me young *Volans*. Though such gifts usually come wi' a price. Are ye sure ye no' be leavin' anything out o' yer tale, beguiled or no'? The *Faerrae* are well-known fer their various appetites, they are."

Thaddeus shrugged. "I can't remember anything else, Asullus."

"Hmm. Well, if ye ha' been havin' commerce wi' their likes, then this mark'll usually be one o' two places: One is o'er the heart, an' the other…isn't. Slip yer blanket down a bit, an' let me —ah, I thought me as much. Well, as I said, it do happen sometimes as folk become involved wi' the dancin' an' singin' an' all—an' ye look no more the worse fer the wear o' it—apart from bein' hung o'er the fence an' not dryin' out verra quick-like. Come on, get yerself clad, an' let's go see if there might be summat the Old Man has in his bag o' tricks as can fix a body up, followin' encounters wi' those creatures as be havin' six legs an' such."

Thaddeus got up slowly and dressed, taking his time and moving carefully. He joined Asullus, who had his front legs up on the side of the cart.

"Ah, there it is, laddie, the little black bag. Do ye see it? That's the one we be wantin."

"Asullus, are you sure we're allowed to get into Master Silvestrus' belongings—his personal things?"

"O' course we're no'! On the other hand, how much do ye enjoy yer current state o' feeling? Ye can continue on if ye likes."

An icy chill passed through his gut. He did not believe that he was supposed to be doing this. And if Master Silvestrus caught him out, what would be the consequences? What might happen if one irritated a Sorcerer? On the other hand, he did feel miserable.

"Well, all right. Here." Thaddeus grabbed the bag from the cart then placed it on the ground. Tied with rawhide thongs, the pack was covered with a sturdy, stiff fabric that showed signs of many years' use. A large circle, with an intricate *S* inscribed within, adorned the cover.

"Go ahead, lad, open it up. I know what we be lookin' fer. Seen 'im do it enou' times."

Thaddeus untied and unrolled the pouch. Inside were rows of pockets holding all manner of items.

"That's it. Now fetch out the green stuff. No, no—not that. That's the leaf the Old Man puts in his pipe sometimes followin' a particular hard day. He seems to take pleasure in it, but it smells funny an' makes him act silly. Gives 'im quite an appetite, too, I so swear. It's the green powder, three pockets over, in the glass jar with the stopper. Aye, that's the one. Now take it o'er by the fire."

For a moment, Thaddeus could not decide if the thievery or his body made him more uncomfortable. His stomach churned as he resolutely walked toward the fire. He set the jar down next to it and looked toward Asullus for further direction.

"That's right. Now, take that pot an' put in three cups o' water, then add a pinch o' the powder. That's it. Now, stir it 'round wi' that little stick an' put it on that flat rock near the edge o' the fire. Good. Now, take that cup an' pee in it."

"What?"

"Ye heard me. Pass yer water in it. It's part o' the cure. Just do it, lad, an' put it in the pot, too."

"Asullus! Are you having sport with me?" Thaddeus asked, perplexed.

The mule rolled his eyes. "Ye wishes to wait to find out, lad?"

Thaddeus did as he was told, as the throbbing in his temples increased.

"All right. Now take out that little frog sticker ye ha' an' slice your thumb up along the side. Either one. Good. Then put aboot ten drops into the pot." At Thaddeus' questioning look, he continued. "Well, you suck on it, o' course. It'll stop on its own. Now blow yer nose into the pot. Yes, I'm serious. Just do it, laddie. Ye've come this distance, an' so far, so good. Now ye must say the magic words."

"Magic words? What magic words?"

"I swear, do they no' teach the young anything at all these days? Laddie, ye must concentrate an' use magic words when ye performs magic acts. Sometimes it needs a magic gesture or a magic object, too, an' sometimes no', dependin' on what it is ye be doin'—one's natural strengths an' skills, the difficulty o' what ye be tryin' to accomplish an' so on. With this particular one, methinks only a phrase is required, an' it goes summat like, *Veni, medice!*"

"But Asullus, I'm no Sorcerer. I'm but a mere Apprentice, if that. And I may never be a Sorcerer, even if I was allowed to be one. Besides, you just said the words yourself. Why do I need to?"

"Laddie, ye are the one wi' the inborn talent. 'Tis a gift. Ye ha' it or ye don'. An' ye ha' it. Denyin' it'll no' make it go away. Ye are the Sorcerer here. Meself, I'm just a poor, old, dumb brute tryin' to make his way in the world, beset on every side by—"

"Oh, fine." Thaddeus concentrated, and with a deep breath, uttered, "*Veni, medice!*" Through his discomfort, a great rush permeated his body, and a deep, distant roaring sound thrummed through his head.

"All right. Now were I ye, I'd stand meself back apace."

Hastily Thaddeus stepped back, his eyebrows raised at the sight before him.

Dark green fumes began boiling out of the small cauldron, along with a constantly rising and falling wailing sound that grated on Thaddeus' ears. The smoke began to coalesce as the irritating sound receded, and there, in its midst, appeared a thin man of taller than average height, dressed in green robes, standing on a cloud that matched his robes.

His aloof and disdainful expression alerted Thaddeus as to the man's importance. In his right hand was a skull, and in the crook of his left arm rested a heavy tome.

The figure intoned, "*Ars longa, vita brevis, occasio praeceps, experimentum periculosum, iudicium difficile*—art is long, life is short, opportunity fleeting, experience perilous, judgment difficult…"

The man paused. "Wait a moment! Neither of you, obviously, is Master Silvestrus. Where is he, and what is the meaning of this?" The Learned One's long, pointy beard waggled as he spoke.

Asullus stepped closer to the fire. "Ah, beggin' yer pardon, Revered Sir, but the lad, Thaddeus the Apprentice, is sufferin' mightily, an' we donno' wish to keep ye, knowin' as we do, that ye ha' many more important an' weighty matters to attend to than—"

"Yes, yes, yes. Very well." Setting down the skull and book, the Doctor squinted at Thaddeus. "Ah, I remember you, young Tedius—the human pincushion. All healed up, nicely, too, if I do say so myself. Yes. Now step forward, and let's have a look at you. Hmm…hmm. Now stick out your tongue and say 'Aesculapius.' Hmm. Nothing there. Now turn your head and cough…all right. It appears to be nothing more than a common case of post-acute alcohol intoxication *residuae*, though it seems that the original elixir ingested was derived from nectar, of all things. Interesting."

The medical consultant withdrew two pellets wrapped in purberry leaves from his robes and handed them to Thaddeus. "Here, take two of these with water. Obtain proper rest, diet, and exercise, and you will be right as rain in no time. However, you may call on me again in the morning if you feel no differently."

"Oh, thank ye, Learned Sir! Ye're a blessin' to the lad, ye surely are."

"Nothing at all, nothing at all. But that reminds me. Your Master has run up a bit of a bill here, and I am certain he would like to see it resolved soon. If neither of you parties is prepared to settle this account, perhaps you could arrange for a third party to—*awwkkh!*"

Asullus, apparently deeming the doctoral business concluded, kicked over the pot, and its contents washed into the fire. With a whoosh, the figure and all the smoke vanished instantly. Thaddeus jumped back, startled.

"Look who be callin' who 'Tedius.' Oh, well, lad, the old geezer's a bore, but he usually knows his pharmacy. Just gulp those down an' I expect ye'll be the happier fer it shortly."

By the time the bag of magic ingredients had been rewrapped and replaced in the cart and the area put to rights, Asullus' prediction had come true. All at once, Thaddeus covered his mouth with an unexpected yawn.

"Laddie, I'm thinkin' ye an' me both could do wi' a rest, lookin' toward restorin' the tissues an' such."

As they were getting settled, Thaddeus rolled over to face the gray mule.

"Asullus, I have a question. You seem larger to me than most mules I've seen. How is it that happened to be?"

"Ah, lad, easy enou' question to answer. You see, me father was a Percheron an' me dear mother was, as it happened, a true donkey, makin' me a hinny, if we was to be technical, I suppose. Now, I know what ye be thinkin', but 'tis true an' true. The way 'twas told to me was that they was sharin' a meadow one day when an unexpected storm arose—more like a deluge, don' ye know. An', as these things can go, they found themselves standin' together under the same tree 'til all the elemental hubbub let up. An', well, there ye ha' it. Love, as it turns out, can come an' nudge ye in the ribs at any moment o' any day or night, an' off ye go. So, twelve months later, there I was—part stallion an' part mule, sort of. Who'd ha' supposed it out, yes?

"Sure 'n you're right to wonder though. Many--well most, that is—well, all, really-- o' me kind donno' care so much fer the lasses an' the makin' o' the wee ones an' the like. An' it's summat I've wondered aboot, meself. But if I ha' the straight o' it, when the Lady Lilith was doin' whate'er it was she was doin' to help me speak, it also caused me to git an eye fer the fair ones, an' I been at it e'er since. As it turns out, no' so many there are be expectin' one such as meself to ha' an interest, an' so when I spots me a likely lass, she's sometimes surprised in lookin' o'er her shoulder to see me there, smilin' an' winkin' an' all at her.

"But, sometimes, I do ha' the thought that all this jumpin' aboot an' hair pullin' is no' worth the exertion an' certainly no' the dignity lost in the foolishness. Still, we do keep bein' the moth to the flame, don' we now, in spite o' all that I'm sayin' this minute?"

Thaddeus' long-eared friend finished with a grin, and nothing more was said on the topic. The sun was three-quarters down before either of them roused again.

New firewood had been collected, water fetched from the stream, and the semblance of an evening meal started when Thaddeus saw Asullus suddenly prick up his ears and turn his head to the East.

"Somebody's coming, laddie—two somebodies. Ah, 'tis the Old Man an' yer new classmate, I'll be wagerin.'"

Within moments, the grass rustled, the underbrush parted, and Silvestrus came striding into the glade wielding his staff.

Just behind him trudged a short, pudgy boy. He was dressed in a white linen tunic and trousers. His leather sandals were laced up, and a leather knapsack of provisions rode high on his shoulders. He squinted and looked down at where he was placing his feet. Somewhat shorter than Thaddeus, he had dark brown hair, apple-red cheeks, and eyes that at once looked up and darted curiously around the clearing.

"Ah, Thaddeus, Asullus. Good to see you. All is well, I trust?"

Thaddeus glanced quickly at Asullus, who shook his head slightly, then answered the old Sorcerer. "Welcome back, Master. It's been quiet in your absence—nothing new to report."

"Excellent. The best news days are no-news days. Thaddeus, come here; I want you to meet your new colleague." The old man motioned Thaddeus forward. "Thaddeus, this is Anders of Brightfield Manor. Anders, this is Thaddeus of Beewicke. Meet and be friends."

"Hello." Thaddeus stuck out his hand as he'd seen his elders do.

The smaller boy hesitantly put out his hand as well. "Hullo."

Thaddeus found the short lad reserved but warmed to his unassuming yet friendly manner. "Beewicke is a tiny village, and we don't get out much. Where is Brightfield Manor? Is it a town close to Meadsville?"

"Uh, no. Brightfield Manor is near Meadsville, but it's not really a town. It's the name of the estate where my family home is. I don't know why they call it that, though. There are fields about, but they're not particularly bright. You're from Beewicke? That's where the honey comes from, yes?"

Thaddeus grimaced but nodded. "Oh, yes. That's where the honey comes from. Is it mead your town is named for?"

"Yes. Many of the estates around there ferment your honey to use in the mead vats. Also, several of the families grow barley and hops. We do, at our works—then the brewers turn it into ale and beer, as well as mead. They're always testing it to see if it is good yet—and always laughing and falling down afterward." The boy smiled shyly.

Thaddeus laughed out loud. He liked the new boy very much. He had had a few close friends back in Beewicke but had always wanted more.

The Sorcerer nodded in approval. "Well, you two seem to be getting on. Good. Thaddeus here will help you get things sorted out, Anders. You boys start a leg on dinner. I am going to have a chat with Asullus."

After the old man turned away, Anders, his hazel eyes large and round, stared at Thaddeus. "Did Master Silvestrus say he was going to *chat* with the mule?"

"Yes, he did. You see, the old mule talks—*really*—and not only that…"

It was an hour of questions and answers, back and forth, each boy perpetually interrupting the other. Anders had much to absorb about the group's adventures to date, and Thaddeus was eager to learn about the outside world.

"…so he was talking to Mater and Pater, and then they both agreed I should go with him. I could scarce believe it. They usually want me to stay close to home and the villa—on account, I think, of the trouble I have breathing when I exercise or when it's cold. I have hardly ever been out except to see the vats in the barns during the tapping. And have you noticed the Master's blue ring? It sometimes glows, like when he was talking to my parents," Anders said.

The conversation concerning their experiences proceeded back and forth in a rush with hardly a breath in between.

"—and Asullus is a special mule. He has girlfriends—if you can believe that—and he was raised by an old Witch. She was the one who fixed it so he could speak. And…"

"I always had a lot of tutors. My parents wanted me to know about everything so that I could take over the family business, but I never did think…"

"…and we were attacked by bandits. They shot two arrows into me, but I was healed right away. Then a *Daemon* named Charles came, tall and brown and ugly as mud, and ate them!"

"That is amazing! I do not understand how that could be. But he told me it was a mystery, and I might be a Sorcerer, and I was to meet another boy—he must have meant you—who was also, but he never told Mater that, and that's odd because…"

"…and that first night, I took him to an old standing stone, and it glowed blue just like his ring when he touched it…"

"…then he showed me an old well that had been covered over ever since I was born, and he told me to look into the water, and I thought I saw a face. It was blue and…"

Once the pair had caught up on their various adventures to date, Thaddeus' head spun around, looking for the old mule. He stood up. "Come on, Anders. I'll introduce you to Asullus. He's amazing, and he talks funny. Of course, he is a mule, so he would, true? This girl I met when we were in Figberry, Ethne—she's beautiful—she made him a garland, and he's all googly about it."

The boys made their way across the clearing to where Asullus stood, his head down, facing the forest.

"Asullus! Look, 'tis the other boy the Master spoke of. His name's Anders of Brightfield Manor, and his family makes mead. He's—um, Asullus? Whatever is the matter? You're standing there like a lump."

"Sorry, laddie. I'm no' at me best. The Old Man ha' some words wi' me concernin' gettin' into his private stocks, he did. He don' much care fer it, don' ye know. Donno' worry none, though; I told him 'twas all me idea. Anyways, he gave me a rough-out —deservedly so, I s'pose—an' it's a bit slow in gettin' o'er.

"But here I am going on aboot me, an' we have us a new lad. Anders, do ye say? O' Brightfield Manor? Aye, we been by there before—some years ago. Saw yer folks, I did. Seemed like nice people. Though I would ha' thought they'd be teachin' their son that standin' around wi' his eyes bulging out an' his mouth hangin' open is hardly polite, 'specially on meetin' new folk fer the first time."

"He—he *talks!*"

Thaddeus chuckled.

"Aye, he do, don' he now? Well, in any event, me name be Asullus. I will no' bore ye wi' all the details, as I'm sure the tall lad here has filled ye in. But, aye, I do be speakin', but only as there's summat worth to be speakin' aboot. Which surely has been hard to find in any conversation I've had me so far wi' young honey-knees here. But, if he e'er be givin' ye a hard way to go, Anders of Brightfield, ye can probably get yer investment back by askin' him a bit aboot the blue butterflies."

"Blue butterflies? Thaddeus, what about the blue butterflies?"

Thaddeus turned scarlet again as Asullus grinned.

"Nothing, Anders. Asullus is just making a joke. But come on, we had better finish getting dinner ready, or we will get some of what the Master gave his pet mule here."

"Ye know, laddie, ye no' be so big as I could no' gi' ye a lesson in manners."

"Asullus! Boys! What is taking you so long? And where is the fire?" Silvestrus called from across the campsite.

Asullus turned to trot off. "Oh, me! We'd better be movin', lads. More later."

Following dinner, the group sat around the campfire, bellies full and at peace. The night was ablaze with shooting stars, and Silvestrus told tales of things grand and mysterious, while Asullus related humorous experiences of past travel.

Anders was brought up to date on the group's adventures, while he, in turn, related stories his tutors had told him about the days of the Empire. The moon had passed its zenith by the time they sought their bedrolls.

As Thaddeus drifted off to sleep, he reflected that his new life seemed much less daunting, given that he would not now be facing it alone. He had a friend.

8

The Third One
Tertius

The next day, the party awoke to a heavy drizzle that had begun shortly before rising, complicating their work and dampening spirits.

"Is adventuring always so wet?" Anders asked sharply.

"It is today, Anders," Thaddeus replied with a smile of resignation. "Did you happen to bring along an extra pair of dry stockings?"

"Oh, not to worry. Mater must have stuffed at least twelve pairs into my bag. She's very careful that way." He looked down at his duffel and frowned. "I am fearful, though, that the jar-jam she also packed has got into them, and I'm going to end up with all pink hose."

Thaddeus' smile broadened into a grin.

Across the firepit, Silvestrus sat stirring up the embers from last night's campfire with a long stick, a branch taken from a nearby tree. Thaddeus felt the constant drizzle would surely dampen any blaze his new Master could generate, but the flames quickened respectably and gave off a welcome heat.

The old man looked up at his two recruits and beckoned them over.

"To me, boys. Let us have some morning tea, eh? It will do the constitution well on such an unpleasant day as this looks to be."

Silvestrus took up a corner of his cloak and grasped the handle of a tripod-mounted pot hanging a short distance above the glowing rocks. The old man set the bubbling teapot down next to him and produced three cups, wiping each one out with the hem of his travel cape. He filled all three cups carefully and passed two to the lads, keeping the third for himself.

"Drink up," he said, taking a careful sip.

The two new friends carefully took their tea and savored the aroma before tasting it. The tea was delicious, and it was not long before the boys felt pulses of energy coursing up and down their veins.

After the tea and some small talk, Silvestrus sketched out his plan for the day, then went back into his tent to pack.

Thaddeus led Anders over to where Asullus stood and began the morning care of the beast.

"I donno' suppose either o' ye ha' aboot yer persons any fruit o' the red type?" the old mule inquired hopefully.

"No, Asullus. I'm sorry, but here are some oats. Maybe they'll do for a bit."

Thaddeus held the feedbag up to the mule's mouth and slid the morral's head-strap over his ears. While Asullus tackled the contents, Thaddeus showed Anders how to groom the gray one. As they finished, Silvestrus reemerged from his tent with a bulging leather satchel and set about tightening up his travel gear. At last, he turned to the boys.

"Very well, Apprentices. After you finish up with the mule, gather your things together, and we will be off."

The old Sorcerer sat down to take his leisure on a nearby fallen log and enjoyed a pipe while he waited. The two boys hurried, completing their preparations, after which Thaddeus demonstrated to Anders how to hitch Asullus up to the cart.

Soon all was ready, and the three clambered aboard the wagon and set off north, circling around Meadsville. Following on, the group headed northeast, passing above the tip of the Twin Lakes. Keeping the lakes on their right, they took turns driving the cart, though Asullus kept a steady pace without more than an occasional consultation. The pestering rain gave no sign of letting up.

The troupe rested from time to time, chiefly to stretch and give Asullus a respite. Mostly, however, they talked—or rather, Anders talked.

He clearly loved lecturing about the history of the world, and his tales were supplemented from time to time by the old Sorcerer, who offered elucidation, annotation, and marginalia. But overall, Silvestrus appeared content to let the boy speak, being pleased to alternately smoke his pipe, listen, or nap.

Thaddeus had only ever heard a limited version of the world's history, so he was fascinated by the flow of events starting from before the time of the Empire. He was surprised at how little he knew. His thirst for this new knowledge was like the thirst of sand for water, especially as Anders demonstrated his education.

"Anders, how do you know all these things?"

"My tutors always kept me at it. And I do like reading and writing. It just comes, and it is there when I need it. I don't know how. My chief tutor, Primus, always told me I should think of becoming a scholar and, perhaps, teach at the *Lyceum*. I'm unsure about that now, though. This Sorcery business seems quite interesting so far."

Silvestrus cleared his throat. "Now, Thaddeus and Anders, we will likely not reach Bostle much before nightfall. So, once we arrive, we will make our way to an inn I know of. Neither of you is familiar with the larger cities, so I want you to stay close by while we abide there. Perhaps we will find time to see some of the sights the following day. The day after, we will travel on to Fountaindale, the seat of the Shire, where there will be many more things for you to experience. And one last fish to catch."

Thaddeus and Anders exchanged sharp glances.

One last fish? Another boy?

If so, Thaddeus hoped he would be a good companion. If their Master indicated that he planned to find a new Apprentice in Fountaindale, then it was likely that the boy would be citified. Thaddeus did not care much for that thought, but he supposed the Master must know what he was doing. He decided to leave it at that.

It was twilight when they rode into Bostle. Though some townsfolk with torches passed to and fro, most of the twisted streets were deserted at this time of day. Thaddeus, whose turn it was to drive, halted the cart when signaled by the guards stationed in front of the city's inner gate.

There followed a brief conversation with Silvestrus concerning the group's business, and they were waved on after a cursory inspection. The Sorcerer gave Thaddeus directions, and before long, they pulled up in front of a weathered inn with a sign reading *A Friend in Mead*. The innkeeper, a tall, thin, balding man with an oversized nose, came out rubbing his hands together in anticipation.

"Hail, Master Silvestrus! Another netting accomplished, I see. Well, you will be staying with us, then, of course. Come down, come down. I will have Gregor—*Gregor!*—attend to you." Soon the hostler was at work, putting up the mule and cart in the stable.

Inside, a low-pitched buzz of conversation greeted the group while a blue haze of pipe smoke hung lazily over the tables and benches. A cheery log fire was burning brightly at one end of the room. It was not so far into summer that they did not welcome the heat from the great stone fireplace. Doffing their cloaks, the group found seats near to the fire and shortly gave the innkeeper their orders for the evening meal.

After he left, Thaddeus dug into his leather purse for the gold coins his father had given him and held them out to the Sorcerer.

"Master Silvestrus, here's some money to pay for our meal. I hope it's enough."

"Thank you, Thaddeus, but that will not be necessary. Save that for your…tuition."

"May I see those coins, Thaddeus?" Anders asked in a low voice.

"Certainly. Here."

The squint-eyed youth fingered the coins carefully. As he inspected them, his eyes widened.

"You know, these are old Imperials. They are very worn, but you can tell what they are from the Emperor on the front and the Eagle on the back. Where did you get these?"

"My father gave them to me before I left Beewicke. He thought I should have some money for my travels."

"Thaddeus, these are valuable, especially on account of their age—worth much more than just their face value. I think you should keep them to yourself, and be careful showing them about. If a robber were to see them, he might put a knife to your throat just to get them."

"Oh! I see." Hastily Thaddeus put the coins back in his purse, tying it securely to his belt. "I didn't know cities were so dangerous."

"They can be, boy," Silvestrus said, "but not for us. Here the danger will usually be for others."

"You mean…on account of…Sorcery?" Thaddeus whispered.

"Perhaps, but in point of fact—well, here is our meal. Thank you, Bartsome."

"My honor, Silvestrus." With a bow, the innkeeper left them to enjoy their food.

"Best stew, best bread, all in Bostle's Best. Tuck in, lads, then it is time for repose, with some sightseeing on the morrow."

Out in the stable, Asullus nuzzled the garland he'd been given. The fragrance it emitted was compelling. As he savored it, a small, faraway voice spoke in his head.

"Watch over him, Asullus. Watch over him."

"Aye, lassie, that I will. That I will."

The Imperial Palace, Cinoton
in the Land of the Cin, the Eastlands

Soh-Nahk sat on an overstuffed gilt chair embroidered with peacocks *affrontee*, behind a sandalwood desk with drawers pulled out, sifting through a pile of documents on his lap. Other piles lay scattered on the floor. Two candles set in clay chamber sticks lit the space where he sat, one almost guttered. He stared intently at the parchment he was holding, then, with a sigh, finally put it down.

So…that is why what happened, happened. At last, it was refreshing to learn the truth. Soh-Nahk leaned back and rubbed his neck, grown stiff from the hours of concentration.

If he understood what he was reading—love notes, apparently—then his Great-Father, Soh-Jinge, the Light of Heaven, and current, though aged, Emperor of all Cin, had, after some time, found a defect in his relationship with his wife, Sim-Nahk. This was possibly related to some intensification of Soh-Jinge's feelings toward the Chief Imperial Concubine, San-Hu, though whether causal or an effect only was not clear.

However, these feelings had, apparently, so strengthened that they led to his Great-Mother Sim-Nahk's death—by poisoning. And then to the Emperor's subsequent marriage to the alleged poisoner. Not content with that murder, his step-Great-Mother —assuming she was the culprit—then went on to eliminate Soh-Nahk's parents, Most Favored Imperial Son, Meny-Sen, and his wife, Lea-Noh.

And, from what he could tell, he, his brother, and his sister were also on the list of the soon-to-be dear departed, to leave the way clear for San-Hu's own child to inherit. Fortunately, the terrible Lady had, herself, succumbed—possibly, due to natural causes.

Soh-Nahk remembered his mother, Lea-Noh, a sweet and loving soul who did not deserve to die. And, for the first time, he became aware of new feelings—a rising intense anger and rage—not directed toward his step-Great-Mother, necessarily, but toward the Emperor himself.

According to these letters, he was guilty—guilty of implicitly allowing, if not complicitly ordering, his Great-Mother's and his parents' murder. There was only one consequence to be mandated from all this.

The Emperor must pay.

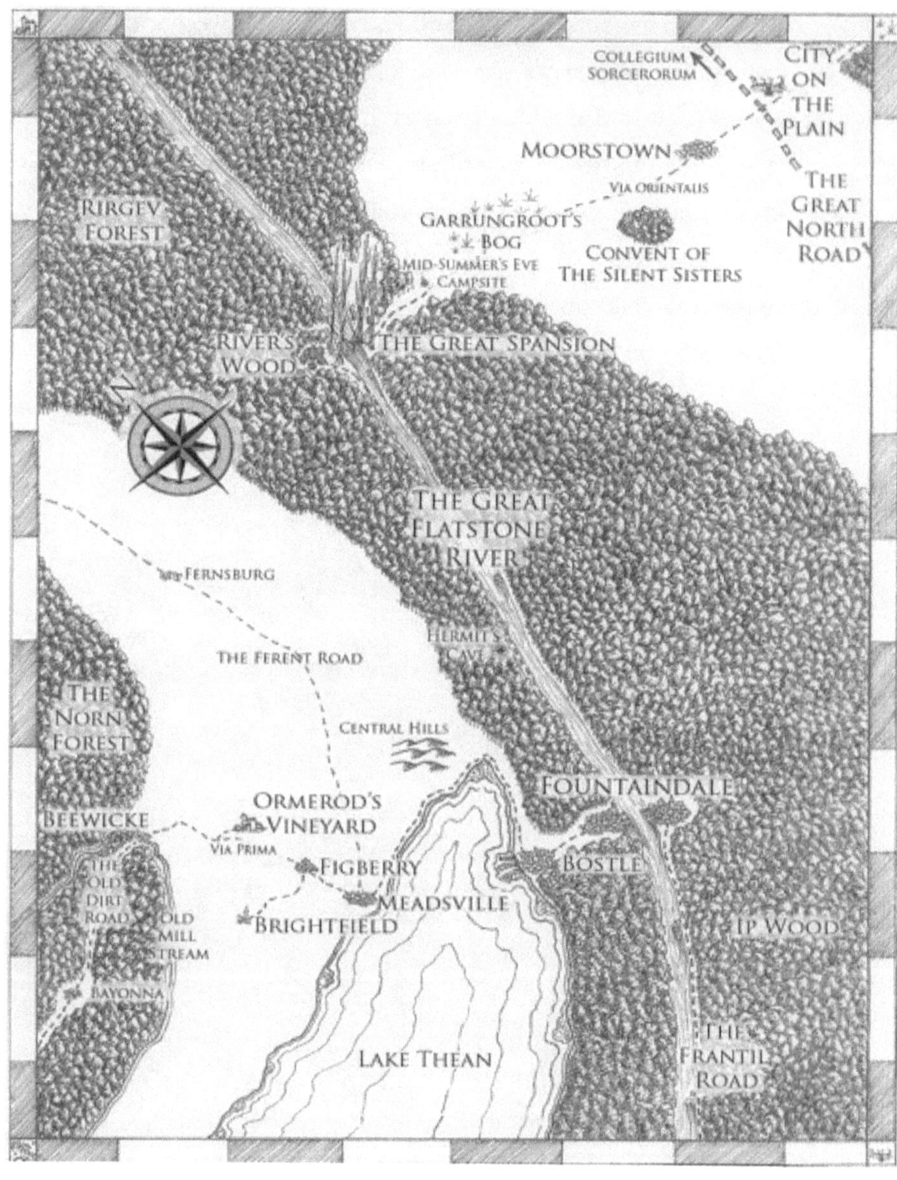
COLLEGIUM SORCERORUM
CITY ON THE PLAIN
THE GREAT NORTH ROAD
MOORSTOWN
VIA ORIENTALIS
RIRGEV FOREST
GARRUNGROOT'S BOG
MID-SUMMER'S EVE CAMPSITE
CONVENT OF THE SILENT SISTERS
RIVER'S WOOD
THE GREAT SPANSION
THE GREAT FLATSTONE RIVER
FERNSBURG
HERMIT'S CAVE
THE FERENT ROAD
THE NORN FOREST
CENTRAL HILLS
FOUNTAINDALE
ORMEROD'S VINEYARD
BEEWICKE
VIA PRIMA
FIGBERRY
BOSTLE
THE OLD DIRT ROAD
OLD MILL STREAM
MEADSVILLE
BRIGHTFIELD
IP WOOD
BAYONNA
LAKE THEAN
THE FRANTIL ROAD

9

The Thief
Fur

The next morning, the boys were up early, pestering their Master to see the city. Amused and indulgent, Silvestrus bade them wash first, then all went down for break-fast. Two platters of flat cakes and sausages with a pitcher of cow's milk rested, waiting, on the trestle top.

As the boys dug in, Anders stared at Thaddeus curiously. "Thaddeus, why don't you put any honey on yours?"

"It's a long story, Anders," Thaddeus remarked grumpily.

"Well, that's all right, Thaddeus, we have time," the scholar replied.

"No, we don't," Thaddeus said under his breath.

Once the platters were clean, and with Silvestrus' nod and an admonition to be wary of strangers who might approach them, the boys left the inn and eagerly explored the town. As they meandered down one of the main streets, goggling at everything, Thaddeus sniffed the air.

"Do you smell it? The fresh-cut timber?"

"Yes," Anders responded, rubbing his nose, suddenly gone itchy. "Clearly, the economy of this place was built on a logging and lumber-milling industry."

Thaddeus pointed to his left. "And look…a lumberyard. See how the workers all have lead markers behind their ears? And they're wearing aprons covered with sawdust. We used to get deliveries from Bostle to our village every so often for the hive-works. It always smelled good and fresh like this."

"To you, perhaps," Anders said, eyes now watering and letting out a sneeze. "I don't think I enjoy it so much."

Seeking to divert his new friend's preoccupation with his nose, Thaddeus nodded toward a group of the city's citizens.

"Look how oddly the people are dressed," Thaddeus said. "Pointy felt hats and bulging pantaloons!"

"We probably look equally odd to them, you know," Anders responded.

After another hour of exploring the city, they had seen more than enough of big houses, sprawling buildings, and strangely dressed people speaking in peculiar accents.

To Anders' nose's relief, the pair headed back to the inn. After getting over his initial astonishment at the bustling town, Thaddeus' mind moved back to his home, and he considered that the familiarity and snugness of his modest Beewicke were much to be preferred.

Following mid-day, the boys took Asullus out for exercise in one of the outlying fields while Silvestrus indulged in his usual afternoon nap. The sun was heading down the sky as they returned to their room to find the old man waiting for them.

"Well, lads, I think we will spend another night here and be off to Fountaindale in the morning."

Following the inn's even-tide offering of game birds on squire's rice, the boys sat with their Master on barrels in front of the inn and commented on passersby while Silvestrus had a cup and pipe.

After a time, Thaddeus turned to his short brother. "Anders, tell us some more of your history. It's good to listen to."

"It's not my history, Thaddeus, but…oh, very well."

A thought flittered through Thaddeus' mind that, perhaps, Anders actually enjoyed being asked to recite.

After clearing his throat, Anders started in again on his history lessons.

"So the last Emperor, Tyrannus Superbus—*Imperator Ultimus*—decided to gather together all of the Empire's Legions—the Westlands' entire army—and set out for the East. The Emperor had heard that the wealth and treasure in the Land of the Cin were beyond counting, and he wanted it for himself —as if the riches of the Empire were not enough. It took ten years to assemble, equip, and train the Grand Imperial Army of the Invasion. They say a million men were counted, and they marched steadily for nine months to get there. They even took their Gods with them. Nevertheless, after they crossed the Great Rift Valley, they were never heard from again. It was as if they had disappeared off the face of the earth."

"What happened to them?"

"No one living knows. My tutor, Primus, claims that the Cin came down upon them in an army of millions and ate them all. Others say they lost their way in the Sea of Sands, and their bleached bones lie yet on the shifting dunes. Old Secundus told me that they became cursed because of the Emperor's pride and greed, and they still wander the East as neither dead nor living, seeking vengeance. And they will continue to do so until the end of time."

"Master Silvestrus?" Thaddeus looked at the old man, gazing off in the distance, and seemingly unaware of their conversation. But Thaddeus had a growing sense that his master paid a lot more attention than he let on.

"Yes, Thaddeus?"

"Do you know what happened to the Emperor's army?"

"The Legions of the Lost? Well, some truth may lie in all three explanations. Perhaps they came upon Magicks—Eastern Magicks—things they were not prepared for. The Magicks of the East are different from what we know here, very different. And certain of the

Wise of the Cin knew well how to wield it. It is said that terrible battles were fought, with fire and lightning falling on them from the sky—and *Daemons* and dragons...and the dead. It is always hot in battle, and the blood will boil. Death and terror stalk you everywhere. But the Cin were prepared."

Silvestrus took a deep puff of his pipe and noticed the boys' attention affixed to him. He continued.

"They had spent years preparing. And, yes, Emperor Superbus was proud. Overweening pride, he had." Silvestrus' voice dropped to a whisper as he stared straight ahead. "They were all cut down...one million men. All cut down until they were no more. They bled, they cried, they screamed, they died. We wanted only to—" Silvestrus shook his head. "That is to say, no one knows their fate for certain, as there is no record of any survivors who returned to tell the tale. All that destruction—all that waste. All that..." the old man said with a deep sigh. "Well, it was a long time ago.

"So, boys, it is late, and we will be wanting an early start tomorrow. There's much to do in Fountaindale—and our last fish to catch. I am going up to bed now. Do not be long." The old man stood, stretched, tapped out his pipe, and went inside.

Thaddeus stared at his new friend. "Anders, how long ago was that war?"

"A thousand years, Thaddeus. A thousand years, at least."

"Hmm." He stared into space for a time, then sat up abruptly. "Wait a moment—did he say a new fish? Another one of us?"

"Yes, that, or we're having fish for dinner tomorrow," Anders laughed as he opened the door to the inn.

~

The following day dawned bright and sunny. After a hurried break-fast, the boys gathered their belongings and brought them downstairs while Silvestrus settled up accounts. Inn-Master Bartsome had his hostler Gregor hitch up the cart as the boys carefully stowed the group's baggage.

In moments, they were headed toward Fountaindale. With full stomachs and fair weather, their mood was light. As they went, Silvestrus taught them several traveling songs. Even Asullus joined in—in his own key and time—with what he described as an old standard, *There Once Was a Filly from Natchez*. After their singing concluded, Silvestrus described the territory they were crossing.

"Boys, pay attention and learn. Fountaindale lies on a grand river. It is the hub and final terminus of the great Western trading route. Raw materials and products from the surrounding regions pour into the city for refinement and shipment down the Greater Flatstone River to the Frantilline Coast. Finished goods flow from Fountaindale back to the hinterlands, spreading the artifacts of civilization."

As they rode throughout the long day, fine country villas gradually gave way to stone houses—some two stories high—then they passed great squares and markets and, eventually, imposing buildings that housed the Seat of Government for the entire region. Thaddeus gaped at every-thing, as he had never seen so many people in one place at one time. Crowds were everywhere, rushing and scurrying about. And the sounds —crying, cursing, shouting, laughing—were altogether overwhelming to him.

Anders cleared his throat. "Master Silvestrus, will we be going to an inn here?"

"Yes, but not right away. We have our fishing to do first." With that, the old man stopped the cart, bidding Asullus remain alert, then led his two Apprentices into the midst of the Great Market as if searching for something.

Thaddeus wondered what he was looking for. A hat? A horse?

After a time, the boy noted that they had already passed by some of the same stalls at least once. Then, in the press of the crowd, Thaddeus was jostled by someone. Recalling Anders' words of caution, his hand went quickly to the purse that held the coins his father had given him. It was gone!

A young voice cried out. "Hey! Let me go! Help! Robber!"

"*Tace!*" Silvestrus commanded.

Thaddeus turned to see Silvestrus' arm gripping the wrist of a red-headed boy, who was now silent right enough but violently attempting to break free of the old man's grasp. Clad in a plain, grimy jerkin, both the wearer and the garment looked in need of washing.

"If you continue to struggle, I shall summon the Watch and inform them of your recent activities, young thief. Which of us do you imagine they will believe? And what do you suppose will happen then? The choice is yours."

The youth ceased his efforts to free himself but remained sullen and defiant.

"Excellent. Now give the taller boy here back his purse. And do not attempt to stab me with your knife while doing so." Silvestrus maintained his grip while the dirty-faced youngster, with obvious reluctance, reached into his tunic, withdrew Thaddeus' pouch—cut strings and all—and tossed it to him.

Thaddeus caught the purse and thrust it into his pocket. He then angrily advanced on the boy, ready to settle things then and there.

Silvestrus, however, held up his other hand in restraint.

"Peace, Thaddeus. You have your treasure back, and you are uninjured. Come, let us move off this busy street to a quieter location. That way, we will disturb no one while we become acquainted."

Without relaxing his hold, the old man steered the young thief to a nearby alley while the others followed with the mule and cart. Taking in Silvestrus' glare, the various passersby who had stopped to watch the disturbance turned and went on their way. Silvestrus leaned close to the boy's ear and murmured a word, then stepped back.

"Now, let us see what we have here. Lad, what is your name?"

The boy muttered a profanity.

"Ah, yes, I am familiar with that phrase—one from my youth, but hardly flattering. Let us make another effort. What is your name?"

An alternate short phrase was quoted.

"Hmm, I am not sure that is anatomically possible. But perhaps we should try another tack and strive to elevate the caliber of the conversation a bit. *Spumo!*"

Immediately a gush of white bubbles began spilling out of the boy's mouth as he gagged, spit, and coughed—his face contorted in a terrible grimace. Gurgling sounds impeded his attempt to speak.

After another word from the old man, the frothing dissipated.

"All right, once more. What is your name?"

"You're a Sorcerer!" the boy said accusingly.

"Oh, my, yes, indeed. And you are a thief. Do you wish another demonstration of the Art, or are you feeling more cooperative?"

"Are you going to turn me into a dung beetle, then, and lock me in a cage?" the young pickpocket asked anxiously.

"Now that is a very interesting idea. I will consider it. But, meanwhile, one final time: what is your name?"

The boy's brow furrowed. "Rolland. What's yours, old man?"

"Well, it seems we are going to have to add *respect* to your syllabus, which is growing longer by the second. Although you do have spirit— and courage," he said, surveying the street thief closely. "I will give you that. But to answer your question, my name is Silvestrus. I am a Sorcerer, and I sit on the High Council of the *Collegium Sorcerorum*—the College of Sorcerers—toward which my Apprentices and I are currently making our way."

Rolland's eyes flicked quickly to Thaddeus and Anders, then back to the old traveler.

"Where do you live, young Rolland?"

"Wherever I choose. I am a free man," the boy snapped.

"Are you now? Well, congratulations. And your father? Your mother? Where do they live?"

"They—they're dead. I take care of myself now. I'm one of Faran's Falcons. You have heard of him, I know."

"Not especially, but I would venture a guess that he is the leader of the Young Thieves' Guild in this city."

The boy was taken aback. "How do you know that? I never told you. Do you read minds, too, Sorcerer?"

"Signs, not minds. It is almost the same, sometimes, or so the philosophers say. However, indulge me in some speculation, Rolland." The old man began ticking off points with his free thumb and fingers. "You are an orphan." A momentary look of pain stole across Rolland's features. "You steal to stay alive, serving a bigger thief, who, no doubt, serves an even bigger thief, and so on.

"I would venture you have seen friends caught and lose a hand, an ear or a tongue—or even their heads. You are often in danger and have few things of value that you can claim for all the risks you take. You can neither read nor write. You cannot recall the last time you were truly clean, went without gnawing hunger or enjoyed sleep without care—or the last time someone told you they loved you. Does that more or less sum things up?"

The boy looked down at the ground in silence.

"Yes, I thought so. Well, I have a better offer. I believe you should come with us to the *Collegium*. There you will be fed regularly, you will have a warm place to sleep, and you will be in fear of neither your life nor the gaol. You will not have to do anything particularly onerous, and you will have friends—true friends. Also, you will become literate. And, not incidentally, you will be taught to become a Sorcerer."

The thief's mouth dropped open in astonishment. But his reaction was not more significant than that of the other two boys.

"What? Master, are you certain?" Thaddeus blurted out, surprised. "Not ten minutes past he was trying to rob us of all we had!"

"All the more reason to give him those things of value we do have—literacy, knowledge, insight, wisdom. Then he will not feel he has to steal from us.

"Well, what do you say, Rolland of Fountaindale? Are you game?"

Rolland's eyes narrowed. "What's the hook?"

"The 'hook,' as you put it, is that you will have to apply yourself—your will, and your mind—harder than you have ever done in your life." He paused and stared intently at the boy. "And you will have to obey the other Masters and me."

"I don't think so, Sorcerer. I've seen your kind before, I have. You're a tricksy folk and never say what you mean right out. I don't believe I trust you."

Thaddeus was relieved. He was unsure if he liked this brash, raggedy boy anyway—especially after the scofflaw stole his three gold pieces.

Anders, however, who had been looking thoughtful, quirked a smile. "It's just as well, Master. Asullus would not have wanted to talk with a street urchin such as this, in any case."

Rolland turned to Anders with a challenging gaze. "And just who is this Asullus, and why should I care whether or not he wants to talk with me?"

"Oh, Asullus, there." The young Apprentice from Meadsville gestured over his shoulder at the beast. "He is a mule—a special mule. He talks to us. All the time."

"What? Are you touched by the Gods? Mules don't talk."

"This one does—but only to people he likes. I doubt that would be likely to include you."

"A talking mule! Ha! Trying to put one over on me, are you? Well, I have heard enough. Let go of my arm, old man, and I will be on my way. A talking mule! Do you really think me that barmy?"

Asullus eyed the scruffy boy critically. "Well, laddie, I'd say ye qualify as well as any other I ha' seen wi' me own eyes. An' you could certainly use a bath, I'm thinkin', though soapin' up the face was a good start, don' ye know."

Rolland gasped. "It's a trick! I saw the like with a talking broom at the Shire Fair one year. Some traveling man did it with his voice, Faran said."

Asullus shook his head mournfully. "'Tis the Gods, indeed, who are personally set against the mule, I says. First, I'm accused o' no' speakin', and then I gets accused o' that very same act. An' now, I'm bein' compared to a simple household tool. I'm tellin' all who be listenin' that as soon as we're done here, I'm headin' meself directly back to Cobbly Knob an' the tender care o' Lady Lilith—no more ungrateful an' misbehavin' boys, no more riskin'-me-neck adventures, an' surely no more o' old men who always be makin' me life a misery at every opportunity."

"I still think it's a trick," Rolland said with a scowl.

"Well, Rolland, I believe there is only one way for you to find out for certain. And that is to come with us. A sharp lad such as yourself should have no difficulty parsing out the truth of the matter soon enough. Then, once you are satisfied with what you have learned, you may return home any time you like." Silvestrus regarded the boy carefully. "So, what is your decision?"

"Oh, I'll go with you—by my own choice, you understand —just to discover your tricks and disprove all the nonsense I've heard about Sorcerers and their so-called Magicks. Then, when I return in triumph to Faran's Falcons, everyone will know you and your kind for what you really are."

"Well said, *Magister Furum*. Agreed. Now walk with me and the others to an inn I know here, and we will talk more of *tricks*."

Thaddeus fell in with Anders as they walked behind the Master and the thief. Thaddeus stared intently at the boy thief's back. He was growing accustomed to his new life away from home, but this brought back feelings of doubt.

"Why did you bait that thief with Asullus? I don't think he's a good addition to our group at all. Though I do feel sorry for him, a bit, in that he has no parents."

Anders seemed to be less concerned.

"Hmm, if that's even true, Thaddeus. Well, it seemed to me the Master wanted this boy for some reason. So, it must be important to him, true? And, somehow, I knew it was necessary that the thief make his own choice to come with us. So, I thought of Asullus—a talking mule would make anybody curious. And it occurred to me that if this Rolland was curious enough, he might be more apt to want to come along."

"Well, all right, if you say so, but I still say he's likely to be more trouble than he's worth." Thaddeus was disappointed Anders didn't echo his sentiment or at least validate his fears. *That street thief did just steal from me*, he reminded himself.

The group traveled several *stadia* further until Silvestrus signaled a halt in front of what had been a grand old villa long ago, but now, nestled between a smithy and a bakery, was an inn called *The Sword in the Scone.*

The inn's hostler appeared from around a corner, hailed them, and immediately took charge of Asullus and the cart—though Asullus always maintained this was looking at the process backward—while the rest of the party went inside. The interior was dark and cool with tile floors and great slabs of green marble composing the fireplace, staircase, and half-walls, with the rest finished in a warm, dusky wood that had been polished smooth over decades, perhaps centuries.

The innkeeper was in vigorous conversation with one of the serving maids, but upon spotting Silvestrus and the boys, he gave the girl a peremptory order and made a beeline for the group. He immediately grabbed Rolland by the scruff of the neck.

"Ah, Master Silvestrus! Good to see you again, it is. Ah, so you have caught one of the street hooligans who plague our fair city. 'Tis a shame how they get out and about, bothering innocent travelers and discouraging commerce. But never you mind about him. I will send Aldo here for the Shire Reeve quick as can be. They know how to deal with his sort. It will be short shrift for him. Heh-heh! You won't be stealing from upstanding folks without hands or neck, will you now, boy?"

Silvestrus put a gentle restraining hand on the fat innkeeper's fore-arm. "Oliffe, it is all right. As it turns out, this boy is with us—an old legacy from another time. Appearances can be deceiving."

The innkeeper looked skeptical. "Not to doubt you, Master, but I would swear on my grandmother's trotting harness that I saw this particular redheaded lad before. He sneaks around the clientele, and after every encounter, someone's purse goes missing. Are you certain?"

"Yes, quite certain, good Oliffe. But it is most reassuring that law-abiding citizens such as yourself keep an eagle eye out to protect your town's guests and visitors. I shall be sure to mention it to my brother travelers when next I come to the College."

The innkeeper relaxed his grip on the boy, smiled broadly, and added a quick bow. "It is always an honor to serve the Order. Now, I expect you will be wanting rooms and something to delight the palate from my kitchen. Our room choice is not as it usually is, what with all the logging factors and merchants in town for the Solstice, but I feel sure we can find whatever it is you require."

"My thanks, Master Oliffe. Our needs will include your best room facing the courtyard. Are the baths open at this hour?"

"Yes, indeed, Master Silvestrus. I will send Gertie down with an extra supply of towels, and Aldo will take your things up to our best room. Even-tide will be served at the eighteenth hour, and we have lamb to offer you tonight. Please enjoy your stay and send me word if you need anything else. Your rooms are just up the staircase there, but you know the way."

The innkeeper turned and shouted, "Gertie! Aldo! To me!"

Silvestrus bowed and turned to make his way to the upper story.

"Just what was the nature of your last misunderstanding with Master Oliffe, Rolland?" he asked without glancing back at the boy thief.

"Nothing of the sort he tells. The man is a notorious liar. He claims his receipts for a week last spring went missing. I happened to be passing by the inn on my way to see my auntie—ill with the dengue fever she was—and he spots me and draws the wrong conclusion, shouting for the watch and raising quite a commotion. I think he's the one to blame, actually—I mean, if a man is going to leave his treasures out on the table in plain view, walk away to pester the cook, and then be upset at their absence when he returns, why assign a random passerby the responsibility for his misfortune, when it was his own carelessness as brought about the difficulty in the first place?"

"I understand your reasoning. What was the approximate amount that went missing, would you suppose?"

"Something over thirty Imperials. It'd been a slack week for him, as I recall."

"I see. Well, perhaps we can make it up to Master Oliffe at some point. In the meantime, I think it would be in the best interest of everyone if no more proceeds mysteriously vanished during the time we are guests here. I am certain you grasp my meaning."

The group climbed the grand staircase, with Thaddeus watchfully trailing a bit behind. He had no reason to trust the recently recruited scrawny redhead and a goodly number of reasons to doubt him. They turned down the hall, passing several carved oaken doorways until they came to the last room on the right.

"In here, lads," Silvestrus ordered, opening the door and taking the key from the lock.

Spacious and elegant, the room reminded Thaddeus of the vintner's mansion in Figberry, but even more furniture graced the richly patterned rugs: four beds, each with a delicately carved headboard and an old oaken traveling chest at the foot; two desks; four padded chairs; a small table; and seven floor urns with stands. Thaddeus glanced at Rolland in time to see his calculating eye as he surveyed the room, lips moving as if summing up figures.

"Rolland, what I said about any missing monies also applies to any missing items while we remain at this inn," Silvestrus said over his shoulder as he stood, hands clasped behind his back, in front of the window overlooking the courtyard.

A frown of disappointment crossed the street boy's features, but Thaddeus felt pleasure at the censure. The newly arrived redheaded thief had, after all, robbed him of his father's hard-earned gold. Even though it had been returned, this Rolland did not seem particularly sorry about it. Still, it might be possible that he would turn out to be a generally good traveling companion. But he would have to see. In the meantime, without undue guilt, Thaddeus enjoyed the boy's comeuppance.

"Now, I have a few things to discuss with our host. While I am thus engaged, I think it best if the three of you made your way down to the baths—they are on the lowest level of the inn —and bathe yourselves before even-tide.

"And as for you, Rolland, a change of clothes will be provided. Come back here when you are through. But take your time. You might as well relax and enjoy the moment. Besides, you all could use the experience. Some more than others."

Silvestrus pivoted and left the room only to be replaced by Aldo, who beckoned the boys to follow him downstairs.

The baths, located under the ground floor of the old villa, were faced with green marble up to the cavernous ceiling. Steam rose lazily from the water's calm surface. Two towel-wrapped men—Graecolian merchants by the look of them—were engaged in an intense discussion in a corner enclosed by a ring of heated rocks. Otherwise, the boys had the baths to themselves.

Anders, obviously accustomed to this kind of convenience, took a towel from Aldo, doffed his clothes, and stepped into the water, giving a great sigh of pleasure as the steam enveloped him. Thaddeus shrugged, then aped Anders, joining him in the hot pool. He looked up to Rolland, who remained dry.

After a time, however, Rolland, unwilling to be left behind, gingerly joined his new companions in the bath, albeit with a worried look on his face.

"I think the heated water must come from an underground thermal spring that they tap into and pipe up here," Anders explained, taking a stoppered bottle holding a deep blue liquid from a ledge near the pool and pouring a measure of it into his hand. "Though at home, we heat the water in the pipes themselves." Replacing the bottle, he began rubbing the contents into his hair and soon wore a cap of white bubbles. "Go on, Thaddeus. You, too, Rolland. It's just soap, but it smells good and keeps the bugs off." He passed the bottle to the others, and they again imitated his actions. The shared situation and pleasant sensations worked to loosen the boys' reserve.

Rolland, who had hitherto been silent, spoke up. "So, the old man is going to try to make you two and me into Sorcerers? And he's on the up and up?"

"Oh, yes," Anders answered. "He is. He's a Sorcerer, for sure. I saw him do things. Thaddeus has, too. Come to think of it, so have you—

and not that long ago." He smiled crookedly. "How did that soap taste, anyway?"

Rolland grimaced. "Like *stercus!* I'd like to pay him back for that someday."

"Be careful about trying it anytime soon," Thaddeus said. "He seems pretty alert. I don't think much gets by him."

"So, what's it been like for you two since you started?"

Anders worked up more lather in his hands. "Well, Thaddeus was picked first. In Beewicke—that's his home."

Rolland nodded knowingly. "Oh, the place they get the honey from."

Thaddeus had a sinking feeling that for the rest of his life, it would never be possible to separate himself from Beewicke and its apian confection.

"And he was shot by brigands, and then a *Daemon* came and ate them! Then he was nursed by a beautiful, ah...night lady. Go on, Thaddeus, tell him about that."

"Well, it's not so much. I was just getting my bundle down from the cart when—"

"Oh, and Thaddeus, don't leave out the part about the blue butterflies!"

After savoring the steamy water's pleasure in silence for some time, Anders spoke. "This water is quite nice. Come on—let's go down to the deeper end and practice swimming."

"Uh, you go ahead. I'll wait here," Rolland said, his reluctance betraying his nervousness.

Anders paddled off for the other end of the pool while Thaddeus, acting on a sudden burst of insight, addressed the thief.

"There's probably not a lot of swimming in your line of work here in the city."

"No…uh, none at all, actually."

"Well, I grew up in the backcountry, and our parents were throwing us in the creek from the time we could walk. It's taught me a couple of tricks about making your way about in the water without getting a snootful up your nose. Come on down with me—hold onto the ledge as we go, nice and easy. You can stand, and I can show you what I mean. Then you try, if you like, and see what you make of it."

After a moment, Rolland nodded. Hand over hand, he followed his tall fellow Apprentice. Very soon after, he was splashing about with the others. A smile of accomplishment flashed across his features, followed quickly by an assumed air of indifference as if to keep from showing anyone how he actually felt. After a time, the boys made their way back to the shallow end.

"Thanks," he muttered to Thaddeus as he paddled by.

Sometime later, the trio emerged from the baths, squeaky clean and considerably refreshed.

The boys found their clothes folded and waiting for them close by the heated rocks, and they got dressed. As they headed up the gray slate steps, Anders nudged Thaddeus, nodded in Rolland's direction, and mouthed, "Asullus."

Thaddeus stared at his short friend a moment, then blinked, nodded, and said, "Oh," softly.

"Say, Rolland, why don't you come with us out to see Asullus? There can't be that many talking mules, even in Fountaindale."

Rolland looked at them critically. After considering for a moment, he nodded.

The boys headed up and out to the stable yard. But as they were making their way around the back of the building, four rough-looking youths lounging by the fence that marked the villa's perimeter hailed them. The oldest-looking member of the group stepped forward and confronted the Apprentices.

"Hey, Rufus! You'd better leave off from your patsy friends here. Faran wants to see ya, and he don't look much pleased. Want us to gush this lot here for ya? Looks like they might ha' a copper or two we could be usin.'"

"Leave off, Sagar. I got the edge here, and I'll be lettin' Faran in on the score soon enough."

"Ya know he ain't gonna like that none. An' we can be sure he hears the tale. C'mon, lads, puss-lips here has some new marks and don't seem ta wanna share. Give 'em all a kiss for us, sweet-butt." The ragged group ambled off with exaggerated steps and raucous laughter.

Rolland looked angry, ashamed, and alarmed in turn.

"Boys you know? From…before?" Thaddeus asked.

Rolland nodded. "They're a mean group and they'll try to make trouble for us if they can. Strange, though—until today, those boys were like family to me, but everything seems different now. I can't explain it."

"I know what you mean. I've had the same feeling ever since I left Beewicke." Thaddeus sighed. "I think we're probably all going to need to stick together and look out for each other now."

10

Belief
Fides

As Anders walked along the path with Thaddeus and Rolland, his attention shifted from what they were saying, and he became preoccupied with the grounds around him. He focused his gaze on the soggy, manure-filled yard in front of the stable and the daisy-lined fence surrounding it. As he studied the perimeter, he observed the progress of a sow and the seven smaller versions of herself she was leading across the patch, appearing to carefully follow a particular course.

One of the shoats strayed off the path she'd marked and immediately became bemired up to its nose in the tenacious, smelly, treacherous ooze. The piglet squealed, and the harder it struggled, the more deeply it sank. The mother pig went mad, grunting and nudging at her baby until it was finally able to work itself free. One more foot span further out in either direction from the old sow's track and…

Lost in thought, Anders reflected on the fact that he prided himself in being prepared for any and all eventualities—that is, as far as he possibly could. Those street bullies from earlier had frightened him more than he wished to let the others know. What if he ran into them again? What if he were alone when he did? He glanced again at the row of full-petaled daisies, proud in their yellow-and-white finery, lining the periphery of the fence.
He nodded to himself.

Anders was jarred back to the moment by a sudden movement.

Thaddeus had grabbed Rolland's arm. "Come along; we will go see Asullus. You will not believe some of the things he says."

The three Apprentices rounded the corner of the building and entered the gloomy stable. The musty smell sent Anders into a fit of sneezing. In the last stall, they found Asullus lying on his back, wedged against the stable wall with his feet in the air.

"I've never seen a mule do that before," Rolland observed," unless it was already dead."

"I'll thank ye to keep yer observations on me postures o' repose to yerself, laddie. Ye don' hear me describin' yer every which way when ye be layin' aboot, now do ye?" Asullus rolled over and got to his feet with what passed for a maximum of equine dignity, shook himself, and then sauntered over to the boys.

Surprised, Rolland turned to his new friends. "He does have a lot to say, doesn't he?"

Thaddeus nodded. "You know, Rolland, I remarked on the same thing to Anders not two days ago. In any case, Asullus of Cobbly Knob, let me present Rolland of Fountaindale, Master Acquirer of Small Treasures such as loose coins and the occasional unguarded apple. Rolland of Fountaindale, here stands Asullus, late of Cobbly Knob, our stalwart and boon companion. Meet and be friends."

Rolland bowed. "Your service, honored old mule."

Asullus made a leg. "An' yers as well, young thief."

Thaddeus chuckled. "Asullus, why don't you go with us out to the meadow? Walking a bit will give you a chance to work out, um, any aches in your bones."

"It'd be me pleasure. Lead on, young masters."

Anders, however, spoke up. "You three go on ahead. There's something I have to take care of."

"What?" Thaddeus asked. "Anders, where are you going?"

"Oh, just going to check on some flowers, you know, and some fertilizer. I'll return anon." He excused himself, leaving his newfound friends scratching their heads.

"Now, where's he off to?" Rolland asked.

"I have no idea," Thaddeus said, puzzled. "Usually, he only takes action if he has a reason for it. We'll have to wait and see."

The gray mule spoke. "Ah, ye two, be no a-feared. Though me time in observation's been short, 'tis true, I can tell, yer scholar has a purpose, an' 'tis serious in nature. No doubt, he's figurin' out summat that'll be makin' yer lives better in some way."

It was not long before Anders rejoined the group, though he offered no explanation for his absence. Rolland looked to Thaddeus, who shrugged.

The group set off again.

On their way back to the stable, the three Apprentices took an alleyway shortcut familiar to Rolland. "This is a quick way to the inn," the young thief said.

"Anders," Thaddeus asked. "Will you tell us another of your stories tonight? You know, about the old Empire and all."

"Oh. All right, Thaddeus. I'd be glad to. In fact, I could—"

His speech was suddenly cut off when, rounding a corner, they were confronted by six boys—the four from earlier that day, plus two new toughs. The lads looked arrogant and menacing.

The tallest of the villains spoke over his shoulder. "Hold on, lads! We found the group the man sent us after."

The speaker turned back to address Rolland. "We know a fella as wants to make yer friends' acquaintance, Rufus. So, he asked us to bring them to 'im. Says they got some explainin' to do. Of course yer gang here will need to leave all their possessions, includin' their clothes, right where they stand. And that mule'll come in handy. We can use 'im to haul some of the load across the mountains, then sell him for the glue-pot for a penny or two when we finish with 'im."

Rolland strode forward, thrusting himself between the two groups. "Back away, Sagar! These are my friends, and they have nothing to do with you. I will go see Faran myself, and you'll soon be taking my orders again."

"Friends? Hah! Not a chance true, Red Dog. This ha' got nothin' to do with Faran. This is *extra*—just fer *us*. Things have changed, and yer in for it now. It's high time ya got your comeuppance, anyway, and I been lookin' for a chance to gi' it to ya. All right, me buckos, I'll handle Rufus, here. The rest o' ya bring down young treetop over there and get the short britches. Stooks, you get that old mule. If any of 'em tries to give you a git, use yer knives."

The street boys moved to surround the three Apprentices and Asullus. A knife flashed in Sagar's hand and one just as suddenly in Rolland's. The two crouched, moved toward each other, and began circling. The two larger roughnecks headed for Thaddeus, one with a cudgel and the other with a broken-off shovel handle, while the two shorter toughs turned toward Anders. Then the last thief, a scrawny, pockmarked boy, moved toward Asullus.

Thaddeus saw Anders' gaze swivel between the two advancing toughs.

"I hear your mother likes the taste of manure after she spunks it with your brothers!" he shouted, his pronouncement accompanied by a rude gesture. Then Anders turned and ran out of the alleyway, all elbows and heels. The two thieves gave a howl of rage, drew their knives, and raced after him.

At once, the scrawny one advanced on the mule, grabbing for his halter. "Come 'ere, ya lousy fleabag."

Asullus backed up a step. "Donno' even think aboot puttin' yer scabby touch on me, *Pustula*. Ye'll no' be leavin' here in one piece; I do so promise."

The thief stopped, confused, and looked warily about. He drew his knife and advanced. "I said come here, you stupid ass. If I cut one o' your ears a bit, maybe ye'll hear better after that." He reached out again.

"Don'sayIdidno'warnyeinaccordancewi'alltheruleso'modernwarfare," Asullus barked in one breath. Then, braying loudly and rising up on his hindquarters, he came down hard with both front hooves striking square on the young tough's chest. With a sickening crunch, the boy fell to the pavement like a sack of ripe melons and laid still.

Turning sharply, Asullus galloped toward the other boy with the cudgel, who was threatening Thaddeus. Asullus rode him down, then circled around. "Thaddeus, lad! Get his stick!" the old mule commanded.

Thaddeus dodged sideways, grabbed the club from the ground, and whirled to face the older boy coming at him with the shovel handle. The street thug swung his weapon over his head and down at the Apprentice, attempting to brain him—but met only empty air.

Pivoting around his assailant, Thaddeus struck him in the stomach with all the force he could muster. As the air left the thief, he buckled over in pain and fell to his knees. Thaddeus leaped forward and hit him again with a solid blow to the back of the head. The hapless thief crumpled to the cobblestones and did not move again, either.

Breathing hard, Thaddeus stood in the shock of the moment. He must have just knocked the boy out. He couldn't be…

At once, he came to himself and looked up to see only Sagar left standing. The tall boy had not yet closed with Rolland but was circling him warily, licking his lips.

"What's eatin' at ya, Sagar? Lose your tenders? Yellow your natural color? Asullus! Thaddeus! Get behind him and pin him down so I can carve his tripes out!"

The street boy named Sagar looked around wildly. "The man'll be comin' for you, root-head! The past is shut! Just you wait!"

Now alone, the gang's leader broke and fled down the alley.

Asullus trotted over to join Rolland. "Ye ha' a soft spot in yer heart, I see, laddie, fer this here Sagar, lettin' him go an' all."

"Well, he saved my life once. Now, I guess we're even. Next time, though—"

"Aye, Rolland! Asullus!" Thaddeus called out. "Did you see which way Anders went?"

"I did see him spool 'round the corner as if the *Furiae* themselves were in pursuit, which they was, in a manner o' speakin'."

Come on, after them!" Thaddeus shouted.

Gripping his club even tighter, he ran out of the alley with Rolland at his heels. However, it was Asullus who, galloping past, took the lead and disappeared ahead with the other two trying to catch up. Turning the corner at the back of the inn, the boys skidded to a halt, barely avoiding a collision with the mule, who stood there shaking.

"Haw! Haw! Haw! Oh, good at it, me pride an' joy! Oh, me bright, bonny boy!"

Thaddeus looked past Asullus to see Anders at the far side of the lot, near the stable entrance, laughing while chucking horse turds at the two street boys who were mired to their mid-thighs in mud and manure, immobile, cursing, and shaking their fists.

A delicate trail of white petals from the daisies surrounding the stable yard fence wound its way across the offal. The trail was punctuated by footprints just Anders' size. To either side, off the petal-strewn path, the larger footprints of the two street toughs became deeper and deeper until they ended in the middle of the churned and oozing field.

Whooping with glee, Thaddeus and Rolland jumped up and down, slapping each other's backs and alternately ruffling Asullus' scrubby mane with joy. They, too, soon joined the turd-chucking, calling out deadly insults to the young thugs, along with their congratulations to Anders, who beamed with pleasure.

A shift in the breeze brought the familiar aroma of pipe smoke to Thaddeus' nostrils. Turning, he beheld an important-looking official advancing on them, accompanied by two men at arms in chain mail with drawn swords. Behind them, carefully picking his way over the damp ground, was Master Silvestrus with his pipe.

"All right, what is going on here?" the scowling official said.

After all concerned had given their various versions of events, the two young thieves were hauled out of their predicament and taken into custody, while the Shire Reeve sent one of his men to attend to those left in the alley. The Apprentices returned to the inn escorted by the old Sorcerer, who seemed to be having trouble keeping his lips from twitching.

After changing to fresh garments the boys joined Silvestrus in the common dining area. Amid much boistrous boasting and embroidering of events, the three relived their adventure, the three ate heartily of lamb, braised potatoes, greens, cheeses, and warm loaves of bread. Near to bursting after their sumptuous even-tide, the company made its way to the courtyard, where they took their ease in a recessed corner of the porch.

"You know," Anders said, "it's the funniest thing, but before today, running has always put me in trouble. I felt so short of breath. Mater discouraged it, saying it would make me ill. But today, I felt like I was flying!"

"I would say you had a certain motivation, my boy," the Sorcerer said from out of a cloud of smoke centered around a glowing point of light. "But speaking of such things, I need to tell you about a new wrinkle in the fabric that has come up." Silvestrus reached into his robe and withdrew a careworn brown leather pouch, which he upended on a nearby small table.

Metallic clinking sounds revealed a small pile of triangular golden coins marked by strange insignia.

"Master," Thaddeus said, immediately attentive. "Aren't those golden Dins?"

"Centi-Dins—from the land of the Cin!" Anders blurted out.

"How do you know that?" Thaddeus turned to ask his friend.

"Occasionally, our distillery gets an order for our peach brandy from merchants in the East who visit us, and sometimes they pay us in Dins."

"Anders is right," Rolland added. "I've seen a few of those myself that I lift—that is, from Eastern merchants, too."

"Ah. Very good, boys. You are all correct. After the attack this afternoon, two of the surviving perpetrators were interviewed by the Shire Reeve afterward and with, um, some persuasion, revealed that The Thieves' Guild did not order your altercation through Faran after all. Instead, it was ordered by a stranger—a man posing as a merchant—who is, it seems, an agent working for someone else. Evidently, he offered these local fellows a good deal of reward for the assault."

"They were paid to strike at us?" Anders asked, astounded.

"Yes, apparently."

"Why would anyone want to do that?" Thaddeus asked.

"Well, that is an excellent question and one I intend to answer," Silvestrus said. "But you will recall, Thaddeus, that this is not the first such attempt. Remember the archers who shot you?"

"Yes! They had golden Dins, too, didn't they, Master?"

"Yes, they did. So, it seems someone has marked one of you, or perhaps all three of you. Who and why are unknown thus far."

Rolland, who had been sitting quietly to this moment, looked around the room quickly, then spoke in a low voice. "Whoever it is, he's a dead man, then—along with Sagar and the others—once Faran hears they're working for someone else."

Anders looked to the old man. "What are we to do, Master?"

Silvestrus sighed resolutely. "We go on as we have. My task is to see you safely to the *Collegium,* and that is what I intend to do. I had thought to spend a few days here in Fountaindale, taking in the sights and leaving time for you all to get to know each other before we set out in earnest. But now, after the attack today, it would probably behoove us to leave early in the morning. I do not wish to be looking over my shoulder every time I leave the inn. So off we go. We have been traveling overland, but now I think it prudent to head straight north to River's Wood." Silvestrus cocked his head to one side. "Interesting place, River's Wood…"

"Master?"

"Yes, Anders?"

"If we're not going to travel overland—"

"We will be renting a barge and heading upstream. We will hitch Asullus to the barge, and he will pull us up the river. I will see to the arrangements for our travel first thing in the morning. Well, now, we will need an early start tomorrow, so I think it best if we all turn in. Boys, before you go upstairs, I suggest you go and see to our intrepid mule's comfort. If we are going to require a lot from him over the next several days, then we should at least give him the impression that we are concerned for his welfare." Smiling to himself, Silvestrus went into the inn, stopping briefly to speak with Oliffe before heading up the staircase.

Rolland removed a lantern off a hook hanging from the low porch ceiling, and the boys made their way to the stables.

The redhead spoke first. "Just what part, exactly, of learning to be Sorcerers involves ducking people who're getting paid to be at us all the time?"

"I don't know," Thaddeus replied. "But I wish I did. I have to admit; the Master never mentioned this part of things to Mother and Father. Or to me, either, for that matter."

"You know, I don't believe he knew of it," Anders said. "He seems as surprised as the rest of us."

"Well, his concern is right, considering," Rolland remarked. "I mean that business in the stall was a bit of a close thing. It could've gone the other way, you know."

"Another reason for us all to stick together. But, if it's somebody paying other people to do this, why? What's so special about us?"

"Dunno. Maybe all Apprentices go through this," Rolland said.

"Well, it's not much of a recruiting point, is it now?" Anders sasked drily.

The boys made their way to the back of the stall. Asullus rose to greet them, looking expectantly from Apprentice to Apprentice and considered their offerings.

"Carrots. Hmm. Well, I'll no' be refusin' 'em, but 'tis well known in most circles o' the truly educated that fruit o' the red type do seem better fer the general disposition than the orange. An' that I ha' straight from one o' the very highest himself."

"Oh? And who might that be, old mule?" Rolland asked.

"Meself, o' course. Well, now, laddies, what is it brings ye all the way out here to visit me in me bedroom at this time o' the clock, gi'en all yer day's events an' exertions an' such?"

"Silvestrus wanted us to look in on you and see how you were faring," Thaddeus answered.

"Oh, he did, did he now? Then there's something sinister in the mix, an' that's fer certain. That parsimonious old horse thief will in no way be deviatin' from his dear-held doctrine o' unenlightened self-interest, mark me now. Hmm, I do see it in yer eyes, lookin' at ye from one to another. Well, then, out wi' it, lads."

"You have the right of it, Asullus," Thaddeus said. "Master Silvestrus is going to rent a barge, and he says you're to tow it —with us and our supplies in it—all the way up to River's Wood."

"Really? Did he now? Well, we'll be seein' aboot that, we will! Forced labor, that is. I ha' me rights too, ye know, an' friends in high places, I do. Meself an' the other mules—all together we'll be formin' a solidarity group, we will, to be seein' aboot what our employers can do to us, an' what they canno'. An' then we'll be marchin' on—"

Asullus' attention was suddenly diverted by the appearance of the old hostler and his helper bringing a new horse into the stable.

"Aye, Artie, a new arrival. Just came in. Such a pretty dapple, ain't she now? And perky, too. No, the man said to put her in stall seven, next to the mule. No, I dinna know why but 'tis what he said to do. So those are the orders. Excuse us there, young masters, coming through here."

Asullus continued. "So, as I was sayin', we might be formin' a group, an'—hmm, pretty lass, ain' she now? Where was I? Oh, yes, he canno' be havin' his way wi' us all the time. My, she is a…that is to be sayin'… hmm…

"I tell ye what, lads, this lady looks to be sore alone an' forlorn this night, no doubt scared an' alarmed at all the goings-on an' whatnot, an' in need o' a bit o' comfort, so to say. I'll, uh, get back wi' ye later. Ye'll be needin' yer sleep, o' course, an' we can talk in the mornin', most like."

The stableman led the mare into her stall, saw to her immediate grooming needs, made sure she had water, turned her around, and left the stable.

Asullus' attention was now focused solely on his new stablemate, all other thoughts and considerations apparently having dissipated into the night air.

Rolland nudged Thaddeus and Anders, and all three exchanged knowing looks.

Thaddeus cleared his throat. "All right, Asullus. We can, uh…come back and see you in the morning concerning your rights and all that. Have a good, uh…repose."

"Aye. Thanks be to ye, boys, I—Well, hello there, lassie, me name be Asullus. Now I know ye may be thinkin' I'm a bit short, an' a mule an' all, but donno' be deceived, Missy. There's more here than meets the eye. For example, let me be tellin' ye summat concernin' meself, such as aboot the time when I was facin'—just this afternoon as it turns out— nineteen bloodthirsty villains armed to the teeth wi' swords an' such, who was wantin' nothin' less than to…"

Grinning, the boys left the old mule to his delights and walked back toward the inn over the cobblestone pavement.

"Anders, why are you frowning?" Thaddeus asked as they turned the corner to enter the inn.

"Oh, I was just thinking 'tis too bad we'll not be staying another day in Fountaindale. There seems to be so much to see."

"Not to worry yourself, Anders," Rolland responded. "It's not such a marvel, believe me. I've seen every stinking corner of this piss-hole town, and no one cares if you're being shot at or carved up when taken unawares. Any other place has got to be better—at least I hope so. Else why leave?"

Soon, the three Apprentices arrived at the inn, tramped up the stairs, and, casting doubts aside for the moment, began making plans for the next day and what it might bring.

11

Ogre
Orcus

A rustling sound awakened Thaddeus. When it persisted, he turned his head toward where Rolland slept. The thief's eyes were open, and he gave Thaddeus a nod. Thaddeus cocked his head toward their third companion, who was gently snoring. He seemed to do this more when he was on his back.

"Ssst, Anders. Wake up! Let's go see Asullus," Thaddeus said in a loud whisper.

Anders started to open his eyes, closed them for a moment, then opened them again. "Oh, right. I'm awake, I think."

Rising and stretching, the three Apprentices tramped down the inn's narrow stairway and headed for the stables. They found the mule fast asleep with a fixed grin on his face. He was on his back with his legs in the air. On brief inspection, they found the adjacent stall empty and the dapple mare missing, with no clue as to her whereabouts.

After a moment's consultation, the boys each took out a fresh apple and began crunching on them loudly.

Asullus stirred. "Ah, darlin' Phoebe, ye're a fulsome wench, ye are, but ye ha' done me in entire, an' I admits it freely. But yer fragrance, tho', is to die fer an' be happy in the process, an' reminds me strongly o'—" Asullus' eyes snapped open, "—apples!"

"Good morning, friend Asullus, on this bright and sunny day!" The boys sang out together, grinning from ear to ear.

The old mule snorted, rolled, and rose to a wobbling stance.

After feeding Asullus and seeing to his grooming, the boys put the tools back on the shelf in Asullus' stall. Thaddeus looked up at Rolland for a minute, then Anders. Then his gaze shifted to the gray mule.

"Asullus, may we ask you something?"

At the mule's nod, Thaddeus continued.

"We talked among ourselves about the attack yesterday—and that one before, with the archers, and—"

"P'rhaps ye wishes to know if they be connected, an', if so, how is it that's true?"

"Yes," the three boys said simultaneously.

"Well, I'm assumin' here the Master ha' said, aye, they may be connected. Donno' why, but I'll be takin' care o' it, an' no' to worry, yes?"

"Yes," Thaddeus replied.

"Well, then, what be the rub? Yer Master ha' said all will be well, after all."

"Asullus," Anders spoke up. "Both of those, I think, were close calls. Rolland has rightly said they could have easily gone either way and, well—"

"All right, now, boys. Ye listen up and listen good. Ye have at yer backs one o' the most powerful practitioners o' the craft in the whole world, entire—that bein' yer verra own Master. Believe it when I say, he'll no' let ye come to any harm-wise.

"As to why this fellow from the Eastlands be pickin' on ye, who can know? At least, it does no' seem to be random deeds, don' ye know, but just the one an' his sackful o' three-sided gold. Ye can count on it, that yer Master be thinkin' day an' night aboot this verra problem, an' he'll no let it go till 'tis solved, an' the perpetrator lies cold an' dead in his grave. Mark me now."

The old mule took a long breath and continued.

"Aye, it'll do ye no good to be fussin' and fumin' aboot this matter. So, just be alert, as ye ha' been, stick close to yer Master an' each other an' all will be well. An', I might add, anyone seekin' to harm a hair on yer head'll be havin' to get by me as well. An' good luck to any o' them on that account!"

The boys looked at each other and nodded in agreement.

"Now, that be more like it. Go on aboot yer businesses and donno' worry so. We'll get ye to yer College, this I swear by *Equus*, God o' those wi' four feet an' such."

This reassuring speech garnered Asullus a small assortment of apples offered from now-empty pockets, along with words of thanks.

The boys returned to the inn for break-fast, where they met Silvestrus in the great room. There, the Apprentices gulped down substantial portions of bread, eggs, day-cheese, and pork slab.

Shortly after they sopped up the last bits and licked their fingers, Silvestrus dismissed them. The young Apprentices went up to their room, packed, and came down the stairs, their few belongings stuffed into their knapsacks. Silvestrus settled accounts and bade goodbye to the innkeeper while the Apprentices hitched Asullus to the cart and stowed the group's gear on board.

The party traveled across town, then halted near the river crossing, stopping at a local provisioning merchant, the *Loci Praescripta*, obviously yet another place where Silvestrus was known and his purse welcome.

Mouths agape, Thaddeus and Anders roamed the stacks and piles of goods, stunned at what they took to be an unknowable number of rare and valuable merchandise. Rolland, however, had parted from his companions early on, and they did not see him again until their heads turned toward a conjunction of loud voices and a crop of red hair surrounded by a cluster of bodies from which the voices were emanating.

"Thief! Thief!" the middle-aged man in a brown-and-green-splotched jerkin called out.

"Get off me! No, I don't want to go to the cellar with you! Your breath smells bad!" Rolland said, his voice carrying.

At once, Silvestrus appeared in the midst of the commotion. "Ah, what seems to be the trouble, good Milford?"

"Does this rascal belong to you, Master Silvestrus? Caught him, I did, slipping one of my prize knives up his sleeve. Thought he could get away with it, he did. I'm for sending for the Proctor."

"So I see. Yes, this is one of my boys—foisted off on me by my wife's spinster sister. She sent him to me so that I might break him of some bad habits, but I see there is more to be done! Here, however, is your excellent knife back, Master Milford, and a little bit for the wear, tear, and inconvenience. Now, boy, apologize, and hopefully, there will be no more of this."

Rolland stole Silvestrus a thankful glance, then hung his head convincingly with his lower lip out in a surly pout. He mumbled, "Sorry. Won' do it no more."

"Well, I should think not. I'm not sure what has become of the youth these days, Master Silvestrus. No honor, only trouble. Well, as you have been so generous and upright, we can let this go, but I want no more of this one in my store."

"Duly noted, my good Milford, and my thanks for your generous spirit." With that, the storekeeper instructed his help to tie up the Sorcerer's purchases, which the boys then loaded onto their cart. With a final wave, the group set off, and the gathered onlookers dispersed.

Thaddeus was curious, however, as to how this self-proclaimed "professional thief" could be clumsy enough to be so easily caught in the act.

Silvestrus had driven the cart for only a short time when he stopped and bade the boys rearrange the baggage. "Something is clanking back there. See if you can find it."

The three boys had just begun moving the packed goods around when Anders gasped.

"Thaddeus," he said, "I think I've found the reason for the clanking."

Thaddeus's gaze followed his friend's pointing finger to land upon a pair of large, shiny brass lanterns Silvestrus had admired in the emporium.

"Where in the world did those come from?" Anders asked, astonished.

Thaddeus blinked, then looked up sharply to where Rolland stood, leaning over the old wagon's side-railing.

"Rolland," the tall boy whispered, "do you know anything about this? I don't remember those items being listed on the bill of sale."

"Oh, those," the redhead said, whispering back to Thaddeus. "Well, the Master said he liked their look, so I thought—"

"Ah," Anders said softly. "That business with the knife was a diversion for what you were really up to. Amazing."

Rolland smiled and demonstrated a superior, oh-nothing-to-it attitude, which lasted until Silvestrus, now standing by the cart, crooked his finger at the redhead and involved him in a lengthy discussion regarding decision-making and property rights.

The issue apparently resolved, the group made its way to the north end of the city, where the Sorcerer sought out one of the barge captains and dickered with him for equipment rental.

Asullus, meanwhile, adopted a stolid expression—half long-suffering pain and half beatific martyrdom. But the day, however, was sunny for this time of year, not damp at all, and complemented by a gentle breeze blowing up from the South.

Asullus took to his bondage with a certain stoic inevitability. The cart was loaded aboard the small barge, its wheels lashed tightly between blocks, while the boys secured the provisions on deck.

Silvestrus, last on board, gave the call to Asullus to depart and set about to light his pipe. The old mule began towing the entire assemblage upstream with as much good grace as could be expected, following the well-worn path on the western bank of the river. The four humans settled themselves strategically among the gear to achieve the best possible balance for the craft.

The Greater Flatstone River was calm and flowing smoothly. The spring runoff had spent itself by this time of year. The river folk—those not directly involved in piratical initiatives—generally kept obstructions and hazards such as sunken boats and submerged trees to a minimum.

Once the barge had traveled several leagues, the old man cleared his throat, drew an extra puff, and gestured at the boys with his pipe.

"All right, lads, now gather around here. Make yourselves some comfort on the bundles and attend to me. It is time for your education to begin and for you to get down to the work for which you were chosen."

The three Apprentices settled down as best they could on the group's belongings. Anders looked up to his master with almost rapturous anticipation, while Thaddeus was curious about what he was to learn. On the other hand, Rolland looked willing to listen but had more than a bit of skepticism writ closely on his freckled features.

The old man commenced. "You three are to be Sorcerers one day, and it is my responsibility to see to it that you turn out to be a credit to us all. Therefore, be mindful that I would not enjoy the humiliation that any purposeful failure on your part would cause me in the presence of my peers. And rest assured, I would not take to it kindly."

It seemed to Thaddeus that while the old man gazed at each of them in turn to make his point, his eyes lingered longest on Rolland.

"Bear that in mind and thus apply your best efforts, as I am certain you will, and you will do well. Therefore, absorb what I am about to tell you and try to stay awake.

"Now, as I was explaining briefly to Thaddeus the other day, the talent of Sorcery—and a rare one it is—is bred in the bones. It is a gift one has—or does not have. While a Sorcerer may come from a family of non-Sorcerous lineage, it is unusual."

The old man continued speaking. "Well now, one of the gifts that accompanies the Sorcerous trait is a life span many times that of the non-Sorcerous. No one is sure exactly how long this might be, but records suggest the encompassing of many generations. But, as with all things in this universe, what the Gods giveth, the Gods taketh away—without bothering to consult us mere mortals concerning their various whimsies. So, there is a *hook*, as Rolland would say."

The old man glanced briefly at the young thief and winked.

"The hook is that the very thing that gives a Sorcerer his long years also takes them away, bit by bit. That is, each and every exercise of the Art of Sorcery will diminish the hours and days of your life—and this includes any acts you practice while learning at school. The more complex and demanding the use, the more time, generally, is shorn from your thread."

The old man paused to relight his pipe and glanced to the port side of their barge. Thaddeus, following his gaze, marked several cut tree trunks drifting lazily downstream past their craft.

"For example, suppose a Sorcerer is interested in living the greatest number of years possible. Such a one could accrue an astounding span of decades, even centuries, to himself, but he would be a Sorcerer in name only. He could never use his gift. On the other hand, a Sorcerer could perform the most advanced and amazing things—challenging even divinity itself—but his flame would die out early with, perhaps, less than the life span of an average man."

A frown etched across Rolland's face.

"Yes, Rolland? You have something to say?"

"Well, Master, it just doesn't seem fair—to be given such a gift and not to be able to truly use it, I mean."

"Well, I will explain it as far as I understand it. Given your more—shall we say—commercial background, Rolland, you could think of it as a mercantile transaction. To practice great Art engenders great cost.

Otherwise, I suppose, we would all be living as gods in grand palaces in the clouds with a thousand servants to fulfill our every whim, slaying all our enemies with only a whisper.

"And, no doubt, we would all be bored to tears. Not to say, of course, that certain Sorcerers have not attempted this very thing. However, when they do, they seem not to last very long. Divine on Sun's Day, dead by Moon's Day—with much frenzy in between. In any case, it is, as I have said, a gift. If you would use the gift, you must be willing to accept the price for it. But I digress.

"No one has, so far, been able to factor out just how much the cost is for each individual practitioner. Some Sorcerers, for example, could make a house take wing and fly, losing thirty years of their lifetime allotment. Another, with equal gifts, attempting the same act, would lose, perhaps, only four years. While a third could drop dead on the spot at the first attempt. Also, not only does this cost seem to vary from practitioner to practitioner, but it can vary from time to time in the same practitioner. And no one has yet been able to parse out the whys and wherefores of it. The advantages of youth and vigor seem counterbalanced by the advantages of experience and wisdom."

Thaddeus stirred. "Master?"

"Yes, Thaddeus?"

"Then how do you decide when to use your power?"

"Now, that is a good question, my boy. Let us see what your colleagues would guess. Rolland?"

"Um, only for important things, Master?"

"Good. Anders?"

"Sparingly," Anders said.

"Ha! Good answers both. So, there you have it. Now, where was I? Oh, yes. Although you are born with the gift, for example, that does not mean you can merely shout *'Meretrix!'* and have some sultry siren appear in a cloud of smoke ready to do your slightest bidding. You have to learn how to do what you wish —what things to say. You see, you must first form the act in your mind, then release it through your speech. Occasionally, a gesture is needed as well. Also, it depends on *how* you say what you say. You are obliged, it seems, to use the Imperial speech—*Lingua Imperatoria.* No one knows why. But if another language is used, it will not work in the same way. It may be that this is the reason why the Ancient Ones of the Cin—whose speech is very different from ours here in the West—seem so alien. Perhaps a cleric could tell you the why of it."

Silvestrus took another long puff. "It is not merely thought, word, and gesture, either—sometimes an object or objects are required—a bowl with an unfinished leg, for example. Sometimes a powder, a potion, or certain special ingredients in certain precise combinations—or perhaps even feathers or seeds. Things from *Materna Naturae* that attract your interest may be necessary."

The boys sat silently, digesting this stew of knowledge.

Anders leaned forward. "Master, what you describe sounds very complex and confusing. How is it possible to know, always, what is needful?"

"That is the purpose of the *Collegium,* my boy—or one of its purposes. That is where you will learn what you need to know to answer those questions. But enough talk for this morning. Rolland, signal Asullus to pull over, and let us have our mid-day. Then, perhaps, a nap."

The redheaded thief stuck two fingers between his lips and gave a shrill whistle. Asullus tossed his head and moved to pull the barge over to the bank near a small inlet. The party disembarked and stretched. The boys unhitched the gray mule and gave him his ration of oats and a quick rubdown.

"Ah, 'tis a delight sure when others can know the needs o' the mule an' go aboot swiftly to fulfill the same. Grateful am I, me buckos, fer yer tender ministrations."

After making short work of the mid-day, the Apprentices suggested exploring inland. Since Silvestrus was already drowsing by the small fire they had built, they approached Asullus. But he declined and lay down on the grassy sward.

However, a moment later, his nose twitched, and he raised his head. "I'm thinkin' there's somethin' funny on the air a bit west o' here. It do no' smell too dangerous, but I'd no' go there, were I ye." With that, he lay back down and closed his eyes.

The boys looked at each other, and Thaddeus mouthed the word, *West.*

The other two nodded, and the group quietly left camp, heading away from the river. They struck out cross-country and had hiked about two *mille passuum* when Anders called their attention to a flock of ravens circling just north of them behind a small hillock. The boys turned aside and approached cautiously. Drawing close, they peered around the mound to see the voracious black birds at work on what looked like a massive man's body lying supine amidst the scrub. It was not moving.

Thaddeus surveyed the scene, then spoke softly to his companions. "It's some large manlike creature—I'm not certain what. Let's proceed west for a bit—where it came from, best I can tell—and then we can circle back to here. Keep your voices down—where there's one, sometimes there are two. Follow me." The others nodded and stayed close behind.

Thaddeus used his backwoods tracking skills, leading the boys several *stadia* further west, all the while studying the ground. He found what he was looking for: impressions in the soft earth at regular intervals, bent and broken twigs and grasses, and traces of animal fur on some brambles and burrs. He raised his hand to halt the group and pointed out his findings to the other two boys.

"Look. Here a large creature is running—but not quite a human. Probably that big lump back there that the ravens are pecking at. I believe it was trying to make it to the river. And here's wolf sign—could be a full pack. Perhaps they were chasing it, whatever it was. Looks like it didn't run fast enough, though."

Startled, Rolland glanced at Thaddeus. "Wolves? Here? Now?"

"No. These tracks are at least a day old. Maybe two."

Anders considered the traces. "Well, the wolves aren't around now. Come on, let's see what it is they were after."

The three made their way back to the carcass. As they closed the distance, however, the stench of rotting flesh assailed their nostrils.

"Ye gods! What is that smell? 'Tis worse than that time old Dicey got the pukes and poos at the Pike Street charnel house!" Rolland exclaimed.

Thaddeus nodded and began breathing through his mouth. That seemed to help. Anders rummaged through his pockets, bringing forth a colored cloth which he doused from his water skin, then tying the soaked fabric behind his neck and pulling it down over his mouth and nose.

Rolland picked up several stones from the ground and heaved them at the birds while Anders and Thaddeus alternately waved branches and hooted like an owl to cause a general commotion. The ravens rose in a mass and flew off, cawing curses at the boys. The flies, however, were not so easily discouraged and paid them no mind as they continued their feasting. The boys edged closer to the corpse but had no idea what they were looking at.

The body—or what remained of it—was bipedal and had probably stood at least three paces high. It was solidly built. The head was enormous, with large curving horns jutting out on either side of the skull. The eyes, ears, nose, lips, and tongue were missing. A massive jaw supported two great upward-curving tusks. The creature's arms would have reached below its knees. A rancid, filthy hide, torn and stripped in many places, partially covered the chest and torso. Dried clotted blood coated most of the creature while the remainder had pooled on the surrounding grass. An oversized brassbound cudgel lay off to one side beyond an out-flung arm.

"He was right-handed, anyway," Anders observed.

A broad leather strap slung over the beast's shoulder, draped down the corpse to a small hide pouch, now open, its few contents spilled onto the ground.

Rolland wrinkled his nose. "Well, Thaddeus, what is it? I mean, what was it?"

"Not human; that's for certain. Doubtful it was a giant, either. Not with those horns and tusks. And it looks nothing like that *Daemon* Charles. What do you think, Anders?"

"Not positive, but I think it was an—"

"—ogre," finished Asullus.

The boys whirled to see the old mule standing behind them with the garland around his neck. "I ha' thought I warned ye lads no' to be puttin' yer nose in this direction! 'Tis a lucky piece for ye that yer cousin here ha' giv'n up the ghost. Otherwise, ye'd be in a peach fer certain."

Rolland edged closer. "Asullus, Thaddeus says wolves were chasing it and brought it down, and not that long ago."

"Wolves?" Asullus glanced around quickly. "Aye, I smells 'em now that ye mentions it—o'er the carnage an' such. Well, I'm sure they're long gone by now, havin' completed their e'en-tide."

Thaddeus wondered who it was the mule was trying to convince.

Anders picked up the thread of conversation. "So, it is—or was—an ogre. I didn't know they came so far South, especially at this time of year."

"Usually they do no'. Mayhap he got separated from his clan. Or maybe he was a caste-out. That's as happens sometimes. Anyway, his roamin' days are o'er, an' now he's fer the daisies, eh, Anders?"

The old mule circled the carcass, inspecting it critically. "Young Rolland, come o'er here an' fetch out the sharpest o' the knives ye ha'."

The former thief did as he was told and approached Asullus with his large knife drawn.

"Good. Now cut away that piece o' hide coverin' the place where his legs meet. Do no' be spendin' yer moments gapin' at me, lad—just do it."

The other boys gathered around as Rolland sawed on the stinking pelt, though not closely. The smell, the sight of blackened blood, and the putrefaction discouraged closer examination—even with Anders' natural curiosity.

Thaddeus and his shorter companion were just as glad Rolland had been assigned this task.

Anders backed away a step. "Whee-oosh! What a stink! Overripe!"

"Aye, you have that right, but look at that! *Membrum Sacrum!* I think ye've met your match, Asullus, and then some," Rolland said, pausing in his dissection.

"I do no' know how many times I ha' to be tellin' the youth that it's no' to do wi' the size o' the sloop, but yer skills at settlin' it in the slip. But that said, I'll grant ye his missus'll be missin' him presently these long an' lonely nights. All right, me fine young chirurgeon, I'm needin' ye to carve out this gentleman's bladder, all careful-like, and lay it on the ground here nearby. Begin whene'er ye're ready."

Rolland looked surprised, then grimaced. "Asullus! That's disgusting! Are you sure there's a good reason I'm to cut this?"

"Now, do no' be gettin' all delicate on me, sweet Lucilla. Just ye do it."

"Ugh, washing for a day and a half won't get rid of this smell," Rolland complained as Thaddeus and Anders backed away from him, holding their noses. The boy shook his head but looked to the mule for further direction, which Asullus provided presently.

"All right now, fetch off that strap as is holdin' Sir Handsome's pouch, an' stuff that sweet-smelling orb that ye just removed into it. Also, we might wishes to consider searchin' the area a bit more. Ogres are said to carry treasure with 'em now an' then, they are."

Far in the distance, the group heard a faint, mournful howl, immediately joined by another. Asullus looked quickly in that direction, then back at the group.

"O' course, there be no need now to be dabblin' an' dawdlin' aboot, so 'tis a quick march back to camp fer us. I'm sure the Old Man'll be wantin' to see what it is we ha' found."

Rolland wiped his blade and hands on the grass as best he could. "But Asullus, how'll I get this gut-rot smell off me?"

"O', I don' know, laddie. It might be considered by some to be an improvement o'er yer usual situation, don' ye know. But if 'tis no' to yer companion's likin', then ye could stretch yer noggin a bit to recall we do be travelin' by a river—if that might mean anythin' to ye. Now, off we go."

Another distant howl added an incentive to movement. The boys were distinctly uneasy, though none wanted to show it. They made their hurried return to the riverbank in a much shorter time.

12

A Bladder and a Madman
Vesica Et Vesanus

nce they reached the camp, the boys found Silvestrus sitting on a stump with his pipe in hand.

"I thought for sure he'd either still be gone or sawing logs when we got back," Rolland whispered to Thaddeus.

The tall boy nodded.

"Be careful how you play this," the redhead added.

Thaddeus nodded again.

Silvestrus looked the arrivals over carefully. "I saw you a bit back but heard you farther out than that…and smelled you before you had even turned toward the river. What in the world have you got there?"

"Open up yer pouch an' show him, Red Rose," the mule barked, grinning.

Rolland spilled the pouch's pungent contents onto the ground.

"Ah," Silvestrus said, his eyes lighting up, "an ogre's bladder! However did you boys come by one of those?"

The three Apprentices began talking at once, and soon enough, the old man had the whole story.

"What're we supposed to do with it, Master?" Rolland asked, his face twisted with disgust.

Silvestrus didn't answer immediately, looking thoughtful. After a time, he turned to the old mule and addressed him. "Well, well, Asullus, you remain as resourceful as ever, and you boys are quite clever. We will need to attend to this right away."

He sprang up and walked to the cart where he rummaged for a minute or two before extracting his bag of Sorcery. He lay the bundle on the ground, then untied and unrolled it. After a moment's thought, he selected a purple phial with a cork stopper, a clear crystal bottle filled with a yellow powder and capped with a lead seal, and a small folded parchment. Holding these items carefully, he rose and walked to the campfire.

"Thaddeus and Rolland, take the kettle down to the water's edge and fill it to the brim. Then, Thaddeus, return with it here. Rolland, you remain at the river. And take some soapstone with you. A fair amount. Anders, bring me my staff."

The boys rushed to do the Sorcerer's bidding—Thaddeus and Anders eager and expectant; Rolland, chagrined and resigned.

When the pot was boiling over the fire, Silvestrus added the ingredients in specific proportions and order, and motioned with his staff. He picked up the ogre bladder with a stick and incanted, "*Inverte!*"

The bladder now appeared to have been turned inside out. The sorcerer then deposited it into the kettle.

"This must cook for a while—to cure it," the old man said.

A dripping Rolland came back to the camp, looking like a drowned cat but with most of the stench gone. Rolland toweled off and changed into drier clothes. Thaddeus and Anders filled him in on the proceedings up to that point.

"Yes. I'd gotten a whiff of that pot bubbling as I came to camp. I was hoping that wasn't to be our even-tide," the thief said with a grimace.

Thaddeus smiled, then turned to the gray mule, who had doffed his flowers again. "Asullus, why do you still keep that garland? And how is it that it remains so fresh? And why did you put it on earlier, anyway?"

"Hmm, quite the *quaestor quaesitor*, are ye now? Well, no' that 'tis any o' yer business, but just to be sociable—I ha' kept it because 'tis special to me, considerin' who gave it an' all. Fer example, why do ye still have those curly locks ye carry around in that packet so close to yer heart? Secondly, I don' know why it's persistin' in its freshness, but I'll no' be complainin'. Smells pretty as the lass herself, don' ye know. An' thirdly, 'tis none o' yer concern. There, are ye satisfied now?"

Thaddeus, who had been steadily turning redder, nodded and glanced around before changing the subject. "Think we might get rain tonight?"

Silvestrus prodded the boiling bladder with a stirring pole from time to time as he enjoyed his pipe. When the tobacco finally burned out, he stood, hooked the mass with his stick, and drew it out of the boiling mixture. "*Reverte!*" he commanded, and the bladder turned back outside-in, except it was cleaner.

"We will let it dry overnight; then we may have some use of it tomorrow. Rolland, you could probably use another soak or two, but the afternoon is getting on, so let us resume our journey and see how much further Asullus can tow us before it is time to set our camp for the night."

The mule snorted, muttering something under his breath.

"What was that, Asullus? I did not quite catch what you said," the Sorcerer asked sharply.

"I ha' said, I thought it would probably be clear tonight, though we could ha' rain on the morrow."

"I see. Well, good enough. Come, boys, get to it. We have many more *mille passuum* to cover before we rest."

The barge was quickly reloaded. Thaddeus reattached Asullus' towing tack, making sure the collar was padded in the right places, snugging the cinches, and hitching the tow rope at the best angle.

"Poor old mule," the tall lad said. "More work on little rest."

"Oh, 'tis no great suffering fer this ole body, don' ye see," Asullus replied. "Used to such burdens I am, an' be assured that 'tis meself that will accomplish this labor in much better order than that old scarecrow would, were our positions to be reversed."

The mule snorted in laughter, then turned his head back to Thaddeus. "But, 'tis a treasure sure ye be, lad, bein' concerned an' all fer this old beast. No wonder yer parents kept ye' in the house all those years feedin' ye well, 'stead o' puttin' ye out in the back o' the yard to grow up on yer own."

Once the party resumed its travel upriver, Silvestrus returned to his instruction.

"All right, Apprentices, I have told you all a little about how one comes to obtain the gift of Sorcery. But it occurs to me that you may be curious as to how each of you, specifically, was selected. The answer to this is simple: I do not know. That is to say, I cannot tell you precisely how because I do not truly know. I can tell you, however, that as I have traveled from place to place looking for likely lads, which I do from time to time, I get a nose for who might do and who might not. Each one of you I have observed before."

Thaddeus started and, with eyebrows raised, glanced at Anders and Rolland. They, too, seemed surprised.

"Though you likely will not recollect it. Nor would your parents. What draws my attention is that each of you radiates a natural energy field of sorts. Anyone with a gift for the Art of Sorcery would know another who has it—if they were looking for it. Of course, it helps if one has had experience in doing so. In addition, a special link between a searcher and a likely prospect is useful. At the request of our *Princeps Academiae* —the leader of our Order at the College—I, myself, journey about, casting my net, so to speak. I enjoy it, and it is good exercise. Additionally, it is nice to see the country and meet diverse and interesting folk. And, though I am, by nature, much too modest to admit it, I am rather good at what I do."

Asullus snorted again.

"Though not all may feel so," the Sorcerer added.

Asullus brayed a warning, "Low-hanging branch comin' up. Guard yer heads an' hats—them as has 'em."

Silvestrus looked up, then ducked quickly down as the threatening branch passed directly overhead. Rolland winked at Thaddeus and grinned. Clearly, without the old mule's timely warning, their august mentor would have suffered no small indignity at the hands of the passing foliage.

Silvestrus threw a hard eye in Asullus' direction, *harrumphed*, and returned to his instruction.

"So, we now have set the scene, introduced our actors onto the world stage, and it is time to posit our main thesis. To wit, the key to all this business—the 'critical element,' as Brother Barnabas would put it—is, simply, Belief. To put it plainly, if you are born with the talent, obtain the training, *and* have the Belief, then you can practice Sorcery—*sine qua nihil*. Belief is the third and most important component in our tripodal equation.

"The magic words, gestures, and objects exist only to abet the Belief. But Belief is the key, the cornerstone. During your time at the *Collegium*, you will hear this phrase repeated endlessly by your instructors, myself included. So, be prepared, and know that I speak truly. Listen to me closely: the stronger you Believe in what you are doing, the more you will accomplish, and the more likely you are to accomplish it—*it* being any miracle of one's choice."

Anders half-stood in his excitement, causing the barge to rock. Asullus' eyes widened, if only for a moment.

"Master?" Anders asked. "How can this be? I mean, how can merely believing in something cause it to happen?"

Talking over his companion, Thaddeus interrupted. "Master? Do you mean to say that if—"

Rolland interjected, "But, Master, this makes little sense. How does a person make something real by just thinking it?"

"Yes, well, for all of you skepticism is, generally, a healthy commodity. But, on the other hand, so is quiet acceptance," he added, eyeing each of his Apprentices in turn. It seemed he hoped to postpone further challenges so that he might complete his exposition; however, despite his best efforts, the questions continued. The more explanations and examples the old man offered, the more questions were asked, and the demand for knowledge grew.

After a time of questions and answers, Asullus, who always had one ear cocked to the rear, held a grin.

Thaddeus wondered what was going on in that old gray head of his. Then he noticed that Asullus had begun to whistle a tune.

Thaddeus' smile widened. *Imagine, a whistling mule.*

In time, Master Silvestrus announced that they were just past the halfway point to River's Wood. The party grounded for the night, but not before Silvestrus finally put an end to his Apprentices' constant badgering by glowering sternly at the demanding, skeptical group until they fell silent.

The boys, obliged to accept the admonition, did so with ill grace, resulting in an almost surly display of attitude that lasted until well past even-tide. The Apprentices then tore into the night's fare of bread, cheese, and cured coney, accompanied by the campfire's cheerful popping.

After the utensils were cleaned and stored and the camp restored to order, Silvestrus directed his charges' attention to the task at hand.

"Tomorrow, boys, we will arrive in River's Wood, which I have always considered a rather unusual place. The town's economy is based wholly on timber. However, unlike Bostle, where the lumber is prepared and shipped out, in River's Wood it is centered around the taking of the trees themselves. It is said that, in the distant past, a monastery of sorts stood at River's Wood where there lived a brotherhood of druids—an observance of cadre of tree Sorcerers if you will. They claimed to draw their power from the Earth's arbors and, in turn, devoted themselves to the protection of those selfsame trees, as well as all living things, from the ravages of civilization. However, *Commercium* itself is a powerful God and not so easily thwarted or diverted.

"These days, the population of River's Wood is comprised, by and large, of tree cullers. They are, by some divination, able to deduce which trees to cut and which to spare. The cut trees are sent downstream—you have all seen the great trunks floating by us here on the river—and, in return, they receive certain items from outside their world which they consider important to their needs."

Thaddeus stirred. "Master? Do all the folk harvest trees? Are there none who plant crops or milk cows?"

"Most, but not all. It is a bit of a mystery, but what farms there are, are few—subsistence, primarily—and scattered. As near as I have determined, most folk in River's Wood are remarkably gifted in working with wood. Almost all the artifacts you will find there are wood-based. Little metal—beyond woodworking tools—is available. Even their coinage is made from wood—although they will accept our money in certain of their stores and shops. The work of their carvers and artisans, by the by, is generally of excellent quality and demonstrates high craft."

Silvestrus rekindled his pipe, drew a draught, and continued.

"While you are in River's Wood, however, you must exercise great caution. As a rule, the people there do not look kindly upon strangers, whom they see as wishing only to take financial advantage of them or harm their forests. The townsfolk are a little less likely to trouble a Sorcerer, chiefly because we have never given them any reason to distrust us. But on the whole, they are a suspicious lot. It is best to be polite, respectful, and largely silent. We must quickly conclude any business we have with them and move on."

Rolland abruptly sat up. "Will they try to harm us for gold like the others, Master?"

"No, I do not believe so," the old man replied, "especially if you give them no reason to. Now it is late, and we will need an early start in the morning. Oh, and Rolland, I should probably mention that the last time I was in River's Wood, I did happen to see what was surely the remains of a man nailed to one of their trees leading into the village. Above his head was a meticulously carved sign reading *THIEF.* Well, goodnight, boys. Rest well."

Silvestrus rose, tapped out his pipe on the heel of his sandal, unfurled his bedroll, and laid down to take his rest.

The boys, meantime, were involved in an animated discussion concerning the dangers inherent in mixing with lunatic tree-worshipers. By the time they sought their sleep, they were favoring Rolland's strategy, that detailed a plan whereby harm done to any one of them would result in the survivors setting fire to the entire village and surrounds and watching it all burn to the ground.

Thaddeus first heard the birds begin their daily song toward the end of the last watch. It was only just dawn, and his master had not called him out yet, so he knew he had a little time to remain under his blankets. The night had passed well, though there was one particular root knob he planned on taking his ax to once he was up.

After the boys rose, they loaded up the barge again, and travel resumed until around mid-day when Silvestrus signaled another stop. The look on his face was stark. "We are nearing River's Wood. Rather than pull directly to the dock, perhaps it would be prudent to first scout the surrounding territory. I do not wish to walk into any unforeseen difficulties through ignorance when effort might have prevailed."

The party disembarked, tying the barge to an old willow tree. After partaking of the mid-day meal, the Master and his mule set off to scout the surrounding area, directing the boys to guard the barge but otherwise leaving them to their own devices.

Rolland skipped a flat stone for seven jumps. "Thaddeus, what are we going to do if some of those mad sylvans come down here wanting to know who we are and why we're defiling their land?"

Thaddeus skipped his stone for eight. "A good point. I don't care much for sitting on this barge like a nesting loon. We have no idea who or what may be lurking around these woods."

"Well, if it's information we need," Anders replied, "then we must go and get it ourselves. It surely won't come to us—until i's too late, of course."

Frowning, Rolland looked over at his friend. "What do you mean, 'go and get it'?"

"I mean, my good thief, we should form a scouting party and go see for ourselves."

Thaddeus scoured the ground for another flat stone. "Hmm. I'm partial to that idea, but Master Silvestrus told us to stay here—to make sure no one bothers our possessions. Or us."

"Well, if anyone wishes to bother us, they will come from the North, correct? So, if we head north—quietly and carefully, of course —we should see and hear them long before they see or hear us. Then we can run like the Hells back to the barge, jump in, shove out to the middle of the river, and paddle around in a circle yelling, 'Help! Help!' until the Master returns and sends that *Daemon* you keep talking about after them."

"Right. Good plan, Anders," Rolland said. "You know, Thaddeus, I think the trouble is, he just doesn't look that smart."

Anders made a rude retort.

"Aye, go on, short n' sweet, you don't even know what that means."

"I do so!"

"Come on," Thaddeus said, interrupting the exchange. "There's not much time, and we have no idea what we may run into. We can leave the barge here—it's too heavy to tug along—and we could only see what is by the shore anyway—so let's set out overland."

"Right," Rolland said. "Let's go."

The boys headed due north, parallel to the barge path and keeping close to the forest edge. Their course wound in and out of a string of tall birch trees, white against the darkening forest. Larks sang ahead of them but grew still with their passing, even though their footfalls were muted by the black detritus that lined the trail.

After they'd gone a goodly distance, Thaddeus stopped and sniffed.

"Hold on. Smell that? It smells like a cooking fire. There might be a camp of those River's Woodsmen around here. We should spy them out. Be especially careful. No noise now."

Stealthily creeping forward, the boys came to a thicket and, peering through, they saw—just a stone's throw away—a dilapidated cabin with smoke coming from its chimney. Yet it was not what they saw but what they heard that riveted their attention—a man's angry voice cursing and a dog yelping and whimpering in pain, followed by the repeated staccato sound of a stick or a strap.

"Somebody in there is beating a dog! Come on!" Thaddeus said, hot with anger. Charging the cabin, he banged open the door and rushed into the one-room hut, with Rolland and Anders at his heels.

A small, skinny man, slovenly and unkempt with several day's-growth of stubble, was holding a thick length of willow branch. As the boys watched in horror, he brought the switch down rhythmically on the back of a pale-colored, slat-ribbed, long-haired dog, whose body was already covered with welts and sores. Patches of fur were missing and scabbed out. It cowered from the man and yelped, crying pitifully at every stroke.

Thaddeus' eyes widened in rage as his fists clenched, white-knuckled. "You! Stop! Now!"

Startled, the man whirled around, mouth agape. "Who in the Hells are you?" he bellowed. "What are ye about, breaking into my house?" Brandishing the branch, he advanced on Thaddeus.

Anders and Rolland stepped from behind Thaddeus, ranging themselves on either side. One had a wooden cudgel, and the other a knife held low in each hand.

The man hesitated.

"I know this is your house, but it's not right for you to treat an animal in that way." Thaddeus paused. A quick glance at the only table in the room showed an open stone crock tumbled on its side, its amber liquid dribbling into a puddle. "Especially when you're bleary with drink." Thaddeus noticed the swaying man was red-eyed and slurred in his speech.

"How much I drink is m' business, damn ye! 'Tis *my* house, where I do what I want! And this animal—" he paused, thrusting an outstretched arm at the dog, "—is for beating. Yes, for *beating!*" The dog lay shaking, pressed against the far wall of the hovel.

The man peered at Thaddeus and adopted a crafty look. "Who sent you, eh? Madigan? Well, tell him to go orff himself. 'Tis clear what I am dealing with."

He paused, calculating. "You three—who are you? Just boys from the river? Ye ha' no idea what you got yourselves into. Said you would come, he did…and that she was the key. That beast is *not a dog*—he knew, and I knew. She changes, indeed she does. This dog is a *Daemon!* And I'll beat the *Daemon* out of her! I will!"

The man spun around and raised his arm to strike the cowering dog again, but the boys jumped forward and tackled him, knocking him to the floor.

Anders swung his club, catching the man on the side of the head, stunning him. Thaddeus grabbed the willow rod while Rolland brought his elbow down hard on the man's crotch. The drunk lay unmoving on the floor for several minutes until he stirred and moaned in pain.

Thaddeus stood over him, brandishing the whip. "All right, you. Explain yourself. We are the Apprentices of a mighty Sorcerer, and when he sees this, you'll be lucky not to be blown to bits on the spot!"

The man stared at them in silence before speaking. "Better if 'tis that, then, p'raps. You don't understand…burstin' into me place like ye did. S'truth, she is a *Daemon*! She plays all sweet, but there is summat she wants. And she's set on havin' her way."

The man's eyes bulged, and froth appeared on his lips. "She won't stop 'til she gets it. And then she'll change for certain. Oh, yes, young lads, and that'll be the end for us all. She needs be stopped an' I be the one to do it!"

The drunken man struggled to all fours and, pulling a knife from his boot, lunged at the dog.

Thaddeus stared as if frozen to the spot. But at once, his gaze grew distant as a strange thought surged into his mind. Then a voiced command issued forth through his lips.

"*Fiat Canis!*"

A peculiar roaring rush overtook Thaddeus as he looked at the man on the floor crouching in front of him—except that now it was not a man. He—rather, *it*—was blurring, changing. The man's jaws began to lengthen, as did his ears. His arms grew longer, and he began to grow fur. A tail appeared.

The boys' mouths hung open. Where the man had been, now stood a dog—a cur of mixed breed.

Rolland's eyes then glazed. "*Vermes Venite!*" he shouted.

Suddenly the dog-that-had-been-a-man retched and vomited. A great mass of wriggling worms with bloody suckers and hooks spewed from its mouth.

"*Impetus Pulicium!*" yelled Anders, wearing an identical shocked look.

A swarm of biting insects abruptly materialized above the man-turned-dog and descended upon it.

The canine creature gagged again and vomited more worms. Howling from the insects' torment, it shook its head from side to side, then bolted out of the cabin and dashed toward the woods, pursued by the biting cloud.

The pitiful yelping grew fainter and fainter until the boys could hear it no longer.

A Dog
Canis

ehercle!" Rolland cried, "What happened? What did we do?"

"I think," Thaddeus replied softly, "we just used Sorcery. What a strange feeling." He shook himself. "The dog!"

The boys rushed to kneel around the abused hound. The dog flinched from Thaddeus' careful touch but then lay still, whimpering.

"Anders, get some water," Thaddeus ordered.

Jumping up, Anders' gaze darted around the cabin for a pitcher or bowl.

"Try outside—a rain barrel."

Anders nodded and rushed outside. He was back in a moment with water in a bowl. Thaddeus held it close to the dog's mouth, lightly splashing water against the dog's nose, but the hound seemed too weak to take it. Thaddeus sopped up water with a corner of his tunic and squeezed water onto the canine's tongue. With great effort, the dog lapped it up.

"Poor, poor dog…good dog now. Good dog," Thaddeus intoned, gently stroking the dog's neck. The animal swiveled its head slowly to gaze adoringly at the boy with large and trusting eyes that were rheumy and filmed over.

Rolland turned to Thaddeus. "Well, what are we going to do now? We can't take her with us, and we can't leave her here."

Thaddeus swiveled to look at his friend. "Why can't we take her with us?"

"I can think of about twelve different reasons, all beginning with the words; *Master would not...*"

Anders knelt beside the dog. "Hmm. Are you so certain, Rolland? My guess is that Master Silvestrus likely has a soft spot in his heart for animals. That's just my impression, mind you. I think if we approach him in the right way, he won't object. But we'll be the ones who'll have to look after her—that's certain."

Thaddeus gave him a hopeful look. "Anders, have you ever taken care of any animals—had any pets of your own?"

"Well, no, not really. Mater would not allow any large or rough animals to be around the estate. We did have cats for a while, though, but they don't require much care. And to tell the truth, they don't do much with you, either—unless they want something, that is. After a bit, I started sneezing every time the cats came around, and that was that."

"How about you, Rolland?"

"No. How I was raised—well, it just wasn't a good situation for a dog, a rabbit, or any animal. It probably would have been skinned, cooked, and eaten. Although I'd always wanted one."

"Well, a dog is a lot more work than a cat, I can tell you. I have—or I had—" Thaddeus sighed, then continued, "—a dog. His name's Argus. And you have to do a lot for them—sort of like with Asullus. Water and feed them, groom them, exercise them, and so on. And this poor dog is in a wretched condition. So, she'll need lots of special care and attention —most of it right at first.

"If we take her with us, we all have to agree to help bring her back to good health. Then, we all have to swear to take care of her on a regular basis. Otherwise..." Thaddeus' tone grew solemn. "I will take the dog out back, slit its throat and bury it here."

Rolland blanched. "What? You wouldn't!"

Anders flashed a smile, patting Rolland on the back. "Aye, Rolland of Fountaindale, 'tis a hardhearted thief you are. But Thaddeus has the right of it. And I think he could—and would. We must agree with him on this and not let the animal suffer. All right, count me in. I'm for perpetual dog care duty."

The two country boys looked to the city lad.

"Well, I'm not going to be a party to any dog murder, that's sure," Rolland said. "All right, I'm in, too. But we each have to agree to do our share of the work. No shirking."

"Agreed." Anders nodded.

"Agreed," Thaddeus said.

Thaddeus extended his hand, which Rolland grasped, and it was then covered by Anders' own.

"Done!" they said in unison.

The beaten dog slowly raised its head with what appeared to be a great deal of pain and turned to where the boys' hands were clasped. Remarkably, she gave the three hands a lick as if to seal the bond and then fell back, exhausted and panting.

Thaddeus swallowed, cleared his throat, and assumed a businesslike attitude.

"Right. Now we have work to do. Rolland, why don't you get that axe down from the wall and find a couple of saplings from the woods. We'll have to make a litter for her to lay on so we can move her back to camp. Anders, look around the cabin to see if there are any supplies we could use for the dog. Or for ourselves, for that matter. Load anything you find on one of those blankets over there. Then we can use the other one to stretch between the poles. Meanwhile, I will look her over to see if I can find anything else wrong."

He then addressed the dog, "Lie back, girl. That's right, take it easy now. Don't worry; you're safe. No one will hurt you now—or ever again."

Soon a small pile of assorted goods lay on one of the grimy blankets.

The golden-haired dog lay on the other. Rolland returned with two stout stripped saplings, which he placed on the cabin floor beside the dog. He eyed Anders' collection. "Hmm," he said, then went efficiently around the cabin, searching in a variety of out-of-the-way places.

After a bit of effort, he contributed two knives, a tooled leather belt of good quality, several lengths of rope, a length of harness strapping, and three small purses of coins—one containing thirteen gold half-Imperials.

Anders looked at the pile from the second collection and bowed to Rolland.

"I salute you, *Furis Magister.*"

Rolland made a wave of dismissal. "Nothing anyone couldn't do with a bit of practice."

Thaddeus cast a glance at the clinking purses and acknowledged a nagging sense of discomfort. "Uh, Rolland, should we be taking that money? It belongs to that man."

Anders smiled again. "Thaddeus, you have an interesting sense of comparative morality."

"Excuse me?"

Rolland barked a laugh. "Well, Taddy, considering we just turned its owner into a be-pestered mutt who cannot be using money again in any case, I agree with Anders. If we leave these things here, someone else will take them. Besides, if you wish, you can think of it his contribution to the Perpetual Dog Care Fund—of which I am chief reeve, by the way. We must buy supplies for her, and doing that requires coin. Consider it compensation."

"Not to mention it lends an air of justice to the whole proceeding," Anders added.

Thaddeus rocked an outstretched hand back and forth, as he'd seen his father do, then sharply clapped his hands together. "Points given, good sirs."

Anders continued. "How will we carry her? Toting her several *mille passuum* is going to be tiresome."

"The belt and ropes will make straps to bind the poles. We can sling them over our shoulders and carry the dog in the cradle between," Thaddeus explained patiently. "And, I think, we should also decide on a good and proper name for our new friend. Any suggestions?"

"Bellis. *Bellis perennis*, to be precise—like the daisy," Anders said. "Um…underneath all the filth, blood, sores, and bruises, she has a bright yellow coat. It reminds me of the color of those flowers by that fence at the inn."

"Bellis! Perfect. Bellis, it is," Thaddeus said, nodding.

Rolland nodded as well. "Yes, that fits. Good choice. All right. Well, let's get this litter put together, get Bellis aboard, and get back to camp. We don't want to walk in and find the Master sitting there with a meticulously carved sign reading *EX-APPRENTICES*."

Thaddeus and Rolland rolled the blanket with precision around the poles and tied the rope straps to make the litter. With Bellis lying on the blanket, they slowly raised it to their chests, ducking their necks under the strap loops and gradually letting the weight settle on their shoulders. After setting out, it took some time for them to coordinate their gait to offer the slightest amount of jostling to the dog while minimizing their own fatigue.

Anders brought up the rear, dragging the goods from the cabin. Rolland carried their newfound financial resources in the stoutest of the three purses, tucked deeply inside his tunic as carefully as a mother would carry her baby in a pooka.

They'd only gone a short distance when Anders cleared his throat. "You know, in our rush to tend to Bellis, aren't we overlooking what happened back there?"

Rolland twisted his head to look at Anders. "How do you mean? What was so important?"

"I know," Thaddeus replied. "I said it earlier. We just used Sorcery."

Rolland stopped mid-stride, swaying the litter. "You know, you're right. It's the first time I ever did anything like that."

"Me, too. How about you, Thaddeus?"

"I think I used it before. Asullus had me say some magic words and use a powder when I was feeling sick—you know, to summon that old green physician I told you about."

Anders smiled. "Oh, you mean that time you were…indisposed… from being with the blue butterflies?"

Thaddeus shot him an irritated look. "Yes. But he told me what to say. This time, it just…seemed to come by itself. What did it feel like to you?"

"Strange," Anders said, his smile gone. "All at once, I just knew I had to say something. It came to me of a sudden what to say and how to say it. I've never had that feeling before…all this energy rushed out of me, almost like someone else was doing it."

"Me, too," Rolland said. "I had to say something, to *shout* the words. Then *Vermis Venite* came to my mind. Like the force came from deep inside me. Odd feeling."

"We must tell Master Silvestrus about this. He'll want to know," Thaddeus said.

"Yes. P'raps he will even be pleased with us." Anders said.

"For a change," Rolland amended.

The short scholar paused, then added, "And I'm eager to tell Asullus."

Rolland slid a finger under the strap for a moment to ease the weight. "Speaking of Asullus, what d'you think he will think of Bellis? He doesn't fancy wolves very much now, does he?"

"Oh, once our new friend is healed up and has her strength back, I believe they'll be good friends," Thaddeus said forthrightly.

Anders smiled again. "Yes, you're probably right. Once her diseases are all cured up, only her bark will be worse than her blight."

Rolland groaned. "You know, Anders, that was really pitiful. You'd think some priss from the bookworm factor'd know better than to make such a stupid joke."

"Oh, really? Well, if we are speaking of pitiful, I saw you when we were swimming in the baths at Fountaindale the other day and—"

"Listen! Rolland. Anders. Think here—somehow, we transformed a man into a dog. We're traveling to our camp, and we're carrying a burden. Who knows if the River's Woods people are anywhere about? P'raps they could be following us. We should speak soft and try to make less noise going down our path. If we attract any attention and someone wants to attack us, we would certainly be disadvantaged to confront them."

The others fell silent, knowing he was right. The group continued in this fashion until they arrived back at the barge, relieved to find it and their belongings untouched and their Master still absent.

Gently, the boys placed Bellis down and again gave her water and wee bits of food, only a tiny portion of which she was able to accept. As she could not easily rise, they carefully cleaned away any waste with clean cloths. Next, they tended to her wounds as best they could and groomed her to the extent she permitted. Thaddeus spread several of their blankets on the bed of the cart, and they cautiously placed the golden dog on top of them, with one blanket covering her as well.

After observing Thaddeus' frequent visits to the cart to assess their new companion's status, Rolland remarked to Anders, "That's got to be the most carefully looked-after dog in all the Westlands."

"That's perfectly fine, thief. Perfectly fine."

Back around the fire, Thaddeus, having resumed his seat following his latest trip to check on Bellis' welfare, addressed his fellow Apprentices. "You know, there's no way around it. We'll have to tell Master Silvestrus about our Sorcery—and about why we now have a dog in his wagon."

"We could tell him we were all struck by lightning, and when we awoke, we could do tricks and summon animals," Rolland offered.

Anders scoffed. "Oh, yes, that would be helpful. No," he sighed, "I think we will need to be truthful with him and trust that he'll determine what is best for us in his usual, sober manner."

"Let's hope so," Rolland said.

"Yes," Thaddeus agreed.

The boys fed the dog and checked her wounds, then looked in on her once more before cleaning the campsite and banking the fire. By the time they had finished with even-tide, they had all remarked that Bellis did seem to have perked up a bit, even during the short interval she'd been with them.

"Well, Master, I do believe Charles'll ha' his fill tonight, don' ye know."

"Yes, Asullus, I think you are correct. But the question is, where are these Cinnians coming from?"

The mule snorted. "The Land o' the Cin, I imagines."

A look of annoyance crossed the old Sorcerer's face. He glanced skyward for a moment, then continued. "The more important question, however, is why? But I think I have an idea about that. If by some means, *Daemon*-kind has learned the importance of our boys, then they could simply be employing their Eastern minions to do their dirty work. And I wonder, are they working through the Cinnian Emperor and his Ancient Ones directly? I would give much to know this."

"But, Master, why not just appear themselves, an' do the deed?"

"Asullus," the old man chided, "you know the answer to that already. The *Daemon* cannot come to the surface in the flesh. He is trapped. And even if he managed, by some means, to break through, the Lady herself would know, would appear and would settle him out in a jot. The only way I can think of for a *Daemon* to be present at this time is for him to be summoned—much as I do with Charles. But who would summon such a one? The Ancient Ones might have the strength, but the *Daemon* could appear only in their own land—nowhere else. No, it would have to be a Sorcerer of the West. But who would…?" The Sorcerer's voice trailed off as his brows knitted in concentration. "Who would…?"

Silvestrus shook his head and looked about him. "Well, perhaps that's a problem for a different day. Ah, I see we are nearly back to our encampment, old mule. Now, not a word of this to our charges. It is much too early for their involvement in this drama. Much too early."

However, on returning to the barge, Asullus nudged Silvestrus and nodded to the north.

"Ye ha' asked me from time to time to tell ye when we might be in range o' some o' that medicinal herb ye find so useful. Well, unless me snufflin' tool is off, I'd say there'd be a good stand o' it just into the forest field o'er yonder."

"You know, old mule, I am indebted to you once again for your keen olfactory perception. I think we should break out the panniers and go see if there's enough to justify a harvest."

The old man turned to the boys. "Lads, Asullus has detected what must surely be a patch of a rare plant that we use in our Sorcerous rituals from time to time. He and I are going to investigate. I want you to remain by the barge and protect our belongings."

It was near sunset when Silvestrus and Asullus returned with the mule's panniers filled to bursting with the special herb they'd been seeking. Thaddeus thought he recognized it from the Sorcerer's pouch. The foraging must have been particularly enjoyable, as both the old man and mule were given to much hilarity for the rest of the evening.

The boys were somewhat disappointed at Master Silvestrus' reaction to the news about their first use of Sorcery.

"Really? So you say? Is that not remarkable? Did you hear that, Asullus? Well, what do you know…"

The Apprentices were more reassured by the old Sorcerer's response to Bellis. He immediately went to her and petted her, offering soothing words. Even Asullus appeared mildly interested, then made a number of silly comments, repeating a theme of "all the animals in an ark," which he brayed in self-amusement that made sense to no one. When Thaddeus asked his master if he had any powders or potions they could use to heal the dog, Silvestrus said something regarding "time" and "best healer."

Both the mule and the Sorcerer ate heartily at even-tide, then went immediately to their night's rest.

The boys were initially puzzled by this behavior, but Thaddeus watched with interest when Rolland, adopting a shrewd look, strolled over to the panniers, now propped against a tree. He knelt and picked up a bit of the herb, examining it carefully. Tearing off a small leaf, he crushed it, rolled it between his fingers, smelled it, and then touched his tongue to it. Nodding, he stood and tossed the sample aside before rejoining his companions.

Asullus was hitched up and again harnessed to the barge. The old mule had been strangely silent this morning. Thaddeus and Anders wondered if it had to do with the dog's condition, but Rolland ventured the theory that Asullus might be suffering from the aftereffects of yesterday's herb use.

"You know, we may have a problem here. Those herbs the Old Man and the mule brought back last night are from the green lotus plant. People chew it or smoke it, then talk and act stupid. I've tried it myself, but I don't like it because I find it affects my judgment. It made me careless once, and I almost got caught during a chase. And sometimes people start using it and can't stop. I think we should keep an eye on those two and be wary of anything they tell you to do after they've been using it."

The other two Apprentices nodded in agreement and vowed to be alert for any problems with their Master or their Minister of Transport.

THE IMPERIAL PALACE, CINOTON

IN THE LAND OF THE CIN, THE EASTLANDS

Well, it was one thing to think and another to do…

Soh-Nahk intended to kill the old Emperor. All he needed was the opportunity.

Months passed, and the plan slowly took form—like a slowly hardening bronze cast.

THE
GREAT SPANSION

One day, a growing realization became manifest—he could not stop there. Clearly, he must eliminate his older brother as well. Les-Nahk was not fit, nor would he ever be, to become Emperor and rule well the Empire of the Cin. And as for his tender sister, Sim-Lea…well, that decision could wait for a different time. There might be a way to spare her. It would depend on what turn was taken by future events.

Then, he would become Emperor. He knew he was the only one sufficiently competent to rise to the demands of the position. Soh-Nahk sat fantasizing in his apartments. So, now if he were Emperor…now, what was it that he would do?

One thing he thought of immediately had to do with the Soothsayer.

Two weeks prior, he had been on an outing in the capital with his Imperial Security Detail when an old woman with a filmy left eye hailed him from the crowd.

"Most Favored Second Great-Son! Prepare thyself for thy testing!" The woman said these words twice and would say no more. She kept staring at him as he passed by her.

Soh-Nahk was somewhat surprised. At twelve years of age, he did not expect many Cin to recognize him.

"Who is the old woman who speaks to me?" he asked his guard captain.

"I do not know, Highness. Do you wish her…detained?"

"No. But make discreet inquiries and report back to me. And say nothing about this to anyone."

"Yes, Highness," the man replied, bowing his head.

A week later, the old crone knelt before him in a study off the main hall of the Palace that he used for conducting interviews. The same guards surrounded her.

"Who are you, Madam, and why did you speak to me thus when I was in the city?"

"I am Madrin, your Highness, and I would impart information to you that concerns your future."

"My future? Really? Now that is interesting. I would hear this information."

"I shall give it to you gladly, Highness. But it is difficult for me, bent and old as I am, to speak well enough, constrained thusly."

Soh-Nahk considered the old woman. He had to admit that she had captured his attention with her nerve.

"Very well, Madrin, you may rise. Help her." The boy signaled to his guard, who stood back, as their captain assisted the elderly woman to her feet.

The woman stood unsteadily, then slowly straightened, but kept her head down. "Thank you, Highness. May I ask a further favor and sit?"

"Ha!" Soh-Nahk laughed. "A peasant sitting in the presence of a Prince of the Empire? You are bold. I think, too bold. Perhaps I should have the guard remove you from this room, flog your wrinkled old body and leave you out with the palace sweepings."

The old hag had the temerity to look up to the Imperial Great-Son's eyes. Soh-Nahk noted at once that her right eye was filmed over.

Hadn't her left *eye been filmed over when he saw her in the marketplace...*

"This is your palace—or will be one day soon, Highness—and you may order whatever you wish...if you can," the woman replied with the very hint of a smile.

"Hmm. I am curious about you...but not that curious. Guards! Take her away!"

To his amazement, Soh-Nahk realized that none of his Security troops had moved.

"Guards! Did you not hear me? I said—"

"Highness! Ha!" the woman chortled. "Please forgive me for interrupting you but know that they are not capable of doing your bidding at this time…and will not be for some moments to come. As I said, I have some information for you, and I thought it best I deliver it confidentially. But I believe I will sit down to do so. These old bones—"

With that, the woman took a seat, appearing relaxed and at ease, but with no means of visible support—just settling in mid-air.

Soh-Nahk's eyes opened wide.

Magicks! Was she an Ancient One? How was that possible?

Now, he must be more careful.

"How to begin? Well, Highness, I am but a poor old blind woman. On the other hand—" Here, the woman's voice deepened and became husky. "I am, shall we say, an agent of a powerful personage who desires that you have success and prominence in your life."

Swallowing hard, Soh-Nahk spoke as calmly as he could manage. "Very well. I am in support of those values. What have you to tell me?"

"Your Highness, you will succeed in becoming Emperor and rule over all the Land of the Cin. However, the length of your reign will depend upon another."

"Someone I know?" he questioned.

"No, not at all. At least not yet. The problem is that we know *where* this one is and *what* is likely to happen. But not, precisely, *who* this one is. But then…no one knows everything." Here the old lady let out a cackle that caused the hairs at the back of the boy's neck to stand straight out.

"How does that help me, then?" the Imperial Great Son asked brusquely.

"Patience, Highness. Much will be required of you in this. There are four who will come. Four of four directions. North is your greatest threat—but the other three support him. But who is North? The little prince? The red thief? The clever scholar? The beekeeper? We do not know yet."

"Interesting, but unclear," Soh-Nahk said, intrigued.

"Ah, but because we do not know yet, it does not mean that we will not know ever, your Highness. Look to the Westlands. Look to the Sorcerer who travels collecting his charges—the Wooden One—he with a '*Daemon* on a string.' If you find him, you will find three of the four. And if you find the three, you will find the One. And, if you find the One, kill him at once. That is my advice."

With a grimace, the Soothsayer shifted in her position. "Ah, this has grown hard for me. Farewell, your Highness. You will not remember all, but you will remember enough. We will…not…meet again. And, your Highness, take the Tunnel. You must take the Tunnel."

With that, the old woman gave a loud groan and collapsed to the mosaic-tiled floor. A moment later, the Guard Detail swayed, shook themselves, and came back to attention.

The captain spoke up immediately. "Are you well, Highness? I don't know…I feel odd. I—"

"Not to worry, Captain. Madam, fare you well?"

The old woman struggled to her feet again with some assistance from the captain. She shook her head as if clearing it from cobwebs; then, all at once, she looked down to the floor.

"I said, Madrin, are you well?" Soh-Nahk asked of her again.

"Aye, well enough, your Highness. I must confess, I am not sure of what I said. I have these spells every so often…and I remember little of them—only that they are important and that I must speak."

"Interesting. Yes, now that you mention it, my memory of your sayings seems to be fading also. Hmm." He tapped his head. "Ah, well enough. I think we are done here. Captain, see this woman out and give her fair coin for her trouble. Farewell, Madrin."

The lady bowed with as much grace as she was able. "Fare thee well, your Highness."

Once the guard captain had returned, Soh-Nahk had him dismiss the others, then indicated the captain should join him in a side room, off the main hall.

"Captain, listen carefully to me. My Great-Father once employed a Spy Master—Solon was his name, I think."

"Yes, Highness. I remember him from my youth. I believe he is retired now."

"Yes, that is what I recall. I once heard Great-Father say that he was living at some distance from Cinoton."

"Yes, Highness. At Tobruk, I believe."

"Yes. Good. Bring him to the country lodge on the Imperial estate at Mullin. I wish to speak with him."

"Very well, Highness. I will leave at once."

"No, Captain. I want no attention brought to this matter. In fact, I wish you to take with you all the members of your squad that are here with you today, but in such a way that few others, if any, will notice or think it more than just an exercise. Therefore, pick your time of departure with the utmost care. Do you follow me so far?"

"Yes, Highness. Quite so."

"When all is in readiness, personally advance to me a note indicating a meeting place at the estate, but somewhere off the palace grounds. Do not be concerned regarding my safety in this. I shall take all precautions necessary. See that Solon is there. Then leave us. I will make arrangements to find my way back."

"Very well, Highness, but your security—"

"On this occasion, Captain, that must be my responsibility and mine alone."

After a moment, the captain nodded. "As you wish, Highness."

"Very good, Captain. Now you may leave."

At once, the Guardsman saluted, bowed, and turned to exit the small room.

"Just one thing more, then, Captain." The officer halted in mid-stride.

Soh-Nahk continued. "Those squad members who were here with us today and who will accompany you to Tobruk: I do not wish to see them again afterward. Nor does anyone else."

The captain stood still, absorbing the information and its implications bit by bit.

"I'm certain you understand me, Captain, because any misunderstanding would result in great unhappiness to you and those who love you, I'm sure. Have you any questions?"

"No, Highness. None," the guard captain said at once.

"Good. Then you are dismissed."

Soh-Nahk watched the guard captain depart, then fell into deep and profound thought.

Who was that old woman, really, and who had sent her? Someone powerful, naturally…but who?

He knew—or knew of—all the powerful people in Cinoton and some from beyond. And this business in no way smacked of the Ancient Ones.

So, who? Something otherworldly?

He did not tend to give credence to such notions, yet he was, he admitted, curious.

In any case, she seemed to expect that he was to rule. So, there was no reason not to explore her notion of the threat of the Westlands. On that, she had been quite definite.

Well, now it would be up to Solon. He would do this thing.

14

River's Wood
Fluminis Lignum

A familiar song awakened Thaddeus. He determined by their calls that a brown bush warbler, two Northern chickadees, and a pair of doves were nearest the tent. Opening his eyes slowly, he propped his head upon his elbow. Soft streams of light entered the canvas through small tears in the fabric here and there. Judging from the tent holes, it must be late morning.

Sometimes he wondered whether the holes made the light straight or whether light was just like that. He'd have to ask Anders; he would know.

A low murmur of voices now reached his ears from nearby. With his foot, he pulled back the tent's flap enough to take in the scene outside. Silvestrus was in earnest conversation with the verdant physician who had assisted Thaddeus with his post-nectar ills. They hadn't noticed that he was awake; instead, both were bent over Bellis. She looked a little brighter, appearing to mark the to-and-fro of the old men's conversation with a concerned expression on her muzzle by first gazing at one and then the other.

A moment passed, and he was startled by a kick on his leg. He turned to catch the attention of Anders, who smiled and surreptitiously nodded in Rolland's direction. Thaddeus turned his head and caught Rolland's gaze; he still had his bedroll tucked up to his chin. The young thief winked.

Thaddeus held his forefinger to his lips. Both boys nodded and carefully turned to regard their Master's negotiations with the powdery *Medicus.* The conversation was difficult to hear, and occasional gusts of wind made it even more so, but with concentration, they could just distinguish what was being said —at least by the Sorcerer.

"…and that is what I told the boys last night. I am certain her injuries will heal well enough with time, but I am more interested in how this adventure came about in the first place. It is not the physical I am concerned with. There seems to be more here than meets the eye. So, you are sure you found nothing else of note in your examination…?

"No, I do not mean to question you. It is just that I must be sure. Well, then, that leaves but few other explanations. I mean, why would these normally sensible lads—yes, yes, I know, but they have seen only fifteen or so summers—intercede the way they did and in that particular manner? And look at the result. This is unusual. I am afraid we will have to seek out some of the Elders in River's Wood and ask their opinion. I dislike doing this, but I see nothing else for it. Very well, thank you again for your assistance, good Doctor. Your ministrations are always of the greatest value… Ah, unfortunately, I do not have that precise amount with me at this moment, but perhaps I can find something here in my robes."

Silvestrus made a small gesture and continued speaking. "By the by, my thanks for your earlier intervention with my Apprentice and the old mule." Then, as the boys watched, the old man reached behind him. Instantly, a small leather pouch materialized in his hand, which he then gave to the waiting physician. "You are welcome, Learned Sir. Yes, I will have the balance for you very soon. *Ave!*"

With that, the medical apparition vanished in a cloud of emerald-green smoke. Silvestrus muttered to himself, then sat thoughtfully for a moment before he turned to the boys.

"Come over here, lads—seeing as how you are all awake. We have a puzzle on our hands." He looked back toward the hound.

Chagrined at being found out so easily, the boys hastily scrambled to join their Master.

"My nose tells me there is more to this dog—what is it you call her?" Before anyone could answer, he went on. "Oh, yes, Bellis—there is more than presently meets the eye. Consider, for example, your response to her situation and to what lengths you went to defend her. And, lest we forget one modest detail, for all of you, it involved the use of Sorcery—with two of you employing it for the very first time. Does not that strike you as odd? And all for a dog? Not to demean her obvious sweet nature—I am quite taken with her myself—but you threw yourselves into a perilous situation, and you cannot account for what prompted you to take the actions you did, except for a *feeling*. Lads, that is most imprecise and requires further study."

The old Sorcerer glanced at the sun's position in the sky, then turned his gaze back to his charges.

"Since it is too late for break-fast in any case, tell me, each of you in turn, exactly what you recall of the circumstances in your adventure with the dog. All that you thought and what you felt. Be sure to leave nothing out. Thaddeus, you begin."

There followed at least an hour of discussion, but according to Silvestrus, no further light was shed on the matter. At the conclusion, the Sorcerer spoke.

"Boys, I am inclined to allow Bellis to accompany us, but you must remain alert for any further peculiar behavior and let me know of it at once."

A rumble from Rolland's stomach signaled it was time to trade the discussion for mid-day, which was quickly prepared and efficiently consumed.

Afterward, Silvestrus instructed his Apprentices to pack up their possessions, dress the campsite and move everything onto the barge. Bellis appeared a little stronger now, taking to the ministrations on her behalf with a mixture of good grace and apparent gratitude, at least as much as her strength allowed. The boys had devised a plan of frequent watering and food preparation that she was, so far, tolerating well. Careful brushing had removed all but the most stubborn of the dirt, crusts, burrs, tangles, and inhabitants.

Asullus was hitched up and again harnessed to the barge. The mule had been strangely silent this morning. Thaddeus wondered if it had to do with the dog's condition.

The last leg of the trip upriver was short, and, rounding a broad bend, they beheld River's Wood. All the buildings, which Silvestrus had described as *quaint*, were constructed of wood. Some hung out over the bank's edge, but none of the structures stood taller than two levels. The sound of working rough-cut saws was continual. Many tree trunks were already floating slowly downstream past their vantage point, and more were stacked in loosely organized piles along either side of the river.

Several townsmen were walking about, talking, or tending the cut trees, but no women were seen among them. All the men wore similar garb—tanned hide breeches and tunics, some with rows of fringe at the cuffs or hem. Their feet were shod in soft-leather slippers, with gloves of the same material. All had beards and wore their jet-black hair long, both adornments tied back with rawhide thongs. No elderly folk were seen on the streets, and an uncommon number of dogs was running loose. Interestingly, most of these canines appeared to have a significant amount of wolf blood in them.

Thaddeus found the surroundings eerie and more than a little unsettling.

Asullus towed the small barge to a docking area, then stood stock still, eyes rolling, while their craft was made fast to the dock. The old man waded ashore to supervise the boys as they disembarked, unhitched the old mule, unloaded the cart, and rehitched Asullus to it. Bellis was placed in the tumbrel and made as comfortable as possible with her head propped over the cart's side, so that she could see the town and all the goings-on.

Asullus looked around nervously. "I'll be lettin' ye know, I'm no' so fond o' such cities as are full o' carnivores."

Silvestrus came and stood by his mule. "Be at peace, Asullus. None here will harm you as long as the boys and I have breath in our bodies."

The boys nodded reassuringly, looking as fiercely determined as their Master.

"All right. Then I'm thinkin', let's conclude our business here an' be off, quick as a wink an' maybe quicker."

Silvestrus fetched his staff from the cart. "Thaddeus, come and take hold of Asullus' bridle while we walk. Rolland, Anders, grab your walking staffs from the cart and place yourselves one on either side. I, myself, will lead this parade. Now all of you remember your manners and smile for the citizens."

With that, the old Sorcerer led his small cadre up to the transport factor's office at the head of the docks, where he made arrangements for the barge's return downstream at the next running. From there, the group wound its way up the crooked mud-and-woodchip streets, heading toward the largest building in the town. No sawmills were evident, but the populace all carried axes or crosscuts, and the sound and smell of worked wood came from every direction.

As they passed the various stores and dwellings, Thaddeus became aware that the townsfolk stopped what they were doing and stared as soon as they came into view. He realized a look of recognition dawned upon them, and they gazed down deferentially as the company passed. Several gave brief bows. The odd behavior was puzzling to him.

Rolland looked on the scene with a calculating eye. "They seem to do a good business here. I wonder where they keep the proceeds?"

"Why do you worry about the proceeds?" Anders asked.

"Well, in a town like this, there's bound to be lots of interesting things to buy—a trinket or or two to remind us of our trip, maybe."

"Rolland, the first rule of spending is to acquire only those items that are practical, long-lasting, and necessary," Anders remarked.

"That's three rules, Anders, not one. And what's the fun in that?"

"You would go to all that trouble just for some wooden pence?" Thaddeus asked.

Rolland frowned. "Ah, yes—you're right. Never mind. By the by, Taddy, our young golden miss here, seems to be perking up a bit at all the attention. Think you we should let her down to walk a bit?"

"Hmm. Not yet, Rolland. And p'raps not here. Time enough for that later," the Beewicke lad replied.

Soon enough, the group arrived in front of what Thaddeus took to be the town hall. The hewn timbers supporting the structure were massive and adzed smooth. The tall boy could detect no use of screws or nails in any part of the edifice he could see. He was impressed. The townsfolk seemed to know their lumber and framing well.

He stepped forward as Silvestrus faced the building and spoke softly out of the corner of his mouth.

"Wait here. Do nothing. If the people want to stare, let them stare. I do not believe I will be long. Perhaps you might feed the dog again." With that, he disappeared into the imposing timbered structure.

The boys stood steadfast around Asullus and the cart. Bellis seemed accepting of what was transpiring and appeared to note the proceedings with interest. Rolland dug out a small portion of leftover food for the dog and offered her more water, which she accepted with enthusiasm. A promising sign—clearly, Bellis was on the mend. Anders gently stroked the dog's head, and she gave his hand a quick lick, then resumed her perusal of the town's activities.

The River's Wood folk who walked by continued to behave strangely. None spoke to them or seemed friendly, but their reactions were essentially identical to people they had passed earlier. All eyes were immediately drawn to the little group. The people would stop and stare, then lower their heads as if in respect before proceeding on their various ways.

Every villager they saw was accompanied by one or more of the large, dark wolfish dogs, each of which nodded at them in ways similar to that of their masters. Thaddeus looked at Rolland, who shrugged. Asullus remained silent throughout their vigil but glanced around frequently, his eyes wary.

No one felt like talking. It was as if a weight pressed down on them, enforcing silence.

After a time, Silvestrus emerged from the timber-framed townhouse. "Well, boys, I am not certain how much l have learned, but this is clearly an intriguing place. Did anything curious transpire while I was inside?"

"The townsfolk are acting oddly, Master," Anders related. The scholar Apprentice went on to describe the behavior of the men walking by, which Silvestrus seemed to find of interest.

"Well, well, and well. This deserves much thought." The old Sorcerer's gaze shifted to Bellis, who gazed back. "Well, well, and well."

"Master, where do we go now?" Anders asked.

"We, ah, we will cross the river over the Great Wood Spansion uptown a ways, then stop at a supply store I know of on the other side. Originally, I had thought to spend the night here, but something tells me it would be wiser to get some miles behind us before sunset. There is, however, an inn close by the general store that has a rather good bear stew we might try. I do not mind a last full belly before heading out into the wilderness for a time. Come lads, follow me."

Rolland looked at Thaddeus. "Bear stew?" he mouthed, then made a face.

Anders caught his look and whispered, "You know, back at Brightfield about this time of day, Mater would be setting the cooks to making some soft bread and raisin pudding. Something tells me it might be wise for me to reconsider teaching at the *Lyceum* after all."

The party made their way further up the twisting dirt-chip roads until they reached the Great Wood Spansion. A Toll Master turned out of his watch station and approached the group. On gazing at the wagon, he behaved much as the other townspeople had and stood mutely, looking steadily at Silvestrus.

After a moment's hesitation, Silvestrus produced a pouch from his robes and passed two coins to the man. The man regarded the money briefly, then nodded toward the other side of the bridge. He bowed in the direction of the boys and cart before returning to his watch station.

Silvestrus signaled his charges to proceed, and they crossed the great log arch, which, at its highest point, rose some thirty strides above the river's surface. The Apprentices stared in awe at the towering log structure. They kept in close formation, artificial smiles struck across their faces while remaining silent, their eyes continually scanning their surroundings. Thaddeus had such a grip on his staff that his hand began to ache.

As soon as they cleared the bridge, the boys let out a collective sigh of relief.

Silvestrus guided them to the supply store. At the entrance, he turned to the boys.

"Thaddeus and Anders, you stay here and look after things. Rolland, you come with me to help carry things—oh, and Rolland, we already have sufficient brass lanterns for now."

Reddening to his roots, the thief said only, "Yes, Master."

Thaddeus walked back to the cart to check on Bellis. The dog, with effort, extended her neck for a scratch, which the boy was glad to supply. While continuing to pet Bellis, Thaddeus turned to the mule.

"How're you doing, Asullus? You've been very quiet this morning."

"Aye. Well, I canno' say as I'm entirely comfortable here, but I'll manage, soon as we are shut o' this place. How is our Queenie doin' now, think ye? Seems she looks a little less peaked."

"She's better. She's eating, and she seems less afraid. In fact, she seems very interested in all that's going on."

"Aye, I ha' noticed. Interestin' behavior in a beat-up dog, would ye no' say? I ha' to speak me piece, though—ye three lads did well by her yesterday. Had I been there, I'd ha' no' stopped with just transformin' that no-father into a cur but probably would ha' killed him dead. 'Tis fortunate fer him he was only transformed—or maybe no', all things considered."

Just then, two townsmen came out of the store, speaking quietly to each other and carrying supplies. They stopped abruptly when they saw the boys by the cart and repeated the same action of obeisance the group had witnessed previously before going on their way.

Anders looked after them as they walked down the street. "I wish I knew what all that meant. Just what, or whom, are they acknowledging? The Master is inside, as he was each time before, so those bows can't be for him, nor for Rolland. I don't think this cart is a Holy Relic of any sort. So that leaves just you, me, and Asullus."

"And Bellis, of course," Thaddeus added.

Their speculations were interrupted by the return of Silvestrus carrying his staff and Rolland carrying a bulging mountain of goods in both arms, staggering under its weight. Thaddeus and Anders rushed to give him a hand. He was red-faced and appeared about to share his opinion of his maltreatment when Anders gingerly stepped on his foot and whispered, "Later, friend thief. This may not be the best time."

Rolland glared at Anders, then nodded and made his way to the cart where he and the others stowed the supplies.

The boys resumed their strategic positions and followed the old Sorcerer as he set off up the street, taking a left turn at the first intersecting road. Two *stadia* further brought them to a plainly built planked inn, the *Quercus Antiqua*. Under the pretext of inspecting the positioning of the goods in the cart, Silvestrus spoke in a low voice.

"Now, boys, we are going in for even-tide. The cart is positioned so we may observe it through the front window of the inn there—assuming we will have the right table, which I believe we will. Asullus, keep your eyes peeled and bray if any trouble arises. Pay especial mind to Bellis. Boys, behave yourselves and keep your wits about you. This is our last stop in River's Wood, so let us not stir up any beehives, eh, Thaddeus? And, by the way, I really do recommend the bear stew."

The party entered the inn and waited for their eyes to adjust to the gloom of the drab interior. The beamed ceiling, rough-hewn tables, and wood-chip-strewn floor did nothing to dispel their first impression. The room was immersed in a blue haze, which Thaddeus initially attributed to the pipe-smoking patrons. Still, his nose detected a different, more pungent aroma, which Silvestrus identified as emanating from the numerous bear-grease candles flickering smokily on tables and ledges.

The low hum of voices suddenly stilled, and a hush fell over the common room as all eyes turned toward them. Thaddeus noted Silvestrus' interest in a bearded local with a tankard, sitting in front of the large window that looked out onto the yard where Asullus and Bellis sat patiently waiting. The man at the desired table sat holding a quill in his hand with various parchments scattered about. Several crumpled pieces of composition littered the floor. The prospective author, concentrating on his writing, did not seem to be in any hurry to leave.

"*Alvis Defundat!*" the Sorcerer said under his breath.

Suddenly, the man at the table sat bolt upright with a look of distress on his face. He quickly gathered up his writing materials and threw a few coins on the table. The old Sorcerer watched the scribe struggling to grab up all of his papers as he exited, bolting for the door.

"I regret doing that. However—" Silvestrus gestured toward the desired table.

They headed toward the vacated bench-board, but the bartender reached it first, scooped up the coins, gave the table a swift wipe with his shoulder towel, and silently indicated they should sit.

Silvestrus, Thaddeus, and Anders opted for the bear stew, while Rolland ordered only cheese and bread. Throughout their even-tide, they were acutely aware of the quiet and the surreptitious glances directed their way by the majority of the buckskin-clad patrons.

"You know, Master," Thaddeus said, "this stew really is good." He ordered a second portion, which he and Anders shared.

Rolland, however, was immune to suggestions he taste the ursine cuisine.

"No, thank you. What next? Will we be expecting portions of badger ribs or, perhaps, panther fillet?"

When they finished eating, Silvestrus signaled it was time to leave. He left a half-Imperial on the table, much to the bartender's apparent delight. The man's shift of attention from the group to the money was the first time in the course of the evening he'd taken his eyes off of them.

Once outside, the Master and his Apprentices resumed their march. The group turned onto a street with the grand name of *Via Orientalis,* which soon ended in an overgrown trail once they were past the outskirts of the town. Silvestrus continued to lead them away from River's Wood, speaking over his shoulder.

"Our next stop is not until Moorstown—some distance from here. We will be going cross-country until we reach it. So, place yourselves in a hearty woodsman's frame of mind for the next several days. Off we go."

The boys exchanged resigned looks but dutifully followed the old Sorcerer's pace.

A bold voice intruded on Thaddeus' reverie.

"Hey, look where you're going, Long-Pole! You almost stepped in some trail poo," Rolland jibed. "Probably left by that bear you just ate. Serves you right."

15

Balls and Girls I
Pilae et Puellae I

In camp the following morning, the lad from Beewicke was joined at the fire by the young scholar.

"You know, Thaddeus, I think our Bellis is regaining her strength and healing up nicely," Anders observed.

"Yes, you're right. She's a good dog," Thaddeus responded.

"She has a good tender," Anders said, smiling at his brother Apprentice.

"We have all tended her," Thaddeus said, slightly embarrassed.

"Yes, but I believe she responds to some more than others."

"Well, if so, it's only because I had a dog before."

"Of course. Clearly the only reason," Anders replied with a chuckle. "Whatever you say."

Bellis' relationship with Asullus was more formal, constituted by what appeared to be growing mutual respect. The mule declined to speculate further on the dog's situation, and the boys soon wearied of asking him to elaborate.

Thaddeus approached his master with curiosity. "Master Silvestrus? I—that is—we were wondering about Bellis' odd history, since River's Wood, and with us. For example, look at her interaction with Asullus and how she seems to communicate, and all the rest. Do you think there's anything, well…sorcerous…at play with her?"

"Do you mean, Thaddeus, do I consider her to be a Sorceress? No, I do not."

Thaddeus couldn't decide if that was a message that signaled the end of the inquiry or whether his master was just expressing his professional opinion.

"I mean to say, Master, that she seems strange and—"

"There are many strange things in heaven and Earth, Thaddeus — more than can be accounted for in our philosophy, I would wager. Now, have you boys had a chance to set right the camp yet this morning?"

That reminder ended the discussion, and the Apprentices were thus condemned to murmur amongst themselves until they, too, tired of the topic. With no further marked demonstrations concerning Bellis, they soon turned to other issues.

Following break-fast on the day after their interlude in River's Wood, Silvestrus went to the cart, rummaged about, and retrieved the ogre's bladder.

Rolland, tending the campfire, nudged Thaddeus, who squatted beside him.

"Psst, Thaddeus. The Old Man's got out the dead ogre's piece. What do you think he might be planning?"

"I have no idea. Usually, he tells us first when it has to do with us. Any thoughts?"

The redheaded thief shook his head as Anders joined them, curious as well.

The Sorcerer walked over to the boys, dropped the bladder down in front of them, and addressed his Apprentices, who appeared anxious to understand the mysteries concerning the magical creature's inner organ.

"Boys, we shall take advantage of our recent acquisition here by incorporating it into a pre-study of things that will be critical to your future training, such as the formulation and implementation of battle preparation and exercise of the body—called kickball or, more formally, *Pila Ludere.* Asullus, join us, please. This is a good day for us to have some fun."

"What does an ogre's bladder have to do with fun?" Anders asked under his breath.

"I don't know. I was about to ask you the same question," Thaddeus replied.

"What is he on about?" Rolland asked in a loud whisper.

"I'm not sure, Rolland, but we best to do what he says. So far, he's been on the square with us. Yes?"

"Maybe," Rolland said.

Soon enough, the old Sorcerer moved to a point roughly midway in the meadow near the camp where they had pitched their tents. He summoned the boys and the mule to him. Instantly two sets of upright poles appeared, separated by approximately one hundred paces. Unbidden, Bellis padded quietly over to lie down on the outskirts of the pole-bounded area, appearing to show great interest in the proceedings.

Silvestrus continued. "All right. Now I am going to enlighten you as to the fundamentals of *Pila Ludere*—an activity involving a different kind of Sorcery, so to speak. For this exercise, our goodly beast of burden and I will form a team that we shall call the *Maximi.* You three shall form a second team, the *Minimi.* Now, stand in a line—you, Thaddeus, next to Anders, and you, Rolland, over there—between myself and those two poles to the North. Yes, that is good."

Silvestrus held up the drooping bladder in one hand, passed his other hand over it in an arcing motion, and intoned, "*Inflatus Sis!*" The bladder instantly inflated into a globular shape, approximately three hand-spans across.

"This is a contest, the object of which is to see which team can kick this ball through the opponents' guard the most times within a certain passage of the sun. Each time the ball passes through the other team's guard, the team that has done the kicking earns one point. The team with the highest number of points when the game is completed is declared champion of the match, and the losing team must then perform some bidding decreed by the winning team for the remainder of the day."

The boys nodded to each other.

"Any questions?" the old man asked.

"Um, no, Master," the boys said together.

"Good. Now Asullus, come stand behind me." Silvestrus hitched up his robes, which showed his thin white legs, then bent down to untie his sandals. He threw these to the side, well away from the field of play. "I run better in bare feet, as it were," he explained. "Are you ready, then? All right, let us commence." He gave out a piercing whistle and tossed the ball, roughly halfway between himself and the line of Apprentices. "*Incipe!*"

Immediately, Silvestrus ran up and kicked the ball bladder forcefully between Anders' legs, then ran swiftly past him, turned, and kicked the ball back over the boys' heads where it dropped close to the waiting mule.

"Asullus! *Calcitra!*"

The ball rolled to a stop in front of the mule, who turned around and kicked it squarely with both hind legs. The ball sailed back high over the boys' heads in the opposite direction, bounced several times, and rolled straight through the poles down the middle.

"One to nothing! Good shot, old friend!" the Sorcerer chortled. He retrieved the ball and called out to his Apprentices, whose mouths were hanging open, as he passed. "Let us show a little more effort, eh, lads? Do try to make a game of it, will you?"

At the end of the morning's exercise, the final score of the first game was twelve to zero.

"Well done, boys," Silvestrus said slyly. "That is, more or less."

A second game left the *Minimi* losing again. Silvestrus declared he had not used Sorcery. "There was no need," he said.

"I'm no athlete, it's true," Anders confessed after the second game, "so don't count on me in any strategies. But, given that, I would wager that experience and treachery are more likely to triumph over youth and energy than the reverse. The answer, therefore, seems to me to point to the employment of such useful devices as deviousness, misdirection, combining our skills, and likely-to-be-undetected cheating. Basically, out-and-out perfidy."

"I, for one, favor that approach," Rolland said enthusiastically. "We do that, and the next time, the victory will be ours."

After a third losing game, the boys held a conference.

"Rolland, Thaddeus, listen. I think proximity is lending itself to informal observation here."

"How is that, Anders?" Rolland asked.

"Because we are practicing so close by, our Master is spying on us to gain the advantage."

"Bollocks!" Rolland exclaimed. "The old gassier! He's as devious as the crew I left back in Fountaindale."

Thaddeus did not argue with this assessment.

But even Rolland had to agree that Master Silvestrus showed a fair degree of restraint in appreciating his victories. However, the boys were required to spend the night in watch-shifts rather than rely upon—as they had previously—the Sorcerous warding of the camp.

"*Psst!* Rolland! Wake up! It's your turn to stand watch," Anders said, nudging with his sandal his snoring companion wrapped up in his camp blanket. At once, Rolland bounced out of his bedroll and sprang to a half-crouch, knife brandished in either hand. It took a moment for his eyes to come into focus; then, he shook his head.

"Anders, I swear to the Gods, if you put your foot anywhere near my bottom again, you're going to lose some toes. What in bloody Hells do you want, and it'd better be good."

"It's your turn for the watch," Anders told him.

"Gods' stones! How do you know that?"

"The stars. You see, the moon is in the seventh house and Jupiter—"

"All right, all right. I'm awake. How long do I have to do this?"

"Four hours. Then you can put your foot in Thaddeus' bottom, as it will then be his turn," Anders added with a laugh.

"Right. This standing watch business is for the dung pile. I never signed up for this."

Anders adopted a pious tone. "What cannot be cured must be endured, friend thief. Good night. Ah, those blankets are going to feel warm and sleep welcoming. *Ave.*"

Rolland responded with dark thoughts, cursing under his breath.

Following the next morning's break-fast, the boys quickly completed their chores, seeing to the needs of both the mule and the dog. Still making good progress, Bellis now walked most of the way—usually at Thaddeus' heels. She was gaining weight; her sores and bruises were nearly healed, and a new golden coat was slowly emerging from beneath the damaged areas.

The demonstrations of affection the dog received were accompanied by various treats, which supplemented her weight-gain regimen. Silvestrus proved non-critical of these indulgences and, in truth, was one of the worst offenders.

The group strode along, ranged alertly around the cart. Silvestrus had taken to perching on the cart seat, holding the reins, with Bellis keeping up as best she could afoot. The hiking toughened the boys, and even Anders had increased his stamina. Whether this was by chance or design, Silvestrus did not comment. His voiced rationale was simply that the extra weight of the new supplies stowed in the cart placed an additional strain on Asullus. The boys' walking rather than riding was, therefore, a consideration for the old mule.

Asullus, however, seemed never to be one not to take advantage of a situation that allowed him to give voice to life's apparent inequities.

"No' that I be one to complain, but sure, an' as all can see, once again the mule, it is, do ha' to bear the burden o' the Masters as are willin' to take advantage o' his good nature, sacrificin' his deserved leisure by fillin' his days up wi' unendin' labor, toil, an' the like."

Silvestrus did not continue his formal instruction, stating that it would be the task of the *Collegium*. On any other topic, he was open, sensitive, and flexible; unless it concerned *Pila Ludere*. On that topic, he was adamantly mute.

That afternoon, the boys made their fourth attempt at the game, employing several new strategies. These were chiefly contrived from the combined inventive efforts of the crafty and duplicitous brewer's son and the treacherous and amoral redheaded street thief. Their success was not worse than their first trial, nor, however, any better—resulting in yet another humiliation.

At a strategy session afterward, they realized a practice area some distance from the camp was in order. It was not that they thought Silvestrus would purposefully use any information he might gain from casually spying on them to his advantage—such as they suspected he had done earlier—as much as that it would be complicated for him not to do so. Since a good portion of the afternoon remained—it had not taken very long for Silvestrus to administer his educational chastisement—the boys asked permission to explore a bit further east.

"East? You wish to explore to the east?" Master Silvestrus closed his eyes for a long moment. Then he opened them and smiled. "Very well, to the east it is. Remember, though, to be always alert and on your guard.

One is never aware what one may come up against in the forests. Oh, and be wary of any who might seem to be from the East." This final warning was one on which the old Sorcerer did not further elaborate.

The old man's Apprentices assured him of their caution, then set off, with Bellis at their heels. The bright, sunshiny day lifted their spirits. Soon they were striding along, alternately discussing combat strategy for the next game—Rolland had secured the ogre's bladder with no one the wiser—and rehearsing various traveling songs.

The trail, essentially a deer track, led into a forested area. Shortly after, the boys were under a thick copse of trees, and Thaddeus, in the lead, raised his hand to signal a stop. He pointed up and to the left. A cloud of flying insects was hovering around one of the trees off the path, emitting a low buzzing sound.

"They're swarming," Thaddeus said. "The hive is getting ready to split."

"What's swarming?" Rolland asked.

"Bees. Right, Thaddeus?" Anders asked.

"Yes. That's right," Thaddeus confirmed.

Anders nodded. "Primus told me, in my studies on natural philosophy, that when a beehive is ready to split, it's because the Princess of the hive is in rebellion against the Queen, each having her own adherents, to see who will rule between them. And the one who loses must take all her loyal subjects and leave to establish a new queendom elsewhere."

"Well, yes, in a manner of speaking, but—" Thaddeus began.

"And when that happens, the hives are left temporarily unguarded, and it's easy to get the honey."

"Well, I'm not so sure about that, Anders. I—"

"So, Thaddeus, can we get some honey? You would know how," Anders asked.

"Well, I don't really—"

"*Pssst!*" hissed Rolland. "Look at Bellis!"

Bellis stood frozen with her tail straight back and right paw elevated. Her head held forward with her eyes fixated on something beyond what the boys could perceive.

Thaddeus' eyebrows raised. "She's pointing," he whispered, "but look —not at the bees." He crept forward in the direction Bellis was pointing, and Rolland and Anders joined him.

Ahead was a small clearing. As they closed the distance, the sound of growling reached their ears.

Thaddeus parted the last bush, and the three Apprentices peered through. At the far end of an open space, a young tree was barely supporting the weight of what appeared to be three older children clinging to its upper branches.

Directly beneath them, three *passae* down, two forest lions —young females—paced with upward glances at their cornered prey. The lions could not climb high enough to get to the three, nor could the three trapped above leave their perches. The lions growled and snarled in frustration at the impasse while the treed trio gave them peremptory commands.

"Shoo!" said one.

"Scat!" shouted a second.

"Go away!" commanded the third.

Thaddeus turned to his companions. "We must help those children!"

"What do you want us to do, Thaddeus? Throw this ogre's bladder at them?" Then, Rolland's eyes grew narrow and shrewd. "Wait. Those aren't children, Thaddeus; those are *girls!*"

"*Iovis!* You're right! What are they doing out here?"

Anders peered ahead, squinting. "Are any of them short?"

Thaddeus' head was down, his brows knitted together in concentration. Then he straightened. "Hmm. I have an idea that may work. Rolland, you and Anders wait here and keep watch. Those girls seem safe enough for now, so don't do anything to draw the lions' attention to yourselves. I'll be back in a trice." With that, Thaddeus soundlessly slipped back into the woods, retracing his earlier path.

Within a few moments, Bellis joined Rolland and Anders. Her hackles were up. She was growling.

Rolland stroked her head and urgently whispered, "Shh! Bellis! Be still!"

Anders put his arm around the dog and murmured to her in low tones while they waited.

From behind them came a steadily increasing buzzing sound along with cracking noises—as if someone was not watching where he was stepping.

Anders turned and let out a yelp. "Yow! Rolland!"

Rolland spun around to a figure coming straight through the brush. It was tall and covered with furry, undulating skin. The boys backed away in alarm, but Bellis cocked her head at the new arrival, then sat back on her haunches, her tongue lolling.

Anders gasped. "Look, Rolland, it's Thaddeus! Those are his sandals!"

As the figure made its way past them into the clearing, the sunlight illuminated it, revealing that every square thumb-span of its body was covered with swarming bees, all buzzing loudly.

"Make some noise," Thaddeus rasped at them through clenched teeth.

Anders and Rolland whooped and shouted, and Bellis joined in, barking and growling. The bee-coated Beewickean shuffled on.

Distracted by the uproar, the two lionesses turned to stare at the figure approaching them. They appeared confused, looking undecided about what to do. The three girls in the tree pointed at the lurching apian creature and gestured excitedly.

Overcoming their timidity, the lions began to move stealthily toward the buzzing man-form, crouching low and swishing their tails. When they were ten paces away, the figure stopped and slowly raised its extended arm, pointing at the lions.

At his signal, the bees sprang off Thaddeus and dove toward the pair of hunting cats. The lionesses, yelping in pain, were stung dozens of times from nose to tail and, after only a brief moment, bolted for the woods, hotly pursued by their angry attackers.

Unharmed, Thaddeus watched the lions' frantic retreat with no small measure of satisfaction.

Anders and Rolland burst from the bushes, whooping with delight, and ran to their comrade, nearly knocking him over with their slaps of congratulations.

"Thaddeus, that was wonderful!" Anders beamed, and Rolland nodded in agreement, grinning from ear to ear.

"Oh, it was nothing," Thaddeus said, both pleased and embarrassed. "Just something I learned this while tending the hives for Magister Apiarius back home."

Suddenly, Anders slapped his forehead. "The girls!"

The three boys dashed toward the tree, only to find the last of the group scrambling down from the lowest branch.

Thaddeus strode forward. "Are you all right?"

The shortest of the group, a pale girl slightly rounder than the others with two dark braids curled in a circle at the nape of her neck, glared at their erstwhile deliverers. "Of course, we're all right! What did you expect? And what possessed you to interfere? We had the situation well in hand. We were about to begin our conjuring when you interrupted with your silly trick and threw everything off!"

Of middling height, the second girl wore her brown hair in a single braid that fell to her waist. A spattering of freckles danced across her nose. She nodded with dignity, but her solemnity was betrayed by a flash of mischief in her eyes.

The third girl, a tall honey-blonde, did not nod but gave Thaddeus a shy smile. Her hair also fell to her waist, rippling in the gentle breeze, held back by a leather thong.

Without the courtesy of any warning whatsoever, Thaddeus was abruptly engulfed in a slough of confusion.

Rolland spoke up with some heat. "Excuse us, but the last time I saw you, you were yelling 'Scat' at two *lions*, who, by the way, seemed not at all impressed with your *conjuring*—distracted by their plans for even-tide, no doubt."

The short girl stepped forward, fists balled at her sides, but the middle girl placed a restraining hand on her arm. "Perhaps we are forgetting our manners, Nannsi. These boys do seem to have come here to help— whatever the flaws in their plan—and 'tis not polite to dismiss them so uncharitably."

Having finished her speech, the medium-height girl smiled —not a shy smile but a radiant one that—Rolland noticed—seemed to brighten the clearing.

"Wait a moment," Anders said. "Did you say *conjuring?* But you can't be Sorceresses—hmm, that's hard to say, you know—but you can't be…they…them…those…"

Frowning, the middle girl stepped forward, fists placed firmly on her hips. "And why can we not? Are you, perhaps, referring to some long-forgotten and obscure Law of Nature? But it's unlikely the three of you …country gentlemen…would know much about that."

Rolland also took a step and leaned forward. "Well, not that I enjoy pointing out another's ignorance, but we are Sorcerers, you know. We are traveling with our Master, the Great Silvestrus. Furthermore, be advised that the last person to annoy us will now end his days as a cur, with fleas and worms for companions."

The short girl, Nannsi, jumped in. "The Great Silvestrus?" She gave a thoughtful look and continued, "I am truly sorry. I did not realize you were members of a traveling troupe. What time are your performances? Are any to be starting soon? As for your flea-bitten and worm-infested cur, I presume you refer to the bitch at your feet. My advice to you is that you should take better care of it."

The hackles rose along Bellis' back, and she let out a low growl.

The tall girl stood forward. "Now, Nannsi, I'm sure this is a wonderful dog. She reminds me of my Daisy back home." She knelt before Bellis and put her hand out, palm up, for her to smell, then gently stroked the golden coat. Bellis stopped growling and wagged her tail. "Though it looks like she has had a hard time recently." The girl threw a stern glance at Thaddeus. "Not any of your doing, I assume."

Thaddeus flushed. "No. We found her being beaten by a crazed man in River's Wood. It was he we changed into a cur. This is Bellis, and she's one of the sweetest dogs you'll ever know." He knelt on Bellis' near side and scratched her behind her ears. "Oh, and my name is Thaddeus," he said to the tall girl.

She responded, "My name is Marsia. You have met Nannsi already, and my other companion is Sonnia. It is true; we are familiar with the Art. We ourselves are traveling with our Instructress, Mistress Geanninia. Actually, we are on our way to the *Ludia*—our school—for training. We had just encamped for the day when Mistress Geanninia went into one of her spells—"

"*Psst!* Marsia! We should not tell them about our Mistress' gifts!" Nannsi said fiercely.

"It's all right, Nannsi. These boys appear honorable and are themselves of the Art—or the Sisterhood, as we call it." The girl ducked her head to hide a smile. "In any case, after she came to herself, she said she had to meet someone, mounted her horse, Bucephalus, and headed southwest. She bade us stay together in camp. But it has been such a beautiful day. Anyway, we were enjoying ourselves and became inattentive until those two lions bounded out of the brush and gave us a start.

We were able to get up that tree and were preparing to use our skills when your timely intercession saved us the trouble. A rather clever intervention, that." The girl looked probingly into Thaddeus' eyes. "Where did you learn to control bees in such a way?"

"He's from Beewicke," Anders explained immediately. "He knows all about bees!"

Thaddeus let out a muted grunt and glared at Anders.

"Ah, Beewicke," Sonnia replied sagely, "the small village that produces such excellent honey, harvested by the peasants there. It is said that those who live with bees have a sweet disposition. Is that true, Thaddeus of Beewicke?" The girl gazed at him smokily.

"Well, I—"

"Sonnia, Marsia, we have business to attend to," Nannsi interrupted sternly. "Perhaps some of these boys may have a modicum of intelligence and know what they are about." Her eyes swiveled briefly to Anders. "But our need now is to find our Mistress. Standing around gibbering on over honey will not accomplish this."

"If I may suggest, um, Nannsi," Anders said deferentially to the girl who was just his height. "If your Mistress is indeed traveling to the southwest, then she will run directly into our camp. If you like, we would be pleased to guide you there so that you may be reunited with her."

"A good suggestion, friend Anders, if I may call you that. However, our belongings are back at our own camp, and we should not leave them unattended any longer than necessary."

"We could go to your camp with you," Thaddeus offered, "and help you pack everything up so you can carry it to our camp."

Sonnia smiled again, dazzling the Apprentices. "That's a very sweet suggestion, Thaddeus of Beewicke. We accept."

"But—" Rolland began but winced as Anders' foot came down directly on his instep.

Thaddeus nodded. "All right, but let's be quick about it. Master Silvestrus will not like it that we're gone so long, and sooner or later, those hungry lionesses will recall that they're still wanting supper."

"Very well," Marsia said. "Follow us."

As the group made its way to the girls' camp, Rolland caught up with Thaddeus.

"Do you think we should go back to our camp first and get the cart? These frilly types are likely to have nothing but dresses and fancies without number, and they have undoubtedly made no serious provision for carrying them—probably, they have some old goat and a wagon. They will slow us down, complaining all the way while they carry all their things."

"Ah, let's see what the situation is first. It's getting on. Perhaps the girls won't want to take too much."

"If you say so," Rolland said, still doubtful.

16

Balls and Girls II
Pilae et Puellae II

When the group arrived at the campsite, Thaddeus was surprised to see three small silk tents blazing with bright colors, facing a larger, multihued tent. Resting outside each tent was an oaken chest filled, he imagined, with what must be each girl's belongings.

The camp was laid out in a regular order while off to one side a taut line stretched between two trees to which were tethered three of the most beautiful horses Thaddeus had ever seen—with nary a goat nor wagon in sight.

Sonnia waved a hand. "This is our camp. Our surroundings are primitive here, so please forgive the untidiness"

Thaddeus was curious as to what untidiness she referred.

Marsia moved to stand next to Thaddeus. She could look him in the eye—he thought her quite tall for a girl. While Sonnia's smile burst forth to engulf everyone, Marsia's smile was more demure, close, and intimate. Anders' recitation of his old tutor's declamation about the two horns of a dilemma flitted across Thaddeus' mind.

"Bellis seems to care for you," she said. "She walks at your heel, and her eyes seldom look elsewhere. You must have made a good impression."

"Uh, thank you. I grew up with a dog, and I like them very much. How long have you been practicing Sorcery, then?"

"Oh, I'm the last bit of fourteen. My fifteenth birthday is next month."

Thaddeus looked slightly confused. *What did she mean by that? That's not what I asked, was it?*

"All three of us are of an age. The Mistress came and collected each this past spring, and we have been with her ever since, learning the preliminaries. Now, though, she says 'tis time we went to the School; so here we are, traveling across the country. Our academy is on the Great Sea Coast, due west of here. A rainy climate, I understand, just like the rest of Northfast." She made a face. "Do you also go to a school? Is that where your Master is taking you?"

Thaddeus found himself willing to answer any questions the tall girl asked, even if it took all afternoon...or longer.

Anders and Nannsi were in deep discussion, apparently concerned with the logistics of packing and travel.

Sonnia, who had come to join her taller friend, glanced sideways at Marsia and spoke, interrupting her conversation with Thaddeus. "Nannsi and Anders asked that we join them with, um, Rolland. It's about our traveling arrangements." The two followed Sonnia back to the middle of the camp.

Anders stood in front of the little group like a chief scribe at a factor's office.

"Nannsi says she and the other girls can pack some of their gear and compress it very tightly. Also, they each have carry packs, which will fit on our backs while we walk. Their horses can take some of the heavy things. Isn't that a good plan?" Despite Anders' silly grin, his new companion, the dark and formidable Nannsi, nodded earnestly in approval.

Rolland sputtered, looking as if he'd swallowed a pear whole—his face matching his hair within seconds.

Thaddeus ignored him, looking only at Marsia, who gave him an encouraging smile. Then he addressed the group. "All right. We'll follow that plan. For now," he added.

As Rolland's mouth flew open to protest, Thaddeus continued, "We can't spend the rest of the afternoon arguing. It's getting late, and we need to head back to our campsite. Let's go."

As they prepared to leave, Thaddeus realized he'd been giving orders as if he were the leader. He had no idea what possessed him to think he was in charge, but no one had raised any objections. They went about their assigned tasks quickly and without complaint, even the erstwhile street thief.

Soon, the party of six was on its way back to the young Sorcerers' campsite—three girls riding, smiling, and chitchatting, and three boys trudging, grunting, and grumbling. The girls had described to their male counterparts the interesting spells their Mistress had worked for compacting their possessions, gear, and luggage into bundles small enough to fit each girl's grip. However, though the size was smaller, the mass, as Anders described it, remained unchanged. The Mistress' possessions were likewise compacted, and parceled out among the three horses.

As they came into the clearing of the Sorcerer's camp, they found Silvestrus sharing a cup and pipe with a handsome, slender woman. Her sleek black leather riding habit was partially covered by a forest-green cloak that sported an intricate golden brooch at the shoulder. With a white blaze at each temple, her rich, lustrous midnight hair was pulled back in a large bun.

As they were introduced, Thaddeus noted her eyes—one green and one brown—just like his master's, but in reverse. Sitting easily by Master Silvestrus on an ancient fallen tree trunk, she radiated a regal dignity.

Thaddeus at once thought her to be a great lady. Of interest, however, was the way she spoke with the old Sorcerer. To Thaddeus' eyes, the two seemed to be friends of longstanding, and the woman seemed neither surprised nor concerned at the group's sudden appearance.

Once within personal distance, the Mistress rose and greeted him and the other boys warmly. In the same way, Thaddeus observed that

Master Silvestrus was likewise gracious, charming, and welcoming toward the girls.

The woman spoke in a rich contralto. "Thank you, gentlemen, for rescuing my girls from their dire circumstances." The girls, standing directly behind their Mistress, rolled their eyes.

The older woman glanced briefly sideways before clearing her throat. "Though, perhaps, such efforts might not have been necessary had they followed their instructions a touch more literally. On the other hand, I suppose, had they done so, this…chance encounter…and the opportunity to make new friends and renew old acquaintances might not have come to pass."

The lady's eyes flicked to Silvestrus, and Thaddeus marked the slight flush that sped momentarily across her features.

"Mistress Geanninia and I are old friends, lads," Silvestrus announced, "and our students have often gotten together from time to time over the years, despite the great distance between the *Collegium* and the *Ludia*. All the more pleasure to be taken in these chance meetings, as she has said.

"In any case, we have been talking and, given the fact that this is the day before Midsummer's Eve, she has agreed to share our humble camp for the next half-week. I am delighted for her acceptance and expect that you will extend every courtesy to herself and her young charges. That said, Mistress Geanninia, perhaps you will allow me a moment with my Apprentices, so we can best organize our camp to accommodate you and your students with as much comfort as possible."

When Mistress Geanninia smiled and gave a nod of assent, the old man signaled the boys to accompany him over to where Asullus was tethered, the old mule craning his neck to get a better look at the new equine arrivals. Mistress Geanninia's chestnut stallion, Bucephalus, stood off to one side, seemingly interested in neither the girls' horses nor the Sorcerer's mule. He exuded an aloof air and had a decided curl to his lip, as if he held the entire proceedings in disdain, which, being the *Ludia* Principal's stallion he probably did.

Master Silvestrus bade the boys gather with him around Asullus. "Now, Apprentices, attend to me most carefully. Be aware that you are now in the presence of the most formidable Sorceress in the Westlands, as well as her charges. It is imperative you all remain at your best manners. Any untoward behaviors on your part will reflect directly back on me. And I am sure you understand how things would prevail after that point."

These admonitions were standard fare by now to Thaddeus' mind. Being an intelligent and unassuming type, he saw no benefit in causing the Master to be unhappy with him in the slightest.

Following his warning, the old man advised the Apprentices regarding instructions concerning preparations for even-tide. Master Silvestrus then turned the boys over to Mistress Geanninia's guidance, as, with guests present, an extra effort in hospitality was expected.

The male and female Apprentices were divided into work teams. Thaddeus and Sonnia were dispatched to the forested area north of the camp and advised to seek, identify, and return with several varieties of foodstuffs—herbs, as well as garnishes and condiments. Thaddeus had noted Sonnia speaking with Mistress Geanninia shortly before the task teams were named. He paid it no mind at the time. Sonnia, on the other hand, did not seem in the least bit discomfited by their assignment— instead, she appeared to demonstrate a degree of interest in it.

After Nannsi and Anders were assigned to menu planning and meal preparation, he could see that the two were equally enthusiastic. Judging from their reactions, Thaddeus had the idea that this was a fortuitous pairing indeed.

This left Rolland and Marsia to see to the needs of the horses as well as grounds cleanup, neatening the camp, and sleeping arrangements. After this last posting, he saw the redhead's shoulders slump down, and he looked to be muttering curses under his breath.

Thaddeus attributed Rolland's surliness to his delegation as large animal caregiver and domestic servant—roles for which the worldly urbanite had never expressed any enthusiasm whatsoever. Marsia glanced at the thief and sighed, then squared her shoulders and went about her duties, uncomplaining. Thaddeus was not sure what her reaction signified.

Thaddeus strapped the wicker panniers to hang astride Asullus and walked into the forest with Sonnia. Obeying an internal impulse, he looked back over his shoulder at Marsia to see that she returned his glance and gave him a small wave. He felt a rush of feelings welling up inside him—confusion, certainly, but also, he thought, an eagerness of the warm sort.

As Thaddeus and Sonnia walked, they talked. Rolland had told Thaddeus that if he ever felt he might be getting himself into some kind of uncertain situation, it was always wisest to ask questions. People tend to think you know more about things than you do, he explained, when you ask them questions, and they often enjoy answering them.

"So, Sonnia, where are you from?" Thaddeus began.

"I'm from Frantilla. That's on the coast," she replied with another of her sun-shaming smiles.

"Oh, yes, yes. That is the city sharing a name with the country, is it not?"

"Well, to be precise, the country is called Frantill-a, while the city is Frantill-*i*-a."

"Oh, yes, of course. And it's on the coast. So, there's commercial fishing and a trading port there, right?" Thaddeus' mind was working at a fever's pitch to recall some of Master Silvestrus' geography recitations. The girl nodded in agreement.

"Do you have any brothers or sisters, then?"

"I have an older brother, Gregorian, but he's been off to school these past two years. Do you have any brothers or sisters?"

"Well, no. But I have a dog," he replied. *Stupid peasant*, he berated himself savagely. "So, then, what does your father do for a trade?"

"Oh, well, he does not ply a trade, you might say. He is a merchant leading the port authority."

"You're rich, then?" Thaddeus asked. A moment later, he tore into himself again. *Ignorant dolt!*

The girl laughed gently at what he immediately assumed was his gaff, but then she smiled. "We do well enough, but there are no princes in the family if that's what you mean."

In his discomfort, Thaddeus looked back to check on Asullus, but the old mule was plodding along behind them, head down and silent. Now that was odd. Usually, he'd have had ten or twelve things to say by now.

Thaddeus' further questioning revealed that she resembled her mother, and her father could deny her nothing. The girl was always fascinated with the sea and an excellent swimmer, regularly beating her brother and his friends in local competitions. Sonnia also studied various forms of sea life and was considered the family scholar.

Thaddeus judged her quick, clever, humorous, and interesting—and she had that radiant smile. He began to try to say things he hoped she'd find amusing just to see that smile again.

"So, Friend Thaddeus, you have been especially nosy about my life—" here Thaddeus' head went down in embarrassment until Sonnia put an encouraging hand on his arm, "—so what of yourself? Aside from the known fact that you are from the land of honey?"

Sonnia, for her part, seemed openly curious about him. He began to imagine himself as one of her sea creatures stretched out on a cedar plank in her study with a pin in each limb holding him down while she regarded his internal organs one by one. That Silvestrus had picked him first of the three boys seemed to impress her. Conversely, the story of the brigands and the *Daemon* Charles drew no more than a noncommittal response.

"Oh? Do you say? How interesting."

Thaddeus shook his head—as if *Daemon*-summoning was an every-day occurrence.

On other topics, she had more to say. "And you think the people in River's Wood are wolf-like? I wonder how that could be. Well, perhaps I shall find out and be able to tell you later. Mistress Geanninia has told us we are to go to that village next. You know, Thaddeus, perhaps you are part of the mystery there in some way."

Thaddeus blinked. He, part of a mystery? He did not understand how that was possible. He was just lucky to be there at all.

The pair stopped to pluck some greystone mushrooms to add to the other listed items by Anders and Nannsi to be harvested. Asullus' panniers were beginning to give off an eld and earthy smell, what with all these contents.

The tall Apprentice found his smile-flashing companion stimulating, as she was up to the herb-gathering and seemingly to any other challenge. But then his mind turned to her shy and sweeter companion, the tall girl, Marsia. Comparing Sonnia with Marsia was like comparing a lively dancing tune to a slow piece for swaying in the moonlight.

Which to choose, if choosing only one?

Asullus continued to remain uncharacteristically quiet during the foraging. After the initial shock of witnessing the mule's gift of language, Sonnia fired a barrage of questions at him. Once her curiosity offered by this diversion was satisfied, however, she resolutely turned her attention back to Thaddeus.

It was late afternoon by the time they made their way back to camp. Marsia spied them first and called out to the others. Many changes had been made to the grounds in the interim. The amenities now included neatly erected tents, a roaring fire, horses that had been fed, groomed, and tethered for the night. A large bubbling cauldron emitting a delicious aroma promised culinary delight.

Seeing the ongoing preparations for even-tide made Thaddeus' stomach growl and his mouth water. He had not realized he was so hungry. Nannsi and Anders conferred on the far side of the fire, noticeably close in proximity, heads inclined together while sorting through their supplies. They beckoned the forest foragers upon catching sight of them.

"Ah, our last ingredients," Anders declared, heading straight for the panniers. As he rummaged through the containers, he called off the various items to Nannsi, who replied *aye* or *nay* on which were needed. Having completed their inventory, the pair toted their bounty to the pot.

To Thaddeus' raised eyebrows, Sonnia responded with yet another smile. He unburdened Asullus while Sonnia went off to speak with Marsia. Master Silvestrus and Mistress Geanninia were still in conversation, strolling about the grounds.

Asullus looked in the direction Sonnia had gone, then spoke to Thaddeus softly. "Ye'll be wantin' to watch that one, laddie. She strikes me as the type as is lookin' fer the best vessel available in which to be placin' all her wants an' ambitions. Ye goes in that direction, an' ye'll be an important fellow, no doubt, achievin' quite a resume, an' the giddy heights o' courtly society an' all. But I do no' think ye'll be havin' any lastin' warm an' cozy times by the fireplace, dandlin' yer great-children on yer knee while growin' old together—if any o' that be important to ye. But that's just me opinion. Best do as seems wisest to yerself."

Thaddeus suspected Asullus must have been studying them the whole time they were together. *I am so dull about such things*, he thought.

"Thank you, Asullus. You're a good friend," Thaddeus said, patting the mule's neck.

"Donno' be mentionin' it, me bucko. I know ye'd do the same fer me was we to be reversed. An' it happens summat that an old mule's eyes do see a bit more o' the pot than the lad in the soup already," he said with a wink.

"I think that deserves an apple," Thaddeus said over his shoulder on his way to the food sack.

"Now ye' be talkin', laddie!" Asullus called after him.

Thaddeus rummaged in the rucksack and tossed an apple to the old gray one, who caught it in midair and began munching contentedly.

17

Balls and Girls III
Pilae et Puellae III

The redheaded youth suddenly stood up from where he'd been toiling over the camp's refuse trench and threw his shovel down, lacing the air with curses. Heat radiating palpably from his body, he strode over to a nearby tree stump, then flung himself down on it, putting his head in his hands.

Thaddeus espied his friend's distress and approached him.

"This is ridiculous! A man of my talents, shoveling manure! 'Friend Rolland, go here, do this. Friend Rolland, go there, do that'—and that's just Nannsi! Even Anders has turned himself to the ladies' rule. How can that bookworm betray us so?"

"I hate to remind you of your words," Thaddeus said, suppressing a grin, "but if I remember correctly, you did agree, when you came with us, to do as you were told."

"Well, yes. But how was I to know it would include servant's work? What has that got to do with learning Sorcery, anyway?"

"You have a point, though I believe Master Silvestrus has us all doing a lot more for ourselves lately. Have you noticed how we do everything by physical labor, and now we're even standing watches—with no wards? I'm beginning to think it's all part of our training in some way."

"Well, maybe. But maybe it's as he said. Why reduce his years further by casting spells just to make us comfortable? *Pfah!*"

"If he has a good reason for not protecting the camp with wards, I trust him, Rolland."

"True enough, Taddy. By the way, I think you have yourself a person of interest in our new company."

"Oh? Really? You must mean Bellis. Marsia told me she thinks the dog is particularly attentive, even devoted. But I told her it's just that I'm used to dogs. That's it, I'm sure."

"That's not who I meant, you backcountry dolt. I mean the tall girl."

Thaddeus' eyebrows raised. "Marsia?"

"The same. She looked in the direction you'd gone for five minutes after you were out of sight. Then all afternoon, it was: 'Have you known Friend Thaddeus long? What does he like to do? Has he used any Sorcery yet? Does he have anyone special back home?'—and on and on. Frankly, after an hour, you become a very boring topic of conversation." Rolland lost his sour face and grinned.

"Oh. Well, I think you're overplaying it a bit. I barely know her. She's been pleasant, I suppose. And she does have those dimples, you see. And her hair does seem shiny, you know."

Thaddeus looked in the direction of Marsia's tent for a moment, then abruptly shook his head and turned back to his friend. "But that has got nothing to do with anything. She's just one of the girls."

"Hah!" Rolland scoffed. "*Stercus Tauri!* Oh, by the by, what do you think of Sonnia? She looks rather interesting."

"Well, she's got that wide smile, and she seems very bright, but I don't know otherwise. Why do you ask? Do you like her?"

"What? Me, like her? Uh, no. Why would I like her? I just thought, maybe—she's interesting. You know, Marsia talked about you when you were gone, so I thought maybe…"

Thaddeus looked thoughtful, trying to recall his afternoon in more detail. "I don't remember her saying anything about you, Rolland. Mainly, she just kept asking me questions."

Thaddeus observed Rolland look down for the barest second; then, his head bobbed quickly up again. "Very well. Who cares anyway? So, um, why was she asking you all those questions in the first place?"

"Asullus told me she's ambitious and might want to use one of us to advance herself and her position."

"Asullus told you? Is he now a *Homo Iudicare*, knowing humans so well?"

"Well, he has a different perspective, but what he says makes sense. I was glad for the counsel."

"That accounts for the apple, then." Rolland sighed and stood. "Uh-oh, here comes our side-switcher."

"Hullo, Thaddeus, Rolland," Anders said, coming to a stop before them. "Thanks for your help in getting those herbs and garnishes. Well, what do you think of her? Isn't she wonderful?"

"Mistress Geanninia?" Rolland asked. "Well, she seems nice enough, but she's a little old for you, don't you think?"

Anders glared at his cut-purse friend disdainfully. "Even you are not that thick, Rolland. No, I mean *Nannsi*, of course. She's quite intelligent and knows a great deal about Sorcery already. And…she seems to like me!"

"Well," Rolland replied, "there should always be at least one person in your life who remains oblivious to your obvious faults—excepting your parents, of course."

Ignoring the redhead, Anders turned to Thaddeus, an unspoken plea for support on his face.

"Anders, I think you two might have been cut from the same bolt of cloth, so to speak. You both seem to have a like approach to things and a similar manner. You even resemble one another. I mean, except for the fact that she's a girl, of course."

"They do look a bit alike, now that you mention it," Rolland said, cocking his head to one side, considering. "Anders, is it true your father traveled widely?"

Rolland immediately put up two hands, palms outward to forestall Anders' advance on him. "Peace! Peace! So from whence does this Goddess of Organization hail, Bossyville?"

"For your information, she's from Zorbas, in Graecolia, in the Nearer Westlands. Her father's an important figure in the government there. If you can imagine, she has seven brothers and sisters, but they're all tall and fair. She says she's the runt of the litter, and she is the only one of them who practices the Art. She told me Mistress Geanninia came to her father's guest house and met the family this past spring. She seemed interested in Nannsi right away—as if she'd known her before—though Nannsi swears that it was the first time she'd ever seen her Mistress. I guess her parents did not wish her to go, but they suddenly changed their minds after Mistress Geanninia spoke to them privately."

"You know," Thaddeus said, quietly intent on Anders' tidings, "there's something familiar about all that."

"Yes, I believe you're right. Hmm. Anyway, we're getting on well. So, what do you think of her?"

The unguarded petition in his friend's eyes was compelling. "I think she's just right for you—perfect, in fact. I think you should pursue her. Don't you think so, Rolland?" The look he directed the redhead's way was impossible to misinterpret.

Rolland nodded and managed an encouraging smile. "Oh, yes, indeed. Just the girl for you. Made in the Heavens, for certain."

"Good. I think so, too. Well, you both may want to get washed up. Even-tide will be ready soon. I hope you both like it; it's a special stew Nannsi and the girls created for us. How clever of them. And it contains no harmful meat—just rutabagas and some of the things you found in the forest. Isn't that interesting?"

Rolland looked hard at Thaddeus while Thaddeus mouthed *you promised*, hoping the thief would observe all of Master Silvestrus' cautions.

Thaddeus turned back to Anders. "Yes, Anders, it is interesting. I'm sure everything will turn out well. Don't you agree, Rolland?"

The redhead replied through clenched teeth. "Yes, it will all be well, I'm certain."

At even-tide, the contents of the steaming cauldron, with its unfamiliar smells, were dished out into wooden bowls. While the girls and Anders ate quickly and Thaddeus ate bravely, Rolland ate sparingly and failed to ask for seconds. As the Apprentices attacked the unique even-tide, they talked.

Anders leaned slightly in toward Nannsi, speaking softly. "You know, it is said that Graecolia can be somewhat of a risky place. My tutor has told me it has pirates. I trust you are in no danger where you live."

"You're very thoughtful, Friend Anders," the short girl replied, smiling at him. "But, not to worry. We don't live anywhere near the capital, Illyria, where most of the trouble is."

Smiling and relieved, Anders nodded.

Rolland sat across from Anders and Nannsi and next to Sonnia. Her interest, however, seemed to be fixed on Thaddeus, who sat to her right. It was during a moment when she turned her attention back to her bowl for another bite that Rolland struck.

"So, um, Sonnia, I hear you collect sea life and such," he ventured. The medium-height girl put down her spoon and gave the redhead a penetrating look as if she were judging something. A small smile flickered quickly across her face, then was gone.

"Why, yes, I have an interest in the sea. I have dissected all manner of sea life for my studies. I like to find out why creatures do what they do."

Rolland looked suddenly uneasy while Sonnia gave him one of her brilliant smiles. In the next moment, however, she had abruptly turned her head away from Rolland and back to Thaddeus, whose own attention was focused on the girl to his right.

"So, your father teaches at a local college, then?" Thaddeus asked Marsia.

"Yes, he's a Professor there. Mother used to say that he would have been more suited doing anything else, but he loves sharing knowledge."

"He must be a very smart man."

"Oh, new things are not so hard to learn," Sonnia said, inserting herself into the conversation. "It's just a matter of someone taking the time to instruct you."

Listening to Sonnia, Thaddeus nodded, hoping to imply that he knew what she was talking about. Marsia frowned for a moment, then dipped her spoon back into her bowl for another mouthful.

Midway through the repast, Thaddeus got up as if to relieve himself, leaving the others chatting around the firepit, and headed instead for his pack, where he retrieved the rind of cheese he'd stashed earlier. He thought he might share it with Rolland. On his way back, he noted Asullus standing off by himself and joined him.

"Aye, Asullus, why the long face?"

"Ye'll be notin' that I ha' heard that particular joke now near on to a thousand times, yet e'ery new boy thinks he's the Paraclete o' Wit an' Wisdom in bringin' it up. So, what can I do fer ye, Bee Master?"

"I saw you standing here all alone. Why aren't you mixing with the horses?"

"Ah, well, as a rule, yer purebreds here donno' care to mix wi' the likes o' meself, though things are sometimes different when it's one to one. Besides, 'tis no' all so interestin' bein' 'mongst a bunch o' hay-munchers. The conversations do seem to be a bit limited, so I says, leave 'em be. No' nearly worth the effort."

"Well, if you're not occupied elsewhere, why don't you come back with me and dazzle all the two-legs with your displays of ready wit and mulish charm?"

"*Harrumph.* Well now, donno' mind if I do. Beats standin' here as a target fer them early summer bugs as does bite an' itch, e'en if it do mean sharin' me evenin' with humans."

Thaddeus made his way back to the campfire with Asullus ambling behind. Though dark by now, the setting sun had turned the entire sky a deep scarlet. Tomorrow would be a beautiful day. A few more steps took him near to the ring of logs where the plank board dining table had been set up. He cleared his throat.

"Master, Mistress, everyone, I hope you don't mind, but I've asked Asullus to join us. He looked lonely and bored over there, and I thought he might brighten our evening a bit."

Asullus snorted his hellos.

Of the group, only Nannsi and Marsia had not spoken with him at any length. The two girls' reactions differed. Where Nannsi seemed to regard him as an interesting oddity and looked for practical uses for his talent, Marsia appeared to warm to him immediately and began looking about for a currycomb with which to groom him.

Mistress Geanninia greeted him by name. "Hello, Asullus. It has been a while. You are in good health, I trust?"

"Aye, Mistress. Master here has been seein' to me every want an' whim, don' ye know. I must say, though, that ye looks as ravishin' as always, an' as I ha' tol' ye on occasions previous, were I no' o' the mulish persuasion—" Asullus winked, then looked down.

Mistress Geanninia's smile deepened. "And if I were of the mulish persuasion, dearest Asullus, I would take you up on it in an eye-blink."

Everyone laughed, Silvestrus most of all. Asullus sat back on his haunches and joined in readily on the give-and-take.

At the conclusion of the meal, Master Silvestrus and Mistress Geanninia rose and, each taking a bowl of fruit, made their way to the logs rolled up near the firepit's crackling, smoky contents and took seats. The six Apprentices followed suit with their bowls in hand.

The pairing up, which had begun during even-tide, continued around the fireplace. Anders and Nannsi sat next to the adult Sorcerers—he excited and expositing while she was accepting and confident.

In the meantime, Thaddeus found himself sitting on one of the logs next to Marsia, a plate of fruit on his knees, a cup in one hand, and his knife in the other. It was a juggling act, trying to eat and talk at the same time without spilling and making a boneheaded botcher of himself in front of her.

"And have you then begun your studies in Sorcery?" Sonnia asked, interrupting the seated couple for the third time.

"No, not really. I mean, Master Silvestrus has told us some things, but he says we must wait to begin our formal training until once we have reached the *Collegium*," Thaddeus replied a bit briskly. At once, he regretted his tone. He did not mean to snap, but he knew who he wanted to talk to at the moment—and it was not Sonnia.

Rolland, sitting next to Sonnia, broke in immediately. "We have been playing *Pila Ludere*, however," he said hopefully.

"Ah, yes," Sonnia said wisely, "the field ball game. I understand, Friend Thaddeus, that it involves bladder kicking," Sonnia said.

Thaddeus struggled to appear genial.

The group fell silent and looked to Thaddeus for a reply. "Um, not exactly. It's ball-kicking, really—a game our Master taught us. In this case, the ball was made from an ogre's bladder, but I think, though, a proper ball could be made of almost anything and would do just as well."

Sonnia leaned forward. "Oh, an ogre's bladder. You had to have killed it, of course. It must have been dangerous."

Rolland's head suddenly shot up, pouncing on the opportunity. He leaned forward eagerly. "Well, now, as to that. 'Tis a daring tale indeed. We came upon it all unexpectedly. It was running hard—straight at us— roaring defiance, when—"

Thaddeus sighed and interrupted. "The ogre was dead already, Sonnia. Asullus told Rolland how to carve the bladder out of the beast, and Master Silvestrus prepared it so we could use it. Then he explained the rules and showed us how to play. We've played four games already and we were on our way to practice today when we met you."

Rolland's head dropped down once again. It appeared things were not going as he would have wished.

"You've played four games? With whom did you play?" Sonnia asked.

"Uh, well, Master Silvestrus. And, Asullus," Thaddeus responded.

"You played against your Master and the mule?"

"Yes, that's right."

"Just you?"

"No. Rolland, Anders, and I all played."

"So, you three boys played against your Master and Asullus?"

"Yes."

"And what was the outcome of these games?"

"We've lost four times out of four tries so far."

"You lost all?"

"Yes."

"I see. This sounds like a very interesting game. Would it be possible for Marsia, Nannsi, and me to play?"

Thaddeus was confused. "You want to have your own game?" Surely, she did not mean…

"No. We want to play you in your game."

"What? I don't think that would be fair. I mean, you're girls, and—"

Suddenly Nannsi, as if conjured, was standing two thumb-lengths from him, her hands planted firmly on her hips. "Excuse me?"

"Well, I mean—"

"Do you think we would do any worse against you than you have done against an old man—oh! Your pardon, Master Silvestrus!"

"Not to worry, sweet one. I have taken no wound," the old man said, smiling.

"—and a mule?" Nannsi finished.

"Well, I…that is—"

Rolland stepped forward. "It's all right, Thaddeus. We would be delighted to play against you girls. But, you know, we ought to try to make it a little more interesting—add some incentive for the sake of amusement, you see. I propose that we play the game with you, with all glory and praise to the winners. But the losers must do all the meal, horse, and ground chores around the camp for as long as we stay together. Unless, of course, you would feel uncomfortable in taking this wager?"

The three girls looked at each other then in unison cried, "Done!"

Mistress Geanninia leaned over and whispered something to Master Silvestrus, and they both chuckled.

Asullus shook his head, muttering under his breath. "I hates to say this, meself, but ye young lads may be ruin' the day ye made this particular wager. I ha' no good feelin' aboot it at all."

Rolland, however, was elated. "Now, finally a chance to set things to rights!"

Thaddeus was less optimistic but still confident. He was conflicted, though, over the thought of triumphing over the girls, particularly Marsia, in front of the entire group. His concern, however, seemed minor when he saw the anguish and soul-searing Anders was going through. The youth was actually wringing his hands.

Rolland patted Anders on the shoulder. "Don't worry, Friend Anders. By this time tomorrow night, we'll be sitting pretty, taking our ease and enjoying the day's outcome. Mark my words--you can count on it!"

18

Contest!
Certamine!

haddeus opened his eyes the next morning wide and expectant. During the part of his sleep where he reasoned out the upcoming day's plans, he had determined that he could spend the morning, once chores were done, talking with Marsia —or listening to Marsia—or just being with Marsia. It was no matter what they did, only that they were together.

With anticipation sitting so closely on his shoulder, he quietly made his way out of the tent he shared with the boys and went over to the large goatskin bag hanging from the brass tripod near the fire. The bag itself was covered with dew, which he swiped with his hands and then applied to his face. Even though they were almost two-thirds of the way through *Iunius*, the water was quite cool.

The logs in the firepit were still smoking from the night before, and neither movement nor sound was coming from the girls' tents. After arguing with himself about being over-bold, he eventually tiptoed closer to their area but could still detect no signs of life. Disappointment began to replace anticipation.

Behind him, he heard a rustle.

First Anders and then Rolland stumbled up from their bedrolls, made their way to the edge of the nearby forest to relieve themselves, and returned.

"Morning," Thaddeus said.

Anders yawned. "Morning. Are the girls in their tents?"

"Gone, I think. Mayhap they're out looking for flowers."

Rolland nodded. "Aye, Thaddeus, the ogre's bladder is missing from where I left it last night. Could they have taken it?"

"Possibly. Could it be they were serious about wanting to play us in *Pila Ludere* after all? Hmm. Let's go and ask Asullus. Maybe he saw them go."

The boys picked their way through the dew-laden grass over to where the gray mule stood, tied up separately from the horses. Asullus, himself, had actually asked to be tethered, even though, of course, it was not necessary.

Thaddeus was curious as to the old mule's choices.

"Well, now, ye know there's ne'er been an animal as skittish or sensitive to class an' so on as yer basic horse-types. An' ye'll also be notin' as to how they feel aboot the lowly mule. So, should they be seein' themselves tied up to a rope an' meself standin' free to come an' go as I please, they'd be apt to get a mite uppity aboot the entire matter an' take it out on us all. Besides which, lads, as Thaddeus knows quite well, I can slip me rope any time I needs to, should the occasion arise."

Thaddeus nodded, then looked around the campsite but did not see their golden dog.

"Have any of you seen Bellis this morning?"

"No," said Anders.

"Me either, Taddy," Rolland replied.

Thaddeus looked worried. Their golden dog was almost completely recovered from her ordeal and spent most of her time near her humans, wherever they were. It was unusual for her to be gone from camp now.

"You know, Thaddeus," Anders said, "you should't be concerned. The recent advent of four extra pairs of willing hands has clearly sent our good dog into *Caelum Caninum*. She would't leave all that to wander off—of that, I am sure."

"Yes," Rolland added, "our only worry is that all the extra tail-wagging might cause that particular member to fall off one day soon."

Asullus looked hopefully at the trio. "So, me lads. Ye are all up early—fer boys, that is. I don' suppose ye ha' brought any—" The old mule deftly snapped an apple out of the air, which Thaddeus had tossed his way.

The boys clustered around, stroking him and producing more apples after the first had disappeared.

"Asullus, did you happen to see Nannsi and the girls earlier?" Anders asked. "They might still be in their tents—we don't wish to disturb them if they are. Also, we can't find our ogre's bladder. They wouldn't have taken it…would they?"

"Aye. Nay. Aye. Any other questions, laddie?"

Rolland's mouth dropped open in surprise. "Those girls took our ogre's bladder? What on earth for? Is it some sort of trick? Ah, mayhap they are trying to get out of that bet they made with us by hiding the ball."

"Eh, I donno' think that'd be the way o' it, me young thief. The lasses rolled out at first light, dressed as if they were to be spendin' the day on the trail. They seemed plenty cheerful, gabbin' 'mongst themselves, an' they took special care to lay ahold o' yer bladder. I believe I did hear more than one o' 'em mention the word 'practice,' should that mean anythin' to ye. They first considered saddlin' up their 'mounts,' as they calls 'em—interestin' use o' the word there—but decided to walk out instead an' headed up the northern pathway yonder. Yer sweet, golden Queenie went wi' 'em as well, don' ye know, trottin' along as pleased as can be."

Rolland laughed. "Well, it seems they intend to take the bet seriously. But why take Bellis? Anders, what do you make of it?"

"It's as you said. They do intend to take it seriously. Bellis probably went along because she wanted to follow the only humans awake to pet her at that hour."

Rolland snorted. "*Pfah!* I'm truly amazed they would go to all that trouble just to be beaten and make themselves look foolish in front of everyone. But I'll enjoy a little service around here after the wager is lost. Yes, indeed."

"Ah, Rufus, an' ha' ye ne'er heard o' the ol' chestnut concernin' pride comin' previous to a fallin' down? I ha' seen me summat o' the world o'er the years, lads, an' I be here to tell all who be listenin' that unwarranted overconfidence ha' lost more contests than lack o' skills an' adverse refereein' taken all together."

"But Asullus, they are *girls*. Girls are not a fair match for us," the redheaded boy persisted.

"As to the former, aye, an' be thankin' yer lucky stars fer it. As to the latter, I am inclined to agree wi' ye, though p'rhaps not as ye're intendin'. Well, no matter, boys—whatever will be, will be a pickle, howe'er ye wants to slice it, as I always says. An' if ye're lookin' for an extra piece o' advice, ye might be considerin' gettin' a fire goin' an' seein' to break-fast. Will no' hurt any o' ye to do it, an' pleasin' the Master an' Mistress is ne'er a bad idea, neither."

With some reluctance, the boys concurred and returned to the firepit to begin morning preparations. Soon thereafter, Master Silvestrus rose from his bedroll, and Mistress Geanninia emerged from her tent. The two shared a quiet moment of greeting, then went separately to wash and prepare. By the time they returned, the boys had a good start on the morning meal.

Silvestrus sat down on his log to eat. After a bite or two, he cleared his throat. "This Mid-Summer's Eve will be a lovely day and an interesting night. A shower of stars appeared in the West last evening just at mid-night. Later, a chorus of three frogs sang their dolorous song in unison and harmony. Then a boulder from that foothill just south of us rolled gently down the slope—and rolled back up again."

At this last statement, all eyes were upon him.

"Master," Anders spoke up, "what do these strange things mean? Are these portents or forewarnings of great or terrible events?"

"It is certainly interesting, is it not? I think tonight will be the—ah, Mistress Geanninia, please join us. I was just telling the boys we should have a splendid Midsummer's Eve this night."

"Good morning, gentlemen. Oh my, yes. My three charges and I all have maiden's signs this day. 'Tis unusual, all at once. I was awakened at dawn by a *baa*-ing sound, and when I looked out the back of the tent, a blood-red goat was eating the grass into the shape of a perfect circle. And when he had finished, he ambled slowly into the forest until I could see him no longer. I fell back asleep, but when I awoke an hour ago, one of the *Pixae* was sitting on my hairbrush, grinning at me and braiding several loose strands. As soon as he knew I had seen him, he vanished."

The hair on the back of Thaddeus' arms stood up. "Mistress Geanninia? Do you think these events have a special meaning?"

"Dear boy, I agree with Master Silvestrus: It certainly bodes for an interesting day and night. And I would not dare to miss it for the world!"

Anders took a step forward. "Mistress Geanninia, when we woke this morning, the girls were already gone. This has nothing to do with the odd day, does it?"

"Ah, Anders, your concern for others is a credit to you. However, I believe you may rest your mind about this, young sir. The girls told me last night they wished for a little exercise this morning. They have not gone far, I believe. And I am sure they will be safe."

Silvestrus cleared his throat again. "Lads, I have a thought. It is possible, as you have suggested, these peculiar happenings have some purpose connected with Midsummer's Eve. It is also possible they are just ordinary, random, magical occurrences, and we are only paying more attention to them because of the time of year. But, perhaps not. What we need is more information. After you three clean yourselves and the camp from break-fast, I propose that you take Asullus out with you and scout the area widely—the woods, hillocks, all around—looking for any further signs of import. Report back to us here at mid-day. Perhaps we will have some answers by then."

The boys looked at each other with rising excitement. "Yes, Master," they all said at once. Silvestrus nodded and headed back to his tent, abruptly disappearing inside.

"You know," Thaddeus said, "After we finish up our camp chores and tend to Asullus, we should look for any signs of *Faerrae*. And there might even be some *Aelvae*."

Rolland nodded vigorously. "That would be a wondrous thing. I've never seen any Fey before."

"I have an idea," Anders said. "Let us begin by sweeping the area in an expanding spiral, starting from camp. That way, we can be certain, then, not to miss anything."

"We should make sure and take our knives with us, though," Rolland cautioned, adopting a professional air. "There could always be something mysterious and possibly dangerous out there, and we need to be prepared."

The Apprentices seemed proud of their Master's confidence in their ability to carry out the task.

After completing their chores, the boys and Asullus set out, their steps light and their hearts full of the morning. The scent from the pine wafted in the air, spread by a slight breeze.

Oddly, the exact spiral path which Anders had proposed appeared before them. Taking this as an important portent, the group wound itself farther and farther from their Sorcerous camp.

Waist-high growths of grass gave way to stands of young birch and, after a short while, old forest growth. As the trees grew taller, the breezes became less, and soon all was still.

The old man took a sip of wine from his golden goblet, then set it back down on the short table next to the oversized cot draped with fine linens and comforters. He turned to look at his companion.

"Ginny, our times together are too short and the intervals between them too long."

"There is a remedy for that, my love, as you well know," the lady with the raven-colored tresses and white at her temples said.

"Yes, but at what cost? If either of us gives up our position, an entire class of Sorcerers will be sacrificed. And then what will stand between us and the coming storm?"

"Am I not worth such a sacrifice, then?"

"Of course you are. Shall we just run off now?"

The great lady broke into a rich laugh. "Sometimes, I cannot tell when you are teasing me and when you are serious."

"There is a way to discover the truth here, dearest. Simply arise and start packing."

The woman sipped wine from her goblet. "Hmm. Not today, I think. I believe I would rather stay here with you right now. 'Tis more comfortable." Putting down her glass, Geanninia turned to face her lover. "What further thoughts have you about who is after your lads?"

"Someone, or something, from the East, I think—perhaps, even from the Cin."

"Really? The Cin? That would have to mean the Old Emperor … and that seems unlikely."

"It is. No, I do not believe it is coming from Soh-Jinge. Someone else high in the Imperial Family, though."

"Do you think one of the Ancient Ones is involved?"

"Possibly. And, perhaps even a *Daemon* or two."

"Truly? If so, what should we do?"

"The same as before: Keep our eyes peeled and the boys and girls safe. Who or whatever is doing this shall not find us such easy fish."

Mistress Geanninia sighed. "So many troubles coming at such a late and inconvenient time."

"We have time, dear one," the old man said, smiling.

"Oh? But won't our dear Apprentices be returning one of these hours?"

Silvestrus closed his eyes, concentrating. "Yes, but not for a while yet. Speaking of our charges, what think you of this group so far?"

"They seem to be as you had predicted. That Rolland makes me smile, with his back-alley and thieving ways. Your Anders is brilliant, as you said. Much, I think, will rest on his shoulders. And, then Thaddeus. Even I am impressed. He is quite a treasure, certainly."

"You have said your Marsia is to be with him?"

"Such was the reading that time. But, as you know, these things are not always set in stone. For a time, I thought Sonnia might be his agent, but I think I see her more with the redhead."

"Really? I am not so certain of that. They seem to me to be more like oil and water."

"Hmm. Well, we shall see," the lady replied.

"Then there is Nannsi. Ha! She and Anders are like two peas in a pod."

"Yes, and that is well. What of the Mauretesian, Prince Zoarr? He is a year younger than his class. Has that been a problem?"

"No," Silvestrus said. "He has settled in nicely, even though early. What about your last one, the other Graecolian girl?"

"I don't know. It is somewhat of a mystery to me, I must admit. But if it is meant to happen, then it will, as we both know. I must tell you, however, each of them reminds me of a different piece of you. Only logical, I suppose. How long have you been at this now?"

"Does it matter?" Silvestrus asked.

"No, not in the slightest. But I wonder, sometimes, how you feel about all your efforts at progeny? It rests on your shoulders, you know, when it comes down to it. You're responsible, in a manner of speaking, for most of us, yes?"

"Hmm. Who can keep the count? Besides, I would rather live in the present. Especially right now."

"Then why don't you draw closer and explain this present-living concept to me in more detail?"

"Delighted to, Ginny. Delighted."

Once the camp was out of sight, Rolland broke into song.

"Rolland, what are you singing?" Thaddeus asked.

"Oh, it's an old song we used to sing in the Guild called 'Step Well, John Lightly, the Horse Has Been Nigh.'"

"It sounds a good and lively tune. How does it go?"

This tune was followed by another, then another. Little seemed wrong with their journey of exploration.

Eventually, Asullus spoke up. "Well, now, that was easy, was it no'?"

Anders glanced at their companion. "What was easy, Asullus?"

"Why the ease o' gettin' ye lads out o' the way, o' course."

"Getting who out of what way, old mule?"

"Are ye deaf? Ye boys. Gettin' ye boys out o' the way—away from camp, don' ye know." Three blank expressions greeted him. He rolled his eyes heavenward. "I'm no' sure why I keep meself tryin' so hard these days. Me years is gettin' longer, no appreciation is ever shown an' the lads is gettin' denser. It's Master Silvestrus. He was wantin' ye out o' the way."

"Why would Master Silvestrus want us out of the way?" Thaddeus asked. "I don't understand."

"It is, p'rhaps, because they all be innocents. Aye, that must be it, I am sure. The Master wants ye out o' the way, lads, so he an' the Mistress can be together, cordial-like."

Thaddeus' eyes widened. "What?"

"No!" Anders exclaimed.

Rolland remarked confidently, "That's nonsense, Asullus."

"Oh, now, fourteen years each an' they all knows so much! Remarkable. I takes it all back aboot the stupidity an' such. Must ha' been thinkin' on some *other* fourteen-year old Apprentices I be knowin' at this time."

"Asullus, are you serious?"

"Quite so, laddie. Like I'll be tellin' ye, soon as ye puts yer eyeballs back in their sockets an' yer tongue back 'tween yer cheeks. Master an' Mistress ha' been wantin' as to ha' some time together, just they two. Ye ha' surely noticed that they be friends o' old, aye? Well, 'tis true—they goes back quite a-ways. Was real close at one point, as I ha' heard the tale. Then summat happened. I ne'er did hear the what o' it. No' me business anyways. An' then they drew apart. But every now an' then, they runs into each other—like now, by p'rhaps no accident at all—an' I suppose the old flames be comin' back from the embers, don' ye know. An' at such times they puts a high priority on their privacy, which even ye can surely understand, limited tho' ye be. So, here it is, Mid-Summer's Eve, a beautiful day wi' the same kind o' night predicted, an', like any old couple as has a history, they wishes to be alone fer as long as can be. Now, if ye still do no' understand, then I'll be callin' o' our revered Medico to dose ye wi' some evil brew 'cause ye must ha' some sort o' serious brain fever that warrants immediate attention, I dares to say."

"Oh…I see," Thaddeus said while the others nodded.

"Oh, an' they see! Praise be, vision is restored. So, as I was sayin', we ha' us a little hikin' to do whilst the two old friends is renewin' their friendship."

"That's all this trip is, then?" Rolland said with frustration. "We have to go tramping through the grass and bugs and burrs all morning just so those two can—"

"Whup! Watch yerself, young master. Let us be respectful an' all. Ye niver knows when, as yer life unwinds its coil, ye might be findin' yerself in the exact same position an' such."

The boy blushed. "Very well, but honestly—"

"Besides which, I do no' think 'tis all subterfuge. I would no' be surprised at all that we find ourselves summat o' interest. 'Tis Mid-Summer's Eve, after all, an' on this day, any manner o' curious thing can occur. Why, I remembers once, when as a youth I happened to find meself down on the Frantilline Coast on this very day years past wi' a young filly just come to country, who was black as midnight, 'ceptin' her tail, which was, itself, striped. And therein lies a tale, so to speak. Y'see, her uncle on her mother's side had a hag fer a mistress, an' she, herself, used to…"

Asullus' narrative of astonishing beings and events lasted long enough to serve to distract his charges from their current concerns and draw them into a less resistant frame of mind. Soon the boys were looking earnestly about for anything that might seem as wondrous as the tales the old mule told.

Following a brief search, Thaddeus had easily found the girls' trail and addressed the group.

"Judging by their traces, it's likely they are just past these bushes and over the next hillock. The question is, should we visit them? Mayhap they might like some help in learning how to play the game."

Asullus immediately spoke up. "'Tis no sportin' form to be spyin' on yer upcomin' adversaries' strategies, don' ye know. Me advice is to continue on as we ha' an' hope fer the best."

Rolland replied in agreement. "It's unnecessary, anyway, given what I can assure you will be the outcome of the game."

"Very well. I'm for continuing our search for any *Faerrae* sign as the Master has requested," Thaddeus said. "And I think Asullus is right. Let the girls be."

Anders, uncharacteristically, challenged the majority view. "I think what Thaddeus said at first was right. Maybe the girls would like some help. We should at least go look to see what they are about."

Rolland sniggered. "Aw, go on, Stumpy. You're just hoping they're playing without clothes, and you want to see Nannsi."

Anders stood up on his toes. "I do not! Why would you say such a thing?" The shorter boy's immediate and violent denial only seemed to confirm the redhead's suspicion, causing the latter to grin broadly.

Veering away from the direction of the girls' practice, they continued on in their excursion. It was a hairsbreadth from mid-day when the group finally returned to camp.

Having approached the camp singing and thrashing about loudly, they found Master Silvestrus and Mistress Geanninia as they had left them—sitting on the same log, talking. Their trip, they reported, had, disappointingly, uncovered nothing of note except the usual scratches and bruises that beating about the bush tended to produce.

Thaddeus put several more logs on the campfire in advance of mid-day's preparation. As he went to join his master, a familiar sound drew his immediate attention.

"Those are voices," he announced. "Girls' voices. To my ears, they are…laughing."

Mistress Geanninia and Master Silvestrus shared a look while Anders' head snapped around.

"Is it Nannsi, then? Oh, good. She's back—I mean, they've returned. Let's see what they think we might have for our meal."

Thaddeus stood rooted to the spot, straining his eyes to look for one girl in particular, while Rolland, off to the side, both rolled his eyes and shook his head.

It was but a few moments later when the girls entered the camp. Each of them had a sheen of sweat from exertion. Nannsi carried the ogre's bladder casually in the crook of her arm.

Bellis detached herself from the group and sauntered over to Thaddeus for some attention—and treats. Thaddeus wondered briefly if it was because of her affection for him, returning after a morning's absence, or whether she had wrung the ladies dry during her time with them and was now looking for fresh resources.

"Ah, so now I know where our ball got to. You've been carrying it around all morning," Rolland said with an impudent grin.

"We were doing more than just carrying it around, as perhaps you will learn later this afternoon," Nannsi responded loftily.

The boys laughed. "Ooooo!" they said in unison.

Rolland scoffed. "Well, it's good luck you have so much spirit left. That will serve you well as you prepare our mid-day. It's only good sense to begin practicing something that you needs must be doing over and over soon—honing your skills, so to speak."

Sonnia lifted one eyebrow in a challenging gaze. "How interesting that you use a sentence with the words *good sense* in it. One would think—"

"Ah, ladies and gentlemen all," Silvestrus inserted. "How well it is to see both groups back from your morning exertions. I have no doubt you have all learned things of great interest to you this day. We eagerly await the recitation of your reports. But first, as to the mid-day, in acknowledgment of it being Mid-Summer's Eve's Day…my, that is a clumsy phrase, is it not? Mistress Geanninia and I would like all of you to be our guests at a feast we will prepare. But first, you should wash up and rejoin us as soon as may be."

The boys headed for the water bag and splashed themselves.

"Aye, don't draw the water down overmuch—we'll just have to go fill it up again," Rolland cautioned.

The girls had dispersed each to their own tents, then reemerged shortly, now dressed as when they had first met the boys.

The procession over to stand by their Master and Mistress was marked by an undulating attraction and repulsion between the two trios. Clearly, the lads and lasses wanted to be together, but they did not wish to show that they did.

"Excellent," Silvestrus said, smiling. "Now—are you ready, Ginny? One, two, three—*Convivium Sit!*"

"*Epulae Sint!*" Mistress Geanninia added with a clap of her hands.

A long wooden table flanked by sturdy oaken chairs abruptly appeared before the assembled group. On the large snowy-white linen which covered it were set earthenware plates, crockery, and utensils— enough for eight with pewter mugs for all. Steaming platters piled high with a variety of hearty foods were sitting at intervals, interspersed with plates of cold cuts, warm loaves of various breads, and sweat-beaded terra-cotta pitchers of what smelled like mulled cider.

To his surprise, Rolland found what appeared to be a large wooden bowl of bear stew in front of his place, while Thaddeus found a dripping honeycomb nestled in a shallow clay dish. Soft groans escaped both boys' lips almost simultaneously.

"For you, dear boy," Mistress Geanninia said to Thaddeus, the whiteness of her teeth matching perfectly the sprays of snow-white locks flaring from her temples.

"Please be seated," Master Silvestrus invited, with a wave of his hand.

Following the meal and an hour of conversation, Master Silvestrus finally rose, cleared his throat, and announced, "We are present on this fine day to witness a significant contest of will and stamina with fell fate hanging in the balance. This afternoon will witness a championship contest of *Pila Ludere* matching the fair *Virgines* against the stalwart *Minimi.*"

The old man bowed deeply and swept his arm wide, acknowledging each team. "Our *Arbiter* for this afternoon's laurel wreaths will be Asullus, late of Cobbly Knob. Mistress Geanninia and I will comprise your atten- tive, appreciative, and enthusiastic audience. We will now repair to the playing field, and may the better team end up administering an educational and heartfelt drubbing to their opponents. Ladies and gentlemen, if you please."

Mistress Geanninia walked to the field on Silvestrus' arm, and they took their places on the sidelines—each conjuring a comfortable chair on which to sit.

Thaddeus gathered Anders and Rolland with his eyes. "All right, there goes the Master. Let's go over to the field." The tall Apprentice looked ahead.

"There. The girls are already up. It looks like they're going to have Nannsi guard their goal, with Marsia and Sonnia in the front."

"What do you think Master Silvestrus was going on about?" Anders asked as they walked to a spot several paces back where they could talk without fear of listeners. "He was laying it on a bit thick."

"No matter," Rolland replied. "Besides, I think he knows we'll be the winners doing the drubbing. Speaking of drubbing, Anders, so help me to all the Gods above, if you misplay so Nannsi can get an advantage, I vow I will skin you within an inch of your life, and I'll use my dullest blade. *Intellegis*?"

"Oh, all right. But—"

"No buts, Anders. I'm serious."

"Very well."

"Look," Thaddeus said. "Here comes Asullus."

Asullus appeared, wearing his white garland and dribbling the ogre's bladder on alternate hooves toward the waiting players.

"Right. Gather 'round, ye lot. Now, I knows ye all be familiar, generally, wi' the various ins an' outs o' the game, so I'll no' be wastin' me time on that topic. Master Silvestrus has well-instructed me in terms o' what's a foul an' what's a mere bendin' o' the path. So, do no' be tryin' yer tricksies wi' me, or it'll go ill wi' ye.

"Now, the Master has promised me fifty apples after the game fer me hard work, unirregardless o' who wins, so no tryin' to influence me unduly. I will gi' ye fair callin' an' show ye no discernible bias nor neglect. If ye hears me brayin', that's the signal to let ye know I saw what it was ye did, an' it's goin' to cost ye. Otherwise, keep playin' till I says stop. The ladies will defend the goal to the North an' the louts, the reverse. Oh, an' do no' forget, no hands may be used, so none o' ye will be pickin' up the ball. All else, help yerselves. The game will end at the settin' o' the sun unless I calls it previous. Now, assume yer positions."

The three boys drew together in front of their goal.

"Thaddeus, what's your strategy here?" Anders asked.

"Rolland and I'll play close to the line. That way, we can get the ball away, kick it down to their goal, and score. Anders, you guard our goal and don't let anyone through. If anybody gets close, use that thumping shove you put Master Silvestrus down with the other day."

"I didn't knock down the Master! I wouldn't do that! I … uh, fell."

Rolland snorted. "Of course. Anders, never try to lie—especially to me. You're terrible at it. Hah! Now, let's show these sugar-bosoms why men rule the world!" He clapped his hands, and the other boys followed suit.

"All right, Thaddeus, we're ready!"

The three took their positions, confidently anticipating the worst the girls could offer.

Asullus' gentle kick nudged the ball slowly forward. It came to rest midway between the two sides.

"*Initium!*" the mule called out.

19

Midsummer Night's Eve
Sub Diem Media AeState

Thaddeus captured his fellow Apprentices' gazes and nodded toward the girls.

"See where they stand and follow them closely." That was advice he was more than willing to follow—even if it was his own.

Marsia, Nannsi, and Sonnia spread out in formation, dancing in place. None wore sandals. Thaddeus was acutely aware of their short tunics. He saw they allowed the girls to run fleetly up and down the field with ease. He acknowledged to himself that he did not mind seeing Marsia attired so, but it was distracting. Thaddeus wondered briefly if they were doing this on purpose.

As soon as Asullus gave the call, Rolland sprinted toward the ball, but Sonnia arrived first and kicked it over to Marsia. More shifting back and forth of the ball occurred between the two women warriors.

"Thaddeus, look!" Anders said from back in front of the goal. "They're kicking the ball to each other. They *have* been practicing!"

Thaddeus nodded and ran to try to head off one of the kicks between the two girls out front, but they slipped lightly and swiftly around their heavier, slower opponents. Thaddeus considered that while he and his brothers were stronger, the girls were faster. He also realized that the boys would have no mercy from their opponents.

Thaddeus rounded on Marsia and kicked the ball away from her. At once, however, he was suddenly struck from behind by Sonnia. The off-balance boys' captain was bowled over, with the light-brown-haired girl falling heavily on top of him.

"Asullus!" Rolland yelled. "Did you see that? That's against the rules!"

"As no one seems to ha' serious injury, laddie, I suggests ye play on," the old gray mule replied.

Sonnia, smiling her beguiling smile, ran a muddy finger down Thaddeus' nose before jumping up, laughing, and running off, kicking the ball. On his feet an instant later, Thaddeus turned to see Nannsi with the ball heading resolutely toward the boys' goal.

As Nannsi kicked the ogre's bladder, Anders bravely threw himself in front of her to block the ball, only to receive the vesical sphere full force in the face. Immediately, a fountain of blood gushed from his nose. Nannsi abandoned the ball game at once to carefully tend to his battle wound—with gentle hands, dabbing cloth, and soothing words.

On the field, Rolland tore after Sonnia. He was the fleetest of the boys and, catching up with her, tripped her neatly, causing her to fall.

"There!" he yelled, draped in righteous indignation. "How does that fit you for a dress?"

At once, Asullus brayed, "I ha' seen what it is ye ha' done, thief. This be the third time ye ha' sinned an' now ye're out for three hundred heartbeats."

As yelling at the beast of burden brought no change in the verdict, nor did it allow the game to continue, Rolland swallowed hard and went to the sidelines for the penalty. This situation was not helped by the out-thrust tongue Sonnia showed him when she thought their *Arbiter* was not looking.

With an hour left of sunlight, Asullus called for a break in the game. Thaddeus led the boys over to the edge-line of the playing field, where his team collapsed for several minutes before having the strength to pass around their water skin.

"Two scores for them, and we have nothing! Those girls have been playing together without telling us," Rolland said, looking disgusted.

"Yeah," Anders said, his bandaged nose causing his voice to sound funny.

"That's what Nannsi told me. Mistress Geanninia has introduced the game to them earlier, on their way here, and they've practice their kickball many times since, though she said their ball was made of fabric rather than an ogre's bladder."

"Well, it's not going to help them one whit," Rolland exclaimed. "Now we know what to expect, and now they pay."

Thaddeus found himself to be less optimistic than Rolland and more doubtful. After taking a swig from the water bag, Thaddeus looked across the way to glimpse Master Silvestrus and Mistress Geanninia gazing into each other's eyes and speaking earnestly. He next glanced fleetingly at the girls standing together under a nearby ginkgo biloba tree.

Asullus brayed, recalling the two teams to the field. The play teetered back and forth for the next half hour.

Thaddeus, at last, was able to close the distance on Marsia as she streaked down the field with the Beewickean right behind her. In the heat of the moment, he was torn between stealing the ball from her versus somehow plowing right into her.

His hesitation, however, allowed her to score. Just afterward, he thought from Marsia's flushed face and lowered eyes that she might be harboring a similar notion.

After the girls' initial onslaught, the boys were steadily able to recover their balance and tie the score toward the end of the game. Then, with the sinking of the sun came the critical moment—the leader of each team, face to face, striving for control over the ball in front of the boys' goal with neither side able to gain an advantage as time was running out.

At that moment, Bellis, who had been lying quietly at Master Silvestrus' feet intently watching the game, leaped up and dashed into the midst of the melee.

"Bellis!" Rolland yelled. "What are you doing? Get back to the sidelines!"

Thaddeus ran after the dog. "Hold on—I'll get her. Bellis! Bellis! Heel!"

The girls ran after the golden dog as well, but despite both sides yelling, she snatched up the ogre's bladder in her bared teeth and dashed straight between the Apprentices' goal posts, tail streaming behind, as the last remnant of the sun's red disc sank beneath the horizon.

"*Heus!*" Asullus barked. "*Debellatum Est!* Girls win!"

Pandemonium ensued with the three girls jumping up and down, whooping in triumph and hugging each other, while the Master and Mistress laughed and toasted their frosted wine glasses together.

Calmly surveying the chaos, the golden dog Bellis sat on her haunches at the far side of the goalposts panting, the ogre's bladder between her front legs, tongue lolling and looking very pleased with herself.

Rolland, shaken, descended on the old mule in a rush, waving his arms and shouting, his two teammates running up behind him. Asullus, however, stood sturdy and staunch, remaining impervious to his pleas, threats, and exhortations.

"That wasn't a fair goal!" Rolland yelled.

"Why not, laddie?" Asullus asked.

"Because she's a dog!"

"None ha' said the game was limited to humans."

"Well, she can't come in at the last moment like that!" Rolland said, not ready to give up.

"No rule aboot when somebody can come in or no', don' ye know," Asullus replied patiently.

"But she can't play for them!" the redhead persisted.

"She's a girl, an' 'tis a girls' team."

"She's an extra—that makes it three versus four!"

"None ha' said the numbers fer each team must sum the same, Rufus."

"She did pick up the ball with her teeth," Anders pointed out.

"I ha' said only ye could no' use yer hands. Ne'er said a word aboot teeth, did I now?"

"That's not fair!" Rolland said, returning to his argument.

"*Pfah!* Ye be confusin' unfavorable outcome wi' dis-equity," Asullus responded.

"I thought you were our friend!"

"I ha' heard this before, methinks. I ha' gi'en ye fair judgments, young masters. P'rhaps ye're disappointed that ye ha' been outfoxed. Should ha' asked more questions, ye should. Although ye'll be rememberin' I did tell ye I had a bad feelin' aboot this to-do from the beginnin'. No' to say I told ye so, but I did tell ye so.

"Now, if ye be lookin' fer another piece o' free advice, I'd say, swallow yer gorge, go give the ladies yer congratulations, an' start doin' their biddin' per yer agreement. Probably time to start that sort o' thing, anyway. After a while, they'll leave off their crowin' an' be nice to ye once again. Ye'll have learned some valuable lessons, an' ye'll like it when next they treat ye well. Besides, 'tis Midsummer's Eve, an' ye niver can know what's goin' to come o' that."

Thaddeus stood, taking in the scene, chest heaving. His thoughts and feelings were very mixed. It was not that he hadn't wanted to win; he had. Though, to be honest, a part of him hadn't…that is, if it would make Marsia happy, which it apparently did.

But to win like this? *Hmm.* Well, maybe it was best, after all.

Who could have seen this—a dog winning the game? A small smile crept across his face. It *was* funny…

Hearing the girls' laughter in the background interrupted his thoughts. Thaddeus looked across the field to where the girls had finally ended the celebration and were moving apart. Marsia knelt to pet Bellis, then looked over to Thaddeus with a shy smile.

Nannsi marched to where Anders was bent over with his hands on his knees, breathing heavily through his mouth. "Here, Friend Anders. Let me have a look at that nose."

Sonnia herself danced lightly behind a dejected Rolland, saying not a word but smiling all the while.

A voice called out. It was Master Silvestrus, with Mistress Geanninia at his side.

"Apprentices all! Come, gather 'round. We have an announcement."

The six youths and one dog dutifully made their way over to where their Sorcerous mentors stood under the shade of an ancient oak tree.

"That was a wonderful display. Well fought and well done. Good effort from all of you—winners and others alike. Now, as it happens, this being Midsummer's Eve, Mistress Geanninia and I have certain Sorcerous rituals to perform to mark the occasion. We shall, therefore, have to take our leave of you for the duration of the evening. After you are cleaned up from your recent exertions, you should find enough provision remains from the mid-day to make you comfortable. We, however, must fast as required by the Rites.

"We shall make the camp secure before we leave. If you encounter difficulty, pray solicit Asullus, who will find us. Now, I understand you boys have made a wager with the young ladies, the terms of which you must now follow. I am sure everyone will steadfastly fulfill any oaths and obligations they have contracted. Otherwise, I bid you good evening and—"

Mistress Geanninia turned to whisper in his ear.

"Ah, yes. Thank you, Ginny. I am reminded to advise you concerning things you may experience this eve:

"Some may be real; some may be Fey,
Some tell tomorrow; some view today,
Some show the past, some are those last,
Some you may hear, but only if near,
Some need your act, but only post-fact,
Some are to see, so attention's the key,
Some may alarm, but none will cause harm,
Any fogging your senses will just confuse tenses,
These visions a-borning, hold power till morning."

"Hmm. I think that is it. *Ave!*" With that, he and Mistress Geanninia walked north into the woods.

Puzzled and uncertain, the rest of the group looked at each other.

"Thaddeus," Rolland whispered urgently. "What was that rubbish about? What are we supposed to do now?"

"Thaddeus, shouldn't we ask the Master more about this?" Anders queried anxiously.

The tall Apprentice began to reply. "Well, I—" but he was cut off.

Nannsi strode up to the Apprentices. "Very well, you three, now here is what you are to do. First, Friend Thaddeus, you will…"

The young woman sat in front of her mirror, curling her waist-length raven locks with a heated iron. *Almost done.*

She glanced critically at her application of face paint. *Good.* The colors matched those of the day's flowers.

For a moment, she wondered briefly how much of her life had been spent in front of a looking glass. Still, she had always been taught that—sometimes quite pointedly—appearances mattered. In her trade, it could mean the difference between whether one ate or did not. Or, more seriously, whether one received a beating or did not. Fortunately, she had a certain aptitude, so she ate regularly and did not suffer violence.

Her life had changed, however. Now she sat at a mirror in a villa in the middle of a great vineyard. Who would have thought it, all those many months ago back in Fountaindale, working at the House of Lilies? Not herself, certainly.

Coughing lightly into a speckled linen, she wiped her lips. This was a change as well, albeit an unwelcome one.

She surmised she provided the house staff with all manner of tantalizing gossip with which to pass the tedious hours of their tedious lives. Frowning, she chided herself—that was unkind. Who was she to be critical of others? Still, she heard them chittering to one another often enough these days.

Everything had happened so quickly. All those years of memorizing prophecy, then the loss of her mother, and her subsequent sale to the flesh factor—the go-between—in Fountaindale. She shook her head. Those were horrible years indeed. Only the camaraderie of the other girls…and those few boys…had helped her through those terrible days, especially at first.

Well, the past was the past, and well and done.

And then there was Ormerod.

A slight man, shrewd in his craft and business but in other ways— well, no one was perfect. He was kindly enough, though, and treated her well. In fact, it had been his idea to spirit her off to his villa. Of course, he could have just bought out her contract, but Ethne was unsure whether even he had such coin. She had to acknowledge she was good at her profession, just as everyone said.

Besides, she knew she had to leave. The prophecy was specific—*the vintner*—not just any wine merchant. He was to be her major stepping-stone to the next rung of the ladder.

First, the villa and then the boy…

And so, one day, there he was, in the back of a cart, needing to be carried up the stairs. She sighed. Only that one night and one day. That's all she was to have for now.

Imagine, though, that this might lead to an Emperor. That would be doing well for a girl from the House of Lilies…very well, indeed.

The warmth that remained from the late afternoon sunbathed the tall youth carrying a large straw hamper, jammed to overflowing with kindling and small sticks slung over one shoulder. He stopped near Mistress Geanninia's tent and laid his burden down, then wiped the sweat from his brow with his trail rag.

After a moment, he placed the rag under the spot where the hamper's strap had been digging into his shoulder. He supposed his discomfort was his own fault. He had purposefully overfilled the basket, hoping a second trip would not be needed.

Several steps later, behind the Mistress' tent, he spied Rolland sitting on a log, head in his hands, cursing softly to himself. Thaddeus slipped quietly up behind him.

"Aha, Friend Rolland! Laze about now, is it?"

Rolland jumped as if stung and looked around wildly. "Thaddeus! Don't do that!"

"All right. But you did look odd. Why are you hiding out behind the tent?"

"Because…I'm hiding out behind the tent. Why else? Those girls have been directing me mercilessly—especially that Sonnia. She's played the 'do my bidding' game all day, and now she is deviling me with questions befitting an idiot. 'Oh, Nannsi, what did you think of the game, dear? Do you think the boys may actually appear for our next match?

They do not seem to have been in attendance for the game today.' It's been constant like that all bloody afternoon and my patience is gone. So, I'm taking a rest. I still can't believe they won."

Thaddeus smiled to himself. He truly had not minded the loss all that much, considering the opportunity it had provided him to be close to Marsia for a fleeting two hours. Powerful feelings were at work here, and he had no will to try to stop them. Indeed, he was at peace with the onslaught.

Suddenly the image of Ethne flew to his mind. He felt a pang of guilt but then came a dawning revelation. He had loved Ethne, but in a different way, almost as a caregiver with a tender ward. But Marsia…oh, she was beautiful like a hidden lily—something rare and treasured.

A strident voice broke in on Thaddeus' musings. "Aye, Thaddeus! Pay attention! I said, what do you think we should do about this?" Rolland demanded.

"Um, nothing, I reckon, Rolland. It's as Asullus said—" He tried to copy Asullus' voice. "The game's o'er, an' we've learned summat." He sighed. "I guess now it's time to 'make honey from bitter-flower,' as my father used to say."

"*Pfah!* It's always honey with you, Thaddeus!" Gradually, Rolland's expression began to change, and a small smile tugged at the corners of his mouth.

"Rolland, I've been with you long enough to recognize that look. What are you on about?"

"Never you mind, Taddy. Nothing terrible. Besides, I think you'd rather not know."

"Be careful, then. You don't want the Master coming down your throat searching for your tonsils when he gets back."

"Not to worry, Bee-Master, I'm always careful."

Shaking his head, Thaddeus resumed his trek to the fire pit with his burden.

It was on the return from his third trip to the woods—at Nannsi's insistence—he found Rolland dressing the fire. One of the larger panniers lay open on the ground beside him, its contents unceremoniously dumped onto the burning logs. The fire, roaring several moments previously, had now diminished to a smoking heap. Rolland tossed more kindling and sticks over the layers of greenery, hiding it from view. The ex-thief looked up at Thaddeus' approach and grinned.

Thaddeus eyed his friend dubiously. "Rolland, what are you doing?"

"Evening the score, Taddy. Just evening the score."

Thaddeus started. "Oh, that's not the Master's special pipe weed, is it?"

"Not yet. I'm saving the Master from himself. I told you if he goes funny he may not be able to stop using it. So now, we'll get rid of it for him."

"Uh, have you thought this out? I mean, he really doesn't seem to like it when one of us gets into his supplies. He almost took Asullus apart last week for that very thing."

"Thaddeus, you worry too much. This is a service to our Master. It may also have some beneficial effect on the girls' attitudes as well.'"

"Just exactly what beneficial effect do you mean?" Thaddeus asked, suddenly feeling protective of the tall girl who had come to occupy a large portion of his thoughts lately.

"Oh, nothing serious. If anything, it'll just make them giggle. They're in Mistress Geanninia's tent preparing for Midsummer's Night's Eve's ceremonies—whatever they are.

"Oh, and Thaddeus, my lad, a word of advice. Were I you, I'd stand back a little from the fire tonight—out of the smoke. You see it's—uh-oh, here they come. Shh."

The Mistress' tent flap was thrown back, and the three girls emerged, dressed in sable robes with belts of white rope. All were barefoot in the emerging evening. Nannsi carried a small lute and pick, Sonnia bore a wooden flute with a silver bell, and Marsia grasped a tambourine with black silken streamers. The girls walked in single file toward the fire with great dignity of purpose.

Anders—looking like a raccoon because of his bludgeoning at the game—returned from burying the garbage left from even-tide and joined his two fellow Apprentices.

With the slightest of smiles in his direction, Nannsi addressed the group.

"As your Master said earlier, this is a special time: Midsummer's Eve. It is paramount that certain rites and ceremonies take place to acknowledge the importance of this day. After all, should the summer fail, the harvest will fail. Should the harvest fail—well, I'm sure even you can puzzle out how disastrous that would be. In any event, just as your Master and our Mistress have their parts to play on this occasion, so, too, do the three of us, though in a smaller way. Our Mistress has given us strict instructions concerning the rituals to be performed this evening, and that is why we have these instruments, and that is why we are dressed thusly."

Rolland gave his diminutive friend a dig in the ribs. "Sorry, Anders," he whispered, grinning, "Looks like it's clothes tonight, too."

Anders shot him a venomous look, causing the redhead to grin even more broadly.

"Though there may be changes later, depending on how our rites are received, we will begin tonight's celebration with solemn music and dance. We will call upon the *Igenium Ignis* and invoke the wisdom to guide us. You would be well-advised to stay clear of our work. And, please, do not interfere. You may, however, observe the ritual if you wish. Just do not interrupt, ask questions, or make noise. Once we begin, it is imperative that we complete the rite as prescribed. Sonnia, Marsia, come. Let us take our places."

Thaddeus signaled Anders and Rolland to step back several paces. He remained observant and curious as the girls formed an equilateral triangle around the fire, instruments at the ready.

Bellis, who had walked over to stand by Thaddeus, sat down on her haunches and placed her head against his leg. He reached down absently and scratched her behind the ears. At once, the dog began to whimper, and Thaddeus looked down to find Bellis' attention fixed on the heavens overhead.

He gazed upward and gasped in surprise. "Anders, Rolland," he whispered, pointing. "Look up at the sky."

The boys looked heavenward into curtains of iridescent blues and greens dancing across the nighttime sky, from horizon to horizon. The eerie light shimmered and wavered, never still, like a clothesline-pinned blanket on a windy day.

The girls began their ritual with odd, haunting music that rose from each instrument before blending together in subtle phrase and form. The music spun and wavered as they wove a stately dance with a measured pace around the fire.

Thaddeus' attention was interrupted and pulled skyward again, where he beheld the veil of shimmering light now parting down the middle as if it were a curtain opening. The tempo of the girls' music increased.

Overhead the boys watched, seeing first a few, next a shower, then a storm of shooting stars issuing from the dark vault between the parted banks of lights. The streaking stars, initially all white, gradually burned in intense colors they could not describe. Stunned, they were transfixed. None had ever witnessed such a sight before.

Without warning, a loud detonation and echo sounded off to the left.

"Did you see that?" Anders whispered. "One of those streaking stars flew into the woods and exploded! Look at those sparks!" Anders' eyes were round with wonder.

More streaks flew by and crashed, the bright explosions lighting up the landscape. Thaddeus flinched reflexively when a tiny missile shot by just in front of his nose.

As it zipped past, parting the fire's fragrant smoke, time froze for him. He gasped as he gazed at a little man perched atop the star, riding it down as if in slow motion. But it was no sort of man Thaddeus had ever seen. This little creature, no more than two thumb-lengths tall, sat astride a fireball half the size of Thaddeus' fist. He was scrawny with outsized batwings, clawed hands and feet, and curving nose and chin, both so long and narrow that they met in front of his face. He wore a crazed expression, and flames from his burning mane shot out behind him. A high-pitched cackling followed him down until the star collided with a large oak, tearing a sizable hole through the tree trunk, and exploding into countless fiery fragments with a deafening roar.

Thaddeus had bunched his muscles, ready to shout for them all to run, when the celestial storm stopped abruptly. The boy returned his gaze to the girls' dance to see sparks issuing from their fire as well, but these sparks were looping and twisting, spiraling out of the flames, higher and wider. It was as if they were keeping time with the accelerating tempo of the music.

Thaddeus' concentration on what he was experiencing distracted him from the others, and he began to lose track of his friends. One particularly large spark captured his attention as it flew out of the fire, bowing and weaving in a dance. When it passed near him, on impulse, he held up an outstretched hand, and it settled on his palm.

Looking down, he beheld a fire *Pixae* sitting astride a minuscule winged salamander. The *Pixae* looked up at him and smiled. He thought it might be female but could not be sure. The next second, the *Pixae* and the enkindled amphibian leaped from his hand and soared off into the forest.

Bemused, Thaddeus stared after them for a moment.

Bellis barked, then nudged his leg. But then it wasn't a nudge any-more—it was a prod. And there was a voice.

"Thaddeus."

20

Dreams I
Somnia I

Thaddeus stood before the smoking fire, feeling a tug at his leg. He reached down to stroke Bellis' head, but it felt odd. He looked down to see, not Bellis, but a small blonde girl with large brown eyes smiling up at him and raising her hand for his.

"Where did you come from?" Thaddeus asked while searching for his companions. No one else was in sight. He thought she looked offended by the question. In her eyes, he saw a startling combination of both sweet innocence and ancient wisdom. Her smile, however, was compelling. Although he could not help but smile back at her, he was taken by a vague sense of alarm.

What was a little girl doing out here?

"And who are you, little one?" he asked.

"You know me, Thaddeus of Beewicke," she said, her tone quite formal. "Though, perhaps, not exactly like this. I have come to take you away with me."

"You have? Away to where? What is your name?"

"Yes. You will see. And I am Luperca," the child replied. "Come. Hold on to my hand." He hesitated, and she gazed at him directly. "What? Are you afraid, Thaddeus of Beewicke?"

"No, I don't think so. It's just…so odd." Thaddeus shook his head, trying to clear his thoughts, but it had no effect. "What's happening to me?" His attention returned to the little girl. "Where did you come from? Why are you doing this?"

"From very nearby. Because I can, of course. After all, it is Mid-Summer's Eve. Come, Thaddeus, *Amicus Faerrarum*, come with me." The little girl clasped his hand firmly and began tugging him toward the woods. "We will go in there."

Thaddeus stopped. "Wait. What about the others? Where are they?"

"They will each have their own experiences. Some may be shared. Come."

The pull from the small girl's hand was insistent. He put first one foot down, then another, then another. Within moments, they were making their way down a winding road. Thaddeus soon lost all sense of direction and had no idea where he was.

"You know," she said after they had walked for what seemed a goodly distance, "It's at times like these, people often ask, 'What will become of me?' You've not done this, however, but I thought perhaps you might be curious…"

Her voice seemed to melt into the air. No matter how he tried to understand her words and keep his attention focused, her words disintegrated into insubstantial wisps of smoke, dissolving into the air. Thaddeus tried to keep his wits about him. What was the little girl going on about? *How curious….*

He stopped abruptly when the girl halted and swept her arm wide, revealing the path opening out onto a small plain.

"Wait here," she said, then vanished back into the forest.

Thaddeus did as she bade and waited. Within moments, his attention was drawn to a tiny figure moving toward him through the tall grass. As it advanced, it grew in size. Thaddeus stared as the figure resolved into a towering man-shape, though it was not a man.

Tall it was—as tall as two men standing one atop the other—and broad, with yellowed, upturned tusks protruding from its lower jaw and great curved horns jutting out from either side of its head. It was dressed in skins and carried a massive, brassbound club.

Gods! Was it an ogre? Was it that ogre—the one from River's Wood?

Thaddeus turned in alarm. "Luperca! Luperca! Where are you?" But the girl was nowhere to be found.

The creature advanced, but it was soon apparent it neither heard nor saw Thaddeus. It seemed to be searching the immediate area, its gaze sweeping back and forth until it stopped by a small outcrop of boulders. It put down its club and knelt, its snout sniffing vigorously, apparently tracing a scent on the ground.

Then the creature reached a massive arm into an opening in the earth between the rocks. After feeling about, it withdrew its arm. In its grasp were two wolf cubs, one black and one yellow. The ogre casually dropped the pair and reached back into the den—for den it surely was —and dragged out three more pups, then three more after that. When it seemed satisfied that it had all of them, the creature stood, then took up its great cudgel and killed them.

Disbelieving and horrified, Thaddeus stared. How could this be happening? He tried to throw himself forward but found he could not move, not even a twitch.

The monster's chest convulsed rhythmically in what might have been a coarse laugh.

Then, suddenly, the beast paused and looked sharply over its shoulder as if listening. It sniffed the air, glanced around wildly, and, holding its club close to its torso, sprang into a lumbering run, heading away from the den.

A few moments later, a pack of wolves arrived at the scene, led by a great golden female, her jet-black consort right behind her. They went immediately to the bodies of the pups, frantically nuzzling and licking their dead whelps. After a moment, the leader threw back her head and uttered what Thaddeus knew must be a long, keening howl, though he heard no sound.

The rest of the pack joined in the eerily silent concert. Moments later, she started circling the area, nose to the ground. She howled once more, though now her lips were turned up in a snarl.

He sensed what she was feeling; the beast had killed their cubs! The pack howled with rage—the same rage Thaddeus now felt slamming through his body. It was as if the pack's feelings were becoming his feelings —as if he were becoming one with them.

The golden pack leader rushed off at full speed in the direction the ogre had taken, her pack in pursuit. As she ran, the pack arrayed themselves on either flank, and the entire group swept off and vanished in the long grass.

Thaddeus felt dizzy, disoriented. He put his hands to his head to stop the spinning, but his hands did not feel normal. *They were changing…*

He bent forward. He thought he should be running.

To his surprise, he *was* running, but not alone.

Abruptly, he found himself to be one with the wolves—racing over the ogre's trail. He knew what they were after and why—just as he knew how it would end. Rushing over the uneven ground, hatred pounding in his heart, his shoulders jostling against his pack mates, and blood lust rising in his throat.

Within moments, the pack caught up with the desperately running creature, which stopped and turned to face them, a look of inevitability writ large upon its heavy features. The ogre swung its massive club rhythmically in a large figure-eight arc.

The golden female and her coal-black mate flew through the air, lunging directly for the ogre's throat, one on either side, while the others dashed in to hamstring it and bring it down. The ogre swung his club with a *whoosh* of air, its force clearly audible. It caught the black wolf on the side of its head with a resounding crack, sending it sprawling. The wolf did not get up.

The ogre got no chance for another swing as Thaddeus surged forward and bit through one of its knees. The creature toppled to the ground with a thud, thrashed briefly, then laid still.

After a time, the wolves had taken their fill.

Thaddeus found the taste of blood both exciting and satisfying. Abruptly, however, his mouth became dry, as if he was eating only air. He looked up. His pack mates began to waver and dissolve. In a moment, the wolves were gone.

Thaddeus blinked. Somehow, he was again in his human shape, looking down at the ogre's bloody corpse. A shudder ran through him, and he closed his eyes and shook his head. But when he opened his eyes back up, the vision remained. He could not tear his eyes away from the monstrous form, and the havoc wreaked upon it.

However, as he stared, the creature clambered slowly and laboriously to its feet. It looked directly at Thaddeus for a long moment, then reached down, put its hand into its lower body, and ripped out what looked like its bladder, fully cured and inflated.

The monster rolled the object toward him, where it came to rest at his feet. The ogre sighed, lay back down where it had fallen, and closed its eyes. A moment later, a pair of curious crows landed lightly on its chest.

Thaddeus looked sideways as a movement to his left caught his eye.

A procession of wolves had emerged from the forest and made its way toward a great boulder that stood in the center of the meadow. On top of the boulder, with stoic dignity, stood the great pack leader. Thaddeus blinked as the golden female gazed directly at him, as if in recognition.

The grass rippled with the slinking forms until the entire area was filled—first with wolves, then with dark, wolf-like dogs. Thaddeus remembered with a shudder that Asullus had told him that he thought the whole town had a wolfish smell to it—for those with two legs as well as four. Finally, members of the other dog families joined the gathering. All seemed to be paying homage to the golden one, standing regally on the rock as if on a throne.

The young boy blinked again. The images of the dogs and wolves began to shimmer, then fade. The boulder and surrounding plains blurred, and in their places, a forest arose. He looked around for Luperca but could not find her.

"Luperca," he called. "Luperca!" But the little girl did not appear.

After taking a few steps, he again found the forest path, which was shimmering now in the light of the full moon. He glanced back over his shoulder, but the plain had disappeared, and only a few tufts of long grass were left among the trees.

Thaddeus followed the downward-sloping trail until it opened onto a wide expanse of a rocky, boulder-strewn shore lined by waves that stretched toward the horizon. He breathed in the salty tang as flocks of gulls wheeled and soared overhead, calling loudly.

A deep, rasping noise startled him. The noise was followed by a low-pitched roar. As he drew nearer, the roaring grew louder. It seemed to be two pitches—one a higher, piercing cry, and the other, a bass rumbling sound. As he rounded one of the larger boulders, he beheld a sight for which he was completely unprepared.

Down at the edge of the shore, two magnificent creatures faced each other. Remembering the detailed descriptions from Asullus's lessons; the immense beasts could only be…*dragons.*

Thaddeus noted that the creature to his left was smaller, more delicate —if such a word could be applied to a dragon—and it was sea-green in color. That must be a female, he guessed.

The second dragon, larger and more robust, was blood-red and reared up to the right. The red male seemed to be pressing his suit to the green one, but after a time, it was clear she was rejecting him. With a final toss of her magnificent head and flowing mane, the proud green dragon turned about and strode away with great dignity. Thaddeus observed carefully.

At once, the male, apparently enraged by her action, and, roaring a challenge to the heavens, began to transform himself. Within moments, a giant red warrior holding a cruelly bladed crimson spear stood where the dragon had presented just before.

Suddenly, he rushed forward, hurling his weapon toward the retreating female's arched back. Not sensing the danger, the green dragon took the fell lance directly between her shoulder blades and reared up—a wailing bellow issued from the creature's dagger-toothed maw.

The green dragon clawed at the pointed shaft protruding from her chest and thrashed about, growing weaker by the second. Finally, she fell onto her side with a reverberating crash, where she, too, underwent a transformation. In place of the creature now appeared a comely woman, who lay grasping the spear with both hands.

For an instant, he thought she called out to him: "Thaddeus!"

He realized it would be only a matter of time before she died if no one came to her assistance. Rushing forward, he ran to aid her, but a large wave welled up and swept onto the land, obliterating everything in its path. Backing hurriedly away from the incoming wall of water, Thaddeus found the coastal scene had suddenly changed back to the more familiar forest, and the *Dracones* were gone.

Shaking his head in wonder, he resumed his journey, judging nothing was to be gained by standing still. He was also uncertain whether he could find his way back to where he started, even if he wished to do so. Continuing to follow the path around a great curve, he came upon a scene that looked more familiar.

Between two tall, moss-covered trees stretched a huge web made from a shimmering substance as thick as ropes or vines. In the center of the net, an enormous black spider, clearly angry, was lashing out with its several legs at a myriad of swooping, darting winged men and women, all blue, who were taunting it.

The largest of the blue swarm detached itself from the azure mass and fluttered down to Thaddeus, landing on a fallen branch in front of him. Even with this advantage, she barely came up to his chest.

"Thaddeus of Beewicke, welcome. Behold your Queen."

He recognized the figure at once—Caerulea, Queen of the Butterflies.

She had changed, though, since he'd last seen her. Her abdomen was now swollen and protuberant. He feared she was ill. He remembered when he was a small boy, his mother's only sister, Aunt Auricia, had developed a growth like that and had come to live with them for a while. Later, she had become more seriously ill, turned yellow, and died in the spring.

Caerulea, however, did not look sick. As far as he could tell, she seemed to glow with health—for a great-winged, blue person.

She took his hand in hers. "I know you have not much time this night, fair Thaddeus, so I will tell you that all is well, though My Lord Spadix has, of late, been in a right state. Well, that is his fault, is it not? Perhaps he should not spend so many evenings away from his Queen, chasing about all night with common moths. It may be possible that even a Lord can learn a lesson."

The regal blue lady smiled, and standing on tiptoe, kissed Thaddeus firmly on the mouth. Thaddeus became aware of a rush of new feelings. Immediately, those feelings of peace he had experienced all those days ago returned. The sentiments echoed those he experienced at the end of his adventure of the spider and the blue butterflies. All was well; all was complete.

It was the *Faerrae.* Of that, he was sure.

"I know you must go, brave Thaddeus. Worry not. I will send word when all is complete." With that, she leaped into the air and resumed her circling flight around the spider with her court in tow, as the entire company bared their wiggling bottoms at the enraged but impotent arachnid.

Thaddeus waved to the *Lepidopterae* and continued his journey. "It's like a great circle," he said aloud as he moved away from the woodland scene. He stole a look back over his shoulder to see the web, spider, and butterflies shrinking in size, rapidly growing smaller and smaller.

Presently, the path opened up into a sprawling meadow where a riot of blooming flowers covered every inch of the broad expanse. It struck Thaddeus as strange—what flowers remained open at night? The bright, vivid colors were a counterpoint to the heady fragrance wafting across the field to him—intoxicating, transporting.

In the midst of the meadow, a slight, blossom-bedecked figure faced away from him—her white, gauzy raiment fluttering lazily in the light breeze. He gasped in recognition at the sight of the long black curls trailing down to her waist—he knew her.

"Ethne!" he called.

The figure turned and rushed toward him, smiling and laughing. She flung herself into his arms. "Thaddeus, my beloved! I hoped you would come!" With that, she drew him close and pulled his head down for a long, lingering kiss.

This was no longer the pale, sickly girl from a city's back alleyway he had remembered. Instead, she was a vigorous, mature woman full of strength, energy, and the fire of life. He pushed her to arm's length to drink in the sight of her. Her cheeks were rose-blushed, and her eyes sparkled.

"Ethne! How did—I mean…what is happening?"

"Oh, my dearest, I am as you see me this night—as you would wish to see me and as I wish to be seen by you. I am a dream come to you. Shhh, don't speak. We have moments only." She again pulled him to her. "Oh, if only it could go on like this…"

Suddenly, her body began to change, growing smaller, thinner, turning in upon itself. She coughed.

"Oh, my love…" Her abdomen began to swell, but, unlike the Queen of the Butterflies, it did not cause her to look flushed and vibrantly healthy. Instead, it was as if some giant parasite was gnawing on her insides, consuming her from within.

"Oh, my love… We have—we have no more time, my sweet." A spasm of deep coughing wracked her now-frail body. Blood trickled from her mouth. "I have no more…time. All my strength is gone. I have given it to…another. I managed to do it, my love —for us…for us all. You will see…you will…"

The healthy color bleached out of her face, and her skin stretched, thinning. Her bones protruded. Her flesh became transparent. She grew thinner and thinner until she dissolved into an ashy mist and was gone. The flowers from her hair, her neck, her gown—all that was left—fluttered slowly to the ground.

"No! No! Ethne! Come back!"

Thaddeus sank to his knees, put his hands to his face, and wept. Great wracking sobs shook his body. He cried until he was spent.

His first love was lost to him. There would not be another.

THE IMPERIAL PALACE, CINOTON

IN THE LAND OF THE CIN, THE EASTLANDS

The patter of the rain was loud enough to be heard on the tin roof of the small shed behind the storage building, adjacent to the Imperial summer retreat house west of the capital.

Looking both irritated and wary, a grizzled old man sat across from the boy wrapped in the hood and cloak. Each knew the other, but by reputation only. And, as far as each could determine, they had both arrived alone.

"Master Solon, I am glad that you came."

"Of course, Highness. I am always pleased to respond in this way to Imperial invitations, especially those delivered with such enthusiasm."

Soh-Nahk smiled. "Just so. Now, I have a mission of the utmost importance for you to undertake. It is also one which demands the greatest confidence. No one must know of this or realize what we endeavor to do. No one."

"Hmm. If I were a betting man, Highness, I would venture to say that this, uh, mission, is one that concerns, shall we say, you, particularly, and not, perhaps, your Great-Father or others of the Imperial Family?"

"Yes, Solon."

"I see. Then, I take it, discovery would be unwelcome."

"Most unwelcome, Solon. In fact, fatal, I imagine."

"Very well, if the current Emperor—may he live forever—is not to be involved here, then, perhaps some future Emperor may be."

"Solon, I believe you have a very keen eye for the nuances of royal succession."

"Thank you, Highness. One does one's best. How, then, might this one be of service to such a person?"

"Heed me, Solon. I have recently been given reason to believe that a threat to the Empire arises in the Westlands. It is said, as I understand it, this threat is in the form of four boys. There is, at this time, a Sorcerer of the *Collegium Sorcerorum*, who seeks to recruit these same boys to become, I assume, his Apprentices.

"Although all four threaten the Empire, one, in particular, is especially so marked. I have little information to give you about them, save their reported occupations. One is a princeling, one a street thief, one a scholar, and one a peasant—a keeper of bees, I am told. The Sorcerer who seeks to recruit them is identified as 'the Wooden One' and is described as having a '*Daemon* on a string,' whatever that may mean. Your mission, therefore, is to find and identify these persons and remove them as threats to the Empire."

"I see. That is little information, Highness, but sufficient, I think, to make a start. Of course, Highness, you understand there will be a cost attached to travel, necessary equipment, and other expenses."

"Your needs will be met, Solon. It will be necessary, however, that they be met most discreetly. I'm sure you understand."

"Yes, Highness. Of course." The old man's eyes drifted to the door. "And the guard captain who brought me here?" He spoke with a questioning look, tilting his head.

"He has worked long and hard in the service of the Empire and, I'm certain, yearns for a…rest."

"Yes, Highness. Of course." The man stood and bowed. "You will be hearing from me when I have something to report."

Soh-Nahk nodded, and the man disappeared out the door.

Well, that was one less concern to worry about.

If a threat existed, the Most Favored Second Great-Son was sure it would now be summarily dealt with.

21

Dreams II
Somnia II

After a time, Thaddeus opened his eyes. His heart throbbed with sorrow, a sharp ache in his chest. Rising from his knees, he wobbled about in a circle.

"Ethne! Ethne!" He called her name over and over as if his voice could bring her back to him. There was no answer. Frantically, he gazed all around him.

The meadow, once green and fecund, was now brown, sere, and withered. Dun-colored rocks poked raggedly through the ground while dust plumes swirled by on random gusts of wind. Thaddeus stumbled forward, dead leaves and twigs crunching under his feet.

Just ahead, a flash of ivory caught his eye.

He lurched forward and found a single white flower—a rose. He bent over and picked it up, inhaling its fragrance. It was hers. Cradling it carefully, he scrubbed the tears from his eyes, heaved a great sigh, and strode away with only the moonlight for a companion.

After a time, he found himself walking along a dusty road, where a weathered fence appeared, and proceeded to keep him company on one side. He gazed longingly at the rose.

He glanced about uncertainly, then passed by an ancient willow, its gnarled roots sunk into the bank of a narrow, gurgling creek. At a bright peel of laughter, he glanced up to see a lithe young girl disappear behind the tree only to peek out at him a moment later from the other side of the trunk Her olive-colored hair and bark-like skin marked her a dryad, and the willow, her tree. He did not stop, however, but moved on.

As Thaddeus walked, he tried to quell the pain of a loss he had experienced not once but twice. And if a part of him had thought that the second time through lessened the sting and the tearing, he was wrong. But as he made his way, he reflected that the relatively peaceful and familiar woods and accompanying road worked to soothe his jangled and confused feelings. It brought to mind his times with Asullus. Somehow, the old mule always seemed to help him make sense of things. He wished he could talk with him now.

He estimated an hour had passed by the moon's course when, coming around a bend, he spied an old barn standing at one end of a field. The fence curved gradually away from the road to end at the far corner of the ancient structure, inviting him to follow. A lane marked the path leading to the barn.

In front of the yawning entrance, a man with a wooden pitchfork was heaving piles of hay from the ground onto a sturdy wagon. A mule's harness hung on a peg outside the barn with a wooden plow parked beneath it.

Thaddeus wondered fleetingly why a man would be working a farm by moonlight.

As Thaddeus approached, the man speared his fork into the ground and, leaning on it, took out a handkerchief and mopped his brow. He fetched a large red apple from his tunic, polished it for a moment on his leather vest, and took a bite with a satisfying crunch.

The worker was short and bowlegged but solidly built. He moved with a plodding strength born of practiced toil, and his dark gray hair and short beard accentuated his long face. Particularly arresting were his large brown eyes that appeared to miss nothing. Though Thaddeus had never seen the man before, he nevertheless seemed familiar.

"Hello," Thaddeus said, raising a hand in greeting.

"Hullo, lad. Care fer one?" The farmer held out a second apple while taking another bite of his own.

Thaddeus shook his head. "No, thank you kindly."

The extra apple disappeared back into the man's vest.

"Is this your barn, sir?" Thaddeus asked.

"Nay. It belongs to one R. Locksley. But I tends to it fer 'im. What do ye here, young master? An' by the by, ye need no' be callin' me 'sir' an' the like. Will ye no' know to whom ye're speakin'?"

"I've been walking this road for a time. Do you know where it leads?"

"Aye, that I do, but it might depend a bit on yer destination. Do ye know where it is ye're bound?"

"Well, not exactly. It's all so strange. First I was with…" Thaddeus' voice trailed off. "Your pardon, I don't mean to be rude, but haven't we met before? I feel I should know you."

"Aye, well that would no' surprise me, 'specially at a time like this. 'Tis true enough, though—I ha' been around, I has. An' sometimes it may depend upon the light. Ye know, someone may look different from what ye're expectin', though 'tis still the same one on the inside."

Thaddeus' thoughts drifted off again.

The mule-tack…it put him in mind of…

Images of his childhood with trusted older friends came to mind. *Who was this?*

When he came back to himself, he was staring at the white rose in his hand.

The farmer cleared his throat and gestured toward the flower. "I note ye've been to see the Lass. More to her than meets the eye, an' that's certain. Has a powerful strong love, she does. Would no' startle me to discover something verra grand comin' from all that."

The farmer shifted his weight from the pitchfork. As he did so, a stray shaft of moonlight glinted off a necklace he wore. Thaddeus had not noticed it before, but now he found it spellbinding—white globes of fire on an intricately worked chain.

Why would a farmer be wearing such a necklace? Especially one like that?

The farmer caught Thaddeus' stare. "I see ye're admirin' me garnish. 'Tis the Lady, herself, as has gi'en it to me. Well, 'tis a pretty one to be true. An' ye niver knows when such a thing might come to be quite handy on down the line. But me wager is ye did no' come so far as this to be discussin' me personal choices in adornments. So, laddie, how is it I may help ye? Fer I am inclined to do so, I vow."

"I, um, I think I'm lost." Thaddeus shook his head in confusion.

The farmer nodded, a twinkle in his eye. "I believes I knows what ye're sayin', lad. Come on, then, lad, an' follow me."

The worker led him around behind the barn to where the fence opened onto a large worked field, beyond which rose a densely wooded area. They headed toward the trees.

As they passed through the gate, Thaddeus noted a figure sitting on a stump off to the side, apparently eating his lunch—probably a farmhand. As they passed the figure, however, Thaddeus' impression changed drastically. The man was massive, with brown, bulging arms and chest, had talons for fingers, and was dressed in a simple field hand's smock capped by a tattered straw hat. The old farmer nodded to him, and the worker held up a hand in return. The hand he gestured with was holding a half-eaten arm.

Thaddeus blinked and looked again, but the stump, the creature, and the arm had vanished.

"Pay it no mind, lad," the old farmer said over his shoulder without looking back. "Once ye ha' seen one, ye ha' seen 'em all."

Thaddeus and the older man continued across the recently tilled field, making their way toward the edge of the forested area. The tall boy's mind churned with a parade of confusing and contradictory elements. He kept walking, hoping to see something he recognized.

Nothing.

Without knowing when it started, Thaddeus became aware of a buzzing sound—growing in intensity with each step he took. Though much louder than what he was accustomed to, he recognized it. Within minutes, the sound was so loud as to be painful to his ears. Thaddeus pushed through the last screen of bushes and tree limbs and came to a stop at the edge of a large glade in which there were thousands of milling bees.

These were not just any bees, though. These bees were huge—the size of horses.

He blinked and surveyed his surroundings to make sure his perspective hadn't changed, but everything else seemed as it should. The leaves were the right size, the twigs were the right size, and he was the right size. Only the bees were out of proportion.

The buzzing sound steadily increased in volume until it became deafening. He looked up to see hundreds of the extraordinary creatures flying around in an intricate pattern he recognized as the signal for *danger and opportunity.* He craned his neck and stared into the maelstrom as far up as light and distance allowed. All the insects seemed busy.

Thaddeus froze as the largest bee by far flew down and hovered in front of him, surveying him with its multifaceted eyes, its wings beating too rapidly to see. He knew he had nothing to fear—at least that was what he hoped. Who could tell what was right in this place?

The chittering sounds it made constituted speech—regal speech. It was a language he understood.

"Thaddeus of Beewicke, I am Princess here. We know you of old. For ten generations in our reckoning, you have gently tended our sisters. And we have paid our obligation by fighting for you these days past. I am come to tell you not to tarry here. Your time is incomplete. Therefore, proceed through our glade with haste. Affairs of great importance— some to you, some to us—await you on the other side. None will hinder you. Farewell."

The giant form abruptly lifted and flew upward in ever-widening circles, followed by her entire retinue, until she was lost to sight.

Thaddeus made his way carefully to the center of the clearing, now eerily empty. He wondered what other fantastical phenomena he might witness.

His guide's voice came to him. "Cautious be ye concernin' those things as what it 'tis ye wishes fer, lad." With that, the laborer turned and vanished into the forest.

Thaddeus sighed and continued walking. He came to a crossing of several paths. As he could not tell one from the other, he chose the one just to the left of center, as it seemed the most inviting, and followed its twists and turns, which soon sloped upward.

Again, the young Apprentice sensed water, but this time, it was the sea. Knee-high branch grass suddenly ended on a prominent cliff overlooking a rocky shoreline where gray-flecked, black waves crashed in never-ending succession against the cliff's base. A smooth stone, hand-sized, dislodged by his foot from his abrupt stop, plunged down to the shore. A distant crack verified it had struck one of the boulders below.

Of a sudden, at some distance ahead of him, he beheld a sturdy stone tower, altogether striking to his eye, rising to a height of five floors if he had counted the lighted, spaced windows correctly. Sitting close to the cliff edge, it was the tallest building Thaddeus had ever seen. A bare thread of a path wound its faint way up to the structure's base.

Squinting, Thaddeus made out a small door that appeared to be partially open from the pale glow emanating from it. Striding purposefully toward the faint light brought him to the tower entrance.

The pronounced salty tang in the air made him lick his lips. He looked about but saw no one.

"Halloo!" he called, then waited. He received no answer. "Halloo!" he called again, more loudly. There was still no response.

Perhaps it was abandoned, he considered, but how, then, the light— and where did it originate?

A third call brought the same response. Shrugging, Thaddeus entered.

The silver moonbeams stopped abruptly at the massive doorway, replaced by flickering light shed by torches set in sconces at intervals along the wall. Several doors led off the entry room, and a stairway curved upward.

He went to the first door and gently pressed his hand to the latch. It did not move. He then tried the others, one by one. None of the doors responded to him. Hesitating, he then sighed and headed up the stairs. The stairway wound round and round, up the inner aspect of the outer wall. At each level was a small landing with a door leading to the interior, but they, too, were unyielding—except for the last one, which stood ajar.

Thaddeus gently squeezed through the opening and found himself in a short hallway with several more doors on either side. Only the last one was open.

Walking cautiously down the hall, he peered into the room. The large, airy suite was appointed with fine comfortable furniture, rugs, and accoutrements—clearly suitable for a lord's estate, he thought. His eyes swept the room and stopped at the far end where a solemn tableau was taking place amidst the shadows.

A huge bed of some rich dark wood was standing out from the far wall, illuminated by a single large candle burning brightly at the head-board. Only one figure, the bed's occupant, was discernible.

The bedridden form, a frail and wasted elderly woman, lay unmoving, her mouth open. Her face and hands had a chalky white cast, and at first, Thaddeus feared she was dead. He took a timid step forward. When he paused to concentrate, he detected slow, shallow breathing. Her arms, outside the fine white linen coverlet, framed her body. Her right hand was clasped by another hand outlined by the flickering candles surrounding the bedside.

Thaddeus saw that the larger hand—a man's—belonged to a dim figure obscured in the shadows. The blurred figure's arm was clothed in dark green with a swatch of thick fur bordering the sleeve. The man's hand, though strong and firm, was also aged. A large gold ring, set with a glinting greenstone, encircled his fourth finger.

Thaddeus knew in an instant he must be her husband, though he wasn't aware of how he came by that understanding. The man to whom the arm belonged was kneeling by the bed, but Thaddeus could not see his face, as it was hidden in the crook of the man's other arm, his body wracked and heaving.

Somehow—he knew not how—he felt deeply connected to this man.

As his eyes adjusted to the dark, Thaddeus became aware of twelve other figures gathered at the deathbed vigil—men and women in equal number. All were tall—some dark, others fair—and in their middle years. As a group, they were refined of feature and elegantly dressed— all but one of the men wore medallions, ribbons, and sashes, and they carried swords of various descriptions. The remaining man wore a dark robe with a cowl that hid his features. The comely women were likewise dressed elaborately in colorful gowns, most of them ribbon-bedecked as well. The most senior-looking man stood next to the kneeling lord with a hand placed comfortingly on his shaking shoulders.

A moment passed, and the elderly woman's breathing slowed further, then ceased. As one, the men and women ranged around the bed bowed their heads.

"She has died," Thaddeus said in a whisper and offered a brief Prayer for the Dead.

When he looked up, however, he was startled to see the old woman's head turned toward him and, eyes now open, staring at him intently. The boy jumped as if stung.

A smile spread across the woman's face as Thaddeus fought to regain control of his galloping heart. He knew he recognized her but could not remember why she was familiar.

The ring of mourners remained immobile in their grief, seemingly unaware of the dramatic change in the deceased's condition. The woman released her grip from the man and, gazing at him tenderly, brushed his beard-covered cheek with her hand. She then sat up and pushed herself off the bed. Standing for a moment in her night shift, she walked across the floor and came to a halt in front of the gaping Apprentice.

Although the woman's figure had clearly walked toward him, a quick glance back at the bed showed Thaddeus her corpse remained composed and had not moved from its place of rest.

The woman was tall yet looked up to Thaddeus. Her smile was somehow familiar, and, after a moment, she spoke.

"Be not alarmed, Thaddeus of Beewicke. I know you, though you know me not. I wish none but the best for thee. My time with you this night is limited, however, and I am constrained from speaking all I know. This is very difficult for me, but I would give it all up again to see you as you are now. Follow me closely. I have something of great import to show you."

The woman turned and walked to the doorway, where she paused to beckon the young Apprentice. Gathering himself, Thaddeus stepped forward and followed boldly after her. The figure left the room, heading confidently down the circling stairway, with Thaddeus obediently behind her.

They made their way out of the tower and traced the path back to the woods, where more paths than Thaddeus recalled branched off the main trail. As they passed by one, the sound of raucous laughter caught his attention, and he paused to stare.

A short distance down this path, a roaring bonfire blazed, in front of which there were three figures—young women, none of whom wore so much as a stitch—gyrating wildly in time to the pulsating flames, flinging themselves about and laughing with abandon.

Behind the group stood an ancient beech tree to which was attached a short, young man—*ah, Anders!*—bound chin to ankles with ropes, suspended halfway up the trunk in an inverted position. This circumstance did not seem to trouble the tethered boy, who was grinning and laughing along with the girls, keeping time to the dance by bobbing his head rhythmically.

At once, Thaddeus began to make his way over to his fellow Apprentice but stopped abruptly. Anders certainly appeared in no danger. In fact, Thaddeus had never witnessed his first friend as so giddy and joyous. Still, the tall lad desperately wanted to talk to someone he trusted about the night's strange events.

Was this all the result of Midsummer's Eve?

Glancing again at the boy he knew to be his first friend, it occurred to him that what he was seeing was truly a comical scene. After a moment's consideration, he determined that he should probably not interrupt. He laughed to himself. "Well, Anders, you finally got your wish."

Thaddeus turned away from the scene by the fire to find the tall female spirit looking at him with a wry smile. "And do you crave, then, to join them, Thaddeus of Beewicke?"

Chagrined, Thaddeus ducked his head as his cheeks flamed. "Uh, no, no…uh, we should press on. I'm certain it's getting late."

Not for all the sage in Calumnia would he have admitted that the thought had, ever so briefly, crossed his mind.

The two walked on silently. Thaddeus noted the elderly figure had an easy, though mysterious, grace about her. Regarding her more closely, he guessed she'd been bewitchingly beautiful in her youth.

Soon, the forest gave way to rockier terrain with, at first, large stones, then great boulders littering the landscape. The air grew steadily warmer and arid. Thaddeus' nose began to burn. Finally, the lip of a huge rocky ridge reared up, blocking their path.

The apparition turned to face her charge. "I must leave you now, young Thaddeus. Proceed on up just over the edge of this ridge. There you may receive enlightenment."

She did not move to leave him but stood gazing at him quietly. Tears welled in her eyes. She reached up and gently stroked the side of his face in the manner she had done to the man at her bedside.

"It is so hard," she whispered, then turned and walked back down into the shadows and was gone.

22

Dreams III
Somnia III

Perplexed, Thaddeus stared at the spot where the specter of the old woman had stood, then swiveled his head to look ahead to the rocky ridge.

Who was she? She had looked so familiar, but try as he might, he could not recall anyone like her. He knew no elderly women except those few from his village. And none of them looked like this woman.

What was it she wanted him to see?

Thaddeus shook himself, then squared his shoulders and climbed to the edge of the rock formation. Mounting the crest of the ridge, he looked down upon an immense circular crater spread out before him. He could barely make out the far rim. Great stone spires, like giant spikes, rose from the floor of the basin at irregular intervals. Hot gases and vapors vented from cracks and fumaroles in the tortured surface.

At the center of the depression, an immense pool of bubbling molten rock in violent reds, yellows, and whites was punctuated by great gouts of fire that leaped skyward every few seconds. Intense heat licked his face and hands, almost forcing him backward.

Now his nose really burned. He feared his skin might begin to peel off. An image of the old fire-eater at the Country Faire sprang to his mind. He had shown young Thaddeus the yellow-white powder of his trade once between performances, and he had called it the perfume of his profession.

As he took it all in, his arm flung up to protect his eyes, a great shadow descended upon the scene, and the night grew darker. The moon faded as if a great cloud had passed in front of it. Even the fires died down.

Thaddeus looked about him warily, his heart racing, at the boiling stones and the blackening sky.

Not knowing what else to do, he sat down on a small boulder near the edge of the crater and gazed at the center of the pit. As he stared, the darkness began to resolve into the form of an outline of a tremendous figure, hazy at first, then sharpening and solidifying. The being, at first, reminded him of Charles, the *Daemon*—but much, much bigger—truly enormous and titanic, first blotting out the moonlight, and then the entire sky. It reared up and farther up, displayed massive ribbed wings and talons, yellow slits for eyes, and a sinuous forked tongue that flicked in and out. The immense being seemed unaware of Thaddeus' presence.

The boy broke out in a cold sweat.

It must be a colossus—just like those stories Mother used to tell. It would be better were I not here. It does not see me. I am too small, thank the gods.

As the figure filled in and became even more solid, Thaddeus began to be aware of a sense—he did not know how to put it any other way— of great evil. The colossus' attention focused on its tightly closed fist. After a time, the titanic being's hand slowly opened. As it did, an intense, brilliant white light spilled out between its clawed fingers. The glare was so bright Thaddeus could not bear to look at it directly.

Then another feeling washed over him—as if it were an antidote to the evil—something of hope, it seemed.

The creature gazed down at the piercing white light radiating from its palm, regarding the light for a long moment. Then, as if having made a decision, it raised its other arm in a great arc and smote it down upon the glistering light with a cosmic, shattering force. The result was instantaneous, spectacular, and cataclysmic—as if the entire universe was exploding.

Thaddeus started so violently he fell backward off the boulder.

Regaining his seat, he discovered that the explosion had shattered the great being itself, which, with a world-shaking bellow, was torn asunder into an infinite number of bits and pieces. These fragments flew apart in all directions, filling the night sky from horizon to horizon as they streamed outward at speeds faster than Thaddeus could comprehend.

He stared as each dark speck grew in size and brightness, forming different shapes—some were globes, others an ellipse or spiral. Occasionally, at the very center of each, black pits began to distort and grow into miniature replicas of the colossal figure itself, which gobbled up the small fiery balls nearest them as fast as they could dip them up with one clawed hand after another.

A movement caught his eye. One of the rock-globes, a bright orange, sped toward the center of the nearest cluster in the spiral. As it drew nearer, he saw still-smaller *Daemons* covering the globe. It was headed toward one of the circling bodies—the third one in—four times its size.

In a titanic explosion, the smaller orange *Daemon*-plagued ball struck the larger red globe. Following the immense detonation, the surfaces of both bodies began to crumble and explode outward, flames shooting out from the two worlds. The cataclysm all but vaporized the smaller orange rock. Then, mingled and united with the detritus from the collision thrown up from the surface of the larger rock, it formed a ring around the remnant of the red globe.

Unless his eyes were playing tricks, the *Daemons* on the smaller orange rock had all been propelled forward into the boiling center of the larger red body by the force of the impact. Before any of the maniacal survivors could escape, they were sealed beneath the raging fires by a mixture of molten rock and iron.

"Like honey poured over ants," Thaddeus said aloud.

The infernal beings were now trapped inside the center of the larger red sphere. Had that been their plan, the boy wondered, or had something gone terribly wrong?

The encircled red rock gradually cooled, and more changes occurred. The flotsam and jetsam from the tremendous impact that formed the ring coalesced into a smaller pale globe that gradually pulled away from the bloodied rock, coming to circle its large red partner, with one face perpetually turned toward it.

The greater change, however, occurred to the large red ball itself. As the globe cooled, storms scoured its surface. With time, the color of the rock changed. What had at first been a tortured red ball turned into, first, a green sphere, then, finally, a shining blue globe, layered over with wisps of white. It was truly beautiful. Again, Thaddeus felt a sense of hope.

But not all was peaceful.

Every so often, an eruption took place on the surface of the azure globe. Mouth open, Thaddeus stared, incredulous at what he had witnessed.

Then he blinked, suddenly comprehending what he had just observed. "The *Daemons*—they don't like being trapped inside. They want to be free."

"Aye, lad. 'Tis the way o' things, ain' it now?"

Startled, Thaddeus whirled to face the farmer, who stood in a casual pose, chewing on a blade of grass.

"Sorry, boy. Did no' mean to disturb ye, but 'tis late an' it occurred to me that ye've seen a great deal tonight an' like to be tirin' in the process, p'rhaps wishin' fer yer covers an' whatnot. If I ha' the right o' it, then come along, an' I'll be seein' ye safely back to yer camp."

"Excuse me. That is…did you see that? What was it? And how did you find me? Um, do you know the mule, Asullus, by chance? You remind me of him, I think."

"So many questions ye ha', laddie. But donno' worry. 'Tis always better to ask than no'. Howe'er, such answers as ye seek may be comin' to ye o'er time in any case, don' ye know. In the meantime, better ye be concentratin' on followin' me steps. 'Tis no ordinary night we ha' an' considerin' things as we go along may provide ye some benefit, ye see."

A thousand more questions occurred to Thaddeus to ask, but as the young Apprentice walked behind his guide, yawning repeatedly, he became less and less sure of what he wanted to know. The path continued its gentle arc, and, passing by a grove of crimson maples, Thaddeus caught sight of a boy with red hair.

Rolland!

A large blanket was laid out on the grass by a copse of trees, and a generous-sized open hamper attested to the remains of a hearty luncheon. In the middle of the blanket, Thaddeus recognized Rolland, who sat with two others. One was a middle-aged woman with fiery red hair, who kneeled behind him, smiling and massaging his neck in a maternal way. The other figure, also middle-aged, was a dark-headed man sporting several nautical-themed tattoos on his exposed arms. The resemblance among them was obviously more than chance.

Rolland and the man were gazing down at a playing board with little carved figures upon it that lay on the blanket between them. From time to time, one or the other reached down and moved a figure on the board.

As he had with Anders, Thaddeus had an impulse to go to his friend and ask him about the night, but the closeness of the three figures on the blanket brought to Thaddeus' mind that of a family, so he was reluctant to disturb them. Somehow it didn't seem that it would be right to do so.

In the distance, a rooster crowed.

"Aye, lad, we'll be needin' to pick up the pace a bit. I ha' to get back meself. I'm certain there'll be no one o' the party wishin' to see me in this fashion, an' that's the sure o' it."

Thaddeus trudged along behind his bandy-legged guide, his mind churning and bubbling like the molten rocks and stones he'd seen just earlier. What an odd collection of visions he'd seen—or, he wondered, someone had made sure he had seen them.

His heart ached when he thought of Ethne, but then his thoughts readily moved on to Marsia, Geanninia's Apprentice. Was he so disloyal? Then there was the farmer who seemed so familiar, and the lady who died, yet didn't, and the birth of a world in tumult. Thaddeus found himself quite overwhelmed. As he could not make a lick of sense of any of it, he would have to decide to…but his musings were interrupted once again by a yawn.

No decisions now, then. Actually, bed sounded good…very good, in fact.

The farmer came to a halt at the edge of the forest, leaned an arm against a large tree trunk, and looked to the clearing, pointing out the campsite. "There ye be, laddie. Now try an' get some rest. 'Tis niver a good go to expect to work marvels when ye be at the point o' physical collapse. Good repose to ye." With that, the older man turned back toward the wood and vanished.

The Apprentice stood looking after the spot where the farmer had disappeared, uncertain about what he should do. Seeking his bedroll sounded best, as he was beyond tired. He was not used to staying up till all hours unless he was on watch, and even then, it was hard.

Rolland did not mind keeping late company, but he was not Rolland. It was not only the fatigue; it was the experience—or rather, the sum—of all the experiences of the evening. He needed to clear his mind before he retired, or his brain's swirling contents would allow him no rest at all, despite his exhaustion.

Thaddeus sat down on a nearby log by a stand of walnut trees, still considering the evening's events. Many small *Faerrae* folks —field *Pixae* by their appearance—gyred and gimbled amidst the morning dew drops by his feet, but he paid them no mind.

He wondered if the others had returned. He was at the point of looking in their tents when a trumpeting bird sound off to the West caught Thaddeus' attention. His head snapped up to see a giant black swan with a tiny rider approaching from the sky, winging into the meadow next to the camp. After the beautiful sable bird glided to a smooth landing, a small figure slid gracefully off its back, stroked the bird's neck affectionately, and then headed for the tents.

As Thaddeus studied the scene, he realized that the swan's rider was one of the girls. Judging from her height, he deduced that it had to be Nannsi. The girl turned at her tent flap and waved as the swan leaped into the air and flew back the way it had come. Staring after the beautiful bird, she nodded once and entered her tent.

The tent flap had just dropped shut behind her when, from the East, a thudding of hooves heralded a brilliant horse-drawn carriage, bright with lights and flowers. The glowing conveyance slowed to a stop at the edge of the camp, and a uniformed footman hopped down to open the carriage door, where he handed Sonnia down. He then bowed gracefully and hoisted himself onto the rear of the carriage, which turned in an artful circle and swept out of sight. Sonnia was dressed in an ornate *stola,* her hair piled high atop her head in an intricate coiffure set off with a glittering tiara. Smiling wistfully, she watched the carriage depart and then she, too, sought her tent.

Thaddeus peered into the distance, wondering how Marsia would make her appearance. Perhaps he could catch her attention before she went into her tent, and maybe they could talk.

Thaddeus smiled at the thought; he would enjoy speaking with Marsia. He was, therefore, startled to hear her voice behind him.

"Hello, Thaddeus. Oh, I am sorry to disturb you. I didn't mean to take you unawares."

"Marsia. Oh, hello. I returned not too long ago…I think." Thaddeus shifted to allow her a place to sit next to him on the log. The tall girl smiled and seated herself next to him, with what he considered to be infinite grace.

"I just left the forest and saw you sitting here, so I thought I'd join you. How was your evening? Did you see anything strange? I certainly did." Marsia's tone was matter-of-fact.

Thaddeus' heart began to race, and his mouth was suddenly dry. The moonlight was fading, and the rosy colors of dawn tinted the eastern sky. He was pleased she'd sought him out, and he desperately wanted to tell someone what he'd seen—especially her. But he did not think she would like him to remind her of her dance in front of Anders. And he was hesitant to tell her of his adventure in the strange tower with the old woman, even though a part of him felt he should. He was glad for her company. Still, in the end, he remained strangely silent on the topic.

"I…oh, I'm not certain what I saw. It's all been very strange. I don't even know where to begin," the country boy replied.

"It's all right; I feel the same way. It was interesting, though, yes? Part dream, part smoke, I think."

Thaddeus nodded, gazing into Marsia's eyes. And for a moment, he thought he saw…something strange. For a moment, he was certain he saw something swirling in her eyes, a quick flash of light, a figure in smoke. A vision of an elderly woman dying, but then leading him out to witness worlds in collision. For a second, she seemed to be someone he knew, but as she appeared, she left just as quickly. Incredulous, he blinked, and the image was gone. He was once again staring at the calm, bright gaze of his fellow Apprentice.

The rooster crowed for the second time.

"Well, it's probably best seek our beds. Good repose, Thaddeus. I will see you in the morning." She stood.

"Good repose to you, too, Marsia. We'd little time to talk, though," he added hurriedly.

"Ah, it's not the number of words, is it?" Marsia bestowed a smile on him and headed for her tent. At the entrance, she turned to him and waved before ducking inside.

Bemused, Thaddeus sat for a moment. There was something about her, an unknown quality that stirred his feelings. Something quite powerful. He slowly stood, then stretched and yawned.

He was sure about one thing—he could not think any more about the preceding night lest his head explode. Without volition, his feet turned toward his patiently waiting bedroll.

As he was about to slip under his covers, he lurched up at the distant sound of blaring trumpets that rang out over the campsite.

From around one of the hillocks to the south emerged a grand procession with a magnificent golden chariot in the lead drawn by four matching emerald-green firedrakes, each roaring and belching flames every few steps. All manner of Fey folk accompanied the chariot, including nymphs strewing rose petals in its path, winged *Spritae* blowing elaborate fanfares on long polished brass and silver horns, and *Aelvae* choristers following, raising ethereal voices on high, declaring for the celebrants.

Standing at the reins was a strong-sinewed man with dark hair and beard who wore a golden coronet upon his brow and was dressed in robes of white samite. The black-haired lady standing proudly at his side was similarly attired with a golden diadem circling her forehead. One arm was locked through that of her escort, with the other gracefully poised on the chariot's rail.

Thaddeus rubbed his eyes and watched transfixed as the stately procession crossed the short plain until it vanished behind the last hillock on the far side of the camp.

Moments passed before a movement at the other side of the hill caught his attention. But only two people emerged, and he knew them instantly.

They walked slowly, as befitted their age. A tall, older man in a worn traveling robe and a just-past-middle-age woman in black, leaning on his arm, made their way to the campsite.

At her tent, Mistress Geanninia bade a good repose to Master Silvestrus. She disappeared inside, and the old Sorcerer went to his bedroll. Turning, he caught sight of Thaddeus and gestured, pointing to the boy's blankets.

Neither Anders nor Rolland had returned, but for some reason, he felt no fear for them. Sighing, he made his way to his bedding, pulled the covers up around his ears, and plunged into a deep and dreamless sleep. Just before he dozed off, he thought he heard a rooster crow for the third time.

A light wind brushed Thaddeus' face, and he awoke to the low murmur of voices. He opened his eyes lazily. The sky, an incredible robin's-egg blue, was interspersed with fluffy puffs of brilliant white clouds.

Turning on his side, he observed Master Silvestrus deep in conversation with Asullus. But of his fellows, there was not a trace, and the ladies' tent flaps were still closed. Murky cobwebs lingered in his brain. It came to him that he should remember the events of the previous night, but it all eluded him. Instead, he stretched and slowly rose to his feet, then walked over to join the others.

"Good morrow, lad. Slept well, I trust? Intriguing night, do you not agree?" The old man smiled to himself.

Thaddeus sighed, still waking up, still unable to recall anything about the previous evening.

"On another matter," Silvestrus continued, "I have a task for you. I would like you to go and scout about for your two comrades. They seem to be lost. I do not fear for them, certainly, but boys your age should never miss a good break-fast, especially following a long night in the woods, as it were. Asullus will go with you."

"Yes, Master. Right away," Thaddeus said, grateful for the diversion. He walked over to the old mule.

Asullus nodded a greeting, jerked his head toward the North, and they started walking.

"Ye know, laddie, if an' when we e'er get to the *Collegium*, ye'll be arrivin' replete wi' legends concernin' yerselves already in place, methinks."

"I don't follow you, Asullus."

"Oh, don' ye now? Well, 'tis simple enough. How many o' yer friends from back home would ye say ha' fought robbers, seen *Daemons*, wooed lassies, courted butterflies, killed street villains, rescued wolf-dogs, transformed religious madmen, and played at ogre's bladder—an' all in a few days o' time? No' so many, I'd be wagerin'."

The mule snorted with laughter. "No, no' so many at all. They'll be tellin' tales aboot this trip fer years to come. Heh, heh, heh. 'Course I ha' to be sayin'—an' 'tis a surprise to me entire—the Old Man is takin' it all in good stride. He seems to ha' a tolerance fer yer bewilderin' gaffs an' gaws like might be expected o' a proud an' dotin' great-pa, don' ye know. Quite amazin' it all is. I ha' meself seen him flay a man alive fer much less. Much less."

Thaddeus gulped. "Well, I hadn't thought of it like that; I'm only an Apprentice. But, you know, these things just happened. I mean, it wasn't as if it was all of a-purpose, just—"

"O' course. None there'd be who'd plan such an itinerary. But all the same, this be no common series o' events, e'en on trips such as these. An' as I told ye in the beginnin', I ha' been on a fair few o' them o'er the years meself. No, laddie, there's summat special goin' aboot, make no mistake."

"You mean those men from the East who've been following us?" Thaddeus asked the old mule.

"*Sst! Sssh!* No' so loud, boy. These woods be like all woods, havin' ears an' such. So ye knows aboot the Cin an' the gold, do ye? Well, 'tis to the good, says I. Who's wise walkin' into a trap wi' eyes closed, eh? I tell ye true—'tis a race to the College we're in now, wi' the question bein': Who is it will get there first? Mark me words—but do no' repeat 'em."

Asullus steadfastly refused to say more on the topic despite Thaddeus' many burning questions. Finally, looking first to his right, then to his left, he winked at his charge. "But let me add, in spite o' what ye usually be used to hearin' me say, this ol' mule be havin' quite a time wi' it all. Quite a time, indeed.

"Well, enough aboot that. Let's be lookin' out fer the other two young Masters. Elsewise, we'll just ha' to go back, get two more, an' start all o'er again. Way too much work fer an old servitor such as meself. Here, let's try this trail."

The pair headed into the woods and took the path Asullus suggested. Closely spaced, overarching elms obliterated the morning sun's rays, and the forest became simultaneously both dark and quiet. Thaddeus noted vines beginning to festoon the tree limbs, with flowers peeping out and moss hanging down. The blossoms' sweet perfume added to the sense of closeness he had. The young Apprentice felt the effect as eerily different from the forests at home but not alarming. The scene was beautiful in its own way.

Asullus looked around as if to assure himself that Thaddeus was close by and safe. The boy reached out and patted Asullus' shoulder. The mule glanced sideways, gave another wink, and returned to scanning the forest path.

Asullus sniffed the air and nodded. Soon Thaddeus smelled smoke as well.

A few minutes later, they came upon the smoldering remains of a bonfire and found Anders fast asleep at the foot of an ancient bristlecone pine tree. Rope burns marked his wrists and ankles, but he seemed to be in one piece otherwise. He was smiling as he snored.

Thaddeus knelt down and gently poked his friend a few times. "Anders? Anders! Wake up! Nannsi's here, and she wants to see you!"

The pudgy boy's eyes flicked open. "Wha? Nannsi! Oh, it's you, Thaddeus. I thought you said—oh, um, what? Oh, hello, Asullus. What are you two doing here? Where is everybody?" Anders rubbed his eyes. "I was just…just…hmm…"

Asullus prodded him with a hoof. "Quick as a snake he is, as I ha' said on many occasions. No wonder he's to be a Sorcerer. Come on, lad, 'tis time fer ye to sweep yer cobwebs away an' come wi' us in lookin' fer that thievin' an' purse-snatchin' partner o' yers. If ye're here, he's bound to be around an' aboot as well."

Thaddeus gave his young friend a hand as he rose to his feet.

Anders kneaded his back as if getting out the kinks, then looked at his fellow Apprentice, all manner of questions in his eyes.

"Later," Thaddeus mouthed.

Anders seemed to consider the situation, nodded in agreement, and the three set off back down the track the mule had indicated.

23

Affairs of the Heart
Amores

As the trio walked along the forest path, Anders expounded in glowing terms once again on Nannsi's virtues, proceeding to list them in detail.

"…and not only that, Thaddeus, but you know she's the smartest one in her class—oh, though I'm sure Marsia is just as bright, of course. And it only takes Nannsi one diameter of the sun's width to completely dress her hair buns. Isn't that amazing? Then, just the other day…"

Thaddeus felt that his friend's dissertation was a distraction from finding Rolland. For some reason, he had begun to think of himself as being responsible for the general welfare of his brother Apprentices. The thought suddenly flashed into his mind that this seemed to have started around the time the others began following his "orders."

How—and better, *why*—this had all happened was a mystery to him. He would need to puzzle this all out sometime, but in the meantime, he needed to find his thief.

As soon as Anders took a breath, Thaddeus interjected, "So, Anders, are those rope burns I see at your wrists and neck? How did you happen by those?"

The dissertation halted abruptly. "What? Oh. Well, you know how it is in the forest; something is forever happening to someone. Say, 'tis that a purberry bush over there?"

The path curved off to the left, with a smaller trail diverging to the right. Asullus stopped and sniffed the air, then inclined his head to the left. "I ha' the most serious feelin' our prize be down this path, laddies," he said.

Thaddeus walked ahead and soon found the redheaded Apprentice asleep beneath an old beech tree. As Thaddeus knelt down to stir his friend, he noted dried tear tracks running down the boy's face. After a gentle shake, the former thief opened his red, swollen eyes. He quickly glanced around.

"Thaddeus, a moment. P-please," he whispered.

Thaddeus blinked but stood up quickly and turned to the other two.

"Anders, Asullus, follow me over here while Rolland is getting his wits together. I want to show you something very important. You see, last night I saw a Great *Daemon*. It was the biggest thing I have ever seen, and it filled the entire sky. It was just over here in this hollow, I believe. Did either of you see it? There were showers of other *Daemons* too, all over, and…"

Thaddeus, still talking, led the two back down the path.

Anders, looking concerned, stopped. "Thaddeus, what was that all about? Is Rolland not well? Is there something we should do?"

"Ne'er ye mind, laddie," Asullus interjected, "yer thief'll be right as rain in no time. 'Tis lucky fer all o' ye that ye ha' one another. 'Tis a rare thing, indeed, an' perhaps one o' the few areas in life where ye boys are excellin' o'er the common sticks an' stones as always is to be found on the ground, I must say. 'Tis proud I am o' ye all. Well, yes—that is fer now."

Rolland joined the group after a few minutes, his usual jaunty smile in place, and all trace of any other mood vanished entirely.

"Rolland, what did you see last night?" Anders asked, unwilling to let go of his worry.

"Oh, nothing out of the ordinary, I'd say," the thief responded.

"Nothing out of the ordinary?" Anders asked, incredulous. "How can you say that? It was bizarre. I hope Nannsi—I mean, the girls—are all right."

"Not to worry, short one. I'm sure the situation is all under control."

"Thaddeus, do you hear what he is saying? Rolland, are you sure you were not struck in the head?"

"Anders," Thaddeus interrupted. "Peace. Rolland said he was fine and noted nothing strange. I did, but he says he did not. Perhaps it's best to leave well enough alone."

"Well, I dunno. It seems to me that if we were all involved in something so mysterious, the least we could do is share our moments. That way, we'd be sure to know more about…things," the scholar insisted.

A look of irritation flashed across Rolland's features as he turned to face his friend. "Anders, I said nothing was—wait! Anders, what's wrong with your neck and wrists? Are those burn marks?"

Anders did not respond except to say, "Hmm. You know, we saw an old purberry bush back there a while ago."

Asullus abruptly broke in. "All right, lads. Enou' o' the chitchat. Past the time to be back at the camp, I trow."

The rest of the trip back to the campsite was spent largely in silence. When they returned, Mistress Geanninia and the girls were up and had begun preparing a combined late break-fast and early mid-day. Without discussion, the boys joined in, fetching wood and water and performing whatever tasks seemed needful.

Thaddeus stole glances at Marsia rather often. On other days he would have wondered at his own behaviors, but today all he could feel was that he could not get enough of her vision. Again, it was similar to how he had felt about Ethne—yet somehow different. He could not sort it out, but once, when he caught her eye, she smiled shyly at him. His heart fluttered.

The Master and his Mistress sat on their usual log and approvingly watched their charges willingly work together.

At table, the conversation among the young workers was tentative, for the most part, as if each were sharing something intensely personal. Some of their night's experiences were drawn out, some encouraged, and some coached. Each tale was different from the others.

Haltingly, Thaddeus began with his experience of his time after he came upon the five-story Tower of the North. The others immediately quieted to listen.

"…I lost sight of all of you and, um, followed a road that, after a while, led me to a ridge overlooking a great pit of molten rock. At once, above it all, there appeared a titanic figure. I felt a great presence of evil when I gazed upon it."

The others gasped as he continued.

"It was so big that it filled up the sky. Then, all of a sudden, it smote its own hand and exploded into bits, too many to count. Each bit went on to form great spheres—which were red at first, then other colors. There were bits of *Daemons* as well—they were trapped inside some of the spheres, I saw. But there was also this feeling of…hope. And, almost… peace. It was all quite confusing."

Anders jumped up excitedly. "Thaddeus, it sounds to me like you saw **A** at the beginning of the world!"

"**A**? Who's **A**?" Rolland asked.

"**A**," Nannsi answered with a slight touch of condescension, "according to ancient texts, is, as Friend Anders has said, a great daemon personage present at the beginning of things."

"There was an evil creature at the beginning of things? Whatever is the point of that?" Rolland scoffed.

"It accounts for why there are unseemly beings and affairs in the world, of course," Nannsi replied loftily, "and unseemly people," she looked pointedly in the direction of—but not directly at—Rolland. Sonnia chuckled as Rolland reddened slightly.

"But, also, it's why there is hope and peace, as Thaddeus has said," Marsia broke in, speaking bravely, then blushing ever so slightly.

"Very well, then," Rolland said, switching to the offensive with a smirk. "What did you see, Friend Anders? More ancient texts?"

Startled at being called on, Anders answered the question after a moment, "Oh, well, nothing to speak of, not really. I, uh, was at some sort of school, I think…teaching, as it comes to that."

"More than that, I believe," Nannsi said. "These visions are thought to be prophetic, you know, and Friend Anders saw himself on the faculty of a prestigious center of learning where, at a relatively young age, he becomes a respected Master and, later, a beloved one as well."

Now, it was Anders' turn to blush.

"What of you, Sonnia?" Rolland asked a bit flippantly. "Were you teaching somewhere, too?"

"No," she said disdainfully, then began to smile almost dreamily. "I was involved in a torrid assignation with a wealthy and powerful noble, court intrigues, and the subtle wielding of vast political power."

"Yes," Rolland said impudently. "I can understand how that would be."

Sonnia turned away from the thief with her nose up in the air and had nothing further to say to him. After a moment, she asked, "Nannsi, dear, tell us what *you* saw."

Nannsi seemed a bit more reluctant to describe her experiences. "Well, there was nothing so grand for me. But I did spend a time in pursuit of the finer arts—that is, singing and dancing, mostly."

Strangely, still red-faced, Anders looked away whenever she spoke of these things. Nannsi later added details concerning sensations of flying and observations of bird lore.

"Oh, that sounds lovely," Sonnia said with her sparkling smile. "And tell us, Sister Marsia, about your experiences."

At this invitation, Thaddeus became especially attentive.

"Oh, sakes. My experiences were all rather humdrum, really—just things involving family matters, mostly." She glanced up at Thaddeus and blushed.

Thaddeus was debating with himself whether to ask Rolland. While the situation would argue for everyone to participate, he remembered his friend's response and hesitated to demand that he go to an uncomfortable place again. Rolland, however, spoke up, perhaps seeking to forestall that very situation.

"So, for me, it was nothing out of the ordinary. Um, something like Marsia said. Just family things."

Sonnia initially looked ready to pin the redhead down a bit more. Evidently, she thought the better of it and pressed for nothing.

The Master and Mistress had sat quietly during their students' recitals, sipping from goblets of spelled, chilled wine. On occasion, one would lean toward the other and whisper some comment. At times, the words would elicit a nod, a knowing smile, or a quiet laugh.

Finally, after Rolland's turn, Master Silvestrus cleared his throat, and the table again became quiet.

"Thank you one and all for relating—to a greater or lesser degree—your extraordinary experiences from last night. Having experienced many such nights over time myself, I believe, and I'm sure Mistress Geanninia would agree." he nodded to his striking colleague, "that much has been learned, even if presented to each of you in a possibly odd and unfamiliar context. My advice for you is to take from your experiences whatever seems relevant and useful. And as for the rest, make of it what you will, either as to butter your bread with or to use to wrap up your fish innards. The choice is yours."

Following this, Mistress Geanninia began speaking without missing a stride.

"I heartily endorse Master Silvestrus' advice and would add only that, perhaps, what is of most value here in what you have encountered is the beginning of that greatest of all strivings—the understanding of yourself. This process will be a journey and challenge to occupy you all the years of your life, and most worthy it is. And, not only have you received that gift but, with it, also the beginning of the understanding of one another. Keep these discoveries closest to you, grow them well, and the benefit will be yours."

The midsummer's day was pleasantly warm, and after cleaning up the meal's remains and squaring away the campsite, the boys and girls petitioned for an impromptu game of *Pila Ludere*. Asullus was prevailed upon to reprise his role as *Arbiter*, and even Master Silvestrus and Mistress Geanninia were persuaded to participate. The latter showed a measure of leg with her skirts hiked up.

"I could run a pace or two when I was a slip of a girl at school, you see," she said.

One difference, however, was that the players in this game changed sides regularly, depending on the score. The intensity of the contest was just as high-pitched as before, and after one particularly close call, the *Ludia*'s Mistress even had it out, nose to nose with Asullus.

"*Tsk-tsk*. Such language," Rolland said, grinning for once, while the three boys stood casually with their arms folded, watching the theater.

"So that's how you pronounce it," Anders observed clinically. "I've always wondered."

The mule, however, was unmoved by any profane threats. "A feisty one ye be, darlin', but 'twill do ye no good to spell me in such a way. Who would it be, then, should ye ha' a need in the future, agree to carryin' all yer sacks, incidentals, and unmentionables, as ye travel 'twixt here an' there, eh? Meantime, I suggests ye return to the line an' we'll all continue wi' this contest o' exceptional valor an' stamina."

For her part, Bellis raced in and out among the players, scoring at will for either side whenever she could steal the ball. After the fourth such occurrence, Thaddeus took it upon himself to chastise the golden dog.

"Bellis! Why are you being a bad dog? You can't just run off with the ball anytime you want to!" For his effort, the tall Apprentice received a canine face-wash, and play resumed as before.

Anders cheated shamelessly and, on one occasion, even nudged the ball away from Rolland, who was counting on him to kick it to him. Nannsi immediately swooped in to make the score.

Anders ran up to her, beaming, unable to conceal his delight.

"You marvelous boy!" Nannsi chortled and, grabbing him by his ears, rewarded him with an enthusiastic buss in front of everyone. The scholarly Apprentice turned progressive shades of red.

"Unprincipled traitor," Rolland growled, turning his back on his peer.

Though Asullus asked slyly—several times—if Anders favored exacting a penalty against Nannsi for her illegal goal, the smitten boy consistently declined.

Late in the game, Thaddeus pounded up behind Marsia, who was trying to keep the ball away from Anders. Thaddeus subtly interposed himself between the pair, giving the tall girl an opening to rush ahead, which she immediately did.

As they ran, side by side, Marsia grinned at him. "Here," she said, kicking him the ball.

Thaddeus grinned back, dribbled down the field, then kicked it back to her. "Here, yourself," he said. Running flat out, the two outdistanced all the others and scored a goal at the opposite end of the field. Thaddeus considered this the highlight of the day.

The sun was setting when Asullus called the game over, declaring it a tie, though both Rolland and Anders challenged the mule's arithmetic —for different reasons.

The sweating players walked back to the campsite talking in small groups and separated by gender to refresh themselves. The group rejoined afterward and took charge, once again, of preparing the evening meal.

After even-tide, Thaddeus and Marsia sat together on their log in front of the campfire.

"That was fun today," Thaddeus said.

"Yes," Marsia said, smiling. "You run very fast."

Slightly embarrassed, the Beewickean replied, "Yes, well, back in my village I was…I mean, it's just something I… Well, you run very fast, too. I mean, you run fast." He thanked the gods he had been able to stop himself soon enough not to add, *for a girl.*

Marsia smiled again, dimples showing, then abruptly looked down.

"Marsia, is something wrong?"

"Oh, no. I was just remembering; Mistress Geanninia told us we'd be having to leave for the *Ludia* tomorrow."

"Oh," Thaddeus said. "Really? It's to be so soon? I—oh—"

"Yes, well, it's to be what it's to be. My mother used to tell me that." The honey blonde shifted her braid back over her shoulder, then smiled bravely. "So you are from Beewicke, then. What is it like there?"

Rolland had been so bold as to sit next to Sonnia. He smiled at her, but she seemed preoccupied. Not one to give up easily, he made a valiant effort at conversing.

"Um, hello. Thaddeus and Marsia over there seem to be growing closer, eh?"

Sonnia gave him a penetrating stare. "Yes."

"Oh," Rolland replied. He thought Sonnia was impatient with the proceedings as if she wanted to be off and about the rest of her life-to-be. His own thoughts were elsewhere, however, and his tongue uncharacteristically quiet. He was glad for the distraction when Nannsi turned to speak to Anders, who had come to sit by her.

"Now, Friend Anders, we will be leaving tomorrow morning with Mistress Geanninia and—" She noted her partner's face falling but pushed her hand out. "Not to worry. I am certain there will be a need for our two classes to congregate together once again in the relatively near future. In the meantime, it occurs to me that you will benefit from a review of some strategies for you to apply once you reach your *Collegium Sorcerorum…*"

It was clear that, once begun, no natural force on earth could prevent the short girl from her full recitation, were there any who would even consider the attempt.

"First," Nannsi began, "it will be necessary for you to get your proper rest each night—one of your obvious sensitivities. Use repose to your advantage so that your brain may be restored to meet the challenges of the next day. Second, you must eat your needful meals in full at each setting. The diligent pursuit of your studies will, no doubt, tempt you to miss these opportunities for nourishment, but it is important that you do not cheat your physical self of its due sustenance. Third…"

Nannsi continued, giving Anders summary lists of what she considered essential requirements, and cautions to keep in mind to steer him through his next several years of study.

For his part, Anders listened quite attentively, his chin in his hand. He seemed not to mind that the content of what he was absorbing placed a very distant second to the form in which it was being dictated. Clearly, Anders was besotted with the dark-haired girl as she spoke on and on.

As the boys threw more logs into the firepit, Master Silvestrus went to his tent, returning in a moment with a hefty purple-dyed leather flagon and embossed wooden case, from which he produced eight pewter goblets. With Mistress Geanninia's assistance, he unstopped the large flask and portioned out equal amounts of its dark liquid. As he poured, they were dispersed one by one, along with advice to go lightly.

The Master then stood, and with the leaping fire at his back, declared that the evening would be dedicated to wondrous tale-spinning and other diverse entertainment. To set the mood, he offered up a harrowing adventure concerning a spotted troll, a mermaid, and a mad centaur.

The Mistress, in turn, told a story of a tragic love triangle among a virgin, a knight's squire, and a nymph, which resulted in much eye-dabbing toward the end.

Thaddeus gave an amusing account of a lost cave bear cub and a village beehive. For his part, Rolland casually walked his way around the circle of the audience making lighthearted jests and performing sleight-of-hand displays while methodically, and without notice, relieving his audience one by one of their valuables, displaying them at the end to the astonished group.

Anders spoke from his store of historical lore, and the girls performed an intricate pageant of song with dance. Thaddeus thought they were very good, and clapped loudly along with Anders.

Eventually, Silvestrus again rose and gave a benediction to the evening.

"Ah, Apprentices, all good things must run to their natural conclusion, and we now find ourselves at ours. Tomorrow we must sunder our glad company and go our own ways, according to our appointed tasks. As solace, I can only say that our retained memories will stand in for true experience until we may next meet. But I have always found that the more vivid and wonderful the memories, the more often they can be reexperienced. And, sometimes, in that way, a measure of the original pleasure can be retained."

He cast an intimate glance at the Mistress. "As for myself, I will now drag my weary bones to a well-deserved rest, and I imagine the lovely Mistress Geanninia will wish to do the same. However, there yet remain a few last tasks for you lads and lasses to accomplish before retiring.

"Rolland, I would ask that you and Sonnia clear up the grounds here at the campsite before turning in. Anders, Nannsi, perhaps I could prevail upon you two to make a sweep of the South side of the camp and around the nearest hillock for any possessions overlooked there or back at the playing field. Thaddeus, Marsia, if you both would be so kind as to check on Asullus and the horses before you retire, and also see to the North side and the near forest area. Something may have been left there inadvertently. Now, thank you all, and good repose."

Thaddeus, clad in his coarse cloth tunic and trousers, and Marsia, wearing a sturdy country dress with tiny flowers at the neck, walked side by side along the tree-lined path dappled gray and black in the bright moonlight. Thaddeus was at once acutely aware of their proximity but simultaneously trying to give the impression of taking no account of it whatsoever. Her scent wafted to him as the distance between them steadily diminished. He experienced it as nothing so much as the *Pixae* fields at midsummer.

Almost by accident, their hands brushed. All hazard at play, he gently clasped her soft hand. To his surprise, she did not tear it away but grasped his gently in return.

After a moment, they slowed, then stopped, facing each other.

He noticed her height once more, especially now that they were so close. It occurred to him that he liked tallness in a girl —quite a bit, actually. Marsia had her hair in a braid this night, hanging just below her waist. He liked that, too. Although he had earlier noted that her eyes were green, here in the night, they looked dark. Then he noticed they were looking at him. They seemed by degrees, kind, soft, and what he would have sworn was inviting. He knew he should speak, but he knew not what he should say. The moment demanded of him, however.

"I—it was wonderful meeting you, and I hope, I mean, maybe..." Thaddeus' heart pounded in his chest, and his pulse roared in his ears. He savaged himself for talking as an utter oaf. *Fool! Dolt! Sounding like Jack Simple at the Faire!* He expected Marsia to turn on her heel and walk away in despair at his backcountry clumsiness, and he would not have blamed her if she had.

Against all logic, however, she moved forward and kissed him full upon the lips.

She then stepped back a pace and reached into a pocket of her dress before taking a deep breath. "Thaddeus, I have come, in this short time, to feel toward you in a very special way. In my family, when we have met a person we like—like very much—it is customary to give that person a gift. I have something that would please me if you would accept it."

She opened her hand upon which lay a small greenstone. "I don't know if it is so, but my Great-mother told me that this greenstone has been in our family for many years, and it is said to have certain felicitous powers when used by someone with the talent of Sorcery. I'm unaware of what these powers might be, but I think this stone may sometimes influence how people regard us. I would like you to have it."

A lump formed in Thaddeus' throat, and he swallowed hard.

How could this beautiful girl think to give a backcountry boy like him such an undeserved favor?

"Oh, Marsia, I can't take something that your Great-mother gave you. It's a priceless gem, I'm certain, and it should be kept in your family."

"Well, perhaps it will be—but, please, do not spurn my gift. I greatly desire that you have it—for a remembrance."

Thaddeus could only stare at the ground while waves of shame welled up inside him. "I—I have nothing of any value to give you in return."

"Yes, you do, Thaddeus. More than you know. And perhaps you already have." She smiled again, then moved toward him and gave him another kiss. His head swam, and he could hardly stand—honey-knees, indeed.

After a moment, Marsia spoke. "We should probably be getting back. I would hate for them to have the bother of looking for us." However, she did not move away immediately, but stood looking deeply into his eyes.

She then reached up and gently stroked the side of his face.

A roaring began in his ears—not the roaring of the Sorcery so recently learned, but that of a far more ancient and powerful magic.

The small, golden-haired girl stood in the shadow of one of the old oaks watching the young lovers kissing. Luperca sighed.

What was her future mate doing with that tall, gangling girl?

Of course, she knew the answer to her question, but that made it no easier to accept. Once Old Mattom the Wise of River's Wood, Chief Druid Madigan's father, had told her about the stranger who would one day rescue her and by whom she would birth a High Priestess. It had merely been a matter of waiting. But she had made too many assumptions and had not asked nearly enough questions.

For example, she had assumed her new mate would come to her rather than the reverse. Also, she had thought she would have this mate to herself rather than have to share him. And, she had assumed that once they met, he would know her for who she was, and they would never be parted thereafter.

Well, silly self. None of this was working out the way it should, and she was not very pleased with any of it. But the fault was not his—or at least, not entirely.

She sighed again.

He was clearly going to go on to the *Collegium* and remain for his years of training. True, she could go there and stay with him as Bel-lis—*how she'd come to treasure that name*—but it was always cold, dark, and windy that far north. And winter was coming, which would make it even worse. Not that she could not abide the frozen wastes—after all, she had been born in that setting—and she would be spending most of her time snuggled up by the fire in the Apprentice's quarters. But she would still have to go outside sometimes, and the back-and-forth of such climactic extremes was almost worse than the constant winter.

Also, she was positive the Masters there would be as intolerant of her true wolf form in the dormitories as they would be of her tawny-braided siren form.

Of course, the boy would have to leave the College eventually. And what were a few years to a wolf? She would be waiting for him, but not right at his doorstep. The time would be right eventually, and she would find him, just like she'd found him the first time—but this time without some madman beating her nigh to death.

That had not been pleasant.

Indeed, that alcoholic Corrigan had reaped a richly deserved reward.

It was unfortunate she had allowed herself to become so careless in her excitement to meet the promised boy that the madman had caught her out. Subsequently, she had to suffer the consequences of a beating; and that constituted what Mother would call an *education.*

Her thoughts returned to the tall, freckled boy. He was so handsome, so brave, so gentle—and so powerful. He reminded her of Father. What a story they had already experienced—ogres, maniacs, *Pila Ludere,* and all the rest. He made her current consort, Black Tooth, seem rather dull and humdrum by comparison.

Well, there was nothing for it but to wait. She needed to have another litter soon, in any case, to replace the one she'd lost to the ogre. Maybe she'd have two or three—it would give her something to do while waiting for her Thaddeus. And if she had to share him after they had their daughter, well—she'd have to think about that.

In an instant, the little girl vanished, and in her place stood the great golden pack leader. Sniffing the air one last time, she turned and made her way westward. It was long past time to return to her den and be about her lupine business. Her pack needed a keen nose on their courses if they were to continue their current prosperity.

It was her responsibility, after all.

24

Blue Nose
Nasus Caeruleus

Thaddeus and his brothers hurried from one chore to another in a flurry of activity.

"Come on, let's go!" Thaddeus called. "The Master has said he wants the camp cleaned up soonest."

"All right, all right. I'm moving, and for this time of day, that's good," Rolland responded.

The girls had bridled and saddled their horses, with Marsia seeing personally to Bucephalus. The boys helped take down, shake out, and fold all the tenting, coil the ropes and place them in the travel boxes. Hungry, Thaddeus and his fellow Apprentices had dug into their store of leftovers.

Thaddeus shyly approached Marsia and held out a parchment-wrapped parcel.

"Hello. How are you? I hope you slept well. I did. It looks like the Master and Mistress want to be moving apace on their journey. Um, we had some food left from last night, and I thought you might like something for break-fast."

Marsia looked briefly at the proffered packet, then up to meet Thaddeus' eyes. She smiled.

"Hello, Thaddeus. We slept well, and I am fine.

That is very thoughtful of you to consider sharing your break-fast, but we have already partaken. Mistress Geanninia is very strict about 'following the rules,' you see. But I—"

"Marsia," Sonnia called out, "could you please come and help me with this chest?"

A question instantly intruded itself into Thaddeus' conscious mind as to whether or not she was taking Marsia away a-purpose.

A quick frown of irritation fluttered across the tall girl's features, but she immediately recaptured her smile.

"I must go. Perhaps we will have a chance to talk more later." The tall girl smiled stoically and walked off, carrying Thaddeus' heart with her. Thereafter, Thaddeus and Marsia had time for only snatches of conversation. Most of their communication occurred visually.

On one such occasion, as he was storing the tents on the wagon, Thaddeus looked over and caught Marsia's eye. He gave her a quick wave, then patted his purse holding the greenstone, so Marsia would know her treasured gift was being kept safe. Marsia blushed slightly but then nodded and gave him a secret smile.

Thaddeus nodded back, then walked over to the campfire site to wet it down with the wash water and bury the still-smoldering ashes. He arrived to find Nannsi in earnest conversation with Anders.

"Now…Anders, remember, when you put on your socks this winter, especially on the coldest days, to turn them inside out first. That way, the seams will be on the outside and not irritate the tips of the toes. Also, when you doff your boots at night, place them by—but not overly near—the fire. Otherwise, if they are too close, the leather will become stiff and useless."

Nannsi continued to add to the list of admonitions, often stopping to fuss over him, plucking off any stray blades of grass from his tunic she could find. He listened attentively, endured patiently, and offered no protest, only adding occasionally, "Yes, I will."

On conclusion, she added, "He's only a boy. I'm sure he can hardly strap his sandals," saying this to no one in particular.

After her call to Marsia, Sonnia paid absolutely no attention to Thaddeus. She was the first packed and arrayed by her horse in her traveling robe, pacing back and forth, and impatiently slapping her riding gloves against her palm.

Rolland was even quieter and more withdrawn than he had been the night before. Thaddeus approached him.

"Rolland. Are things well with you?"

The redheaded thief glanced quickly at Sonnia across the way, then looked back to his tall fellow Apprentice and nodded with an unconvincing grin.

"I'm well, Thaddeus. Could scarcely be better."

Thaddeus cocked an eyebrow in disbelief, but as no more was forthcoming from his friend, he let the moment pass and moved on.

Mistress Geanninia made her way over to the horse tether where all the mounts were hitched and came to a stop in front of the old gray mule, contentedly munching on his portion of dried hay.

Asullus looked up at her approach. "Yes, Mistress? How is it I may be o' service to ye this fair day?"

"No service is requested, good Asullus. I am here to apologize to you for the little outburst during our game of the previous day. I seek to make amends." As she spoke, she produced a shiny red apple, and extended it forward as a peace offering.

"Ah, sweet lady, we're too well-known to one another to be fussin' the one day an' sayin' *so sorry* the next. On the other hand, I'll no' be insultin' yer fair self by ignorin' the savory prize ye be presentin' to this old body, don' ye know." Asullus gently took the fruit of the red type in his mouth and crunched down with delight while the Mistress of the *Ludia* sweetly stroked his mane.

After finishing with Asullus and making one last inspection of the campsite, Mistress Geanninia lined up her girls, after which Master Silvestrus marched down the row, pressing hands and presenting a whiskered cheek for a quick buss to each in turn.

For her part, Mistress Geanninia embraced the boys warmly, one by one. "Ah, Anders, have no concern. You will do well. Very well, in fact," the Mistress said. Then, smiling slyly, she added, "Especially considering all the good advice you have been given recently."

The scholar blushed and made a leg, bowing in respect.

She spent a longer time in earnest discussion with Rolland. "Rolland, you must listen to me," the Mistress said in a low tone. "Should a time come when all seems darkest with no dawn in sight, then straightaway approach your friends and the Master. They have a great love for you, though you may not yet be prepared to accept this. Take that advantage, and it will save and sustain thee, should the situation warrant." The thief nodded, ostensibly accepting her advice.

After leaving him, Mistress Geanninia had a slightly worried look. But when she arrived at Thaddeus, she relaxed, kissed his cheek warmly, and whispered, "People to whom we are important never forget us, dear boy."

The ladies mounted their horses and turned them toward the West, setting off in single file with Mistress Geanninia in the lead. Thaddeus watched Nannsi, constantly glancing over her shoulder at Anders and dabbing her eyes. He then observed Anders, who looked utterly miserable.

Sonnia, in the meantime, rode line-straight, head held high, looking only ahead. He thought Rolland might have taken to her during the holiday, but she had given not the slightest sign of interest. Thaddeus wondered if Rolland was feeling anything like Anders did, but the thief did not indicate how he felt either way.

Thaddeus' primary focus, however, was on Marsia. She looked steadfastly back, waving and smiling bravely until distance took her. Thaddeus windmilled his arm in great arcs until it ached as much as his heart.

After the girls were out of sight, Thaddeus turned and went to his pack for a final inspection. He was in a black pit of despair with an empty hollowness gnawing at him from within. *If I had never met her, there would be no pain in me. Yet, I cannot think of never having met her.*

Thaddeus fumbled inside his tunic for his purse, withdrew it, then fished out the greenstone Marsia had given him. He gazed at it for several heartbeats, then softly rubbed it between his thumb and forefinger. After a moment, he sighed and put it back in the purse and the purse back in his shirt and moved on to finish his work.

Tying a final knot in his camp kit, Thaddeus looked up to witness Rolland, his pack slung over one shoulder, disappearing north into the wooded area. Seeing that Master Silvestrus and Anders were involved in discussion with Asullus, he sprinted after his friend and soon caught up to him.

"Rolland. Rolland! Wait! Where are you going?" As the thief did not respond, he increased his pace and soon overtook the redhead, grabbing him by the arm.

"Get off me!" Rolland cried, shaking loose Thaddeus' grip.

"Rolland, what are you doing?"

"I'm getting the Hells out of here, you backcountry turd-head! What does it look like?"

"Yes, I can see that. But why?"

Rolland stopped and turned toward his fellow Apprentice. "It's no good! It's not going to work! I don't belong here! Faran was right—I belong in the gutter!"

Thaddeus was shocked at the intensity of his friend's pain. "Rolland, wait! I don't know what any of this is about, but I think I should tell you—last night, I saw you with…some people. A lady and a man. They sort of looked like you. I was thinking they were your family. Does that have anything to do with it?"

Thaddeus observed Rolland staring at the ground. It was then he heard a sob escape his brother Apprentice.

A familiar voice intruded upon their conversation.

"Thaddeus. Rolland. Good. I was looking for you both. Thaddeus, please return to the campsite and assist Anders with the last of the preparations. We leave shortly. Rolland, I would speak with you."

"Yes, Master." Thaddeus gave his friend a last glance, turned, and ran back to the camp, a wild jumble of emotions coursing through his chest.

On arrival, he immediately hailed Anders and told him what he'd witnessed.

Anders whistled. "I'm not surprised. I was talking with the Master when all of a sudden, he looked past me toward the woods and took off in a line like one of your bees."

Anders sighed and continued. "So, Rolland was that upset? It's too bad he and Sonnia didn't get on better. It might have helped distract him. You know, though, I believe you're right, it must have something to do with his family. You remember when we first met him and how he looked when the Master talked to him about those things?"

"Yes, that's right. Has Asullus said anything?"

"Only, 'Ah, no' to worry, laddie. The Old Man knows what it is he's aboot,'" Anders said in perfect imitation of the steadfast gray mule.

Thaddeus glanced over to see Asullus standing stock-still, gazing northward.

"Thaddeus. Give me a hand getting these cook pots and supplies into the cart, will you? I think it would be good for us to look busy when they get back," Anders said.

"Yes. I agree."

Silvestrus came striding out of the woods with an impassive expression on his face, but it was some moments before they caught sight of their urban colleague. Rolland emerged from the wooded area, head bent. He was walking slowly and seemed to have some sort of blue scarf dangling down his chest.

After a few more strides, Anders let out a gasp. "*Iovis!* Thaddeus! What is that blue thing on Rolland's face?"

Thaddeus gulped. "Oh, Anders, that's not a thing; it's his nose!"

Coming closer, it was clear that Rolland now sported a foot-long, bright blue proboscis.

The boys immediately looked to their Master, but he'd gotten out his pipe and was smoking while he checked the cart contents, seemingly oblivious to any external concerns. Their eyes swiveled back to their friend, but just as they stepped forward, Asullus bolted for the boy. Eating the distance in no time, he skidded to a halt just in front of the redhead, turning his body so it was interposed between Rolland and the rest of the camp. He talked rapidly to Rolland in low tones, then listened.

Suddenly, Rolland threw his arms around the old mule's neck, burying his face in Asullus' shoulder and crying out in loud, heart-wrenching sobs. Asullus turned to fix Silvestrus with a baleful stare. The boys had never seen the old mule look so angry. Then the animal turned back to the weeping boy and resumed talking softly to him.

After a moment's hesitation, Thaddeus said, "Come on, Anders."

They had covered half the distance when Asullus gently separated himself from the young thief and trotted toward them.

"Comforting yer friend is the name o' the plan fer this day, lads. But should any o' ye say one disparagin' thing or be makin' one jest at his expense—well, I'm just blowin' me smoke. Neither one o' ye would e'er do such a thing, I'd bet me tail. I am, howe'er, goin' this minute to be havin' me piece out wi' the Old Rooster o'er there. Ye go on, now. Yer thief'll be needin' yer kindly words, an' more, yer kindly ears."

Both boys nodded and started toward their red-haired friend.

"What shall we say, Thaddeus?" Anders whispered, concerned.

"Nothing. We should probably do what Asullus told us. Say nothing and just listen."

Ahead, Rolland awaited them with downcast eyes.

"…I don't remember them at all. I was a mere babe." Rolland sat on the grass facing his two friends as he spoke, plucking grass stems aimlessly, twiddling them in his fingers for a moment, then discarding them. His azure nose hung down his chest.

"The only thing I had from my mother were two small portraits she had made—miniatures, she called them—little oval paintings in pewter frames about the size of an egg. A street artist made them for her. I know because Faran showed me the pictures once I was older. He sold the frames but thought I should have the pictures—or maybe he just wasn't able to flog the portraits. I tore them up a couple of years ago when I was angry once, but that is how I know what they looked like.

"My father was a sailor, and my mother was a flower girl—at least, that's what they called it. But I learned what that meant later on. I was told he shipped out on a merchantman in *Plutonius* and was lost at sea when I was merely a babe. My mother was stabbed to death by some drunken customer a year or so later. Faran had been her…business manager…and he had the man flayed alive. He told me once she said the few months with my father were her happiest ever until I came along and I made her life worthwhile.

"After she died, some of the other ladies raised me up beside their own brats. 'Twas the way things worked. When I was old enough to run fast and keep secrets, Faran took over my training. Hard times it was, but there was a bond amongst us outcasts. We always stood up for each other. No one ever thought of leaving. At least not till the Old Man and you Merry Andrews showed up." Rolland shook his head.

"I was as loyal to that bunch as any ever in my life—they were my family. But then I meet you, and in the space of five minutes, I was ready to chuck it all to follow some dream. That's not natural, you know, but I never thought about that till now."

Anders nodded. "It was the same for each of us, Rolland. We were in our homes, reasonably content with our lives, and then all at once those we love suddenly said, 'Oh, it's all right. Go away with this nice man. And good luck to you.'"

"The ring!" Thaddeus said. "I think it has something to do with that blue ring of his. I would bet my staff on it. Each time we—or those we were with—needed convincing of something, that ring glowed."

Thaddeus reached into his tunic and brought out his pouch, dumping the contents on the grass—three old coins and the small greenstone. He held up the last for the others to see.

"Marsia gave me this last night. She said it was old and had been in her family for a long time. She said stones like this could influence people. I wonder if our Master's ring-stone does the same?"

"Interesting idea," Anders said. "Let me see it, Taddy." Thaddeus passed his gift to his friend, who held it up to the sun, squinting. "Hmm, I can't tell anything about it one way or another. It's a little warm, but that could be from being close to your body."

He passed it to Rolland, who peered at it closely, then shook his head and handed it back to Thaddeus. The young beekeeper scooped up his coins and put his treasures back into the pouch and the pouch into his tunic.

"He can be a sneaky old crust, that's for certain," Thaddeus said. "Say, Rolland, you don't have to tell us if you don't want to, but why did—"

"Oh, that's my *comeuppance*, he called it." Rolland gestured at his bright blue nose. "For all my past sins and for trying to leave. He said this would teach me to set a better value on life's gifts. But I don't think he was all that angry with me. Actually, I think he did it to make sure I would stay with all of you."

"How so?" Thaddeus queried.

"Well, I'm not about to go skipping into town dragging this big blue thing between my legs, now am I? He's got my feet nailed to the floor, he does."

"Is it—I mean—does it come off…sometime?" Anders asked tentatively.

"He said, 'when the time is right'—whenever in the Hells that means. Meantime, I got me a bright blue flycatcher."

Anders' eyes widened perceptibly. "Really? Can it do that?"

Thaddeus and Rolland looked at each other and burst out laughing. Rolland snorted.

"Anders, never go to a city market without me. You would come home with nothing but your fingers sticking out of the hole in your pants where your purse and your pickle used to be."

"Well, I fail to see how I might be going to market with you, in any case, Bluenose. Somebody might want to catch you up and mount your member above their mantel, anyway, if not dice it up for stew."

The three boys laughed heartily, and Thaddeus was relieved that things were returning to normal—if not exactly like they used to be. Abruptly, he looked around the campsite, hand shading his eyes.

"Have either of you noticed Bellis lately? I've not seen her since the game."

"No," Rolland said.

"No," Anders added. "But don't worry yourself. She'll show up in plenty of time for the next meal—she's never missed one yet."

While they awaited the order to leave, Thaddeus cast his thoughts about for anything that would take them away from the sadness of loss. Of a sudden, his attention was drawn to the grassy area between the campsite and the forest, which had been trampled down by the constant comings and goings of the past few days. Now that the grass was flattened, it was easier not only to see where the forest path started but easier to follow it, too.

"Anders! You said once in one of those history lessons you're always giving us that the last Emperor—Superbus, was it?"

"Yes."

"Right. The Emperor Tyrannus Superbus, *Imperator Ultimus*. Anyway, you said that when he marched East, he took the whole Imperial Army with him—a million men."

"Yes, that's what Primus told me."

"And they were all lost in the invasion, right?"

"Yes, right."

"A million-man army. Anders, how many men were left at home then? I mean, to defend the Westlands? There wouldn't be that many, could there?"

"No, not many at all. In fact, Primus said that there was great deprivation for many years afterward on that account. What are you getting at, Thaddeus?"

"Well, just this. I mean, if I were the Cin, and an army had come to my homelands to try and annihilate me, but I had figured out a way to eliminate them instead—while keeping all my troops from harm and in one piece—I think I might want some sort of revenge. I believe I would surely give some thought to giving something back to them—especially if I knew their lands were now empty of defenses, while I still had my entire army hale and healthy. But I've never heard a story or mention of the Cin taking revenge, invading—"

"You know, Thaddeus, that's true. I'd never thought of that before."

"Anders, is there any record of the Cin coming West—coming to attack us?"

"No. Not at all. In fact, for the thousand years since Emperor Superbus went East, we've heard nothing from them at all."

"That's sort of strange, don't you think?"

"Yes, it is. It is indeed."

"What made you think of that, Taddy?" Rolland asked.

"I was looking at the trampled grass between here and the woods. It was standing tall when we first came, and you couldn't see anything at all. Now that the grass is beaten down, you can see clearly where the paths begin. It's an easy walk. So, if nothing stands in the way, it would be easy as pie to march in. So, why haven't they?"

"With everything that's happening, why in Hell's name are you worried about whether the grass is flat or not?" Rolland asked.

"Hmm. I'm thinking it would be very unusual for an invasion these days--especially after all this time. If they were going to come at all, wouldn't it have happened by now?"

"What if something was stopping them—something they couldn't change? Then, what if one day they suddenly found a way to overcome it?"

"Well, whether or not that's so, I guarantee they'll not be coming this afternoon. Give it a rest, Thaddeus. All this thinking—you're going to end up hurting yourself."

Anders laughed while Thaddeus smiled ruefully.

Rolland looked up to see Asullus trotting toward them. "Ah. He's probably coming to tell us that the Cin are invading after all, Taddy."

25

The Necessity of Love
Necessitas Caritatis

Asullus cantered over to where the boys were sitting, flicking his tail—in part at the flies, in part at the irritation.

"Well, lads, Master *Spiritus Duri* over there is indicatin' we're to be up an' aboot our business an' on our way. An' no more of this layabout idleness an' more o' the same, don' ye know. I tell ye true that Old Crow can be the most exasperatin' bein' that e'er walked when he's of a mind to. Oh, well, I canno' see no point in arguin' any further wi' him—probably just get us all turned into newts o' one kind or another. So, ye lot, get yer last bits together, an' if one o' ye'll fetch me my harness, I'll meet ye o'er by the cart." With that, the old mule turned and made his way, slowly and deliberately, over to the conveyance, where he stood waiting patiently.

Rolland rose and looked down at the ground with resignation. "Well, we should be at it." He sighed. "It's been a waste of a stop. Better I hadn't been here."

"Rolland," Thaddeus said, concerned. "Stay with us. You should be here. I want you here."

"Me, too," Anders added.

"Really?" Rolland gave each of them a penetrating look.

"Yes, really, Master Thief. Come on, we have work to do," Thaddeus said, giving the redhead a hand up.

When they broke camp, Bellis had still not returned. Asking the Master and Asullus brought no answers; no one had seen her leave. Thaddeus turned to his two brother Apprentices.

"Have either of you seen Bellis? It seems she still hasn't returned."

Anders looked around at the campsite. "You know, Thaddeus, now that she's fully healed, perhaps she has just decided to return to her pack." While Thaddeus accepted the logic of that argument, he missed the golden dog.

"Well, maybe we could look over the area just a bit more just to be certain?"

At this point, Master Silvestrus joined their group. "Boys, I need to remind you: Our moments are passing. We have no further time for fruitless searching. Let us be going."

Rolland walked over to his tall friend and threw a comforting arm around his shoulder. "When the time is right, she'll come back to us. That dog is quite the tracker, you know."

Thaddeus nodded but, he felt at a loss without his canine companion all the same. So much loss. First home and Argus; then Ethne; then Marsia; and now Bellis.

The group was headed east again, greeting the sun. In spite of the trying events of recent days, it was not long before their spirits had risen, and they broke into one of their traveling songs. After a few bars, however, Thaddeus stopped singing and stared at Rolland in surprise. His friend, heretofore a nondescript tenor, had suddenly become a resonant baritone.

Anders, who also appeared to have noticed the difference, caught Thaddeus' eye, winked, and made a curving motion from his brow to his chest, indicating Rolland's new nose, silently positing that the additional volume of air accounted for the improved sound.

Thaddeus grinned and nodded.

As the day was warm, the boys walked, mindful of Asullus' burden, and only Master Silvestrus sat upon the cart seat. Rolland moved to take his usual place in their treks, walking last in order. He had donned a hooded jerkin, pulling the hood down over his face as far as it would go and still allowing him to see the road. It was a poor disguise, but it seemed to make the blue-nosed thief feel better. They met no fellow travelers on the road, however, so such precautions turned out to be unnecessary.

Thaddeus, who had been looking over his shoulder for their missing golden hound since they began their march, finally stopped and stared back at the woods for a time before moving on. "Goodbye, Bellis," he said softly. "Take care of yourself and be safe."

Aside from the occasional rest stop, they did not pause for mid-day but traveled on till near dusk when they camped near a clump of trees off the road. The land was changing, becoming low wetlands and the occasional bog began to replace old-growth forests and rolling hills.

After stopping for the evening, the boys prepared dinner made from several unwary rabbits and local forage—knowledge they had gleaned from the girls. Master Silvestrus had hardly spoken two words all day other than giving instructions, and an uncomfortable silence fell around the even-tide fire.

The Master had brewed some tea for himself with his usual dollop of Beewicke's Best and was sipping as he stared into space. Asullus was munching the local grass somewhat apart from the group, and the three lads were eating quietly.

Thaddeus broke the silence. "Master?"

The old Sorcerer started and looked at his first Apprentice with raised eyebrows. "Yes, Thaddeus?"

"I was wondering… I know you said we'd be receiving further instruction at the *Collegium*, but I have a question."

"You may ask it."

"Back near River's Wood, when Anders and Rolland used Sorcery for the first time, and then, earlier, when I first used Sorcery—how was it we were able to do that? I mean, none of us had ever done any Sorcery before. How could we do it then? Was it something you *did* to us? Or something you *said* that made it so?"

"How could you come to practice Sorcery when you did, and why then—not earlier, not later—those are the questions?"

"Yes, Master."

"All right, fair enough. Hmm, let me see… Very well then, allow me to ask you a question in return. How was it that your father decided to give you your first knife when he did?"

A moment passed before Thaddeus replied, "I was old enough. He felt I was ready, and so did I."

"Very good. And what was it about you that had changed—something that, perhaps, was not there, say, the year before?"

"Um, well, I had grown. I was able to handle it. I could control it safely."

"So, physically, you were ready. Your body had passed a certain threshold. And mentally and emotionally, too, I would wager. You were ready for the experience and the responsibility, yes?"

"Yes, Master."

"It is a similar thing, Thaddeus."

"How is that, Master?"

"Oh, I believe I know," Anders said quietly. "I've been thinking about this Master, does it have anything to do with…death?"

"Go on, Anders," Silvestrus prompted.

"Well, Thaddeus, do you remember those street toughs in Fountaindale?" Anders asked.

"Yes. What about them?" the tall boy replied.

"Well, you killed one," Anders said.

Thaddeus' head jerked up. "What? I never killed anyone in my life! What are you talking about?"

Anders continued. "And, Rolland, if I'm not mistaken, has mentioned that he had, too, back in his old life."

Rolland looked up. "Yes. I'm not proud of it, but it's true. I killed my first man when I was nine. But he was trying to take me to his room, secret-like, and I didn't want to go. Put a knife to him, I did, and then ran like the Hells and never looked back. It was a good knife, too. I hated to lose it."

"Wait a minute, Anders," Thaddeus interrupted, suddenly disquieted. "How do you know I killed that boy? I thought I just knocked him in the head!"

"I overheard the Shire Reeve mentioning it to the Master afterward. But I knew, anyway. On our way back to the inn, they were loading him, along with that boy Asullus struck, onto a hurry-up wagon, and they pulled a canvas over them. They don't do that for people who are still breathing." Anders observed his companion and then hastened to add, "Um, I'm sorry, Thaddeus. I thought you knew."

"I killed that boy? Oh. I did not mean… I do not know. I thought—"

Silvestrus reached out a long arm and placed a supporting hand on his Apprentice's shoulder. "You seem far away, Thaddeus. What troubles you?" the Sorcerer asked.

"I, well, it's…taking a life. I didn't mean to. I was just, just—"

"Defending yourself, Thaddeus," Rolland interrupted. "I knew that boy. Gladitorius, his name was. He was stupid and a bully, like the others that day. I never cared much for him. I tell you true—he meant to kill you. And he would have, too, if you had not gotten him first. He's done the deed before; I've seen him. I promise you, the world is a better place without him in it if that helps."

"Well, yes. I, I… Thank you, Rolland. I—" Thaddeus looked up sharply at Anders. "Wait a moment. I see a problem with your theory. If we are going to use death as our criteria, then just when and where did you kill someone?"

Rolland's head swiveled sharply to consider Anders. He snorted.

"Kill someone? Me?" Anders blinked, surprised. "Oh, no, I never did that. I couldn't. I mean, you know, I wouldn't, not ever… Oh. Hmm, I see what you mean. Well, it can't be that then, can it? So, it must be something else entirely."

"Very good, boys. What you three have worked out so far is correct: Death is not a criterion for Sorcery. So, have you any further thoughts?" Silvestrus asked.

"Thaddeus," the old man said, "you have mentioned something … something that started with 'blue.' Does that call anything to mind?"

"Oh, the blue butterflies? But what would that…oh…" Thaddeus' face flushed.

"Yes. Precisely."

Rolland nodded in understanding, a smirk playing across his lips.

Anders, however, seemed perplexed. "I don't understand."

"It takes sparkin' to make the spark, so to speak, my boy," Rolland offered.

Anders continued to look confused, his head swiveling between his two comrades.

Rolland made a crude hand sign and smirked again.

Anders gasped. "What? You can't be serious!"

"Anders, for all your alleged brilliance, I think you've spent way too much time near the ale vat fumes. Your wits are as addled as the hops. Of course, I am serious! It's what the Master means. You have to have been with someone—you know—like in love. What's the word, uh…?"

"You mean, like joining?" Thaddeus offered.

"Yes, like that—with a girl or whomever—but in a relationship, not in a family, you see. Right, Thaddeus?"

The tall Apprentice nodded slowly, picturing Ethne.

Rolland continued. "I remember my first time. It was three years ago. Molly o' the Willows, her name was. I never learned why they called her that. She was the sweetest girl I ever knew. She took it upon herself to look after several of us in Faran's care back in the early days, but then when I was older… Well, we became special to each other. Just last year, she was bought by some greasy Graecolian merchant, but she later escaped, someone said. I haven't heard any tidings of her since. It was hard to lose her."

Both boys were gazing steadily at Anders, who looked down, his cheeks aflame.

"Well, Anders? You already know about Thaddeus and the blue butterfly lady. I've just told you about my Molly. We all know you've done Sorcery. So…?"

"I, uh…I had a governess, Carolle, who had a niece, Nyree. She… the niece…came to visit her aunt every summer at Brightfield. Had for years. She was a bit older, and…" The young historian ground to a halt, unable to continue.

"Ah, well," Silvestrus intoned, "everyone has things to be held close for a variety of reasons. The point, lads, is that you cannot practice Sorcery without the necessary ingredient of Amor. Why Love is chosen over Death, I cannot say, though I think it a wonderful asymmetry. As for what the Wise think, who can say. There are many, many theories, of course, as you might expect; some so ludicrous as to be downright silly. Perhaps one of you will be able to search it all out someday.

"In any event, inborn talent and native intelligence—your birthrights if you will, combined with your experiences—this one in particular along with a little training for leavening and, of course, Belief—and there you have it, a recipe for a Sorcerer. Take away any single component, and you have an ordinary man. Take away any two, and you have a village fool. Take away three, and you have a tax collector, as my Master was wont to say." Silvestrus laughed heartily at his own jest.

"Master!" Anders' eyes had suddenly grown large, and his call was both plaintive and insistent. "Does it work the same for gi…I mean, would Nannsi have to have…I mean…" Anders floundered.

"Master, I think Anders means, do the ladies require the same experience as well, in order to practice their Sorcery?" Thaddeus stepped in, trying to remain calm, though his heart was racing with concern as well.

"Why, of course. Why would it not? Goose and gander, you know," the old sorcerer replied airily. "But why do you ask? Does it matter? That which binds us both to the earth binds us equally. Either gender may own property. Both sexes bleed when cut. The list goes on."

Anders looked genuinely miserable.

"However, if it is any consolation to you, my recollection of our visit with the young ladies recently is that, while they related numerous accomplishments and achievements, that particular history was not revealed. Nor do I recollect any claim for the use of Sorcery. References, perhaps, but no solid evidence. In addition, my—that is, Mistress Geanninia— made no such reference, and I am sure she would not have failed to note that particular accomplishment."

Anders sighed, letting out the breath he'd been holding, and Thaddeus unclenched his fists.

"There are some differences, however. The girls have the added benefit —a miracle, actually—of being able to harbor life-growth afterward, depending on the circumstances. And while that may be the crowning achievement for most, for others, it may be a disaster. Especially if the girl is too young. So certain precautions are put in place, I believe, by the Heads of their Orders. Alternate paths may allow the ability to use Sorcery without that specific requirement.

"However, it seems that may not be the exact point of the distress to which you are responding. You boys may wish to examine this element within yourselves and try to discover some better understanding of why this should trouble you in the way it apparently does. Introspection is a valuable endeavor and well worth the effort, though few things of import reveal themselves at the beginning—or easily." The old Sorcerer returned to his tea, sipping it slowly until he was finished.

Suddenly their Master stood and stretched. "Well, boys, our trek has been somewhat arduous today, and I am ready for an early repose. Please do not remain astir too long. We will be wanting an early start in the morning." The old man went to accomplish his preliminaries before seeking his bedroll.

The Apprentices were tired but not yet ready for sleep. As they sat around the fire, they talked in low tones and speculated on issues concerning the myriad mysteries of the female gender.

After an hour's time, Rolland abruptly stood and gestured toward the East.

"Thaddeus, do you see that patch of light over toward the horizon? Any idea what it could be?"

Thaddeus followed Rolland's gaze. He could see something—several pale luminescent lights hugging the ground that seemed to move and shift about in the distance.

"Yes, I see it. I don't know what it is, though."

"We should go look. It's not that far off." Rolland gestured for the boys to follow him.

Anders shook his head. "I don't know, Rolland. I don't think the Master would want us to go traipsing about the countryside, especially at night. It could be anything at all—a will-o'-the-wisp or even a boogus."

"All right, *ignave*, stay here and guard the empty camp from the empty countryside. Then you'll be here to explain to the Master where we are when he gets up in an hour to check on things. Meanwhile, Thaddeus and I will be out in that *Aelvae* light, looking for enough sacks to bring home all the treasure."

Anders glanced up in astonishment. "Treasure?"

"What treasure are you talking about, Rolland?" Thaddeus asked.

"Well, my good Beewickean, there's bound to be treasure out there. I mean, those lights are obviously Fey, and the *Faerrae* always have treasure, you know." Rolland warmed to his subject. "And Marsia will certainly love the baubles you find. Too bad Nannsi won't be getting any any." Rolland shot a sly glance at his studious friend.

"I must be mad to consider this. All right! I'll go…but I know we'll get in trouble with the Master. Just a minute," Anders said, turning.

"Where are you going?" Rolland asked.

"To get some rope, so when we get lost, and the Master finds us near death, having ruined everything, I'll be able to show him how you dragged me off with you against my will."

Thaddeus was also a bit suspicious about this adventure. His father always said wild goose plans lead to nothing but trouble.

But *Faerrae* and treasure? The tall boy felt apprehension being rapidly replaced by excitement.

26

The Old Woman of the Tree I
Anicula Arborea I

The boys carefully made their way eastward. Each carried a torch, though only Thaddeus' was lit. He stopped, lifted his torch, surveyed the surrounding terrain, then lowered it to a few handsbreadths off the ground.

"Look," the he said to his companions. "There's no sign of any passage here. No one has been this way unless they were flying."

"Thaddeus, Thaddeus. Everyone knows the *Faerrae* leave no trace when they walk. And it's certain they would be especially careful when they carry their treasure."

"You seem very confidant, talking about treasure and all," Anders said.

"Look you, oh short one, when I'm about that which is valuable in the world, none can doubt my skills."

"Very well, you two. Let us press on. If we don't return to camp soon, the Master is likely to be on us. And there's no treasure in that, for certain," Thaddeus said.

The still-full moon was bright enough. Wisps of fog began to rise from hollows in the terrain, which soon turned the ground damp and slippery. The slightly musty smell of deep moss was both familiar and comforting—forests here in this strange land were, he supposed, like forests every-where. At least, he hoped that was true.

They steadfastly followed the glowing lights, but they were unable to draw closer. It was as if the lights continually receded as they walked forward.

Anders looked up at the star-bedecked night sky. "Thaddeus, judging from the moon's path, we've pursued this tail-chase for at least an hour. We're no closer to those dancing lights than when we set out."

"'Some there are to explain, but most there are to complain,'" Rolland recited.

"You know, Rolland," Thaddeus said, "Anders has a point. In fact—" He halted. "Hold! I think someone's out there," he whispered, peering intently ahead, making out a dim shape on the squishy ground.

"Is he moving?" Anders asked anxiously.

"No. He seems to be waiting." Thaddeus said, eyes fixed on the obscure figure.

"Well, he's sure to have seen our torch by now. Is he alone?" Rolland asked.

"I can only make out one," Thaddeus said.

"What do you think we should do?" Anders asked.

"Well, we might as well go ahead. I agree, Rolland; he must have seen us. Doing anything else would seem suspicious. Now stay close to me. If it gets sticky, make your way back to camp and get the Master. Come on."

Thaddeus once again found himself giving orders as if he were the leader. But he shoved that thought down to mull over later. They had work to do.

Several more paces brought clarity and uneasy laughter.

"Ah. Our stranger is an old scraggly tree. Long dead, by the look of it. See how the branches flare out? Makes it look as if it was reaching for us. Someone should have taken a torch to that thing a long time ago."

A thin, quavering voice spoke out of the night. "Well, that's hardly friendly, considering the circumstances."

The boys jumped.

"Thaddeus! What's that?" Anders called out in alarm.

"*Sssh!* Anders! Stow it! Do you want it to hear us?" Rolland cautioned in a hoarse whisper.

"Wait," Thaddeus said. "Stay together. Let's see what we see," he offered, trying to induce a sense of calm—both in himself and his friends. "Halloo," he said, more bravely than he felt, "who is it that goes there this night?"

A second shape emerged slowly from behind the ancient and hoary tree—a shadow emerging from a shadow. In the moonlight, it had the outline of a person—short with bony hands, hunched shoulders, and dressed in a swath of dark robes. As it stepped nearer, they made out the form of an old woman.

"Your pardon, Mistress," Thaddeus said, recovering quickly. "We were unaware anyone was out and about at this hour."

"Hah! 'Tis a long time since I have been called 'Mistress'—although once, long ago… But speaking of being out and about, how is it that three unlikely lads such as yerselves are here at this hour mucking about in the moonlight?"

As the boys drew closer, they beheld a time-ravaged, pockmarked countenance with milky eyes. The old woman stared sightlessly past them into the distance.

"My apologies, Mistress, but…that is, can you see us? I mean no offense."

"Oh, none taken, good Master. And my name is Merriwhiddle. Never fear, I see right well enough, young Master. I see many things— more things than ye can imagine, I wager. Smells 'em, too."

Thaddeus quickly glanced at his friends, then to the old woman. "Excuse me, ma'am?"

"I said I smell 'em. Ye lot, for example. Let me see…" The old woman tested the air circling around the group, then sniffed each Apprentice in turn. She halted in front of Rolland. "Ye did not get that nose from yer mother, boy. That's Sorcerer's work, that is. Did ye offend one of them, then?"

"Yes, I did, Mistress," he admitted.

"Ha! Ye're lucky to still live. That trumpet, though, is not going to get ye very far with the maidens, I imagine. At least, not with most."

She continued her circuit, stopping abruptly in front of Thaddeus with a sharp intake of breath. "Ye, boy, what is that ye have on yer chest?"

"I am not sure what you mean, Mistress."

"I said, what is that on yer chest, lout?" She grasped the front of Thaddeus' jerkin, and with a quick snap of her wrist, tore it down the middle, exposing his skin.

Thaddeus grabbed the old crone's wrist, but to his astonishment, he could not move it more than a hairbreadth, even with his best effort.

The old woman stood in front of the boy, sightlessly staring at his chest. "*Amicus Faerrarum!*" she spat.

In a blur of movement, Rolland was suddenly behind the old hag with a knife at her throat. "Now, now, Mother. You will ruin my friend's finery if you keep on that way. I suggest you release your hold and stand away. Then we can talk and get to know each other more peaceably."

Merriwhiddle let go her grip, allowing her arm to fall slowly to her side.

Thaddeus stepped back, rubbing his neck. He could not take his eyes away from the mysterious black-garbed crone.

Rolland's attention remained fixed on the old woman. "Very good, Merriwhiddle. Now tell us, Mistress, what do you mean by all this?"

"It is uncomfortable for me to speak with steel at my throat. Perhaps ye could imagine the same were ye an old woman yerself."

"Yes. Of course. You are right." Rolland sheathed his blade and stepped away. "Now tell us your story. But do not bother with invention. I have the Gift of Hearing and the fastest reflexes in Fountaindale. I can make that knife reappear in a gnat's wink."

"Such a polite boy, though *thief* is nearer the mark, I wager. Very well. 'Tis nothing disparaging, young Master. It is just that I was once on the bad side of some *Faerrae* tricks, and I did not relish the experience. I harbor some resentment toward them to this day—and toward those they favor, such as this lad—ill-reasoned, I trow. And 'tis true, this young Master has done me naught of harm, though his mark did give me a turn. But my adventure with the *Faerrae* was long ago, and I did forget myself. It will not happen again; rest assured."

"'Tis naught," Thaddeus said. "I was taken off guard, that's all. You are incredibly strong, Mistress, I must say."

"It comes from years of toil, my boy. Years of toil. Now, how may I help ye, young Masters, for I wager ye are not out here because this land is all that familiar to ye?"

"Well, that's true enough," Anders said, relaxing a bit. "We were trying to find some lights we saw glowing in the distance and—"

"Ah!" the old woman interrupted. "Yes, the Lights of Calling. Fey, they are. Only occur at certain times of the year, they do. It is said that if ye follow them to ground, ye will find something of great value."

"Ha!" Rolland interjected. "Treasure! I knew it. So, how may we find them again? I can't see them now."

"Easy enough, young Masters. I'd accompany ye, myself, but old Merriwhiddle has got a touch of the grippe. My bones complain as well, especially on these damp nights. But I'll be glad to point ye in the right direction. There. See ye that fork in the path? Just bear to the right. Ye'll come across them soon enough, like as not, if they can still be seen. Then follow them to the end, wherever they may lead. Most importantly, make sure ye keep them in sight and don't stray from the path. Or ye could wander the moors forever."

"Wait," Anders spoke up. "If they lead to treasure, why are you here like this, Mistress, instead of warm and dry in your own manor, with servants to look after you?"

"'Tis a smart one, ye are, darling. Well, ye have delved the truth. These lights do yield up treasure, that's certain. But only once to each petitioner. I chose me treasure many years ago when I first came here. But I spent me wealth foolishly as the young are wont to do, and now I have only a pittance remaining." The old woman abruptly drew back, looking alarmed. "Ye'd not take what little Merriwhiddle still has left to her name, would ye now?"

"Oh, no, Mistress!" Thaddeus reassured her. "We're not robbers. We'll gather our rewards from the lights of our own efforts."

"Well, ye have the right of it there, I wager." Merriwhiddle uttered a small laugh—almost a cackle to Thaddeus' ears—and seemed to relax. "Right, then. So, 'tis as I said, lads. Follow the fork to the right, and all will be made clear. Good hunting, young Masters!"

The boys thanked the old crone, turned, and followed the path to the right. Thaddeus glanced back over his shoulder, but the woman was gone.

"Now, she was a strange one for certain. You know, she never did say why she was out here this time of night. Do you think we should— Ow!" Anders slapped at the back of his neck. "I am stung! Oh, 'tis like fire! Why is a hornet out at nighttime? Oh, no, I don't feel so good. I think I should stop…for a minute." He wobbled a step or two, then dropped where he stood with his face planted straight into the mire.

"Anders! Whatever is the matter with y— Ow! Damn! One just got me in the neck! How many of these things are there? Thaddeus! Oh, misery, I feel sick. I—" Rolland slid to the ground in a slow spiral.

"Ow! Hornets!? What do you do? I am a beekeeper! Anders! Rolland! Hold fast; I am coming!" Thaddeus lurched toward his two comrades, but the world began to swim, and he knew no more.

Thaddeus' senses returned to him slowly with an uncertain agony. From what he could discern, he swore it felt as if he was being dragged along the ground by the back of his jerkin. A few moments more, and he realized this was true. His collar choked up against his throat as he swallowed hard. All he could do, however, was make note of it since he could not move any of his limbs by so much as a whisker.

"Big oaf!" a voice above and behind him muttered. "Yes, old Merriwhiddle is strong, but that does not mean she has a liking for yanking an overgrown boy-almost-man half a *mille passuum* because she's enjoying the experience. Whyever did I save the biggest for last? What was I thinking? *Pfah!*" The old woman spat and fell silent as the strange journey continued, her breathing unlabored for all her complaint.

Thaddeus had a thousand questions, but try as he might, he could utter none of them. He was only able to hear, see, and breathe.

"Ah, awake, are ye? Fancy the view from down there, do ye? Ha! Well, ye'll be joining yer friends soon enough. A puzzle ye are, though. My little stingers did not want to bestow their kisses on ye. As a rule, they like to nip. I must ha' a word with them about that. I cannot imagine why they—ah, here we are."

Merriwhiddle dragged Thaddeus to a rock outcropping facing the old, gnarled tree. He was dumped unceremoniously next to Rolland and Anders, who, like him, appeared only able to note their circumstances but not to interact with them.

The old woman stepped into Thaddeus' line of vision and addressed the group.

"All right, me boys, all together again. Happy about that, are ye? Ye, the short, supposedly smart one—too bad ye canna tell the difference between swamp gas and *Faerrae* lights, eh? And ye, big blue-beak, ye should have considered exchanging the Gift of Hearing for the Gift of Listening. When I bade ye follow the lights, ye believed I said *treasure*, but, in truth, what I said was that ye'd find *something of great value*.

What I meant, of course, was *knowledge*. Always of great value, don't ye think? To be sure, there's also *timing*. For example, *when* it is that ye actually receive that knowledge. But 'tis often the way of things—nothing is perfect. Hee hee! Hmm, ye dinna say much, do ye? Ha! Not now, and not later, either, I expect." The old woman laughed again, stroking her chin.

"Now ye lads are an unlikely lot, it appears to me. One *Amicus Faerrarum,* one blue-nose, and one just plain nosy—just as our Visitor said ye'd be. And all with the power of Sorcery—at least a fledgling power, anyway."

Of the myriad of questions that were stirring in Thaddeus' mind, one came immediately to the forefront. *What Visitor? Who played a part in this?*

Merriwhiddle continued, "I doubt ye're all here by chance. Mayhap your Master, if you have one, will be looking for you shortly as soon as he sees ye've run off. But by that time, ye'll all be shriveled husks lying at the bottom of this bog, I vow. Sorry I am to waste good flesh, but I don't want the bother of questions and other troubles. At least me pets and Old Mister Garrungroot here—" she jerked her head at the tree, "—will have their uses for ye. But why am I going on so? First rule of Dark Acts—just be shut and do them. Must be getting old."

Merriwhiddle sniffed the air, turned away from the boys, and a high-pitched keening drone escaped her lips. In response, a soft humming sound commenced, and several mosquitoes alit on Thaddeus' arms and face.

The humming sound escalated and intensified as, at first, hundreds and then thousands joined them. They were biting him everywhere— every hairsbreadth of skin: inside his ears, up his nostrils, on his eyelids. And he could do nothing. As soon as one flew away, engorged and swollen with his life's blood, another ten took its place as wave after wave of them descended.

He began to feel tired, sleepy, and weak. All feeling had left his face and limbs. All sound had been reduced to a droning and humming that went on and on without end.

"Hmm. Not so sure, am I, why you're all so important, but *He* seemed to think so—our Visitor did. Came by a fortnight or so ago, *He* did. Said ye might be coming this way and fer me to keep a keen eye out fer ye. I had a chuckle with that, you know —me, old, blind Merriwhiddle, keeping her eye out. Maybe *He* did mean it, though. Anyway, 'twas clear this one was not bound by any convention or politeness, ye see. *He* just said ye three'd be coming and to take care of it. So, *He* said."

Merriwhiddle scratched her shoulder absently as she watched the waves and waves of her minions settle down to feast on her prey.

"Impressive figure, *He* was. Odd, though. Was all usual lookin' at first—just some poor old soul wand'ring through the bog, holding his robes close to himself. Then, of a sudden, *He* straightened up, grabbed that jewel at *His* chest, and it seemed *He* was, in a burst, all of three paces tall. And *His* voice changed, all friendly-like at first, then raspy-deep and growling. *He* said he'd come this way from the far East and started givin' us orders, *He* did. That's when I started smelling the sulfur. Not too many like that venture this way to see us. Would no' care to cross *Him* once, neither. And not one you could just say no to. No, not at all. Gave no reasons, but I could tell—somethin's in the wind. Yes, somethin' big. Very big. You don't get visits from *His* sort every day, 'tis the truth of it. Even Old Mister Garrungroot seemed taken a bit aback, shifting his roots, sayin' nothin'—just got quiet. And that's not like him when we gets a visitor. Gets all chatty, the Mister does. Not this time, though. No, not at all. After the Visitor left, though, I heard the Old Mister whisper the word '*Daemon*.' That raised a hackle or two on my neck, I'm here to say.

"And, now that I thinks about it, there was something about a direction, too…no, a compass. Took me back to someone I knew once long ago."

The old woman stopped for a moment and sighed. "Anyways, ye three are in the soup, and it has to be. *He* was quite certain about ye and what we was to do when ye came. We both had the feeling there'd be no good coming out of not following *His* orders. Threatened us both, *He* did, and I'm sure *He* meant it. Hmm. Wish I knew more to tell ye, but 'tis the way o' things sometimes. Probably don't matter to ye much now anyway, eh, my dears? Sleep now, and Merriwhiddle'll get ye a blanket of sod when you're done so at least ye can rest soft. But there's no getting you out of this pickle, young Sorcerers."

The old woman let out a cackle as the sky filled with ever more of her servants.

Suddenly, from out of the night, a bellowed spell interrupted the swamp tableaux. "*Sphaerae Ignis!*"

The shouted command coming from behind the boys was immediately followed by a loud retort and a blinding yellow flash with a brief lick of heat that moved out and away from Thaddeus in an ever-expanding globe leaving an acrid smell like after-lightening.

And then it was gone.

Thaddeus became aware that the awful droning had abruptly stopped. The mosquitoes he could still see on his arms were now nothing but burned grit lying lifelessly on his skin. He felt a soft, velvety tickling as a rain of charred insect bits gently drifted down on him from the sky.

"No. No. No! *No!*" Merriwhiddle wailed. "My pets! Ye're all killed! Who—?" The old woman sniffed the air frantically, then stopped. Staring at a space behind Thaddeus' line of vision, she smiled cheerlessly. "Ah… Silvestrus, my old love."

"Hello, Merriwhiddle."

"Oh, I see. Ye've come for your brats, have ye? And do they know they're yer brats, old man, if only a little removed?"

"No, Merriwhiddle, I have not told them yet. I was waiting for a certain time in the future—one different from this one, though."

"I'm sorry to have spoiled it for ye, then." The old woman had a far-away look on her face, and when she spoke again, her tone was almost girlish. "How—how fare ye? Are ye well?"

"I am well, Merriwhiddle. And you?"

"I am as ye see me. Bound in chains to this place and to me Mister here. But ye knew that, already, didn't ye, old man? It was ye as put me here!"

"You came to this of your own free will, Merriwhiddle. You know that. Your eyes were wide open when you struck your bargain."

"Yes, I know the bargain. Knowledge—and power. Enough power to hurt even one of the Great—even one who sits on the Council of the Wise. Do they still call it that, Silvestrus, when ye meet?"

"Yes, they do," Silvestrus said. His voice held an edge of pity.

"The Wise. Ha! A gaggle of old farts, I say!"

The Sorcerer gave a light chuckle. "As tactful as ever, Merriwhiddle. But I must confess, I have little to argue with you there."

"But we do have our arguments, don't we, Silvestrus? Concerning yer Prophecy, for example."

"Merriwhiddle, we have been over that ground a thousand, thousand times. I felt I had no choice—"

"One always has a choice! Ye taught me that! No, I do not blame ye, at least not entirely. It was that slut of an instructress at the school—Geanninia!" The old woman spat again. "It was she who turned yer head. Ye left me for her! And me seven moons gone on me time with yer sprigs in me!" Merriwhiddle's voice rose in timbre, full of passion.

"I am sorry, Merriwhiddle. I truly am. But you knew I had to go. The Prophecy—"

"Don't talk to me of Prophecy! I don't care a fig about those four *whores* who came to ye! It was easy enough to cry *Prophecy* when all they wanted to do was enslave the gullible. They forced ye to leave yer black-haired mistress and thereby create a false sense of a chasm that ye thought only she could fill. So, when ye had done their bidding with me, back to her ye crawled, leaving me. *Me!* Of them all, I was the only one who ever truly loved ye for *who* ye were—not for *what* ye were. And there I was, abandoned—two months later having our daughters, our lovely twin girls. And where were ye? In the arms of that trull!"

"Peace, Merriwhiddle. It was, after all, over five hundred years ago."

"It's like yesterday for me. It is a pain that will never leave me."

"Yes, I heard they were lost. I am truly sorry."

"Lost? Oh, yes, 'tis what ye were told, weren't ye? Ha! It wasn't exactly like that, ye know."

"No, I do not know," Silvestrus replied, his voice suddenly becoming stern. "What do you mean, old woman?"

Merriwhiddle's face turned sly, and her voice took on an icy edge. "Ah, the truth. The truth at last. Yes, ye have it right. To obtain this knowledge and this power, I became bound. But that weren't the only price. There was another; some would say *higher* price. Did it never occur to ye to ask what the cost of this kind of power would be?"

"No. Never. It is a power in which I have no interest."

"No interest? Yet ye are interested in the fate of yer daughters, are ye not? Little Fabia and Fabrica? Yes, I thought so. I can smell it on ye."

"What are you saying, Merriwhiddle?"

"Only that it was an exchange. An exchange in which I willingly partook—as ye so gallantly pointed out. I obtained a life span of no end, my body safe from all external threats—true power—and in return, I gave something of value. Great value."

"Merriwhiddle! What are you saying… But you cannot have done such a thing. They were your children!"

"Only half, old man. Yers was the other half, and *ye* were the one I wanted to hurt. More than anyone else has ever been hurt before. Ye and yer arrogance, yer infidelity, yer haughty power—so casual in its use. I wanted ye to feel as I felt—and now, at long last, I ha' achieved my goal—as *my own prophecy* said I would."

"Oh, Merriwhiddle…you sacrificed our children and threatened the Prophecy…just for spite? So that I would feel what you feel? But I do not feel what you feel, you know. That is unless you feel pity."

"Pity? Don't you throw the word *pity* in my face, ye old fool! Ye're in no position to pity anyone except yerself. It was here I stood that night—right here! All that time ago, shushing them while I slit their soft little throats and watched Mister's greedy roots suck up every last drop that fell upon the ground. After a while, they were still and cold, and I buried them among his tubers—where he told me to. I never thought about them aga—"

Suddenly overcome, the old woman began to weep. After a moment, she gathered herself, scrubbed the tears roughly from her face, and spoke again.

"And now ye know. Now ye have the pain. And now yer precious Prophecy lies in ruins, and it is I, Merriwhiddle, who did this. It is I who have interrupted the chain. Yes, I can tell, ye remember. Ye told me of the Prophecy, the one which you called the *Circuitus Octipes Magnus!* The Great Compass—the Eight-Pointed Star.

"Each point of the Eight had ta' be from one of th' four Cardinal Points or from one of th' four Ordinal Points. So…ye have the *Cardines* already, I presume. Aye, yer precious Apprentices. I can smell the signs. But the four *Ordines*—where will ye get them? I have interrupted that line. Two of the *Ordines* were to have come from us, weren't they? He told me that, the Old Mister. And now they're lost. Yes, I know it from yer sweat. But they are no more. All your scheming and treachery—all for nothing. Ha! It's no more than what ye and yer wretched Prophecy deserve!"

Silvestrus let out a long sigh. "Ah, poor Merriwhiddle. Have you never heard there is more than one way to achieve one's destiny? True, a pair of the *Ordines* were to have been descended from us. Originally. But there is another way. Consider the *Cardines…*"

"What about them?" she demanded in a voice now grown shrill.

"Well, there is nothing to say that the *Ordines* cannot come from but one of the *Cardines*, you know."

The old woman stood in stunned silence as the import of Silvestrus' words washed over her. "But—ah, wait—oh, I sees it! The *Ordines* could, indeed, come from the *Cardines*. But, if so, they would not be human—at least not entirely human. They would have to couple with… others. And who'd ever do that?"

"Stranger things have happened, Merriwhiddle. Do you not recall that verse from our youth? *'The flower, the insect, the serpent, the beast —who, indeed, can encompass them all, in tomorrow's song today?'*"

"Gibberish, old man. But even if it weren't—"

The old woman suddenly turned toward where Thaddeus and his brothers lay paralyzed. "Well, *He* said the Compass was the problem, *He* did. And *He* wants them dead—your precious Apprentices, you know. The East—something about it all coming from the East. But *He* was quite clear. I admit, though, I wasn't expecting you, Silvestrus, to be here. No, not you."

"'*He* who, Merriwhiddle?" Silvestrus asked, impatience in his tone.

"*He* who is. At least that's how *He* introduced *Himself*. Visited the Old Mister and me, *He* did. Said we were to do away with these three. Said *He*'d be disappointed if we failed. Very disappointed. In truth, said *He*'d end us—or send us someone else who would—if we didn't do *His* bidding. Well, I don't normally give a fig about what somebody says, but *He*, now *He* was serious, and I believed *Him*. Hmm. Don't want to let *Him* down now, do I? Hmm."

Merriwhiddle stroked her protruding chin, with her head tilted toward the boys.

"There is still a way to end this once and for all and be certain of it this time." She whipped around to face the tree. "Master and Mister of Old, I call on ye now—"

"Merriwhiddle! Stop! Yes, you have sinned, but that can be addressed. With heartfelt repentance and the correct Rites, there is—"

"Heartfelt repentance, Silvestrus?" The crone laughed scornfully. "I am a good ways beyond that by this time. But now I will show ye my power—what it is I paid for with such a price!"

"Queen of the Midges, do not provoke me further! I would not wish to harm you, but—"

"Harm me? Hardly, old man—or weren't ye listening? Ye cannot harm me. That was a part of my bargain. Attempt to slay me if ye will— arrow, sword, poison, lightning. Choose. I will yet abide."

"But when I said I would harm you, it is not you I would strike. Merriwhiddle—consider what you do." The Sorcerer's tone was pleading now. "For all that we once had. I—"

"Nay. It does not matter what ye say. I have the power now, and ye are a dead man, yer precious brats with ye and the Prophecy after that! Old Master and Mister—Garrungroot! Attend to me and rise ye up! Yer enemies surround ye! Rise up and slay them!" she ended with a great cry.

With effort, Thaddeus forced his eyes open further.

Unless his gaze was betraying him, he saw that the old, gnarled tree was moving, growing in size, and reaching out toward his Master.

27

The Old Woman of the Tree II
Anicula Arborea II

"*Arbor Incendat!*" Silvestrus' voice boomed, reverberating out over the swamp.

Instantly, with a powerful detonation, the ancient tree was engulfed, root to crown, in a great red-orange tongue of flame. A roaring bellow erupted from deep inside the trunk, and the massive tree writhed as if in pain. Still, the tree's howls were but mutters compared to the high-pitched screams of the old woman.

Thaddeus watched with horror as the old woman, herself, first began to smoke, then burst into a blaze, fire pouring from every orifice. The stench of burnt hair and, scorched skin was sickening. Merriwhiddle ran in a circle, arms flailing, crying out in piercing shrieks, flames trailing out behind her like a ragged garment. The dual infernos of the tree and his thrall climbed higher and higher. Finally, overcome, Merriwhiddle collapsed, burning, oily vapors rising upward at the foot of her old tree—or what was left of it. Eventually, only greasy smoke and cinders remained.

"Merriwhiddle. I did love you, you know. Once, I truly did." Silvestrus sat down with a sigh, his head in his hands, lost in thought.

Embers still flickered and snapped as the sky began to lighten in the East. Thaddeus found he could again move. He clenched and released his fist, repeating this as he felt his strength returning.

"Master? Are you well, Master?"

Startled, Silvestrus looked up. "Ah. Sorry, my boy. My thoughts were wandering. Yes, I am well. How do you fare?"

"A little stiff, Master. But it's nothing—except for the itching." Thaddeus scratched fiercely at his arms, clearly miserable with the discomfort.

"Good lad. I will see what I can do about that in a bit. But for now, I recommend you resist abrading your wounds. Well, this was a night to remember and think about, was it not?"

In Thaddeus' opinion, Silvestrus seemed to want to pass over what had just transpired and was not anxious to explain any of it. "Ah, I believe your comrades are coming around as well. Perhaps you could help rouse them. It has been a long night, and I think we would be well-served to return to camp and take what ease we may."

Thaddeus, feeling slightly dizzy, rose with some difficulty and leaned against the trunk of a nearby willow. He put a hand to his swollen face. It was as bumpy as the pebbled path that led to the hives back home. It was also wet, as some of his lesions had begun to weep. He tottered over to his friends and helped them up.

"Is it over?" Anders asked. "I feel awful."

"Not as awful as Merriwhiddle," Rolland murmured under his breath, staring at her smoking remains.

"Save your strength, boys," Silvestrus said. "We have at least an hour's hike back to camp. Time for talk then. And do not scratch. When we get there, I will give you some salve that will help."

Far from clearing his head, the walk back to the camp only caused Thaddeus' head to ache more. Far from feeling better, he felt much worse. By the time they made the camp, the boys had to support each other. He was uncertain whether Silvestrus, lost in thought as usual, was even aware of their condition. He had promised an unguent.

Asullus greeted the party, his eyes full of concern.

"Ho, me lads is back to their safe camp an' wi' a tale or two to tell, I'll wager an'—" The mule's joyful greeting was cut off as he regarded the boys' swollen faces. "So, I see there be a better time fer the story o' yer adventures. Well an' good an' it'll keep 'til tomorrow or another day fer certain."

As soon as they gained the fire ring, the boys collapsed, asking only for relief from the itching. The Sorcerer finally handed them each a large bottle of a peach-colored balm.

Rolland dabbed a small amount of the preparation on his finger, raised it to his nose, and sniffed the concoction briefly. Immediately, he made a face, pinched his nose, and shook his head.

Thaddeus sampled the aroma as well and was reminded of a dead raccoon he had once found under some trees. He imagined it must have been there a while. Only at their Master's command did they apply the pale unguent in great measure from head to toe but then hardly moved until even-tide.

At the nighttime meal, Silvestrus plied with them with conjured foodstuffs, making three passes in the air against the sun's course, his hands clenched with protruding thumbs. After speaking a phrase, a sumptuous feast appeared on a linen cloth spread out before them. The meal contained, not by chance, items known to be favorites of his Apprentices, as well as chicken soup with dumplings.

"Come, lads, we have yet to complete our journey, and you will need fuel for your inner fires," the old man said.

"Master, thank you, but I'm just not hungry," Thaddeus said, never moving from where he lay. His two brothers echoed his comment.

The Master Sorcerer scowled. "Boys, this is not a request. Over here. Eat and drink. Now."

Thaddeus started to get up but groaned and lay back down. The others did not even attempt to move.

Silvestrus shook his head, then poured himself some tea and attended to the boys, lying scattered around the firepit at odd angles. He managed to spoon a small portion of the soup and some tea down each one without any of them retching it back up. It was only a brief time before they all fell into a restless sleep.

When he next awoke, Thaddeus mustered sufficient energy to struggle to a sitting position. The others soon followed suit. "Master?"

"Yes, Thaddeus?" A small smile played across the old Sorcerer's lips.

"I—that is to say…about the old woman, Merriwhiddle—she said something about a Proph—"

"Prophecy. Yes, she did. She said a great many things. And, yes, prophecy was among them. All right, to save time—you all look wretched and in need of a good night's sleep—I assume you were about to ask me about said Prophecy and, perhaps, several other matters she alluded to. Am I correct?"

"Yes, Master."

"Well, I will tell you, though it will take some time. And at this moment, we—all of us—ought to be sleeping to regain our strength." The old man let out a heavy sigh and handed them the already-conjured plates of the boys' favorite foods, still perfectly hot and ready to eat. But they again rejected everything, denying hunger.

Silvestrus shook his head in puzzlement but carried on.

"Since you have asked… This story is a dreary one and is as yet without any resolution."

He lit his pipe and began. "Prophecy, you say. Well, prophecy, as an entity, is highly overrated. These days, every single scroll you read appears to require a prophecy in it somewhere for validation. If you ask me, it is a hackneyed and sorry device and a mere convention—not to mention that the majority of such scrolls are suitable only to wrap fish innards in. This, of course, is because we must wait to look into an event after the fact and verify to see if a prophecy concerning it can be identified. After all, the only way to know a prophecy to be correct is to see how it all ended up. The whole matter begs the question, what good is a prophecy if you only know whether it was accurate after the events it has prophesied have transpired? That is an excellent query with no satisfactory answer.

"Nevertheless, from time to time, a prophecy comes along that seems to have some substance behind it. Such a one, I believe, is the Prophecy to which Merriwhiddle and I were alluding earlier. This Prophecy, a very old one, was given me some years ago by a group of ladies called the *Intelligentiae.* They were four in number—*Ingenia, Argutia, Sapientia,* and *Providentia,* and proclaimed they had been sent by the Lady herself. Immediately, I appreciated what a rare and hazardous circumstance this was likely to be.

"At the time, they told me a great danger lay ahead in the future. That was safe enough, I suppose, as there is *always* some sort of great danger lying ahead in the future. However, they were quite insistent I pay attention to their warnings, saying that the key to defeating the danger once and for all was through the use of the *Circuitus Octipes Magnus*—the great Eight-Pointed Compass."

Thaddeus leaned forward. "Excuse me, Master, but what is a compass?"

Anders looked eager. "If I may, Master? A compass, Thaddeus, is a device made from the clinging iron. It always points North. Navigators and explorers use them often. North and the three other directions inferred from it are known as the *Cardines*—or the Cardinal Points. In between each pair of major compass points is a lesser compass point, an *Ordinis*—or Ordinal Point. There are four of them as well, so it is the eight points together that comprise the Eight-Pointed Star. Is that correct, Master?"

"Of course, my studious Anders. To continue, the Compass of the Eight Sides is an object, certainly, but it is also like a simile—almost a metaphor, actually. In the case of the Prophecy, it is believed to have a specific meaning, that is, to refer to eight living *persons*—who, acting together, will somehow be able to stop this great danger before we all join the ranks of the Eldest—that is, in essence, before we are all *extincte.*

"It was made clear to me that, for some reason, I had been selected to discover the Eight Points and to use all my power to orchestrate their working together to achieve this end. The four ladies even compelled me to go through a particular ritual with them to initiate the process. Merriwhiddle was correct on that point.

"However, preceding the visit of the quartet, I had met Mistress Geanninia, and we had become…close. To underline the seriousness of the situation, the *Intelligentiae* foretold that I would need to put aside this new relationship for a time to start my search for the *Cardines.* This was extremely difficult, as Geanninia and I had become quite fond of one another and had planned to become one. She did not take the news well. Perhaps you have, at some point in your lives, seen a woman put off or thwarted in a relationship? They generally do not favor this and often act accordingly."

"Yes, Master," Rolland said. "Once, a couple of years ago, a girl staying at Faran's, Floria of Copperville, her name was, was deceived by her man, and he left her. Afterward, she tore the place apart, knifed three women, and then killed her ex-beau by slicing off his cobblers and watching him bleed out."

"Yes, quite so. Now imagine a similar situation but with a fully trained, powerful Sorceress."

"Oh, I see," Rolland said, while Anders and Thaddeus nodded their heads in agreement.

"So did we all. Fortunately, I am not without resources, so most of the damage was repaired. But I digress.

"It occurred to me that I might be able to accelerate the pace of this process by using my powers to cause a twinning—if some are good, then more are better, as they say. This was my own idea—a shortcut, if you would—so I could return to my Geanninia. So, I determined to beget twins with Merriwhiddle. It was my attempt at bending Destiny. And, well, it did not turn out so favorably, as you have witnessed.

"You see, I had taken it into my head to make the acquaintance of Merriwhiddle, who seemed to me a likely candidate. As it turned out, she had been a student at the *Ludia* where Geanninia herself was an instructress. But poor Merriwhiddle had experienced a difficult first three years and eventually decided to leave the school and return to her home, leaving her studies incomplete. I followed her there—to the countryside near Moorstown—and struck up an acquaintance. She was a shy girl, but I persisted, and well… You heard what she said."

Silvestrus paused for a moment, cleared his throat, and continued.

"Afterward, the *Intelligentiae* appeared to me one night, and they made it quite clear they were not well pleased with my efforts to circumvent the natural order of things. They said my duty to her was done and recommended I return to Geanninia forthwith. In fact, they strongly advised it, with little room for dispute. I was deeply torn. I had come to care for Merriwhiddle by that time. I loved her after a fashion. And she was pregnant—with our twins, as it turned out." The old man's eyes misted.

"But the four ladies were adamant. I went to Merriwhiddle, and we talked for a day and a night. She was hurt and angry—with reason, it is true—and we were getting nowhere. Then, while I was sleeping, she arose and put a Sorcerous spell on me."

"A Sorcerous spell, Master?" Anders cocked his head to one side and stared at Silvestrus intently. "Of what kind?"

"It is not important. The problem was, she had not enough knowledge and power to do it correctly…and it turned out badly. It took me some time and effort to get back to my proper self, and by then, I had decided to leave. Merriwhiddle was unbending in her wrath and made all manner of threats. But by that time, my heart had turned, and I knew she was not the one for me. So, one morning, I left her a long note and a heavy bag of gold, and I traveled west."

After a long silence, Rolland spoke. "Not my business, Master, but after all that, I'm thinking that getting back into Mistress Geanninia's good graces might have posed a problem or two."

"You have no idea."

"Um, Master," Anders offered, "the woman, Merriwhiddle, seemed to say that her, um, bargain with the Tree Lord, Garrungroot, provided her with invulnerability to all assault. How was it, then, if I may ask, that you were able to defeat…them?"

"Ever curious, Anders. Very well, it was a strategy, actually, both simple and complex. It is true I could not assail her directly—she would have been immune to that—but I could assault her Tree Lord and, through him, overcome her. You see, they had a rather unique bond; what affected the one affected the other. It occurred to me then that if I caused Garrungroot to catch a-fire and be consumed, it was likely to spread to Merriwhiddle, as well, on account of that bond."

"But Master," Anders persisted, "if the Tree could cause the woman to resist a flame, how is it he could succumb to that himself?"

"Excellent question, Apprentice. As it turns out, he, being mostly composed of fibrous wood, was vulnerable, after all, to such an attack and, therefore, due to the bond, she became so as well. But, enough of this sad business, boys."

The old Sorcerer stood and stretched. "Now, with all our scholarly discussion, I dare say you look even worse than before. So, get yourselves to your bedrolls and sleep the sleep of the justly weary."

~

It was approaching mid-day, and the three Apprentices had yet to stir.

Asullus walked over to where Silvestrus was having a pipe. "Ye ha' the look o' concern on yer face. 'Tis somethin' troubling ye regardin' our young lads, then?"

"I do not know, Asullus. Ever since the swamp, they have not been themselves. I had thought the salve, some rest, and the food would remedy the situation, but—" The Sorcerer sighed and looked down at the ground.

"Bein' in charge 'tis a perilous place to be. Now, if all's goin' well, then 'tis cakes all 'round, But when the dough is sour, 'tis no' so wonderful a world. Still, the lads are o' good stock an' blessed wi' keen minds. An' we're no' so far from where we're aimin' to be. I'd say we're likely to make it, by an' large."

The old man rose and patted the mule's neck. "Ah, Asullus, always a comfort you are. So, see you there—they are beginning to move. That is a better sign."

The boys got up slowly and tended to their ablutions with no great enthusiasm. The ointment seemed to have already begun its work, but the boys refused break-fast. Silvestrus regarded the group solemnly as they packed and resumed their journey toward Moorstown.

"Boys, I have not decided as to whether we will go to Moorstown or skirt around it. In part, it will depend on how you are feeling. Our timing is still a close thing. So, let us be about our work then."

The pace was slow and plodding, as if they were ascending a mountain, even though the land was comparatively flat. Silvestrus called an early halt, and again the boys refused anything but water.

"I feel like a cart-and-eight just ran over me, swung around, and did it again," Rolland said to no one in particular.

Anders and Thaddeus nodded dully in agreement. Discussion that evening was limited to essentials, and after another goodly application of Silvestrus' salve, the boys sought their bedrolls early.

Silvestrus made rounds during their sleep, checking on his charges at intervals throughout the night, his look of concern transforming into a frown of concentration.

Again, morning came and went, and again the boys remained abed.

Silvestrus now marked that, although their bites had subsided, they took turns sweating, then shaking—first throwing off their blankets, complaining of burning up, then clasping as much cover to themselves as they could, complaining of freezing cold. They were weak and barely able to leave their bedrolls, all the while clamoring for water. Silvestrus rotated among the group with the water bag, noting that as soon as one's thirst was slaked, another called out.

Asullus paced the campsite back and forth in a frenzy of worry. "Master, what is it as has taken our bonnie boys? I ha' ne'er seen a group o' young 'uns no' already dead so discomposed."

"Ah, Asullus, I think I know, but I hope I am wrong. Well, there is nothing for it but to summon the Good Doctor."

"Oh, well an' good then. Whate'er it may be that'll increase the lads' welfare," said the old mule while rolling his eyes.

As Master Silvestrus barked the command, a green fog appeared and began to take shape, and a minute later, Master Celsius was standing in a cloud of verdant vapors. After Silvestrus had explained their symptoms and the Doctor had performed his examinations, Celsius stood gazing at each of the Apprentices in turn, his hand stroking his beard in thought.

"Well, Silvestrus, for certain it is *Paludis Febricitantem*, or what I call swamp fever. I have never seen such a virulent course of it—and in three at once. You say they were on the moors and were bitten by the mosquitoes there? Ah, yes. Thousands of bites? Well, that accounts for it, I suppose.

"Now as to the cure, that is problematic. I will require the bark from a local willow tree—amongst other ingredients—to make a potion for the boys, but the course of this illness typically waxes and wanes, exacerbates and remits. Even given that these lads are young and healthy, it will be touch-and-go. I will prepare the medicine and leave you with instructions.

"But I must recommend you interrupt your journey and seek without delay the Convent of the Silent Sisters—the *Sorores Silentii*—close on to Moorstown. They stock an excellent vintage in their cellars, by the by, and, of course, they truly do maintain silence—another blessing when it comes to the ladies. Primarily, though, they have had extensive experience in dealing with this malady."

Celsius turned to busy himself with the preparation of his medicinals. Obtaining the willow bark, indigenous to the area, proved to be not difficult, and soon three beakers of a gray-green, foul-smelling brew stood on a rock by the campfire.

"This should do it, Silvestrus," Celsius said, staring thoughtfully at the Sorcerer for a moment before continuing. "I will, of course, be happy to check in on the boys from time to time to note their progress, but 'tis now mostly a matter of dosing and waiting. On another topic, I hesitate to bring this up at such a delicate time, but I don't suppose—"

Silvestrus scowled.

"Yes, well, of course, I understand. Another time. *Vale!*" And the healer was gone in a cloud of green smoke.

Asullus trotted over to the old Sorcerer. "Master, our Medico did no' seem all so confident to me regardin' his current poison, especially concernin' its efficacious effects. I'm wondering if t'would no' be wiser fer ye to use yer own powers to bring the lads around?"

"Indeed, Asullus, I have been debating that very question this recent while. When considering this, I run into the same dilemma as I described to Thaddeus regarding Ethne. To heal one Apprentice of this deadly disease could take a good part of my reserves—but all three at once? I must weigh this against conserving them for the time of need that's coming soon, according to the writings. And yet, my boys, my boys…"

The old man turned away and began pacing back and forth, hands locked behind him.

The gray-green potion, which the Apprentices took only with much gagging and sputtering, seemed, after a time, to ease their symptoms.

"Gods! That's awful!" Rolland exclaimed. "The last time I tasted something this bad was when I stole soured wine from behind the merchant's stall at the market. Closest thing to horse piss, it was."

Anders and Thaddeus laughed weakly. After a minute, all three turned their gaze to their Master, who had suddenly stopped pacing and, with eyes closed, had tilted his head up toward the sky.

After only a moment, the old man abruptly opened his eyes and strode over to the mule.

"Asullus, we must get the lads to the Convent of the Silent Sisters as soon as may be. However, as you can see, they are in no condition to walk. I know it is warm here and the journey long and difficult, but—"

"Ye pay it no mind, Master Silvestrus. I see the direction o' yer wishes, an' I ha' me no objections. Ye load the lads in the cart an' seat yerself up there as well to do the guidin', an' I'll see we get there. I ha' me the remains o' me youth, more or less, an' me strength, which is considerable. The goin' will no' be so speedy, but it'll be sure an' steady, an' we'll all be arrivin' there in one piece."

"You are a good friend, Asullus, and I know you have the best interests of the boys in your heart. No one could ask for more."

"Well, Master, thank ye fer yer kind words, but ye just be puttin' off the inevitable. So, get off yer lazy behind an' put on me harness. Then get those worthless collywobbles up in the cart, an' we'll be on our way, 'stead o' talkin' the day away."

Thaddeus remembered little of the next few days. He was sick, and the bouncing back and forth only made it worse. He had an incredible burning thirst and a vicious headache that threatened to split his brainpan open. The persistent bouts of nausea and vomiting were debilitating. Also, the insult of the warm water, the thin sour broth, and the vile-tasting potion were sufficient to make him vomit repeatedly. He could control neither his bowels nor his bladder.

Every so often, Master Celsius appeared in his green robes, looked into his eyes, and murmured something meant to be reassuring—but it was not. Once, or perhaps twice, it rained, which offered some relief from the heat. Mostly, though, it was a trip of endless misery—alternately shivering and sweating—*rigor et calor*—as Master Celsius said often enough.

Thaddeus' eyes blinked as consciousness slowly came over him. He heard sounds that were different from the usual jingling, jolting, and bumping of the cart. Night birds called, a bell rang, and there were women who talked in whispers, their hushed tones full of concern. He felt as if he were underwater, unable to discern what they were saying.

Gentle hands grasped him, but he could barely move to respond. He was let down from the cart and placed on a litter. He felt himself being transported into a building where it was cool, quiet, and dark. He was carried up some stairs and placed in a room that smelled fresh, like a spring meadow. His clothing was removed, and he was placed in a tub, where he was washed carefully. The moments of awareness, like the nausea, came in waves.

Lifted once again, he was dried and moved to a bed with what felt to be clean sheets.

"Marsia," he managed to say. He was given more broth, but this time it was fresh and flavorful. It grew dark, and after several moments the voices withdrew. He tried conjuring up images of the tall girl in his mind, but he could not, for some reason, and soon faded into a deep sleep.

~

THE IMPERIAL PALACE, CINOTON

IN THE LAND OF THE CIN, THE EASTLANDS

Almost two years had passed since Solon, the retired ex-Spy Master and assassin, had received his secret commission, and it seemed to Soh-Nahk that there was not much to show for all the money he had spent.

And difficult that money had been to obtain.

He suspected few thirteen year olds in the Cinnian Empire could have gained access to sums as large as the ones he had procured—and from a variety of sources as well. A large leak in one jar alerted every-one. But fortunately, occasional dribbles from small bottles here and there alerted almost no one.

Over time, Solon swore that he was drawing closer to his goal: his claims, for example, that he had identified the Sorcerer and the four boys in question. However, little seemed to have come of it all. Half-effort assassination attempts in a royal palace, of all places, a botched attack by hired local archers in a wooded area, and an attempted poisoning… by a tree? Ye gods, what was all this nonsense?

But he had other things to occupy his mind at this time.

For example, the Ancient One, Wy-Jinge, was due to return soon from his two-year trip to the far lands. The trip had been celebrated as an exploration of the Westlands, but Soh-Nahk knew what it really was: a spy mission.

It would be interesting indeed if Wy-Jinge found that the Westlands was a weakened and drowsy opponent. If memory from his instructors served, those people had lost at least a million men in their ill-fated invasion of the Cin those thousand years ago. And they were, by all accounts, still suffering deprivations from it. Depending on Wy-Jinge's findings, they might be a ripe plum for the plucking, perhaps with help from the Ancient Ones.

Soh-Nahk believed some chastisement of those Westlands was in order. They had invaded, unprovoked, led by the useless Emperor, Tyrannus Superbus, who yet sat, drooling, under the old glass dome in the Great Hall of the Palace. If the ancient accounts were to be believed, the old man had been captured by the Cinnian Emperor at the time, En-Jannen, after the last battle of the failed Westlands invasion. After his capture, he was cursed and placed under the dome by Ancient Ones to serve equally as both trophy and warning.

Ancient Ones...

He had always been taught to respect and fear the Ancient Ones. They, it was said, spoke with the *Daemon,* whatever—or whoever—that was. Yet, it was also said that the Ancient Ones, if caught out properly, could be taken by an arrow just as might any other man. An archer merely had to be a little more deliberate in this case.

In the Westlands, it was said that there were Sorcerers. To Soh-Nahk, it sounded like two different names for, essentially, the same type of people. If one matched them all up, one against another, then would they not annihilate each other?

If that would be the case, then the important fact would be how many soldiers one had fighting for oneself, not how many Ancient Ones or Sorcerers were throwing imprecations at one another.

When he became Emperor, perhaps the Westlands might receive that justly deserved chastisement. And why not? He would be Emperor, and, as Emperor, he could do anything he wanted.

And I shall, Soh-Nahk vowed.

CONVENT OF THE SILENT SISTERS
(SORERES SILENTII)

28

The Convent
Conventus

The *Mater Amplior* peered over tented hands, elbows resting on her desk. The middle-aged woman, running to stoutness, but prim and thin-lipped, sat in the Abbess' chair of the *Sorores Silentii* and covertly examined her robes of office. She quickly brushed a minuscule bit of lint from her bleached burlap *palla* and straightened her *mitra*, tucking a wisp of her gray hair back under the lining. She adjusted the golden *Insignia Matris* hanging from its heavy gold neck chain, absently remembering the day she had received this medallion of her Order from her predecessor.

She moved a teacup slightly closer to her inkwell and considered what to expect from her guest, the self-proclaimed Master Silvestrus. Much had happened since he'd first crossed the threshold of their convent's door with his troubles.

And there was much to remember.

It had all begun that night when he had been pounding at the gate with his staff on that wind-whipped evening, urging haste and care all at the same time while ordering her nurses about as if they were his personal body servants.

Harrumph! Her brow furrowed. And how they had all jumped to obey him without question! A neat trick, that. She would give that matter more thoughtful study.

To his credit, the old man definitely seemed to care about his charges. She had noted how, since their entry to the convent, he had spent hardly a moment out of the boys' room—unless chased out.

And what charges… The Warrior, the Scholar, and the Blue-Nosed Ferret, as she'd dubbed them in her mind. The last boy was a study in facial anatomy, to be sure. Where had he come by that bright blue proboscis? Sorcerer's work for certain, but which Sorcerer—and for what reason?

Had it been the old man?

Turning her mind back to her guest…she thought him subtle and imagined him unlikely to suffer fools.

All in all, however, he appeared to regard his sojourn at the convent as an unexpected, though not unpleasant, interruption in his journey. But he clearly had other priorities. He was neither disrespectful nor, in truth, all that respectful. His attitude was similar to that of the Arch Abbess when she came to pay a call: indulgent, socially correct, and faintly mocking.

Yet he was neither angry nor hostile. His dress was careworn, indeed, but fresher now than at first. His silver hair and beard suggested several things, including the need to treat him with deference but also with caution.

And those eyes—one green, one brown. Now, where in the world had they come from? They twinkled easily enough but also proclaimed inner power and a manner quick to anger. It would have been a mistake in the extreme to dismiss him as a mere vagabond.

She did not need to be told that she sat across from a Sorcerer—one of the Council of the Wise if she was not mistaken.

Usually, she was not.

Still, he had been civil, courteous, caring, even charming—for a man. On more than one occasion, she had found herself wondering what would have happened that day thirty years past had she been one hour later to her Novitiate Adorning. Tardiness on that day would have meant expulsion, and expulsion would have meant Kenneth, a house, and children. Well, there she was, forgetting herself again—like some silly novice on her first trip to a large town—all wide eyes and no brains.

And the old man had said that his visit here was a pleasure. *Yes, a pleasure.* And that's what she had felt that day. That is, until later when Sister Orbis had searched out a dusty scroll in the library concerning the Sorcerers of the College—the document that mentioned "Stones of Resonance." Following that, it was but a simple matter of using the correct cleric's phrase.

And in a moment, the power of the stone to charm and influence was checked. She thought her guest much less smug after that.

Catching herself woolgathering, she pulled back to the present moment and observed her visitor, seated across from her, taking his ease.

Now to the task at hand...

"Master Silvestrus, I appreciate your coming in response to my invitation on such short notice." She indicated the serving tray. "Please help yourself to the tea. I have taken the liberty of obtaining some honey from Beewicke as I understand it has become your preference of late. I hope it meets with your approval."

The old man smiled and the Abbess felt a thrill. She immediately chastised herself. *Fool girl!*

"You are just as kind and thoughtful as you have been since our unlooked-for advent on your doorstep, *Mater Amplior*. I shall attempt to repay you for your more-than-generous hospitality in any way within my power."

"That, as they say, Master Silvestrus, is a bargain. What I desire from you is information. You are of the *Collegium Sorcerorum*, are you not?"

Silvestrus nodded.

"And the three boys who accompany you are your Apprentices?"

"That is correct, *Mater Amplior*."

"Oh, please, do not call me that. I have heard nothing else for the past ten years, and it has become a wearying weight over that time. Please call me Melior."

"Of course, Melior."

"Silvestrus, your charges appear to be responding well to our humble ministrations. They are growing in strength daily."

"It is only through the efforts of you and your dedicated staff that this has been possible, Melior."

"Thank you. But the lads are young and full of healing energy. However, perhaps as a consequence of this transformation, certain unusual occurrences have transpired here at the convent, which I feel duty-bound to call to your attention…in the unlikely event that these incidents are at all related to your Apprentices."

"Pray tell, Melior, to which occurrences do you refer?"

The *Mater Amplior* picked up the scroll sitting by her hand, unrolled it, and began to read the inventory to herself. After a moment, she addressed her guest.

"Master Silvestrus, please understand in what follows that I am not proposing that you or your Apprentices have any connection whatsoever with the peculiar happenings we have lately experienced. However, the timing of these events following the arrival of your group suggests a series of otherwise fascinating coincidences. To wit: You and the young lads arrived here the night of six *Septembris* in rather desperate straits, if I remember correctly. Since then, a twelve-day has passed, and now it is the eighteenth.

"At first, nothing seemed amiss. We tended your boys—burning up with fever one minute and in rigors the next. We concurred with Master Celsius' diagnosis of swamp fever. We applied our knowledge of ministrations to your boys, and, thanks be to the Gods, they've all turned the corner. Their speech soon began to make sense. They first accepted soft food, then full meals. Their functions returned. All was proceeding smoothly …until we noted the beginning of…a series of mysteries.

"Sister Cook was the first to bring it to my attention. Of a sudden, over a period of days, small food items began to disappear—buns, apples, tarts. No one was seen. All foodstuffs are under the watchful eye of the kitchen staff from the time the raw produce is brought into stores from the local farms until it enters the Sisters' mess. Yet items continued to disappear. After the passage of another day or two, entire pies went missing, and now, only yesterday, a whole roast pig! We are baffled, Master Silvestrus. Can you think of any conceivable explanation for these amazing events?"

"Normally, Melior, I'd tend to look hardest at the three lads. But I assume this must have crossed your mind as well. And, since you are querying me beyond that, I have reason to believe that you have already ruled them out as major suspects?"

"Yes. But whether fortunately or unfortunately, I cannot say. They, as you know, have been most closely watched since their arrival. Initially, they were too ill to do aught but moan. Now that the crisis has passed, all of them have been able only to make their way to the commode and back. You have been with them as much as we, and together they do not own an unchaperoned moment. While they may have made some initial steps toward the Art, I assume that they are not yet anywhere near to being competent Transpositioners—those who can move instantly from one place to another without the need for intervening travel? No? I thought not. So that takes us back to where we began."

She took a sip of tea and paused before consulting her scroll again. "You know, that honey is truly quite delightful. However, back to the present matter. Not all of these odd occurrences involve food items, though it seems they constitute the over-riding majority of them. Some of the items missing are items of comfort.

"We, as you have no doubt observed by now, are a rather austere order. Our pallets are straw, our walls bare, our feet unshod, our bowls and plates are of stone, our utensils wooden —and so on. While items of comfort are not specifically prohibited here, they are, let us say, discouraged. We are taught that chastisement of the flesh can lead to greater enlightenment of the mind. However, we are also of the human race, and its failings are our failings. It is not unknown, for example, for a footstool or a wall embroidery to be discovered among the possessions of a Sister recently gone to her reward. And those items seem to disappear as soon as they are uncovered—or so I am led to believe.

"Lately, however, it seems that a cunning *Spiritus* has apparently taken a liking to your Apprentices. Several items of comfort have turned up in their possession: down-filled pillows and comforters, tooled doeskin slippers, fine linen nightshirts, to name but a few. The Sisters watching the boys have come to feel that a presence beyond their reckoning is taking a part in your lads' healing process, and they refuse, therefore, to interfere or confiscate this contraband."

"Amazing news, Melior. Quite amazing."

"Yes, quite. Let me hasten to add that not all items of mystery are those suddenly absent. Several relics we had feared lost forever have suddenly appeared lying upon the Statue of Silence in the vestibule. Arconia's Girdle, for example, missing since the sixth century, was suddenly found there. The Scrolls of Antoninus, lost these many decades, appeared there in their original leather casings. And other obscure artifacts have continued to materialize."

The *Mater Amplior* shook her head, then continued.

"Although this aspect is well and good, my most serious concern has been the effect upon the Sisters themselves. They all seem to be distracted lately, almost giddy. They forget the words of the prayers and hymns, and they are negligent in the rituals they have practiced since they became novices. And, most disconcerting of all, Sister Ardens and two others of her cell came to me this very morning, seeking absolution regarding their vows and asking permission to leave the Order! All Sister Ardens could speak of was the finely fashioned sinews of your three boys!"

"Well, Melior, I would hardly hold that against them. I would venture that the boys are indeed handsome enough rogues, as those things go, and the Sisters are still women, come to that."

"Master Silvestrus, Sister Ardens is seventy-eight years old. And the two others not that far behind her!"

"Oh. I see."

"Yes, I'm sure you do." Melior sighed. "I am at a loss to explain any of it. Therefore, I thought I should advise you. You—I believe to be—one of the Wise, and likely an Initiate of the Mysteries as well. I was hoping you would be willing to apply your considerable gifts to this problem, so the rest of us can return to more mundane pursuits…such as solving the difficulty in the plumbing of our Fountain of the Grove, dry these past fifteen months."

"Of course, Melior." Silvestrus paused and gave her a respectful smile. "It shall be as you say. I will begin my investigations at once. By your leave."

With that, the old Sorcerer stood and gave her a deep bow before making his exit.

Melior stared after him absently, regarding the small bare room with its single glowing candle—scented this time, though the *Mater Amplior* could not recall why she had chosen it for this interview. She let out the breath she hadn't been aware she'd been holding and turned to the next scroll on her desk, squinting, suddenly irritated at the crabbed handwriting of the missive's author.

Silvestrus strode down the corridor from Melior's office and passed by the Infirmary from which several voices issued. He recognized the voices as belonging to several Sisters and…was that Celsius?

"…meant nothing by it; it is just a phrase. I—"

"Oh—'Well, what would one expect of women in medicine.' And what sort of phrase is it, goodly physician, that mocks women in the role of the healing arts, might I ask?"

"Well, I dare say, that is not precisely what I—"

"Did you not know that we have dedicated our entire lives to helping those in pain and duress with the Healing Art? And yet you belittle the entire matter?"

"No, no. You misunderstand. I was merely—"

"Being rude, as well as thoughtless, I would say! And where would you be without a woman, eh? Green cloud or not, your foundation is physical, and some woman went through great pain to bring you into this world!"

"Of course. I do not dispute that. I was only—"

"Discounting the value of our profession! And undermining the importance of the contributions of generations of our gender stretching back into the mists of time! Was that your goal, then, oh, Wise Doctor?"

"Ladies, please, it was just that—"

Silvestrus smiled to himself as he strode along. Some things in life, he reflected, were deserved. And some were *well* deserved.

He paused by a sunlit alcove in which sat a large, two-handed floor urn. It was glazed in deep orange with rows of naked black figures chasing about on it engaged in some activity requiring shields, spears, helmets, and bulls. Next to the urn, a small, purple-winged *Spritae* was sound asleep on a ledge, a dollop of drool trickling out of the corner of her mouth.

"Morphia! Awaken! What news have you?"

The tiny winged creature sat up with a start, wiped her chin, then yawned and stretched, gazing lazily at the old man.

"Oh, Master Silvestrus. I thought you might be coming this way, so I waited here for you."

"A fortunate choice, little one. Now, what news have you?"

"Concerning your charges, I assume you mean? They are healing well. I, myself, have seen them up and about, though they detected me not. They are farther along in their recovery than they seem. I believe they are playing yet at being invalid, perhaps to coax further favors and kindnesses from the caregiving Sisters. These women appear to be quite besotted with them—even with the blue-nosed one—rather *especially* with the blue-nosed one. You have not, by chance, given any of them a Stone of Resonance, have you?"

Silvestrus shook his head.

"No? Of course not. Well, in any event, the boys have commandeered the lion's share of attention. And my *Spritae* Sisters and I have discovered that not all of the items suddenly vanished are the work of the redheaded one who flits about reaping as he wills, so that even I am pressed to keep up with him. Interestingly enough, it occurs that several of the Convent's Sisters conspire to spoil the lads with diverse gifts. If you wish to take my advice—and you should—best get your Apprentices out on the road again soon before the whole convent is either in a riot or abandoned entirely."

"Hmm, I think you have the right of it. Now, have you seen any evidence of our sinister force—that Cinnian fellow who proceeds us with his golden Din and seems intent on bringing harm to my Apprentices?"

"None," Morphia declared. "And my Sisters and I have been especially observant for such, though the lingering smell at that Merriwhiddle witch's place suggests quite strongly that their Visitor was *Daemon*-connected, we think. But nothing like that here—then or since."

"Ah. That explains several things. Someone is indeed after our boys—yet he shall not have them! Of that, I am certain. Once we reach Moorstown, I will make some specific inquiries through the Order's Liaison, though that will require some time away. Are you certain that you and your Sisters can watch over them effectively during any absence I may be forced to endure?"

"Worry not, Master Silvestrus. If any threat comes to them, we will know of it much beforehand, shepherd them quickly to safety, and then alert you."

"Very well. Then I believe I will go talk with them concerning leaving."

The diminutive *Faerrae* giggled. "They're all in the South courtyard, taking their ease."

"Thank you, Morphia. Now, if you will make your way to our cart in the stable shed, you will find four slightly sticky stone crocks. You may take one of them for you and your sisters by way of my thanks."

"Ah, yes, the honey! The perfect gift of thanks—we were hoping. Thank you, Master! Call on us again, anytime!"

With a jaunty wave and thrumming of her gossamer wings, the purple *Spritae* launched herself out of the window and was gone in a wink.

THE GRAND CAVERN,

IN THE LAND OF THE *INFERNA*,

AT THE EARTH'S CORE

The *Daemon* council met yet again.

"Quiet! Lord Morag continues to hold the floor," the Great Leader spoke, his voice loud in the chamber.

The highlighted Daemon acknowledged his selection with a nod and turned to address his colleagues in his distinctive, rusted iron-file voice. Absently he scratched his neck, rubbing the site of his old healed wound —a gift from a long-dead challenger who had tasted rather stringy but whose last desperate bite had left him with his residual rasping speech.

"I am here to report that I am making contact, at last, with one of the faculty at a Westlands Institute—one who, I vow, will be our candidate for the recapture of the Tower of the Cin."

"Oh? And what human would that be?" a blue-horned colleague asked.

"One of the Master Sorcerers of the *Collegium Sorcerorum*, no less," Morag replied.

"One of the Master Sorcerers of the College? Truly? Well, Morag, you are to be congratulated. After all these centuries! That is an amazing piece of work for one from such humble and unremarkable beginnings."

Morag smiled, his polished tusks on display.

Soon, when I have the leisure, I will find a way to slay and then eat that one.

"Well," said the chair-daemon, "Perhaps after all these millennia, our dreams might finally be coming true. Wonderful."

"Not only that, but such an achievement might erase the need for any reliance on that hare-brained scheme to have some Eastern teller of fortunes—one Madrin, I believe—compel those Cinnians to try to thwart their old prophecy by means of a boy-Emperor."

"Yes, and whose plan was that, again?" asked another.

"Babaiaga's, wasn't it?"

"That prune-butted old harpy? How was she able to take control of such a one as Madrin in the first place? Especially being shut away as she is."

"I do not know. She is Babaiaga, however, and that I do know—always a power to be reckoned with."

"Well and good. We will give our support, then, to Morag. And we eagerly await his promised outcome of the fall of the College of Sorcerers, the return of the Tower of the East from its current location at the College to Cinoton in Cin, and the reclamation of the Earth and all its delights from that filthy auburn-haired slut, *Mater Naturae*—she who caused our enslavement here in this desolate prison in the first place. May her fat be well-marbled and her flesh taste sweet!"

The entire Council broke out in loud and sustained applause.

29

Encampment I
Castra I

Silvestrus did not want to antagonize the *Mater Amplior*. She and the Sisters had done much good for them, so he did not want to deny their generosity. Taking the next left, he passed through an arch that led into a sunny atrium where he stopped to survey the scene.

There he found Thaddeus under the branches of a great oak, carefully pushing a two-seated swing that was suspended by vines. A pair of giggling Sisters rose higher and higher into the air with each shove, their filthy-soled feet protruding from their long smocks, kicking in delight.

On the other side of the ancient tree, Anders sat on a small marble stool with several scrolls spread out before him on a low stone table. Three of the Sisters sat at his feet on the grass, two considering scrolls of their own while the third appeared to be engaged in gentle disputation with the young scholar.

But it was Rolland who startled him most. The blue-nosed Apprentice lay propped on one side, fully in the sun, on a soft blanket with a pillow under his head and a smaller one next to it for his azure proboscis. Two of the four Sisters around him were busy kneading his back, while another peeled what looked to be ripe purberries, plopping them into his mouth one by one as the fourth sang a melancholy song, accompanying herself on the lyre. She had a lovely voice.

Morphia was right, he thought. *Time to be gone from this place. Long past time.*

"Sisters!"

The women jumped as if stuck from behind with toothpicks.

"If you would all be so good as to excuse us for a time. I would speak with my Apprentices. In private, if you please."

The Sisters scattered, vanishing within a few moments.

"Lads, I…" Silvestrus scanned the boys' expressions.

Attentive and eager, Thaddeus was trying unsuccessfully to stop the vacated swing in its course. Anders, looking a little guilty, quickly rolled up one of the scrolls, which, judging from the glimpse he caught of the llustrations, appeared to concern itself with matters of anatomy. And Rolland, challenging and irritated as if a treat had been unfairly snatched from him, was rapidly stuffing the remaining fruit in his tunic for later consumption.

The old Sorcerer tossed his head back and laughed aloud from pure joy. The boys started laughing, too, if a bit guiltily. It was some time before they regained their composure.

Finally, wiping his eyes, Silvestrus said simply, "I see you are all well. Very well, indeed. It is time we take our leave of this place."

The next day came the farewell, accompanied by many tears and flowers. Pulled by the bedecked and well-groomed mule, the laden cart— accompanied by the invigorated young men—were given a send-off with earnest and heartfelt waves from the Sisters. The boys both enjoyed the adulation and harbored a renewed impatience to be on their way.

Nevertheless, it was sad to depart.

Silvestrus noted that even the *Mater Amplior,* Melior, standing next to the now-gushing Fountain of the Grove, shed a tear, which she quickly wiped away with her pocket linen as the party passed by. With a resound-ing *boom,* the brass-banded oaken gates swung shut behind them.

With the visitors gone, Melior critically surveyed the scene around the courtyard.

The Sisters were now standing quietly, as if not knowing what to do. Some let the bouquets they had held moments before slip from their fingers and fall to the ground. Smiles and tears steadily changed back to somber expressions. It was as if they had forgotten the possibility of a future bright with hope. Eyes once bright and shining now turned dull and downcast.

The close-knit groups of Sisters, recently chirping and buzzing as friends, now dispersed inexorably, as each walked woodenly away in her own direction, silent, with arms folded in her habit, touching nothing. The festive and colorful faire atmosphere had faded into a gray and solitary existence once again.

The *Mater Amplior* sighed deeply. Something important had been lost, she judged, perhaps never to return.

Was it just the exuberance of youth in a group that had enlivened her nurses? Had she been an abbot at a monastery, would her staff of priests have been equally affected by three young women in need coming into their midst?

An interesting question. Probably.

So, youth *and* gender and their loss—all were sufficient to trigger melancholia? Could a life of service prodded by a sense of duty suddenly exposed to what could have been exact a toll on relationships and personal contentment?

A memory came back to her, followed by another, more personal question. Should she have remained with Kenneth, then, and, possibly, even had a family with him? But what of the thousands of lives she had touched over the years at the healing convent? Had she fled toward the cloistered life, away from a secular path?

And if these were the queries she had to deal with…what about the others here and all their possible concerns?

She shook her head. Such thoughts were distractions and should not be allowed to interfere with her work at the mission. But still, she wondered…if one had ever run away from something, was it ever possible to return?

The group took the dusty path leading southeast from the Convent, circling south of Moorstown. The footpath became a trail, joining a shady lane that emptied onto the major road.

Silvestrus spoke to his Apprentices as they walked along by the cart.

"All right, boys. Now we are on the Moorstown Pike, the main West-East road in these parts. This road will, in time, intersect with the major North-South Way: the Great North Road at the Eastern Cross-roads. At that juncture, we will turn due north and embark on the last long leg of our journey to the *Collegium*."

The three Apprentices nodded to show they had heard and under-stood their Master.

Silvestrus calculated as they walked. They had lost almost an entire month with their most recent adventure. The moon was lacking only a day of being full once again. Still, if nothing else interfered, they would be arriving at their destination just in time.

"Master, are we there yet?" Rolland asked.

Silvestrus frowned. "No, Rolland—what with all that has transpired, we are lucky to be here at all. One more interruption, I fear, will make it too close a thing."

However, time constraints or no, the old man refused to set a faster pace. It was true the boys were doing well, but they still needed their rest.

~

The sun had already begun its descent the next day when the party reached the Eastern Crossroads. The boys had walked throughout the morning swinging their staffs about, poking at the foliage as they passed. After mid-day, Thaddeus, well-nigh exhausted, asked his master if the three of them might ride in the back of the cart for the rest of the day's journey.

With Silvestrus' consent, they had spent the afternoon dozing off and on in the jiggling wagon. As they approached their next stop, Silvestrus, beholding the lads beginning to stir, smote the side of the cart with his staff and intoned, "Behold Terminus, the City on the Plain, camp to the ninety-nine Legions of the Empire of the Westlands."

Anders gazed about critically. "Master, there's nothing here. It's just two wide dusty roads meeting, then crossing and going on."

"That is true, Anders. The area is essentially barren except for wild grasses and low scrub, with the occasional rock outcropping," replied the old man.

The boys rolled their eyes at each other. Thaddeus shrugged.

But later, as they partook of the evening meal, Anders swallowed the last of his bread and cleared his throat. "Master, how is it that such a large and important place is abandoned? We've seen no sign of habitation for hours. I would have thought an intersection of that import would have a sizable town or even a city."

"Well, one would think so, but there are none who will live here anymore."

"Anymore, Master?" Thaddeus asked.

"Yes, once, long ago, this was as bustling a thoroughfare and center of government as you might wish for. It was called Terminus. But it has been essentially deserted these past one thousand years—since the Invasion, as a matter of fact. This was the staging area and mobilization point for the Imperial Army's Eastern Campaign; the one Tyrannus led.

It was here that the Commands from all over the Empire converged, joining together before heading East. But after…well, it withered and died."

Rolland's brow furrowed. "Why was that, Master?"

"No one knows exactly, only that not one stone has been left standing upon another."

The boys waited to hear more, but Silvestrus just puffed his pipe. Finally, he spoke. "All right, lads, try to get some rest. I would say you are very nearly back to normal functioning. One more repose should do it, I believe."

After their Master retired, the boys sat around the dying fire contemplating the curious fate of Terminus. The moon shown down on them fully for the first time since Mid-Summer.

"Thaddeus, Anders," Rolland offered, "Take my word or no, but look to the east. Just look! It's the Lights of Calling again."

Anders squinted. "By the Gods, you are right. Well, we certainly know enough to stay away from them now."

Thaddeus gazed east intently. "I'm not so sure about that. Those swamp lights danced and moved. And they had a green cast. This light is steady and blue."

A familiar look stole across Rolland's features. "I think we ought to investigate. There might be—"

Anders jumped up. "No! Absolutely not! Are you mad? Have you learned nothing? We stay here. I don't care if all the treasure of the Cin is out there for the taking. We stay here. Besides, Master would skin us alive—slowly—and with good cause."

"He has a point," Thaddeus concurred. "Fool me the first time, shame on ye. Fool me the second time; shame on me."

"You know, you two pedestrians lack all the essential ingredients for the enjoyment of adventure. With that view of life, you're going to miss out on any number of fine opportunities," Rolland said.

"Such as almost being turned into compost by an irate old witch after being exsanguinated by all the mosquitoes in the world? No, thank you. My Nannsi will still care for me without a bauble or two."

"Very well. Stay here, then. I'm going to have a look. I may—or may not—share my portion of the treasure I find when I return." Rolland leaped to his feet and slipped off into the moonlit shadows.

After waiting ten minutes, Thaddeus threw down the twig he'd been twisting back and forth. Although the Master had never said it in so many words, Thaddeus thought the old man depended on him to keep his brother Apprentices in some sort of order, including seeing to their safety. Also, though he hated to admit it to himself, he did find himself once again, and at odds with his usual degree of common sense, drawn to the word *treasure.*

"*Stercus!* All right, Anders, come on. I'm going to need some help dragging Rolland's remains back here."

The tall Apprentice stood and headed resolutely after Rolland, with his shorter companion muttering expletives, trying his best to keep up. Thaddeus was aware that Anders thought cursing to be coarse and strove to avoid it whenever possible under normal circumstances, which these were not.

They had not gone far when the thief, appearing gray-haired in the moon's cold light, materialized in front of them.

"Come with me," was all he said.

A few more minutes took them down into a gully.

As they walked up and out of it, Rolland swept his arm and stepped back dramatically. "Behold! The City on the Plain."

It was not so much a city as it was a fortress—built entirely of logs. It was the largest structure any of them had ever seen, and it easily dwarfed the Great Spansion in River's Wood. It was huge—perhaps a *mille passuum* or more on each side—and it had all the markings of a military encampment. The tall trees constituting the stockade's bulwark must have been dragged in from a great distance, for the boys had seen no forests for the last few days.

Timber walls the height of three men were reinforced with cross-works, and elevated guard towers were spaced at regular distances along the entire length. A series of three concentric moats with sharpened spikes sticking out at random intervals comprised the perimeter. A broad avenue paved with flat stones —that Anders identified as lava rock, worn smooth by passage and time—led down from a massive double gate.

The avenue ended abruptly a hundred paces from where the boys stood. The entire periphery of the structure sat within a haze of blue-whiteness. The sheeted light extended vertically to a height several paces beyond the highest tower of the fortress. Though the boundary of the haze was sharply demarcated, Anders pointed out that they could see the moon rising over the encampment through the blue-white glow.

As the boys cautiously drew closer, they discerned glowing figures marching back and forth, patrolling the wall. Through the open gates, rows of identical tents were pitched in a square pattern. Other figures walked in and out of the gate in twos and threes—all of them outfitted in what appeared to be antique armor. A patrol paraded in front of a tall pole topped with a pennant bearing the image of an eagle with several unfamiliar markings below it.

Thaddeus nudged Anders. "What do the letters of that insignia on the standard mean? They say *S.P.Q.I.*"

"Um, those are the initials for the old Empire. It stands for *Senatus Populusque Imperatus*—the Senate and the People of the Empire."

"What about the flag?"

"I believe it's the camp's pennant—it identifies the CIst Imperial Legion."

"What number did you say?" Rolland asked.

"The hundred-and-first."

"*Iovis!*" Thaddeus exclaimed. "The Imperial Army had that many Legions?"

"They didn't; there were only ninety-nine legions. There was a hundredth, but it was an honorary legion left at home in Fornia to guard the farther Westlands—mostly toothless old veterans and scullery lads, I believe. There never actually was a hundred-and-first legion. But that isn't the problem at the moment."

"What do you mean?" Thaddeus asked.

"The last Imperial legion marched East *a thousand years ago,* Thaddeus. So, who are those men? And what are they doing there dressed like old Imperial Legionnaires? And what is the meaning of that blue-white haze encompassing the whole encampment?"

Rolland leaned closer, his voice lowering to a loud whisper. "Maybe they're actors putting on a play? Or revelers in some sort of celebration?"

"It seems a bit elaborate for that," Thaddeus said. "Besides, I don't think people usually attend plays in the middle of the night."

"Well, all right, points given. Who do you suggest they are?" Rolland asked.

"I don't know," Thaddeus said.

"I think I know," Anders said, glancing up at the moon.

"Well, who then, Oh Bright One of Brightfield Manor?" Rolland asked.

"*Mortui.* The Dead."

At his words, a group of four soldiers who had been patrolling the glowing blue perimeter stopped and pointed to the boys. The soldiers made no sound but gestured at them to come forward.

Rolland grabbed Thaddeus' wrist. "It's time to leave, Taddy," he said. "We have no business with the Dead."

"I think you may be right," Thaddeus replied.

"Oh, brave thief," Anders said in a mocking tone, "I thought you were the one eager for adventure and treasure?"

"Cut it, Stubby. Nobody comes out well when they fool with spirits. They could float over here and have our souls in an instant. It's what they do, you know."

"Hmm," Anders murmured. "How, exactly, do you know that? Look there. None of them appear to be willing to proceed beyond that blue-white boundary. In fact, I wager that they can't. We could at least move closer to see. If they do seem unfriendly, we can always leave."

"Hells no! It's very hard to leave someplace if an ice-cold dead man's hand has a hold of your spine," Rolland insisted hotly.

"Well, nevertheless, this is interesting. I'm for going forward—at least just a little bit," Anders said.

Feeling slightly shamed by his shorter colleague, Thaddeus looked at Rolland and shrugged.

"All right, you two," Rolland said, "but remember that rope you brought, Anders—so the Master can haul our corpses back to camp if and when he ever finds them."

Thaddeus squared his shoulders and led the way.

The boys halted within hailing distance and were bid forward to the boundary line with another imperious gesture from the soldiers. Rolland, his scarf around his face, stood behind his two friends.

One of the glowing figures strode forward. "Who are you to disturb the peace of our night?"

Though the man spoke Common, his accent was nearly impenetrable. It reminded Thaddeus of the old farmers from the South who periodically made the trek to Beewicke to trade for honey. They were just as difficult to understand.

Thaddeus took a deep breath and stepped forward. "We are Apprentices traveling with our Master, and we went exploring. We saw the light and thought to come and learn its source."

"Your tongue is strange, hard to understand. From whence do you live?"

"We are from…Fountaindale, sir."

"Ha! No need to address this man as *sir*, lad. He is only Marcellus. No makings of an officer there." The man at the patrol leader's elbow guffawed at his own jest while the leader shot him a *we-will-talk-later* look.

"Fountaindale? I have heard naught of it."

"It lies in the…Western Provinces, sir, on the Great River," Anders added quickly.

"The Farther Provinces. I see. Well, that may account for it, but this matter requires investigation. Bernardus, Franciscus, Horatius—you three remain here with these boys. I will go and fetch Helveticus. He will sort this out, I wager." With that, the soldier turned on his heel and strode back up the avenue and through the gates into the fortress.

The older balding man, Horatius, stepped forward. "Young one, you have a strange way of speaking, true, but also the tongue of a scholar on you, should I not miss my mark. Where have you studied?"

"I have only had my tutors, sir, Primus, and Secundus. When I was younger, I even had Tertius, but he left after some trouble with Cook, I think."

"Ah, yes. Well, it is often so. In any case, we are an isolated outpost, and I thirst for news of the outside world. Many there were who came at first, but now, well, it is a mystery. One of several, as it happens. I can't quite seem to remember—"

A new voice broke in on the conversation—a voice accustomed to command.

"What you can't seem to remember is that you are on parade duty, old old Bookworm. Now be gone, all of you. Back to your posts. I will handle this lot fair enough."

Thaddeus turned to note the speaker.

No doubt, this was Helveticus.

30

Encampment II
Castra II

Thaddeus, Anders, and Rolland were careful to stay on the outside of the bright blue-white boundary that demarcated the surrounding grassy scrub from the grounds of the massive, mist-covered wooden fortification.

Anders had warned that they must respect the dividing line. He did not say why they should do that—perhaps he was being overcautious—but Thaddeus had come to well regard his scholarly warnings, even if they were but hunches. Also, by nature, and unlike Rolland, Thaddeus was cautious, almost to a fault, regarding phenomena he did not wholly understand.

The three boys and the three guards, who stood on the other side of the arching blue-white half-dome, turned to consider the new arrival. It occurred to Thaddeus that this soldier must somehow be in charge at the fort, given the confident way he carried himself.

With Marcellus positioned behind him, the new man stood easily, self-assuredly. He was broad and strapping, with close-cropped, iron-gray hair. His slitted eyes were cautious rather than piggish, clever rather than cruel. His warrior's armor, though bright and spotless in the moonlight, had the used look of a professional. He sported a tattoo of a black eagle, wings spread, on his forehead above his right eye.

After he had come to a halt, the four soldiers struck fist to chest in salute, then turned and marched back to the parade ground. The older man looked the Apprentices over thoroughly, taking his time.

Abruptly a voice issued from the imposing figure—a voice like deep gravel.

"You, in the back. Uncover your face. 'Tis no benefit in conversing with one as likes to have something to hide."

"*Ssst!*" Anders whispered. "Do as he says! We want to avoid trouble!"

Rolland, obviously reluctant, hesitated a moment, then slowly complied with the given order and let down his scarf. His proboscis, the blue member appearing grotesque in the pale moonlight, hung limply to his chest. He had been staring at the ground, but now he gradually raised his gaze to regard his inquisitor.

"Sister-to-the-Mother! Whatever is that you sport on your face, young one, in place of a nose?"

Anders interceded quickly. "It's a Sorcerer's curse, sir. He offended one of their Order."

"Ah. Well, we have that in common, do we not?" The large man's arm swept across the entire camp. "We are under a Sorcerer's curse as well. Though I expect we have been at it longer than you three. I judge you all to be mid-young, fourteen or fifteen, is it?"

The boys nodded.

"I have some of the same at home—at least I did." Here the man looked away quickly, then back again. "They would be your age about now. Put me in mind of them, you do." The Legionnaire straightened his shoulders.

"Now to business. I am Helveticus, *Centurio Prior* to this command. Your names, lads?"

"Thaddeus of Beewicke, sir."

"Anders of Brightfield. That's near Meadsville, sir. I mean, if you know where Meadsville is. That is—"

"And I'm Rolland of Fountaindale, as ye heard, sir—uh, I mean, Centurion Major." Rolland, now recovered, interrupted smoothly with a bow. "At your service."

"Hmm. I don't recognize those names, but then there's as many towns to the Empire as stars to the sky as my father was wont to say. A Centurion he was in his time as well, decorated by the Old Emperor himself. But what is it which brings you lads out this night?"

Thaddeus cleared his throat. "We're making our way with our Master to the *Collegium Sorcerorum*, sir. He's back at our camp now."

"Ah, so you're to be Sorcerers yourselves, then? Good lads. 'Tis a noble calling, though fraught with hazard, I hear tell. How is it, though, that one of you who is cursed by a Sorcerer is traveling with a Sorcerer?"

Rolland explained quickly. "It was a thing I brought upon myself. But I will soon find the means to undo it."

"I see," Helveticus said.

Anders interjected with obvious interest. "Excuse me, sir, but I believe you said you were under a curse as well. You seem to have a high opinion of Sorcerers, nonetheless, for one who has suffered at their hands."

"Such a bright lad to pick that out. Well, yes. But you see—Anders, is it?—we have all had some time to think on it, and sometimes a man gets to regretting his past deeds. In any case, we concluded that we had more of the blame in this. That Sorcerer—Silvestrus was his name—he and his colleagues were only doing what the Emperor had commanded them to do—cursing us for our cowardice, and—"

The Centurion Major stopped, peering at them intently. "Whatever is the matter? You all jumped when I mentioned the name of the Sorcerer."

Thaddeus stepped forward. "It's just that our Master's name is Silvestrus—though I'm sure it must be a different man, just one with the same name."

"Well, I know nothing about that, boy. This happened about forty years ago, and those Sorcerers are a long-lived lot, as I hear it."

Anders' eyes widened. "Excuse me, sir. Forty years ago?"

"Yes. It has to be at least that long since we first marched East in the spring."

"Marched East, sir?"

"Yes, East. It cannot be that the news of that managed to miss your Meadsville, wherever that may be. Yes, the Imperial Army of the Invasion. Ten years in the making, boy. Everyone knows of it. We were going East to take back the treasure of the Cin."

"Take back treasure, sir?" Rolland asked, eyes alert.

"Yes, of course. The reason the Cin have so much treasure is that they robbed the Westlands for centuries by selling inferior goods to us at exorbitant prices. Now we will get back what is, after all, rightfully ours." He paused and added with a wry grin, "Well, plus a little extra for the aggravation. I heard Emperor Superbus himself say this when he addressed the troops."

The boys looked at each other, wide-eyed in disbelief. Finally, Anders turned back to the soldier.

"Centurion Major Helveticus. If I'm to understand you correctly, you're saying that your company was part of the Grand Imperial Army on its way to invade the Land of the Cin?"

"Yes, lad. What else could I mean?"

Anders thought furiously as sweat beaded his brow. Calculations did not lie, and there could only be one conclusion. But what a conclusion this was!

He would bet his last copper—if he had a copper—that he was speaking with a spirit, though the *Centurio Prior* looked as alive and solid as any man the boy had ever seen. That is, aside from the blue-white haze. He knew as well as he knew anything that this could be no acting troupe. Therefore, his conclusion: *one thousand years!*

Oh, my gods! It was impossible—yet it must be so.

They had seen their share of marvels, but this one seemed incomprehensible.

Anders wondered how to put his thoughts to words—alive or dead, he reckoned Helveticus had to have feelings. How could he possibly say what he was about to speak to the *Centurion Major?* If the chirurgeon is set to remove someone's arm, it must come off; but some ways to inform the patient were better than others, yes?

He considered and rejected a dozen alternatives before deciding simply to plow ahead.

"Sir, Centurion…I do not know how to say this, but what you describe—well, that happened one thousand years ago. Your Army and your Emperor are…long dead."

Thaddeus' head whipped around to stare stupidly at the young scholar while Rolland's mouth fell open and his eyes bulged.

"Anders! Is your mind broken? That's not possible. I told you I believe this to be just a large set-piece, and these men are actors," Rolland sputtered.

Helveticus' brow furrowed.

"What? Actors? Our company? Our bastion? Oh, no. I have not spent four decades playing at being a soldier, boy, in a paste-wall fort." The grizzled veteran turned back to consider the news. "But our only alternative is, then, to be dead? That canna' be! I tell you truly, we count only thirty-six years since—well, since the Army crossed into the Eastlands."

Anders pressed on. "How do you reckon your time, Centurion Major?"

"Like any other fool alive on this earth, boy. One day each moon."

"Moon, sir?" Rolland asked.

"Yes, moon. Although we've discussed it much among ourselves, we still do not understand it entire, but each day—or night, rather—is marked by a full moon. Thus, we have counted. Horatius, our scholar —the bald fellow here earlier—thinks 'tis part of the Sorcerous curse, somehow. The moon now shows full, and full only, each night."

"In truth, sir, the moon has not changed," Thaddeus supplied. "It shows the four phases as it always has."

Anders furrowed his brow in concentration. "I think I'm beginning to understand. But Centurion Major, you mentioned a curse. Why believe you that you were cursed?"

For the first time, the stalwart figure looked down, plainly uncomfortable.

"Well, lads, I am sorry to say it—sorry indeed. But this company, you see, is made up of…well, cowardly soldiers who proved themselves afraid to fight. None of us are proud of the fact," he hastened to add, "and we shall regret it till the day we die if we are not so already. But there it is. We are all marching East. And word spreads faster than contagion; nothing good will come of this. Our presence is here only for the greed of the Emperor. The Eastern Mages will have our souls.

"Well then, we melt away, one by one, you see—then one night a bright light came upon us, and here we are. So, we organized ourselves against attack as we were trained to do. Built our camp and patrolled it, doing the things soldiers do. At least we try, nowadays, to do well by the Army. No officers, though. Perhaps there were none who left early, but I don't know about that. Or mayhap they are in a different place.

"Still, we are here, and we made our company the 101st Imperial Legion—the Leopard Legion. And here we sit, awaiting our orders. As I said, it's been thirty-six years, and each night is the same—full moon and empty news. Discouraging."

"Of a certainty—it has to be!" Anders broke in, pounding his fist into his palm. "Centurion Major, attend to me, please: each night your moon is full, and you never see a different face of it. That suggests that your nights occur only once every one of our months…which means that a night for you is thirty days for us. So, your thirty-six years is really— hmm, twelve times thirty-six times thirty. That is…twelve thousand nine hundred and sixty full moons, so—yes, that is one thousand years, give or take. Centurion, you are in this world only once each month and only at the full moon. You and your men have been encamped here for a thousand years!"

The rugged veteran staggered back as if struck by a blow. Furious emotions rushed across his face. If the figure before them had looked astounded before, now he looked stricken.

"One thousand years? That means, that means…we are all…dead." His crested helmet slipped out of his hands and fell to the ground. Great tears fell like shining pearls upon the blue-glowing land. After a moment, Helveticus looked up and took the kerchief from around his neck to wipe his eyes and blow his nose.

The Centurion swallowed hard and spoke again. "My poor Marta and the little ones." He took a breath. "And they say the dead do not cry. Ha! You know, boys, I suppose 'tis not so much a shock to me as you might think. Over the years, we have been trying to puzzle out what has happened to us. We wake up every night—or what to us is every night. There is always that full moon, and we are always in this blue-white light. We have not seen the sun since, well, since then. Horatius is the one who has always asked the questions. I think he thought as much. We used to have plenty of visitors…at first. Though it seems they were just looking to loot the camp. 'Tis a strange curse. You come in easily enough, but you cannot leave. Those looters came in, took what they wanted. Sometimes we caught them, sometimes not. The ones that got away made it all the way to the border. But if they took one step over, they vanished! Just like that." The Centurion snapped his fingers.

"Then the next night, we woke up, and we would have a new recruit. Had to arm him, teach him soldiering—they do not like that very much at first—but you can get used to most anything, I believe, given enough time.

"So, our numbers have increased over the years. We started out with just a thousand or so. Now we have close to ten thousand, at last count. And 'tis number enough to constitute a true legion. What the Hells—'tis our legion. We do what we want. Besides, what could they do to us, eh?

"After the Imperial Army left Terminus, the town remained bustling for a time. And we had many recruits. But as the people who had depended on the Army for their livelihood moved away when the troops left, the numbers dwindled. Nowadays, people avoid us. I believe I understand why now—they must take us for haunted spirits.

"Another odd thing. These new ones do not remember much of their previous lives. Just their names and the names of their towns—maybe summat about their families, but 'tis the most of it. Indeed, we are hungry for news." The clean-shaven professional stroked his chin and looked expectantly at Anders, who then spoke up.

"Yes, sir. Your man, Horatius, said much the same thing. Well, there may not be much I can tell, but I can think of some things. May we sit down? It could take a while."

"Of course, lads, make yourselves comfortable." The Centurion squatted on the glowing blue grass while the boys gaped at him on their own greensward. "If circumstances were different, I would invite you to my tent so you could take your ease, but—well, unless you were looking for a lifetime of military service…" Helveticus let his hand fall in a gesture and smiled with resignation. "And I cannot leave this area, either. All of us have tried. We are stuck here, sure as a fly in amber. So, lads, what can you tell me of these last thousand years?"

Anders took a deep breath and began his recitation. Thaddeus and Rolland broke in with commentary from time to time. None of the boys had traveled widely, but they knew their own areas well, and all of them had heard stories of the greater world.

The Centurion was told what the scrolls had said and what Silvestrus had let slip concerning the Imperial Invasion. Toward the end, they added personal bits about themselves—their hopes, dreams, aspirations, and fears.

The Centurion was an avid listener and appeared to absorb all he was told. He asked pertinent questions, understanding military matters well, but held contempt for politics and those who practiced it. He seemed most interested in the lands that were new since his encampment, their names, and their boundaries. And he was intrigued by Thaddeus' speculations concerning the Cin coming West.

"You know, young Thaddeus, I think you may be onto something. 'Tis a strange thing that you have not heard from those *Orientales* in all that time. I tell you true if it were up to me to advise, I would search for a likely young man to rebuild and restore the Empire and get all in readiness. The Cin are bound to come West—especially having had all this time to prepare. And when they do—well, it'd be best to be ready."

Thaddeus grew thoughtful. "Centurion Major Helveticus, what was it like, sir? I mean, when you set out for the East. A million men—what a sight that must have been."

A broad smile immediately brightened the old veteran's features.

"You have the right of it, lad. 'Twas a sight indeed. Columns of soldiers—row on row and rank on rank—in burnished arms, farther than the eye could see in every direction. All the Eagles, all the pennants! Ninety-nine Imperial Legions, all at full strength. We all knew there had been no such assembly in the history of the Imperium—and would be none again. The horns blaring, the drums beating time, the citizens cheering, and throwing bouquets and kisses.

"You see, in over the ten years of preparations, Terminus had grown into a sizable town. Not all military, mind you—that would'na worked by itself. Many, many supporting staff, logistics—farriers, fowlers, fletchers, farmers, faggot peddlers, coopers, their families, and, well, the camp followers, too. The list goes on and on.

"Then that first day of spring, all the auspices were proper, they said. And there was the Emperor, Tyrannus Superbus himself. A handsome man, lads; salt-and-pepper hair, back stiff with pride, golden laurels at his brows, Imperial purple cloak of the finest weave draped from his shoulders and rippling in the wind, standin' tall in a chariot of ivory, enchased with gold and pulled by four of the most perfectly matched white steeds in the West. Then came the speeches, exhortations, priestly blessings, and all manner of rigmarole.

"At last, the Emperor raised his Imperial baton and lowered it toward the East. The command was given, and we stepped off, smart and lively. What a sight! It took the Imperial Army an entire week to evacuate the area. All those brave lads with their hopeful faces. All those..." The Centurion turned his face away as his voice trailed off.

Thaddeus was suddenly aware that the sky had grown lighter with the dawn on its way. He looked Eastward, wondering what would happen now.

Helveticus caught his gaze and nodded toward the East. "Well, lads, I'm guessing 'tis time for us common foot soldiers to sink back into the earth…or wherever it is we go…until next moon. I must thank you for the kindnesses ye've shown me. I will tell the others what I think best for them to know. Be assured you are always welcome here at the 101st Imperial Leopard Legion. I do not know why your Sorcerer chose to curse us in this manner, but perhaps he has something special in mind for us in the future—maybe, somehow, a way to pay our debt, maybe a way to find our rest. Until then, Thaddeus, Anders, and Rolland, know that you can count Helveticus as your friend among the dead, and if you are ever in need where we can render assistance, you have but to come here at the full of the moon, and any aid you ask will be given."

The Centurion extended his hand through the bluish glow to shake each of theirs, but when the boys looked down, they saw only dried, rotted wisps of flesh falling from protruding finger and wrist bones.

Helveticus followed their gaze. He looked sad and, nodding to himself, started to withdraw, but Thaddeus swallowed hard and reached to grasp the skeletal hand and shake it. He then eyed Anders and Rolland, silently urging them to do the same.

Helveticus smiled. "Thank you, lads. Just remember, ask for Centurion Major Helveticus…" The old soldier's form grew dim as he saluted them. Soon he faded completely away, leaving Thaddeus with a feeling of loss he couldn't explain.

As the boys stood in awe of all that had transpired, the sun broached the horizon, and the dawning light slowly illuminated the area.

Of the grand encampment of the 101st Imperial Leopard Legion, no trace remained.

Rolland's mouth, which had gaped open, finally snapped shut. Then he blurted out, "Aye! Hells' caps and boots! That was something! We have to get back to camp and tell Master Silvestrus!"

They all talked at once, shocked and wondering at everything they had seen.

The Apprentices set a good pace back despite lingering fatigue from their recent illness. They expected to find Silvestrus waiting expectantly, Asullus by his side. Instead, they found only a rolled-up scroll peeking out of a felt case, dangling from one of the camp's tripods to greet them.

"Look there, Thaddeus," Anders pointed out. "It must be a message from the Master. I wonder what it is he's left for us."

"Perhaps a spell of some kind," Thaddeus offered.

"Hmm. Maybe, though to leave it out like that seems odd."

"Easy enough to find out," said Rolland, who reached it first.

"Read it to us," Anders said.

"Read it yourself," the thief replied, handing it to the scholar.

"Rolland!" Anders said, exasperated at his friend's behavior.

The thief looked down and coughed. "You know—I…I can't read."

"What?" Thaddeus' eyebrows shot up in disbelief.

"I said I can't read! Are you deaf?"

"Wha—I mean, how can that be?" Thaddeus asked.

Anders placed a restraining hand on his tall friend's wrist. "Thaddeus, I just realized something. Remember when the Master made a list about Rolland's situation in Fountaindale? When we first met him, he mentioned that. It's all right, Rolland. Here, let me read it."

Rolland handed over the scroll, and Anders glanced at the note before addressing his friends. "It says here that the Master has taken the cart with Asullus and gone into Moorstown for supplies. We're to wait for him, get some rest, and perform…let's see…ah, a list of chores. He says the camp is warded; we must take our medicine, not leave the camp again and—well, it goes on in the same way."

Rolland snorted. "Oh, how nice of him to be so concerned about us. Here we were out all night—he had no idea where we were or what kind of peril we might have been in. Then we get back, dead tired, having had truly great adventures with plenty to tell, and he's left us all alone and gone off to buy supplies."

Thaddeus straightened, cocking his head to one side. "We may not be all alone, though." Thaddeus dropped his voice. "Listen, do you hear that? It sounds like breathing—snoring, almost—and it's coming from over there." He pointed. "Come on," he whispered.

A muted, rhythmic buzzing emanated from behind a large rock lying just west of the camp. Thaddeus put a finger to his lips and motioned for the others to follow him. Quietly rounding the rock, the boys spied an open honey crock on its side, a portion of its contents pooled on the ground, and a small figure sound asleep beside it, snoring softly.

The *Spritae*—for Thaddeus could think of nothing else it could be —was very short, an infant's height only, and slim, dressed only in a vestment of leaves that Thaddeus thought might be fig. A young female, he thought. A pair of violet wings lay akimbo beneath her—one folded, one pointing outward. Thaddeus was reminded of an old man he once saw sleeping off a drunken stupor outside a tavern in Fountaindale.

"What should we do, Thaddeus?" Anders whispered, peering more closely. "She's beautiful." The scholar was clearly captivated.

"Anders, she's too short, even for you," Rolland joked, then added slyly. "Besides, what would Nannsi say?"

Anders appeared to struggle to ignore the thief. "What do you think, Thaddeus?"

"Well, she's not here by accident. All the honey crocks are in the cart, and that's with the Master. He wouldn't let one go missing, given how fond he has grown of it. So, he must have given it to her. I think we should wake her up and ask her what's going on. Maybe she can tell us more about where the Master has gone. Maybe she knows something about what's been happening."

Rolland nodded and started forward, sticking out his foot to give the little *Faerrae* a nudge, but Anders stopped him.

"Wait. If we startle her awake, she'll just fly off, and we'll have nothing. Let me think. We need something to keep her here until we can find out what's what. Let's see, what would hold a member of the *Faerrae* folk?"

"How about cobwebs?" Thaddeus offered.

"What?" Rolland asked.

"Cobwebs. I don't know if that would work with this creature, but they worked with Caerulea, and she's Queen of her folk."

"And where are we supposed to get cobwebs at this time of day, Lord Bee Master?" Rolland asked.

"I know," Anders spoke up. "Look around you on the grass. See all the dew? Now look closely. Notice the patches of webs stretched across the blades of grass—you can see them glistening in the sunlight."

"This is ridiculous. Whoever heard of…" Rolland's voice trailed off at the looks from his two friends. "Oh, all right, but this is stupid."

Working quietly, the boys harvested and carefully applied the delicate bindings to their snoring prey in a relatively short time. The *Spritae* did not stir.

"Now give her your nudge, Rolland," Thaddeus ordered.

Rolland gave his brother Apprentices a *why-must-I-do-everything* look before stretching out his leg.

It took three attempts, but the small figure finally opened her bloodshot eyes, closed them again, and then smacked her lips. Abruptly, her eyes snapped open again but now in consternation.

"Oh! Oh! Let me go! Let me go!" she cried, desperately struggling against the shiny silken threads.

"Peace, small one," Thaddeus spoke reassuringly. "None here will harm you. But your presence is a mystery. If you give your oath to stay, answer our questions, and not fly off until we are done, we will release you without penalty."

"Oh! I do give it! I do! Now loose me, please!"

Rolland was at her side in an instant, his hand casually caressing his knife hilt. "Oaths so easily given are oft so easily broken. Look you, little sparrow, one false step, and you will not get above two men's height before this point finds your vitals."

The small figure quieted but regarded the redhead archly. "You may live to regret this threat you make to me, Bluenose."

Surprised, Rolland recoiled. Then, eyebrows furrowed, he made a quick gesture, drawing his thumb across his neck.

In turn, the *Spritae* grasped the air two handbreadths in front of her own nose, and with her other hand, made a downward slicing motion as if severing something she was holding. Then, mustering what dignity she could, she turned her attention to Thaddeus.

"Lord in Beewicke, hear me! I am Morphia, *Spritae* indentured to Silvestrus, Vice-Master of the Council of the Wise of the *Collegium Sorcerorum*. As long as your questions do not conflict with my sworn obligations, I will answer what I can. If I like you, that is. Now loose me."

Thaddeus suppressed a smile. "All right, Morphia. Fairly spoken."

Thaddeus pulled away the restraining fibers until she was entirely free. He held his breath, but she sat quietly, wings slowly fanning, making no move to escape.

"Very good, miss. Now tell us, please, why are you here?"

"Your manners match your stars, Lord in Beewicke. The Lady Ethne has taught you well."

At the mention of the Girl of the Vineyard, both Thaddeus' thoughts and heart sped back to that day that seemed so long ago.

Tilting her head, the *Spritae* continued. "And, I think I like you after all, *Amicus Faerrarum*. Therefore, I will tell you. I am spy to Master Silvestrus. I have been set to watch you all and have reported back to the Master everything you all have done since the very beginning. Everything."

31

Learning to Read
Discere Leger

"**S**py! I *knew* it! I knew we shouldn't trust him! I told you so!" Rolland shouted, pointing an incriminating finger at the diminutive *Faerrae.*

Anders rolled his eyes. "Rolland! Calm down! You never said anything of the sort about trusting the Master—at any time. Now quiet yourself and let me think. Thaddeus, I'd like to know if Morphia's agreement with you to be straightforward might also apply to me."

"I'll ask." He bent down to talk to the *Spritae.* "Morphia, might you be willing to extend our agreement to Anders here as well?"

"Well, all right," she replied after a moment's consideration. "But do not ask me to include—what is it the old mule calls him? Ah, yes—Rufus. I will not speak with him! *Ever!*"

Rolland took a step forward. "Really? Well, you can go put—"

"Rolland! This is not useful. Please allow me to continue," Anders said, scowling at his friend.

Rolland sputtered. "Oh, all right, but if there's one falsehood—"

"Your pardon, Morphia." Anders gave the thief a hard look before turning back to the winged Fey. "You tell us you're indentured to the Master. How did this come to be?"

"It's, um…onaccountofthehoney," she said rapidly under her breath.

"I'm sorry, I didn't quite make that out."

"I said, it's on account of the honey. My sisters and I, um…we have developed a great liking for the honey—just like the Master!" she stated defensively. "And we knew Master Silvestrus of old, of course, and he learned of our…attachment to it. Especially that elixir from Beewicke. And he said he could provide some for us if we might be willing to do little favors for him now and then. At first, we saw no harm in this. After all, to have it given to us saved us the trouble of having to steal it from our cousins, the *Pixae,* or from those stupid humans who harvest it—no offense, Lord in Beewicke!"

The *Spritae* hiccupped and ran her tongue over her lips.

"What we did not know, however, was that the honey has a much different effect on us than on you humans. To wit, once we acquire a taste for it, we cannot do without it. I mean that literally. After a day or two without, we begin to feel ill. We become nauseated; our tummies cramp up terribly, we let loose bad air. Next, we break out in sweats, feel grievously sick, and we fear we will die. Then we *must* have it! It is a plague. I do not know if Master Silvestrus knew that or not. He has never refused us in our need, but we feel we dare not leave him now or refuse any bidding of his for fear of losing our delectable tisane. It is a dreadful dilemma!"

"I know what you're saying," Rolland broke in. "This trouble has cropped up in the Thieves' Guild in Fountaindale from time to time with the red *Papaver Orientalis*—you know, the red poppy. It's the one thing Faran was strictest about." Rolland adopted a serious tone. "You know, if you or your sisters ever want to rid yourselves of its grip—I've seen it done before. I know how to do it, and I'd you, if you'd like."

Morphia gazed at him in amazement. "You would do that for us?"

"Yes. No one should be beholden to another on that kind of basis."

Thaddeus glanced at Anders and nodded, a new level of respect growing in his eyes.

"I should tell you, however, that it won't be pleasant. You won't die, but you might beg for death before it loosens its grip, I vow. But afterward, you'll be free," Rolland said.

"I—I shall think on it and tell my sisters. Thank you."

"Don't mention it." The thief was silent for a moment. "Of course, there might be a time one day—and that day may never come—when I might wish for—"

"Rolland!" Thaddeus and Anders said together.

Immediately, Morphia's wide-eyed gaze was replaced by a calculating, slitted look. "Humans! Of course!"

"Every time Rolland jumps out of his saddle, he always lands on his head," Anders observed. "In any event, Morphia, what was it Master wanted of you concerning us?"

She sniffed dismissively at the redhead, then returned her attention to the scholar. "To spy on you, as I said. He told us of his advancing years and that his stamina and powers were changing with time. He said he was going out to recruit three new Apprentices—and to join one other, I think—who would be vital to some prophecy he knew of. He said that should ill fortune befall any of these Apprentices…well, the consequences would be beyond reckoning."

The purple *Spritae* looked from side to side and adopted a confidential air.

"He also said he thought we were being followed—he did not say by whom—but by some who wished to do harm by upsetting this prophecy. He said maybe the attacks by the brigands and the old witch were part of this. He worries about getting you safely to your College. Therefore, he wishes us to keep an eye on the three of you. But he stressed we must never be detected for fear the knowledge of being watched would begin to change your responses—or something like that—and that would be bad. So, my sisters and I were ordered to follow you, unseen, and report back to him regularly on your whereabouts and circumstances.

"You recall the street brawl in that place called Fountaindale? And how it happened that Master Silvestrus arrived with the Shire Reeve at just the right moment? Well, I had flown to him with the news. And then on Midsummer's—well, what an experience that was!"

Anders looked at Rolland quizzically, but the thief only shook his head.

"So, I kept him abreast of all the happenings. Then when that Merriwhiddle witch caught you out—well, I have never seen him so worried."

"I see," Anders said. "Did he say how long this scrutiny was to continue?"

"Yes. Until you were safely to the College."

"Interesting." Anders tugged at his ear. "Well, Thaddeus, what do you think we should do?"

Thaddeus shook his head. "Nothing."

"What?" Rolland said, astonished.

Thaddeus looked to his redheaded friend. "Nothing. We go on about our business. Consider—tomorrow, we turn and head north. Master has said there are no real towns or villages between the Crossroads and *Arx Montium*—the Mountain Guard. And once we travel through the pass, well, the Master has said we will be within spitting distance of the College. So, we will go on our way doing our Apprentice-best. To do anything different would only reveal our discovery and place Morphia in jeopardy."

Anders nodded. "All right. I agree that makes a certain amount of sense."

"Rolland?" Thaddeus awaited his response, noticing the skeptical look on the thief's face.

Rolland grimaced. "I agree, too, but I would like to know what our little bottle-fly will run and say to the Master when he asks for her report on this morning?"

"Replying only to you, Lord in Beewicke, and ignoring surrounding unimportants…I will say you arrived back safely from the Terminus encampment, and after you took to your bedrolls, I fell asleep as the consequence of a small indulgence."

"Good enough, Morphia. Now go as you please and with our thanks." The little *Spritae* smiled and jumped up, wings buzzing. She made a dash at Thaddeus, but only to kiss his nose. Then she made a loop and, sticking out her tongue at Rolland, laughed and flew off into the forest.

"Peckish little *Faerrae*. Don't count on her keeping her word," Rolland warned.

"Just be sure, Rolland, that you keep yours with her," Anders said sternly.

Thaddeus stretched and yawned. "I don't know about you two, but I'm exhausted. I think we should get some sleep and save the chores for later."

Rolland nodded. "'Tis the first sensible thing you've said all day."

"Perhaps a quick nap would be good. Then we have work to do." Anders stared thoughtfully in the direction the *Spritae* had flown before lying down to seek his rest.

It was bliss, even if only a dream and Rolland was in the midst of it. He was being held snugly and fed the sweetest liqueur. He almost called out, "Mother?"

But the dream faded, and the elements seemed different—the holding seemed more like a binding, and the sweet taste had turned sticky and sour in his mouth.

Waking further did not improve the situation. Moving only con-firmed he was being held in restraints, and the sticky substance felt as if it was smeared over his mouth, also covering the rest of his face and hair, plastering it down to his skull.

Rolland struggled to open his glued-shut eyes, then wished he had not. Resolutely, he opened them again. A quick inspection revealed he was tightly bound in crisscrossed vines. The harder he wrestled, the more tightly he was held. Biting flies buzzed about his face. He could not move his arms to swat them, and he could barely move his head.

"Gods' bollocks!" he shouted in alarm and frustration.

He looked around frantically—was he once again in Merriwhiddle's clutches? He needed help. A foot's pace to the left, a small stick was thrust into the ground at an angle. Impaled on it was a scrap of parchment with a few words scratched on one side. He saw the note, of course, but could not understand its meaning.

Voices on his other side proved, on twisting around, to belong to Thaddeus and Anders. Relief flooded him. Judging by the sun, it was mid-afternoon, and in moments, he would be free. He was hungry, in any case, and tired of this stupid game and whoever had—*oh, yes…*

He now knew who had bound him. He also knew what he was going to do to that small personage.

"Aye! Thaddeus, Anders! Over here!"

The pair of stalwarts glanced at him and waved as they went on with their conversation.

"Aye! What are you two playing at? Come get me free!"

Thaddeus waved again, nodding at something Anders said, and, carrying two empty buckets, headed toward the small creek that flowed by their campsite.

Anders then walked toward Rolland with several rolls of parchment under his arm and two or three sharpened sticks, each blackened at one end, and he knelt down beside him.

"What in Hells are you grinning at, Anders? Untie me, you mother's prat!"

"My goodness, such language. Yes, I will untie you—against my better judgment—but eventually rather than immediately. First, we have some business to transact."

Rolland strained at his bindings, thrashing futilely. "What? What are you talking about? Anders, loose me! Then I'm going to carve that little purple peahen stem to stern and—"

"Rolland! Will you be quiet and listen for a change? Master Silvestrus hasn't yet returned. You were still sleeping when Thaddeus and I awoke and found you thus. I have an idea who might be responsible, as I imagine you do as well. Thaddeus was going to set you free at once. However, I pointed out an opportunity to him, and he agreed to wait."

"You convinced Thaddeus to leave me tied up? Anders, I'm going to slice—"

"You are not going to slice anything. At least not for a while. Not until I release you in any case. Now stop sputtering and listen! You are a danger to our group."

"What? What are you talking—"

"Silence, knave! You're a danger to us. Rather, your ignorance is a danger. And by that, I mean your illiteracy. There may come a time when our survival will depend on your ability to correctly interpret the words of a message. For example, when we were ill recently—what if Master Celsius could only leave written instructions for our care with you? What if Thaddeus and I were too ill to read what the Doctor had written to prepare the necessary potions? Or, just this morning—what if, when we returned from the Terminus camp, Silvestrus' note had contained an urgent warning against danger? You would not have been able to alert us because of your ignorance. I have persuaded Thaddeus that this situation represents an unacceptable risk. Therefore, I have proposed a remedy."

"Oh, really? And what's that? You going to slit my throat?"

Anders paused as if considering this option. "Hmm. Well, now that you mention it…" The young scholar laughed. "No, of course not, you urban urchin. I'm going to teach you to read."

"*Read?*" The astonishment on Rolland's face was almost palpable. "You're keeping me tied up against my will so you can teach me about chicken scratches? You—"

"Ah-ah-ah! Objection and complaint only make the process take longer. Yes, read. That way, if we receive any important messages, we ignore them at our peril rather than have to always rely on you to get us killed. Practical, yes?"

Rolland struggled with his rage for a time, then surrendered, impotent to stop the inevitable. "All right, scholar. Can you at least tell me how long this is going to take?"

"Hmm. Do you see that little sign on the stick by your head?"

"Of course I do! I'm bound, not blind, ass-wipe!"

"Ever the silver-tongue. All right, what does it say?"

"How in the Hells should I know? I can't read, remember?"

"Well, I'll release you when you can tell me what it says."

"What! What in bloody Hells are you about? Release me now! You can't hold me like this, dung-sweat! And, once I am free, Anders, I swear to the gods, you and I will have a reckoning! This can't be happening! I—look, Anders, just release me, eh? I'm your Brother, remember?"

Anders shook his head.

"Hmm, you know, Anders, I can make this worth your while. Thaddeus needn't know. In fact, if you—"

"We don't have all that much time, Rolland, so if you feel a need to comment on every suggestion I make, we'll be here well into dark. Or alternatively, I could always stuff one of our leftover trail rags in your mouth. Have you a preference?"

Rolland huffed and puffed but said nothing.

"Good, silence is always best." Anders rotated the sign on the stick so Rolland could no longer see the writing. He unrolled one of the scrolls of parchment and took up a blackened stick. "Now, attend to me, sirrah, and learn. This is the letter 'A'..."

As it turned out, after a rocky start, Rolland began to view the alphabet and written word as a coded puzzle to be deciphered. Anders smiled, as he had suspected from the beginning that this approach might have the best chance of success.

The scholar was a patient and gifted, if relentless, teacher, while the thief proved a clever and astute, if captive, student. Following a short interruption for even-tide, during which Anders spoon-fed his friend, teacher and student returned to work, lighting candles as darkness advanced.

Thaddeus had taken it upon himself to perform the necessary campsite chores, reasoning, correctly, that he was better suited to that task than to what Anders had called "the pedogoguery."

The moon, still beaming full this second night, shone down with silver light when Anders finally nodded and addressed his student. "All right. We'll see now, yes?" With that, he turned the stick around and held a candle up to it. "Read it."

Rolland sounded out the words hesitantly. "It says, '*Ha! Blue-nose!*'" Rolland's brow furrowed as he continued. "'*How…do…you…like…it? Morp…Morphia.*' Why, that little—"

Catching Anders' expression, Rolland regarded his friend for a long moment, then looked down. He sighed. "I…want to thank you, Anders. This is something I could not—would not—have done on my own. You have given me quite a gift. I, well, that is…thank you."

His short friend reached out and patted his shoulder. "My pleasure, thief. I know you'd do the same for me. There is much more to it, of course, but this is a good start—even for someone with a sky-colored trunk. Now, let's see to those bonds."

Anders fumbled at his belt for his small trail knife, then method-ically severed the confining ropes strand by strand.

Rolland moved slowly and painfully, first rubbing his wrists, then his legs and ankles before shaking his limbs, one at a time. With effort, he rolled onto his stomach and gradually worked himself up onto his knees, where he paused before shoving himself into a standing position. He wobbled at first but was soon moving under his own power. He made his way jerkily over to the hanging water skin and sloshed water liberally over his head and neck.

Thaddeus, who'd been watching the process with interest, came over and clapped him on the back—gently. "I found some wild purberries and washed them. There is yet some honey in the crock Morphia left. What say you to a reward for your efforts before repose?"

"Ah, a good idea, brother mine. Lead the way!"

Moments later, Rolland sat on an old log pushed up by the campfire, stuffing the fruit from his wooden bowl into his mouth with a look of absolute pleasure.

Thaddeus regarded him with concern. "Uh, Rolland, you might want to be a little careful, there, with those berries. Sometimes they can give you a loosening of…you know…down below."

"Nonsense. Nothing this good can treat you that bad," the thief said, licking the berries' accompanying honey off the tips of his fingers, one by one.

"Thaddeus has a point, Rolland," Anders said. "Primus knew quite a bit about herbs, remedies, and the like, and I remember him mentioning much the same to me."

Rolland, however, airily waved his friends' warnings off and continued eating happily.

That night, as the boys sought their covers, clearly heard gurgles began to issue from the redhead's abdomen.

Anders caught Thaddeus' eyes and shook his head. The Beewickean grinned.

"I think it's going to be a long night for someone," Thaddeus said to no one in particular.

The next morning, Rolland glared at Thaddeus. "You could have told me, you know, that eating so many would give me the trots," he said accusingly, for the fourth time that morning.

Thaddeus gave him the same response. "And I *did* tell you—four times, I think—to be careful about eating handful after handful. It's not my fault you trusted your own urban sophistication over my humble backcountry lore."

"Yes, well, if you'd only—"

Thaddeus raised his hand. "Wait. Someone's coming."

Within moments, Silvestrus and Asullus trundled around the bend in the trail with their canvas-covered cart overflowing with all manner of goods, made fast with ropes.

After waving and halloo-ing, the boys rushed to see what their Master had brought them.

"Well, boys, I have purchased some supplies here to keep us warm: tents, blankets, cloaks, boots, gloves, and so on. Where we are headed, it will be cold enough to see your breath some mornings—even at this time of year."

After the excited recruits had superficially sifted through the new stock from the Moorstown emporium, Anders assumed the role of quartermaster and began inventorying and dispensing the supplies. He seemed at his happiest when faced with tasks such as these.

Rolland, now recovered from his alimentary indisposition, observed the distiller's son. "Aye, Thaddeus, what luck we have, aye? A grocer clerk's assistant to make sure we never run out of handkerchiefs."

"Oh, I don't know, Rolland," Thaddeus replied. "The task needs doing and it seems to make him happy. Mayhap it's more useful doing that than spending the night squatting down with your short clothes around your ankles, aye?"

The thief's former sly look was abruptly replaced by a frown.

The boys prepared mid-day and gave Silvestrus a review of their night at Terminus, also mentioning Rolland's new course of study.

"You know, it is an interesting coincidence, is it not, that I share the same name as the Sorcerer who cursed those soldiers of the *Legio Leopardinus*, the Leopard Legion? I am somewhat familiar with curses of that nature, and it is entirely possible that the Centurion Major—Helveticus, was it?—had the right of it. No one in, no one out for as long as the curse lasts—though typically curses are not so open-ended. They usually have some defining point of extinction, though I am not sure what it would be in this case—perhaps some service to a Higher Good? It is hard to know, as their crime was significant—desertion in the line of duty. On the other hand, it could well have saved their lives, that is, if you want to consider it 'saving.' It was quick of you boys to discover how they experience time differently."

"It was Anders who ciphered it out, Master," Thaddeus said.

"Ah, clever Anders. Once more, you are able to use your noggin for something other than a cap-hook. And Rolland, among the *litterati* at last. Good. Very good. If you like, I have some scrolls in my pack which may be of interest to you. You are free to use them in your practice. Only treat these scrolls with care and once you are done, return them whence you obtained them."

"Thank you, Master," both Anders and Rolland replied.

Though they had responded in unison, their expressions were different—Anders' face shone with interested delight, while Rolland's visage reflected hesitation and possible annoyance at the prospect of more schooling.

The old Sorcerer replied, "Quite all right," then nodded to himself as he reached into his robes and withdrew his pipe.

Of purple wings and clinging vines—there was no mention.

32

Reversion
Reverte

As he loosely held the reins, Thaddeus, almost hypnotized, observed Asullus' methodical tail flicks. He had determined that the gray mule swished his tail every seven seconds, whether or not there were any flies in the area.

The tall Apprentice absently wondered if this were a sign of agitation, yet Asullus seemed placid as he pulled the cart and its contents up the wide, dusty road, his pace steady as they plodded along. Thaddeus wondered at times what Asullus might be thinking and whether or not it matched his own thoughts.

The cart wheels, liberally plied with bear grease, did not squeak perceptibly, but the left rear did make a clicking sound which was, in and of itself, mildly mesmerizing.

Thaddeus noted that there was little traffic on the highway despite its name. He wondered if Master Silvestrus might have cast a spell causing people to avoid the road while they were nearby. If so, the question would be why he would do so? Thaddeus had no answer for this. But this and other similar queries that arose in his mind served to while away the time as he reviewed the day's events.

That morning, true to his prediction, the party had turned left and begun the last leg of their journey up the Great North Road. The weather was cool but dry. Thaddeus' eye had detected no presence of animal activity, which had surprised him somewhat. His attention was, however, mainly focused on his brother Apprentices, who walked beside the wagon as he drove it.

Anders persisted in his role as *Praeceptor Legere*, and Rolland continued to impress his tutor with his quickness and aptitude. Once the ex-thief had mastered the rudiments, his thirst for knowledge proved insatiable, as if his ignorance were an intolerable itch he was at last free to scratch. He addressed it with a single-mindedness that daunted even his erstwhile tutor.

"But why does *e* go before *i* when it comes after *c*? That makes no sense," Rolland remarked with a tone combining both defense and belligerence.

"I don't know, Rolland," Anders sputtered. "It's just the rule. That's all you need to know. So, memorize it—because it's important."

"Oh, very well. But I say it's stupid."

Anders shook his head.

Thaddeus smiled to himself. He secretly delighted in his brothers' banter. It was a new and different taste for him based on where and how he had been raised.

At mid-day, Master Silvestrus approached the boys. "Lads, I have found some more scrolls for you to review for your practice. They represent a variety of topics that I believe will prove useful." The old man handed a bundle of parchments to Anders, who received them with a great deal of enthusiasm.

Following their meal, the boys, the mule, and their Master packed their scrolls and the remainder of their belongings and set out once again on the Great North Road.

Thaddeus was uncertain what those who named the roads had in mind when they used the word *great*. To him, it seemed just another rutted, potholed, dusty way, perhaps wider than most and dignified with the title of *highway*.

As the grade was easy and the likelihood of trouble judged low, Master Silvestrus made a place for himself amidst the bundles and was soon asleep in the warm afternoon sun.

Thaddeus walked at Asullus' shoulder as was his custom and was soon joined by the other two Apprentices.

"Aye, Asullus, why didn't you tell us about that *Faerrae,* Morphia—the one who has been spying on us this whole time?" Rolland asked.

"Well, 'tis a fair question. I said nothin' because I was bid to be silent. The Master an' the young *Spritae* met up soon after we left the College this *Mense Maio* past, but left to get her sisters an' so returned to us only after the trouble near on to Ormerod's.

"Howe'er, she an' her crew ha' been wi' us followin' that time. She is a sweet lass, she is, e'en if she be a little flighty—she an' her sisters, who I can ne'er keep straight. They do ha' a taste fer the honey, though, 'tis so. She was ecstatic when she learned we were to be headin' to Beewicke."

Asullus nodded in Thaddeus' direction. "Now as I think on it, I'm wonderin' if the Master ha' that in mind *ab initio*, as he says. In any means, she an' her tribe were willin' to work fer the nectar, an' the Master seemed sure it was their type o' work he needed. I'm tellin' ye, lads, this trip—with ye three in it—was high on his mind from the beginnin'. I mean to say, ye lot are very, very important to him. But as to the why o' it, I'm bejabbered to arrive on any reason fer it."

"Maybe it has something to do with the Prophecy?" Thaddeus ventured.

"What?" Rolland asked.

"The Prophecy. He seems to put a lot of stock in that idea. Perhaps we are involved in it in some way."

Rolland scoffed. "Thaddeus, my friend, the sun has made you soft in the head. Think on what you are saying. How in the world could some junior librarian, a dung-footed hayseed, and a low-life pick-pocket have anything at all to do with something so grand as this Prophecy the Master is always going on about?"

"Rolland, he is not *always* going on about it. Where did you learn to constantly exaggerate, using only absolutes all the bloody time? But I think Thaddeus has a point, though," Anders considered. "Maybe the three of us—whatever our diverse and humble origins—fit into this Prophecy of his in some way. If he considers us that important, it would serve to explain a number of things."

"Ah, me short 'un, the keenness o' yer reasonin' could shear the smallest *atomos*. I think yer scholar's got the right o' it, lads, though I canno' fill in the details. All I know is this trip ha' been different in so many ways from any other we e'er took. An' I be runnin' out o' hooves to count 'em all."

Rolland snorted. "Well, if we are so special, the old Master has a funny way of showing it. We should be treated like lords at the very least. I mean, if we're that important."

Anders waved the comment away. "Rolland, that makes no sense whatsoever. Look at how you're responding now. Do you think that is the kind of person a Sorcerer should be—believing he is wonderful and worthy of special treatment? No, I think the Master's been feeding us humble pie because humble pie is exactly what we need for now."

"Anders has a point," Thaddeus said. "We've been made to do things that help us become more self-sufficient and, as a result, more self-confident, mayhap. It's possible he is doing it all a-purpose."

"All right, all right. But I'd like to know what that little purple kite-wing meant by saying someone was after us and why."

"Hmm, yes. I agree," Thaddeus replied. "I think since it may involve us, maybe we should ask him about it."

"Be careful, Thaddeus," Anders cautioned. "Don't let your druthers get you on his rough side. I think if he wanted us to know, he would have said something by now."

"Well, if I had my druthers, I'd druther be a *prince* and not have to worry about all this foolishness," Rolland said.

"You would rather be a prince?" Anders asked, amused.

"Well, not that I could ever be one or ever even have a chance at knowing one, come to think, but I wouldn't mind trying."

"And I would rather have my Nannsi by me. And you, Thaddeus?"

"I would just as soon know what's in store for us once we get to the College—but have Marsia be the one to tell me," he said with a grin.

As they continued north, Thaddeus realized it was getting cooler. His fingers were stiffening. He was more aware of chills—especially at night. And he could now see his breath.

Master Silvestrus bade Anders break out the heavy cloaks, gloves, and boots. The young clerk thought each of them should sign a chit for their draws, but Rolland flatly refused and just walked off with his treasures.

Following even-tide, Silvestrus smoothed his brows and cleared his throat.

"Boys, if we keep on as we are—weather holding—we should reach *Arx Montium* sometime in the next five to six days. I plan for us to pass through there, then abide in the Forest Surround overnight. From there, it is a relatively short piece to the College.

"Now, once we're there, things will be different for you. Here, you are young lads under my—if I might say—benevolent protection. And you are valued highly in my eyes—believe it or not. There, however, you will stand alone on your own wits.

"You, the *Advenae,* will be beginners—and Initiates to the Mysteries, along with others. You will be subject to the expectations of all those above you, including the *Indiginae*, the Upperclass. That is a very different position from what you have become accustomed to with me. Know, for example, that the common word for the fresh recruits—the *Tirones*—is scum."

Silvestrus cleared his throat and continued. "A fraternity exists there, and a close one at that. However, in some ways, it is like a soap bubble. If you have ever had the experience of holding a soap bubble in your hand and poking a finger or stick into it, you will recall that there is a certain amount of surface tension present until you finally push through to the inside of the bubble. It is the same in any new circumstance, the *Collegium Sorcerorum* not excepted. Keep that in mind and, perhaps, the experience will not be so daunting."

The old man excused himself to take his pipe in solitude.

"Hmm. There's one thing he didn't mention," Anders said thoughtfully after their Master had left them.

"What?" Rolland queried.

"Usually, when you push on a bubble to get inside, it ends up popping in your face."

Once cleanup was completed, Anders and Rolland fell again to examining the scrolls.

"Anders, does *Reverte* mean to go back?"

"Why, yes. As in *revert*, or, perhaps, *restore*. Why?"

Rolland pointed out the unfamiliar words, one by one. "Look at this line. Uh, let's see…to…use with…spell *reverte,* as in to restore…to the original… Anders! I think this is a restoration spell."

"Here, give me that. 'Return to the original…in conjunction with others, depending on strength. Use r*everte*… Intention important to apply when…' Rolland, I believe you are right. Good read. Now go on to the next."

"Wait a moment. Anders, what do reversal spells do?"

"I don't know, exactly. But the texts concerning the various spells we've been reading about so far all seem to imply that they perform according to their title. So, in this case, a reversion, or restoration spell, should put things back the way they were previously. But what's so impor—Oh! I see! Let's look at this a bit more closely."

Thaddeus, who had been listening over his shoulder, joined his friends and reviewed the manuscript. "You're both right. This has got to be a reversion or restoration spell. And I also think you weren't given that scroll by accident. I think the Master has just said to us, 'All right, boys, this is how you do it. Are you game?'" Thaddeus looked penetratingly at his blue-nosed friend. "Well, are you?"

"Yes!"

"Well, why don't you get to it, then?" Thaddeus asked.

"Hells, yes!"

Anders and Thaddeus helped Rolland go over the text several times to ensure he understood what was required and how to go about it.

"Now, Rolland, think back to how you felt the first time you used Sorcery when we met that madman in the cabin with Bellis."

A sharp pang shot through Thaddeus' heart, thinking of his absent golden dog. "I have done Sorcery twice now, and it felt the same both times. Focus on what you want, then give the command. The timing's important, I think, but you must *believe* you can do it—just like the Master says. You'll know when it's right."

The redhead nodded and took a deep breath, concentration furrowing his brow, and pronounced the spell. "*Nasus reverte.*" The blue nose stiffened and stood straight out from his face for a full minute before slowly wilting and falling back to lie limply on his chest.

Rolland hung his head. "It's no good."

Anders took his friend by the arm. "Maybe if we—"

"Forget about it, Anders. Thanks anyway, but it's just not to be. I have a strong feeling that no matter how many times I try it, nothing's going to change."

"Let me finish, dolt! What I was going to say was that maybe if you and I work it together, like the Master and Mistress did for our feast that time, it'll go better."

"Oh, well, all right. You don't mind?"

Anders smiled. "No, Rolland, I don't mind. Now together—go! *Nasus reverte*," the two intoned.

With this effort, the nose again stiffened, then its surface began to ripple, turning from deep blue to light blue to pink and back again, all the while shortening, then lengthening. However, after several moments, the member again fell sagging to his chest, blue as the bluest sky.

The thief kicked a stone, sending it flying. "*Stercus!* Just what does it take to do this?"

"Rolland, remember who it was who put that spell on you. The Master isn't some journeyman conjurer, you know," Anders said.

Thaddeus spoke up. "What if all three of us try it together?"

"Maybe physical contact would help, too, like we did with Bellis," Anders offered. "Here, take hold of my hand. Yes, I am serious. Just do it."

The three boys stood with Rolland's outstretched hand covered by Anders' and then Thaddeus'.

"Good," Thaddeus said. "All together now. Wait for the tension to build. Wait…wait…wait… *Now!*"

In unison, the three boys, eyes tightly shut with concentration, shouted, "**Nasus reverte**!"

The proboscis sprang outward as if stung, its surface rippling and wavering wildly in many shades of blue, changing from one second to the next. Within a minute, the transformation was complete.

The Apprentices stood panting from their effort, perspiration running down their brows. Rolland's face looked as it had when they first met, except now it was cleaner—and full of gratitude.

Rolland touched his nose in wonder, then smiled broadly. "Thank you, thank you! That is two big favors I owe you both now."

"Ha!" Anders grinned. "You've taught me enough about commerce that you can be sure I will collect on them."

"You're welcome, my Brother," Thaddeus said, his tone serious.

Rolland's eyes widened. "You—you mean that?"

"Of course," Thaddeus replied, extending his hand.

Rolland grasped it eagerly.

"I, as well," Anders said, capping the two others as he had in the madman's cabin. "Secundus gave me a scroll once. It was a tale about three men who fought with swords on behalf of a king. But the thing I remember most was that they were very good friends. And they used to say they were all of them for each other and each other for all of them. I think we are just like that."

"Done!" the three said in unison.

A moment later, Master Silvestrus returned from his walk. He stared thoughtfully at each boy in turn and nodded with a smile for Rolland. "Good work, lads. Good work. Well, time for repose, I think. No bright lights tonight, eh, boys? Off you go. Oh, and you might want to try the extra blankets. I think it is going to be a little chilly."

The old Sorcerer's prediction proved accurate, and by morning, the boys were glad for their heavier bedding. The smells of the new tents, clothes, and gear were a delight, as well as excitement in and of themselves. Rolland appeared most taken with their treasures, having said, often enough, that he'd never had anything new in his life unless he'd stolen it from someone else. Anders, raised in the lap of prosperous surfeit, always looked guilty at such times and said nothing. Thaddeus, no stranger to outdoor gear, pronounced the items of the highest quality and appreciated them as much as Rolland but in a different way.

The tall Apprentice noted with interest that performing the same old chores with new tools made the tasks seem to go more quickly and be accomplished with less effort. He was unsure, however, whether this finding was merely an artifact of perception or was really true.

The boys' buoyant spirits lasted throughout the day of travel and into the night. As they prepared again for bed, Silvestrus touched Thaddeus' arm.

"Walk with me, lad, will you?"

Thaddeus' friends continued their preparations without comment as the first Apprentice and his master toured the camp's periphery.

"Thaddeus, are you ready?"

"Ready for what, Master?"

"Ready for what you will find at the College, I would say."

Thaddeus avoided a woodchuck's hole as he considered his response. "I'm not sure, Master. I am worried a bit. I mean, about how I will perform. And if I'll be considered worthy."

His old mentor laughed softly. "Oh, you are worthy, Thaddeus. Never fear, never fear."

"Master, there is one thing, though, I'd like to ask about," the boy queried.

"Yes, and that is?" Silvestrus intoned.

"Well, this business of us being followed by people who want to do us harm."

"And from where did that notion come to you?"

"Oh," Thaddeus said, thinking quickly, "just from things I—that we have seen. Like those brigands at first, then the toughs in Fountaindale, and, finally, Merriwhiddle."

"And you see these separate events as part of some larger plan or purpose?"

"Well, Master, it does make me wonder. I mean, if we're connected to a Prophecy that has any importance, then would there be those elsewhere who would not want the Prophecy to come to fruition?"

"What makes you think that *you* are connected to a Prophecy?" Silvestrus had an edge to his voice, acting as if he had never even mentioned it. Yet, Thaddeus knew that he had for certain described to them the Prophecy in detail.

At once, he felt uneasy. The signals from his Master seemed to say he was sailing on dangerous waters. "Again, nothing especially—just curious."

Silvestrus cleared his throat. "Hmm. Best to set your mind ready to receive the greatest knowledge one can know, as opposed to indulging in unprovable fantasies, my boy." The old man reached into his robes as if searching for his pipe, but his hand came away empty. A brief look of irritation flashed across his features, then was gone. He continued.

"Thaddeus, on a different subject, I notice you picked up a new possession over Midsummer's night. A stone, I believe. A special green-stone, perhaps? I wonder if I might see it?"

Thaddeus drew back slightly. "You want to see it, Master? It's just an old stone."

Thaddeus became aware of a blue light surrounding them.

"Nevertheless, lad, I would like to take a look at it. It may hold some secrets worth knowing. What say you?"

"I, well, I suppose…I mean, uh… No, I don't believe so, Master. I mean no disrespect, but a special…um, a friend gave it to me. I think… I think I should like to keep it."

After a brief moment, the blue light wavered, then vanished. The Sorcerer stopped pacing and faced his Apprentice, his brows knitted together. Thaddeus braced for the storm that he was sure would come. His heart pounded.

Then the old man let out a long breath and shook his head.

"I see. Well, it is always best to respect a friend's gifts. Especially that of a special friend, I suppose. Very well, Thaddeus. But heed my advice. Hold that gift closely. Of course, if you are able to refuse me, I expect you will have little difficulty with others."

He had defied Silvestrus. Yet no punishment was forthcoming.

The old man glanced up at the moon. "Oh, I see the time is growing late. All right, Thaddeus, off to bed with you. There will certainly be more adventures on the morrow. Good repose, lad."

"Good repose, Master." Energized by this small victory, the boy nevertheless kept his composure and made his way back to his tent. Opening the flap, he saw two pairs of eyes reflected in the moonlight.

"Thaddeus, get in here! What did he want?" came Rolland's hoarse whisper.

"Nothing. He seemed to want me to tell him how I felt about coming to the College. But then he asked to see my greenstone—the one Marsia gave me. At first, I was going to, but then I felt I didn't want to show him the stone. So, I said no. Then he said I should get some rest. That was all."

"Thaddeus," Anders hissed. "He was using that blue stone of his on you! We both saw the light. I think he might have been trying to influence you."

"Why would he do that?"

"I don't know, but if you think on it, consider. He has a stone that can get people to do things for him. What if you were he and had discovered that one of your students had a similar stone? What would you do?"

"I'm not sure. Probably try to teach him how to use it."

"Ah," said Rolland, "that is what *you* would do, but you're not a crotchety old Sorcerer, and neither are you concerned with trying to shepherd some earthshaking Prophecy into being."

Anders interjected. "*Ssst!* That's not the half of it, Thaddeus."

"What do you mean?"

"Well, we were lying here watching you through the slit in the tent flap. When he was using the blue stone, did you feel that you really ought to do what he asked?"

"Well, yes, at first…but then the feeling went away. Why do you ask?"

"Because," the young scholar replied, "when the blue light flashed, it was but a moment before we saw a faint green light shining up from inside your tunic. It shone on your neck and chin. We could see it! It had to have been coming from that stone in the pouch inside your jerkin. Thaddeus, Marsia has given you your own Stone of Resonance!"

"Not only that," Rolland added in an awed tone, "but I would bet my last half-copper it was defending you from *his* stone—interfering with its effect, somehow."

Thaddeus' mind whirled with the implications of this discovery. Marsia's greenstone was a *Lapis Imperii*—a Stone of Power—and it was his very own!

Much of the rest of the time before sleep was dedicated to theories concerning this topic. The last thing Thaddeus remembered before he dozed off, however, was a question Rolland posed just before sleep took him.

"But why would the Master use such a stone on his own Apprentice? What does that mean?"

"I'm not sure. I really don't know," Thaddeus said, his head swimming. He slept fitfully.

33

Mountain Guard
Arx Montium

The troop resumed traveling the next day, heading north. They had not gone a half *mille passuum,* however, when clouds began scudding across the sky, dark and threatening, and the rain started to pour. Within a short time, the storm had mired up the clay-based road —slowing the party considerably—and soaked them to the skin. Some-time later, a chill wind descended upon the travelers from the north.

The boys spent their time slipping, sliding, and cursing. Thaddeus, stationed abreast of Asullus, hung onto the mule's bridle, as much to steady himself as his quadrupedal friend.

"Easy there, laddie. If ye falls, ye falls. But do no' be takin' me down wi' ye!"

Thaddeus turned at a snort from behind to find Rolland grinning broadly.

"If you are finding something funny in this weather, then it has to be good, indeed. It's the first time I heard you stop swearing all morning," Thaddeus said.

"The thought occurred to me that out there somewhere…" the redhead waved expansively with his free arm. "Our little violet nixie and her multihued sisters are struggling mightily against the buffeting winds and sodden air. The image has given me a certain sense of warmth and strength to carry on."

"I hope your words don't carry to her, Rolland. It was not so long ago she had you strung up like a roast at the butcher's, you know." Thaddeus grinned.

"Ah, beef. Now there's another warming thought. My idea of paradise —a side of cow, a barrel of ale, a good knife, and leave me alone for an hour," Rolland said, eyes closed.

"My Auntie Silvie says a constant diet of red meat is not good for you and can cause blue spleen," Anders warned condescendingly.

"Oh, well, we all know that is the closest your Auntie Silvie ever came to red meat—from a cow, that is," Rolland said with some irritation.

The lads' heated sparring managed to distract them from the misery of the weather, but it was soon after that Silvestrus called a halt to make camp.

The rain continued in a steady downpour for the remainder of that day, the day after, and the day after that. While the boys were miserable and complained frequently—some more than others—the old Sorcerer and the old mule adopted a philosophical attitude.

"Aye, an' what's to be done concernin' it, anyway? Will ye throw away, p'rhaps, thirteen months o' yer Sorcerous life to cast a rain-away spell just to see to yer local comfort, then? An' besides, ye could all use a good washin' down as it is, I'm thinkin.'"

The routine became depressingly regular. Each day the leaden skies wept openly, allowing not one warming ray to shine through. The party slipped and slid for twenty or so miserable *mille passuum,* then set up camp and tents and groomed the mule as best as they could, stretching a flyleaf over his halter line. They then tried to find some reasonably dry firewood to prepare their meals and attempted to be pleasant to one another until it was time to crawl into bed between wringing wet blankets.

Rolland's freely expressed misgivings regarding his choice to join the party assumed the form of a daily lament.

After the fifth drenching day from Moorstown, the ground started to rise. After that, the weather became colder.

Two days later, the boys awoke to a chilly crispness in the air. Thaddeus stumbled out of his bedding and poked his head through the tent flap to behold a sun-bright morning. To the northeast, a majestic and imposing snow-covered mountain range stretched from horizon to horizon, standing in blindingly white contrast to a brilliant blue sky.

The young Apprentice's heart soared, and all cares and troubles washed away in an instant. He turned back to the tent, poking his fellow Apprentices awake. "Anders! Rolland! Up quick! You must see this!"

Anders sat up, rubbing sleep from his eyes while Rolland quickly put back the dagger that had sprung to his hand.

At the tall boy's prodding, his two friends came out to join him, gazing silently at the grandeur of the not-so-distant mountains.

"Behold *Arx Montium!*—the Mountain Guard!" the deep voice of their Master declaimed behind them. "The great pinnacle and last stanchion of the defense of the West. Or so the story goes. It is beautiful, boys, is it not? No matter how many times I see the magnificence of these peaks, the feeling is always the same." Silvestrus stood, hands on his hips, regarding the towering tops.

Thaddeus considered the old man's craggy profile and that of the mountains were rather similar.

"All right, lads, let us shake a foot. We are almost home now, and our journey is nearly done. Mine, that is. Yours, however, is just beginning." Silvestrus gave a short laugh and turned back to his tent.

The boys looked at each other, the spell broken, shrugged, and began preparations for the day.

"So, Anders," Rolland began somewhat smugly, "you have grounds pickup, and Thaddeus, you have mule preparation."

"And *your* role in this morning's chores?" Thaddeus asked.

"Ah, I am chef of the day. I will seek to create a delightful and delectable break-fast dish to please the most demanding and discriminating palate."

"No, thank you, friend thief. I've had your day-starting culinary surprises before; I'll cook. You do the old mule," Thaddeus said.

"Wait, that's in no way fair!" the redhead protested.

"All right, we can make it fair. I'll arm-wrestle you for it."

Rolland's shoulders slumped. He had experienced this sort of contest with his larger Brother Apprentice before.

"Oh, very well. Hardly sporting, you know," Rolland said.

"A chef should always be stronger," Thaddeus said, smiling.

After morning chores were completed to the Master's satisfaction, the boys packed up the cart and set out on what they hoped was the last leg of their adventure, each of them seemingly lost in thought regarding what they would find at the journey's end.

The road they followed wound back and forth up the skirts of the close-knit foothills, making its way toward the higher ranges. With each winding, they drew closer to the crest and soon became aware that the trail was leading them to what was indeed a gap in the mountains: a pass—that is, a guarded pass. At last, they trudged up to the opening, the path widening into a road paved with stone slabs similar to those at the City on the Plain.

Rising forty paces on either side of the pass, immense pillared walls carved from the living rock formed a columned fortress. Blocking the pass entirely were towering twin gates, massive and foreboding, with great iron hinges and bronze spikes projecting from the surfaces at intervals.

Thaddeus could not understand how even rock could support the weight of the gates, though his eyes told him it clearly did. Battlements and arrow slits revealed the true nature of the architecture and its purpose —as did the armored men intently peering down at the party.

"I count thirteen men-at-arms with crossbows aimed at us, with four men each manning a pair of *balustradae* on either side," Rolland whispered to the Beewickean.

"Then we should probably behave ourselves," Thaddeus said.

A tall man, uniformed in overlapping stiff leather sheathing with a chainmail hood that spilled down his chest, emerged from a sally port built into the base of the great gate, followed by two others, similarly outfitted. All had belted long swords, currently sheathed, and carried themselves as well-practiced professionals. The leader strode toward the party with easy authority, his two arms-men keeping pace behind. Blond curls escaped from beneath the man's hauberk, and a twig of some plant was tied over the left side of his chest as if it were an insignia.

"It's a sprig of broom over his heart," Anders said in a low voice. "He's an officer—and from an important family."

"You learned that from some scroll?" Rolland whispered appreciatively. Anders nodded in return.

As the officer drew nearer, his wariness eased. A handsome man, he smiled and waved a greeting, hailing the group. "Master Silvestrus! Good morrow and well met! Welcome, again, to *Arx Montium*. I see your fishing expedition was successful."

"Greetings to you, Captain Geoffrey. And yes, it worked out rather well, all things considered. New ingredients for our soup of learning, I think." The Sorcerer indicated the boys as the old mule snorted.

"How stand the courses at this time, Captain? Any news of import?"

The young captain ran a finger across his short beard, squinted as he looked west, then turned back to address the old Sorcerer.

"There has been some disturbance, Master Silvestrus, but I am unsure of what to make of it. It was Lord Non-Dar of the Greensward *Aelvae* who first alerted us to this. This was before we received your missive. He told me he had run across several folk who did not seem to 'belong,' as he put it. They scooped up these fellows—three of them, in total, I believe—from just west of here, secured them for the night, with the plan of questioning them in the morning. However, the next day, all three were found, still bound, but with their throats cut."

Silvestrus' eyebrows rose in surprise.

"Now, the strangers were under tight *Aelvae* guard during the night, none of whom said they saw anything. How someone was able to penetrate an *Aelvae* camp, do this deed, then sneak off undetected is a mystery of the deeper sort. Lord Non-Dar was *not* happy about it, I can tell you. He asked me to relay this information to you and let you know he and his folk will keep diligently searching the area until the intruder or intruders are found. Oh, and he asked me to give you these."

The captain fished around in his side pouch for a moment, eventually retrieving three golden coins, which he gave to the Master Sorcerer. They were all triangular in shape.

Silvestrus gazed intently at the bright objects resting in his palm. "Ah, yes. We have seen these before. The Cin, it seems, have come to the Farther Westlands."

"The Cin? Truly, Master Silvestrus? For what possible purpose?"

Silvestrus looked at the captain as if measuring something in his thoughts before answering.

"I am not sure, Captain Geoffrey. Only that they seem to have been following our boys for some reason." The old man suddenly feigned an air of indifference. "Though it seems now that we have nothing to worry about, what with the diligence you, your men, and the *Aelvae* have shown. Other than that matter, any news of import?"

"Nay. Nothing of any consequence, Master Silvestrus. The summer has been quiet here, though we did see quite a display of the Northern-most lights and a rain of falling stars a few weeks back. None of the men could recall ever having witnessed such a spectacle." The young officer's eyes held a questioning look.

The old man did not meet the officer's gaze. "Ah, yes. I believe we witnessed the same phenomenon; surrounding Midsummer's Eve, perhaps if I remember correctly. Such displays are not common, that is true, but they do occur from time to time. I am sure there is a natural explanation for it. Now, tell me, have any of the other Apprentices begun to report to the Collegium as yet?"

"Only the *Advenae,* in groups of two and three, beginning last week —all looking scared." The officer gave the Sorcerer a wink.

"As well they should. None yet of the *Indigenae*—the Upperclass— then?"

"No. I believe the only ones here about are those few who stayed the summer—Prince Zoarr being chief among them, I'd say."

"I see. Well, thank you, Captain. We are, as always, in your debt for the peace your constant vigilance provides."

"My thanks to you, Master Silvestrus. It is an honor to serve the Order. And I do not mind the scenery, either, though the winters are a bit frosty, I must confess one day coming, I will allow myself, one day, the leisure to take a turn to the Southlands. I understand the ladies there, especially among the high, are most comely, with an ear to music—and well-re-sourced."

"An excellent plan, Captain. Were I in your position, the same thought would occur to me. However, should you decide to follow your fortunes in that way, please have a care to train up one of your loyal and competent subalterns to assume your considerable responsibilities prior to commencing your absence from us."

"That I will, Master Silvestrus, on my word. Now, what other service may we provide for you this day?"

"There is no need for you to trouble yourself, Captain. We are just passing through. If there is no objection, we will refresh ourselves in the barracks and see if we can wheedle Cook out of a late mid-day meal in the mess. Then we shall be off. I wish to make the forest surround by repose."

"As regards the commissary, Master Silvestrus, today's selection features Raugauld's culinary masterpiece: hash. Not on the order of that excellent stew you bring us from time to time—"

Rolland made a face to his fellow Apprentices at the reference to the bearish casserole.

"—but filling, nonetheless. Now, however, I must return to my duties, but I will see to it that all are alerted."

The old man nodded. "My most heart-felt thanks, Captain."

Silvestrus signaled to the boys, who fell in once again behind the cart, and the party made its way through the lesser gate door. The guards saluted smartly as they passed.

Thaddeus was not sure what he had expected to see, but what he did see was breathtaking. Gazing northeast, he beheld a vast forested plain stretched out far below them. At the far horizon, he made out a stark white border, though he was not sure if this represented mountains or some other feature.

Glancing around, he found that the mountain gate sheltered a small military garrison with barracks, stables, storage, and administrative buildings, all laid out in straight lines. A squared-off yard was being used by at least two squads of soldiers. One group was drilling with pikes in marching formation while another loosed bolts from crossbows from varying distances at three straw men on uprights.

"All right, lads, we will take mid-day in the mess, with a proper table and chairs for a change." The old man stepped down lightly, handing the reins to Thaddeus. "See to Asullus' needs, square up the cart, and then join me. I will be inside that low building on the right. Do not neglect *latrina et lavatio*—commode and ablutions—afterward. Then come to me."

After rejoining, the Apprentices and their Master were guided to the mess hall, though it was obvious that Silvestrus already knew the way. There was a momentary silence upon their entrance into the moderate-sized and spartan dining hall as the garrison troops marked the visitors' arrival. Low conversations quickly resumed, however, once the Sorcerer and his charges joined the end of the serving line to wait their turn.

Anders, directly behind his master, looked down upon his plate after the cook's assistant had ladled a large quantity of the day's special onto his tin flatware. He turned to his tall brother.

"Yes, it's as the Captain said: hash of some sort."

Thaddeus received his portion, then ducked his head down and inhaled.

"It smells well enough. I think it should be all right," he replied.

"Just so there's no bear meat in it," Rolland added earnestly.

"You boys eat there," Silvestrus said, pointing to an empty patch at the end of one of the benches at a plain, planked table. "I am going to sit over there." The old man indicated what Thaddeus realized must be the officers' table. "I need to have a word with Captain Geoffrey. Now you three stay out of trouble," he added with a stern look before turning on his heel and walking off.

The boys took their assigned seats, got out their knives, and set to work on their simple repast.

One of the grizzled veterans sitting close by turned to regard the boys.

"So, yer're concerned about bears in yer victuals, are ye?" The man spoke with a twinkle in his eye.

Rolland took up the soldier's challenge without batting an eye. "Aye, that's true, officer. We don't hold with the eating of such creatures."

Thaddeus and Anders exchanged looks behind Rolland's back.

"Ah, no officer am I, young 'uns. 'Tis Sergeant Grunius you be speaking with. But perchance give some thought to yer decision about the consuming of the bear. Might it be better for yer to be eating the snarling brown one than to suffer from the reverse?"

Here, the men sitting with Grunius laughed and, after Thaddeus and Anders joined them, Rolland grumbled under his breath and began to aggressively shovel the day's hash into his mouth without looking up.

Following the plain, though generous, mid-day, Master Silvestrus instructed his charges to thank their host for his board and prepare Asullus and the cart for their journey East.

Captain Geoffrey walked with Silvestrus out of the mess hall, up to the courtyard, and through the guard gate.

"Thank you, again, Captain. Your service is always appreciated. I think now that we are beyond the wider world and soon to be safely within the confines of the Forest Surround, our boys will have less to be looking over their shoulders for. Yet I would ask you to remain alert for this next little while, advising me as to anything untoward."

The tall commander smiled and bowed. "Farewell, Master Silvestrus. Have no concern. I will keep an eye out for any Cin or other men of that description. I will send word immediately should any be detected—though, as I have said, none have passed here to my knowledge. Otherwise, have an excellent academic year."

Silvestrus climbed up on the cart as Sergeant Grunius signaled for the guards to open the gate. At his master's nod, Thaddeus clucked and shook the reins lightly. Asullus snorted and moved forward toward the darkening forest.

The trail led rapidly down from *Arx Montium* into the green carpet that spread out before them. In the distance to the North, Thaddeus glimpsed what he took to be the sun glinting off a ringed temple of some sort. Silvestrus turned halfway round from his perch on the cart.

"Well, boys, now we begin the last leg of our journey. It is now straight across this great forest to the *Collegium.* We will follow that path you see going down into the foothills and camp tonight in mid-forest, then press on come morning. If all goes well, we should reach the College, perhaps, by tomorrow afternoon.

Rolland looked up. "Master, the valley below is lush and green. Yet, as we approached Mountain Guard, it seemed as if winter had already come. I don't—"

"Yes, *Arx Montium* is a wall of ice and rock that protects this valley, Rolland. They have four seasons here, like most other places, but the spring here comes earlier, the summer lingers longer, the fall is brighter, and the winter snow is less frigid. This forest lies on the path to a renowned College of Sorcery, after all. I am sure you understand. Well, Asullus, I believe you know the way."

"Aye, as well as yerself, Master, as I think ye know. So, lads, I be an old mule leader, no' a sheepherder. Haw-haw!" Asullus moved sure-footedly down onto the green-carpeted plain, cart and passengers jouncing behind him.

On a sudden impulse, Thaddeus looked back over his shoulder, and he beheld a little purple *Spritae* hovering at tree height off to one side. As soon as she realized she'd been seen, she waved and, in a trice, whirled in midair and was gone.

Thaddeus acknowledged the tiny creature's salutation but suspected she'd not seen it. He thought back to Beewicke and how he had lived his life up to this point, right under the nose of the Fey, but had never seen even one of them. Now, with his eyes opened, he saw them everywhere —spoke with them, even had commerce with them.

Until now, he'd had no idea of the depth and breadth of the world that surrounded him, all unknowing. And this was but a taste, he imagined, of what might come to be.

Thaddeus walked in the woods heading back to camp from where he had relieved himself. On the way, Morphia had materialized from somewhere in the bush, and he had started back in surprise, particularly since he'd just been thinking about her.

Morphia fell to the ground, rolling around, laughing at catching a human in a compromising situation. This seemed to be a favorite pastime of *the wee folk,* as Asullus dubbed them. After, she flew at his shoulder, and they talked as he walked—a rare treat granted only to him.

"But why is it you send off sparks every time you come within a pace of Rolland? Has he done you harm?" Thaddeus asked earnestly.

Small red spots blossomed on the *Spritae*'s cheeks. "No. But I will tell you, Lord in Beewicke, if you shall give me your word you will tell no other. Ever."

"All right, Morphia. I give you my word."

"Very well. It is…my temper, I suppose. At the Convent of the Silent Sisters, I was so irritated that he was almost able to slip beyond me on several occasions. It damaged my pride, and it was embarrassing for me to admit such to Master Silvestrus. Then, Rolland threatened me with his knife. The Fey do not well tolerate such behaviors toward their persons from humans. Additionally, I suppose I chose to believe that it was Rolland's idea to bind me with cobwebs, and I was looking for an opportunity for a fair return.

"But now that we have been together, I…I have come to feel differently about him—about all of you, really. And I am sorry for my *vanitas.* There! That's as much honesty as I choose to give this night, and usually, we Fey do not give any at all." Morphia's eyes were shining brightly.

"Thank you, small one. I shall hold this in my heart always."

34

The Old Man
Senex

"And thank you, again, Morphia," Thaddeus said under his breath. "For all you have done for us. I hope you never want for honey."

"Thaddeus, who are you talking to?" Anders asked.

"I was just saying goodbye to a friend. Morphia was leaving us."

"Oh. I see. Well, I'm sure we'll see her again. So, Taddy, we're almost there. I have to say I'm pretty excited. Are you?"

"Yes. Quite a bit, actually."

"Rolland, how about you? Are you excited?" Anders asked.

"I suppose so. I just hope it's a place where everybody minds their own business. I don't fancy a lot of ignorant questions about this and that."

They walked easily along the forest path and did not stop for even-tide until moonrise. The boys went through their well-practiced camp routines, and in a relatively short time, were sitting on logs around a cheery campfire contentedly picking their teeth.

"Master," the short Apprentice began.

"Yes, Anders?"

"May I ask a question concerning *Arx Montium*?"

"Of course."

"As I understand it, Master, the line of mountains comprising the Great Wall stretches from the gate all the way to the Great Northern Fastness—and from the Southeast to the towering Golden Range. It's but a long line of snow-covered rocks sticking up out of the earth at an angle, cutting in front of the more regular geography. And the only thing, it is said, of any consequence that lies beyond *Arx Montium* is the *Collegium* itself—a peculiar construction of Nature, it seems. Primus even said that he considered the range an 'unnatural formation.' Is that true, Master?"

The Sorcerer puffed his pipe for a moment. "Yes, that would be the right of it." Silence returned to the group.

"Master, would you tell us, then, of the Mountain Guard?"

The old man looked thoughtful for a time, then sighed. "Very well, Anders. I suppose there is no harm to be had in it. So…*Arx Montium*. We have spoken several times of the Invasion of the East under the last Emperor. During the final battle—but several hundred leagues away from where the Imperial Army was being chopped to pieces—a group of Sorcerers from the *Collegium* had made its way, in stealth, to Cinoton, the capital of the Cin. There, they hoped to find some way to render impotent the Magicks' power of the Eastern Mages and save what remained of the Imperial Army. Regrettably, they were altogether unsuccessful.

"It was discovered, however, that the, um, magical energy from which the mages of the East—the Ancient Ones as they are called— seemed to be drawing their power, appeared to have its origin, *omnino*, in an ancient, tall and rather ugly tower—the Tower of the East, as it is known—that sat in the middle of the square of that selfsame city. It was not difficult to identify, as it was bathed in all manner of glowing colors with bursts of lightning and flames shooting out from it at intervals. It seemed to hold a life force of its own.

"The leader of the Imperial Sorcerous raiding party, if you will, was a practitioner named Portoman, one of the truly Wise, gifted with great power and skill. It was he who first broached the idea of making away with the Cinnian Tower. We—that is, he—intuited that the artifact was the source of the Eastern Mages' power, a power so much different from our own, even at its great distance from the battlefield. That being the case, he put forth the argument that removing the Tower from the land of the Cin would be akin to striking away the burning torch set to ignite the bonfire.

"Now, this was a bold and dangerous design. What if Portoman were wrong, and the Tower was in no way connected to the Mages' powers? Then the Sorcerers' quest would have failed, and they would expose themselves, limiting any further attempt to succor the Imperial Army and forestall disaster.

"And what if the Tower could not be destroyed or moved? The same result. And what if the forces with which the Tower were imbued would call an alarm and signal others to come to its aid, or, itself, resist the attempted abduction, and strike out? These and many other questions were considered in urgent debates. They knew lives were being lost by the second, you see.

"In the end, Portoman had his way, and the group of Sorcerers gambled that if it could not be destroyed in time, removing the Cinnian Tower from its lodgings and safeguarding it elsewhere was the best they could hope for. So, the Sorcerers joined together—much as I understand you three did with Rolland's nose—and the Tower was successfully uprooted and made off with."

"Master," Rolland spoke, his eyes alight. "Were the Westlands Sorcerers detected? What happened to them?"

"Of a surety they were detected. How could they not be? A great hue and cry were raised. However, something extraordinary occurred. It was as if water had, of a sudden, been poured over that hypothetical bonfire I alluded to earlier. The Eastern Mages' flames went out, so to speak. Their power seemed to falter, both at the site of the battle and, also, once Portoman and his colleagues had managed to cross the border. They could only continue the pursuit of the Sorcerers as mortal men. No Magicks, no spells were employed. It was as if they had been drained of all force and initiative."

The old man paused to take a swig from a wineskin he'd fetched out from his robes and then stoppered and returned it to the confines of his garment.

"Well, the Westlands Sorcerers were as astounded as the Ancient Ones, I dare say. It was thereby confirmed that the Mages' powers were inextricably intertwined and beholden to the Cinnian Tower—that ugly congregate of stone and mortar."

"So, they made off with their score? They got clean away?" Rolland pressed.

"Yes and no, boy. The surviving Sorcerers were able to make their way back to the Westlands with their great prize, but it was too late to save the Legions of the Imperial Army—which, by that time, already lay butchered in the baking sun."

"Did the Ancient Ones and the Cinnian Army follow the Imperial Sorcerers to try to get their Tower back?" Thaddeus asked.

"No, lad. It was most peculiar. As I have said, once the Westlands' Sorcerers got just beyond the border of the Land of the Cin, the pursuers suddenly and abruptly gave up their pursuit. They just stopped. No one knows why. It is one of the several thousand mysteries that surround that disastrous campaign."

"The 'surviving Sorcerers,' Master?"

"Ah, quick Anders. Yes, not all the Sorcerers survived, so to speak. Portoman himself, alone of the group, did not return home, at least not as you might count such things. At some point in the theft, he was struck with madness and never recovered, despite best efforts to heal him. Adjurford, his second, later postulated that in his role as leader of the attack on the Tower of the Cin, Portoman witnessed or experienced something that overwhelmed him. None there were who could ascertain what had happened."

"And what of the fate of the Tower, Master?"

"Ah, well, that brings us back to *Arx Montium*. The Cinnian Tower —the very Tower of which we have been speaking—stands now, as it has for the last thousand years, on the grounds of the *Collegium Sorcerorum*. Yes, the College has for the past millennium played host to it, where we refer to it as the Tower of the East."

Anders shifted position. "Master, if the Tower has been with the *Collegium* all this time, what has been learned from the study of it?"

"Another good question, Anders. The answer is, however, very little. The knowledge the Tower holds has remained inaccessible. No one has been able to reveal its true function. It has, all this time, remained an enigma woven into a mystery —a riddle, floating in a mist. In recent years, however, one of the junior faculty claims to have teased out some knowledge of its secrets…although…it is difficult to determine the exact verity there."

"Master," Thaddeus queried, "what of the fate of the Emperor, Tyrannus Superbus? Was he killed with his men?"

"No. It is my understanding he was captured—wounded but still fighting. Concerning his subsequent fate, the records are impenetrably silent. All that is known from the few surviving Westlanders with knowledge of the event is that he was yet living when taken away."

"Master, if the Cin have not pursued it in all this time, why is the Mountain Guard fortress still necessary to protect it?"

"Because, Rolland, the fact that they did not come immediately does not mean they will not come eventually. Mountain Guard was created to defend against such an event. Over time, however, only a chosen few of the stewards who now man that fortress actually know the real reason for their task and sacrifice.

"But, the Cin have not come—not yet, at least. And for that, we should all be extremely grateful."

"Master, Thaddeus made the same point these few days past."

"Really? Is this so, Thaddeus? Tell me of your thoughts regarding the matter." Silvestrus stared at him intently. "Be sure to omit nothing."

Feeling exposed and uncomfortable, Thaddeus hesitantly outlined his reasoning.

"Well, Master. You see, it occurred to me that while the Westlands lost a million men a thousand years ago, the Easterners never responded, even though their force, as I understand it, was at the time intact. And that's been the case ever since. So, I was wondering, why haven't they come West? It seems like there'd be nothing to stop them. The *Centurio Prior*, Helveticus, said that if it were up to him, he'd pick out someone to lead the West, just in case the Cin or someone else do decide to come. I don't know about such things, but it sounds right to me to be alert."

Silvestrus listened carefully, then looked down at the ground for a moment before raising his head to reveal a wide smile—one of the first the boys had seen.

"Well done, Thaddeus. You have hit on exactly the problem that has been gnawing at the back of my mind for quite a long time. If anything further occurs to you regarding this matter, let me know immediately."

"Yes, Master."

"Oh, Master?" Anders, head down, looked very uncomfortable. Beads of sweat stood out on his brow despite the temperate evening.

"Yes, Anders," his master said with a certain expectation he always showed toward Anders, whether the boy presented a question or a hypothesis.

"There is a thing I have been puzzling over for some time and I wish to ask you about it. I think I may have the right of it by now, but it may represent knowledge you would rather wish we did not share at this time, or, perhaps, *never*. I am, therefore, hesitant to make mention of it, though you have always taken pains to assure us of the inviolate nature of any quest for knowledge."

"That is quite a preamble, my boy. You should probably get on with it."

"Um, yes, Master. I…that is…I believe that it may be possible… What I mean to say is… Well, to begin with—"

"We are all of us only on this world for a relatively short time, young Anders. But before my own time is gone, I should like to hear your postulation."

"Yes, of course, Master. It is quite to the point. Master—"

"Yes?"

"Master, Ithinkyouweretherethen!" The words tumbled out in a rush.

"What? What did he say, Thaddeus?" Rolland asked, leaning forward.

"He said he thought the Master was there then," Thaddeus replied.

"What? Where? When?" Rolland asked, looking puzzled.

"On the Eastern campaign with the old Emperor Tyrannus Superbus —he was right there, at the Great Invasion of the Cin, I imagine. Right, Anders?" Thaddeus posited.

Anders nodded slowly, not daring to look up.

"What? Anders, have you gone and lost those legendary wits of yours? How in the world can you—?"

Silvestrus was now smiling openly. He held up a hand. "It is all right, Rolland. He is right, you know. How did you find me out, clever boy?"

"What? What? How…?" the thief sputtered in disbelief.

"Rolland, you have taken to saying 'what' quite a lot lately. Why not listen to what Anders has to say?"

Anders swallowed, then continued. "Well, Master, nothing that was major. It was mainly putting together small bits here and there that you have let out—"

Silvestrus nodded. "Perhaps you mean, 'let slip'?"

Anders smiled shyly and continued.

"I first thought about it that night in Meadsville, when you told us about the Eastern Invasion. You were talking about the last battle, and you said…you said, 'they bled, they screamed, they died. We only wanted to…' And you stopped. So…it was after I had rehearsed that phrase over in my mind I thought it sounded to me very much like something someone who had been there might say. However, of course, there was the problem of the thousand-year interval between now and then."

"A formidable problem, I would have thought," the old man said, still smiling.

"Yes, Master. But you, I believe, solved that one by telling us that Sorcerers are long-lived, even up to several hundred years, you said. So, if several hundred years, I thought, then why not a thousand years now and then? Also, during our recent sojourn at Terminus, the Centurion Major, Helveticus, told us it was a Sorcerer named Silvestrus who had cursed them.

"The last bit of thought I needed came just now when you described the events leading up to the establishment of *Arx Montium.* Again, it sounded very much like the kind of detail only one who had been there would possess. Taken all together, well… There it is, I think." Anders spread his hands and shrugged.

"And so, you asked me about *Arx Montium* a-purpose, no doubt. And most of what I told you, you had already known, perhaps, from your erudite and seemingly omniscient tutors. Yes?"

The short boy nodded, reddening.

"Ha! Outfoxed by my own cleverness. Well done, Anders, well done." The young scholar blushed but looked pleased.

Silence again descended on the group, as the realization began to slowly dawn on the Apprentices that they faced a man who had lived in this world for more than ten centuries. The impact of this understanding rendered them silent.

After an extended period, the thief of Fountaindale meekly cleared his throat and spoke. "Master, um, that is, may I ask a question about… about that time?"

"Ah, Rolland. I know you would like to know more—from someone who was there, so to speak. Know, however, that while they concern things of greatness, these memories are not, for me, happy ones. And I am not in the habit of sharing such thoughts with my Apprentices, in any case."

He slapped his knees as if he were about to get up and stop the conversation. But then, he apparently thought better of it.

"However, since a great deal has been shared, I will share a few things more. Take note: it will be up to me to decide which. That said, what is your question?"

"Master, it's as Thaddeus asked—why didn't the Cin ever come West in all this time?"

"No one knows why the Cin have not come West. Indeed nothing has stood in their way these long centuries. Personally, I believe it must have something to do with the Cinnian Tower itself, but I have no idea as to specifics. Perhaps one of you lads will be able to discover it one day. But in the meantime, there is *Arx Montium.* Yes, sturdy and staunch it stands—unmoving, unchanging, unassailable. It also has another useful, if minor, function in that it serves as an excellent deterrent to the idly curious.

"In older times, I understand, commoners would travel from all over the Westlands to the *Collegium* demanding this remedy, or that bag of gold, from the Brothers at the College for any minor frustration or grievance. Nowadays, those who come must have, by definition, demonstrably greater motivation and, therefore, purpose. We, as a result, treat their petitions with greater gravity.

"In any case, that wall possesses only one vulnerability. But it is, of course, something that I never discuss."

The boys looked at him expectantly but knew their Master would not speak further.

With that, Silvestrus laughed to himself and abruptly stood. "All right, my fine young *Advenae,* you have kept me at it long enough and extracted from me already too much in the way of things best kept secret. Now off to your bedrolls with you! Good repose. Tomorrow, the *Collegium!*"

"Oh, um, Master," Rolland called.

Silvestrus turned from the opening of his tent, one hand on the flap. "Yes, Rolland?" he asked wearily. "It is a matter to which great importance is attached, I hope?"

"Master, are we then to hold secret all you have told us?" There was an air of challenge in the young redhead's voice.

Silvestrus merely barked a laugh. "Who is there alive that would dare believe it? Again—and *finally*—good repose!"

It was some time before Thaddeus heard the regular snoring of his two friends. Their discussions concerning this new information had carried on through half the night. But later, when it became quiet, Thaddeus still could not sleep. Too many exciting images were parading through in his mind concerning the events of a millennia ago. It was as if voices from the past were speaking to him.

After a time, though, he stirred and realized that there were actual voices. They were coming from outside the tent. But he could not decipher their meaning. Gingerly, he lifted the edge of the tent a handspan nearest his ear and listened.

"…asleep, as I said. There is no watch, only the three children. Let us be about it and be gone," said a tenor's voice in a silvery tone.

"If you are certain concerning this, then we should proceed," responded a second speaker with a syrupy quality.

"I agree. Such things are best done quickly. Here, give me that. Now stand away. This will not take long," the first voice said matter-of-factly.

Thaddeus was immediately filled with alarm. Intruders in the camp! Could these be the evil men who had been following them all along?

Those who wanted to kill him and his friends? It sounded like they were preparing to make an attack on the Master.

Without thinking, Thaddeus grabbed his dagger, yanked up the tent wall, rolled out, and jumped to his feet in one smooth motion. Only afterward did he consider that he had left two potential allies-in-arms still sleeping.

"Hold, villains!" the young beekeeper cried, brandishing his knife. "Attempt to harm my Master, and you'll have to deal with me!"

Thaddeus, roused for action, even if it meant battle, noted the moonlight shining down—sufficient to illuminate the camp. His first thought was that he had surprised three young boys—of Anders' height or less—who stood gaping at him. One was holding a scroll, while the one on the left proffered a quill and ink bottle, and the third offered his back as a writing table.

The three were attired in forest garb, which caused them to blend in with their surroundings. Each carried a dagger on one hip, and a short sword on the other. Bows and quivers were slung over their backs. They were slight of frame, but as Thaddeus stared, he revised his opinion upward as to their age. Their hair, gossamer and silvery, covered their ears, the points of which, however, protruded proudly therefrom. Their faces were beautiful with delicate, chiseled features.

All this was noted quickly, for, in the next instant, he was on his back with three sharp points at his neck. He could see the intruders more clearly now that they were leaning over him and staring intently.

"Hold, Al-Donn! This boy is *Amicus Faerrarum*!" Though serious in tone, the fellow's voice had a lilting quality to it.

"You are certain, Ko-Thas? He does not appear the type."

"A simple matter to resolve," said the third. With a flick of his wrist, he laid back Thaddeus' tunic to expose the Apprentice's left breast. The three gasped.

Suddenly, Thaddeus was hauled quickly to his feet by six hands.

"Our pardon, Friend. We were intent upon our mission, and our preoccupation with it fostered carelessness. I hope you have taken no hurt." The trio regarded him with concern.

Thaddeus wished to present himself as entirely in control as if it had been his intention all along to lure these strangers into gross over-confidence by allowing himself to appear to have been taken so quickly.

"Oh, not at all. I am well. But, um, who are you, and what do you do here at this hour of the night?"

"As you, yourself, have given us no name, I will assume, for the moment, you are, perhaps, an Apprentice who travels with Master Silvestrus on his way to the *Collegium*. Yes?"

Thaddeus nodded. He felt that these creatures seemed—now—to offer him no immediate threat. He told himself he should probably practice the manners his parents had always expected him to show in public. However, it was also true that, but a moment ago, he had had three *Aelvae* knives at his throat.

"Ah. Then, young one, allow me to introduce myself. I am Non-Dar of the Greensward *Aelvae*. My companions: Al-Donn and Ko-Thas." The speaker fell silent and joined the other two in looking expectantly at the tall Apprentice.

"Oh. I'm Thaddeus, son of Cedric…of Beewicke." He had, of late, become hesitant in adding this last, beginning to dread the response.

"Ah, Beewicke. Yes, where the honey comes from."

A brief grimace stole across the Apprentice's face.

"I thought I noted the fragrance on you. Well met, then, Thaddeus of Beewicke. You ask after our mission. Know that your Master had expressed concern regarding the presence of men of the East—Cin, I believe you call them—in these woods.

"As it chanced, we did, indeed, run into such, lurking about the down-pass from *Arx Montium*. We sought to bring them to Silvestrus for close questioning as to their intentions and motives here, but, alas, they resisted. A few of their fellows were killed, but the remainder we gathered and questioned—with some stringency, it is true. That is until they each, at some time during the night, had their throats cut. By whom or how, we can not determine. Several of us now seek their trail. And it looks as if they either came from or were going to the South-West swamps."

Non-Dar paused to look away, then quickly back again, resuming his report. "Their boldness and temerity are impressive. No one unfriendly to our People has ever before in the history of the *Aelvae* penetrated so far into these woods for any unwelcome purpose."

The speaker stopped to earnestly look the young boy in the eye. "Hear this, Thaddeus of Beewicke, the intruders seem to believe three young boys are their quarry. Therefore, we deem it likely that it is you they seek. And what it is they seek, we are convinced, is your life. And not just for their own wish. They are employed in this by one of the Mighty, though we could not determine who. Or what.

"Knowing this, *Amicus Faerrarum*, proceed with extreme caution, and never leave your Master's side. If they, with their intent, could penetrate even thus far, well..." Non-Dar gravely spread his hands wide, then clapped. "In any event, tell your Master we shall not be slack in our vigilance."

Non-Dar indicated the writing materials held by his cohort and continued. "Given these events, we were traveling close to you this night and thought to leave word with your Master that the Wood is otherwise quiet and the *Orbis Magnus* silent. Finding all asleep, we desired to disturb no one, so we had resolved to leave a message regarding the above. Now that we find you awake and alert, might you be so good as to deliver the message for us?"

"Yes, of course. It would be my pleasure to serve."

Now that everything was explained, the tension drained away from Thaddeus. The *Aelvae,* indeed, did seem benign in their intent. He had simply caught them unawares. He would have acted similarly under the same circumstance. He extended his hand, and the chief *Aelvae* placed the rolled-up script in the Apprentice's palm.

"Ah, excellent. Our thanks. Fare thee well, then, Thaddeus of Beewicke, *Amicus Faerarrum.* Travel with ease in this forest, but beware: Stay close to your Master." In a swirl of shadow, they were gone.

Thaddeus' mind swung about in a whirlpool of emotions. Threats made, threats averted, and then more threats. And, *Aelvae!* He could scarce believe what had just happened to him, let alone think to repeat it. Surely no experience in Beewicke had ever prepared him for tonight's events.

Looking about him, he decided that he was in no position to expect rest, given the events of the long day. He decided he would take a turn about the campsite's periphery. Perhaps that would serve to lessen his excitement and beckon sleep.

He set out to the North and had gone halfway around when his ears detected a muted *crack.* Thaddeus was a skilled enough woodsman to know that only a heavy animal could cause such a sound. And heavier animals, especially those looking for prey, were not so clumsy as to betray their presence with a twig-snap.

He spun to his left, the direction from which the sound had come. Straining his eyes, he could see nothing moving in the moonlight.

What had that been?

He walked stealthily toward the forest edge and examined the ground carefully. He could see nothing.

Wait! Was that a slight movement among the trees?

He whipped his dagger out, then froze, intently scanning the area. No signs. Well, there was nothing for it but to go and look. He took a step.

With a sudden jolt, he felt himself yanked up into the air. Simultaneously, he saw a shadow leap from behind a tree and circle, running behind him. Before he could cry out, he felt a blow to the back of his head.

Then, nothing.

As Thaddeus gradually came to his senses, he saw that the world was upside down. Then, after a moment, he understood that it was he who was upside down—suspended from a tree limb by some tether, the other end of which was wrapped tightly around his left ankle as he dangled and swayed back and forth.

What a milk-liver dolt!

He'd fallen into a trap he was both setting and avoiding almost since he'd learned to walk.

Then, a voice. "Ah, you are awake. Good. There is no need to try to shift around—you will only make yourself dizzy. I will come around into your line of vision."

A man of average height but slightly bent over and walking with a limp hove into Thaddeus' line of sight. He wore a hooded cloak pulled around him and muddied boots. The moonlight revealed the outline of an unremarkable face, with a pair of old, whitened scars tracking across the otherwise smooth visage.

"You are, I believe, the one they call Thaddeus? Yes? Do not worry or be shy in any denial—I have confidence in my sources."

Thaddeus reached up for his ankle to untie the cord that bound him, but it would not budge. After a few moments, fatigue coupled with cramping was the victor, and he straightened back down again to face the earth, where he saw his empty dagger sheath lying close by with his three gold coins and the greenstone directly beneath him. *They must have fallen out of my pouch*, he thought.

"Congratulations, beekeeper! In my best days, I could not have held that pose for as long as you just did." The man smiled.

Who are you? What do you want?

Thaddeus wanted to speak, but his gag prevented him. An inadvertent taste informed him it had been used previously. He hoped the man would continue talking, as he wanted to try to place the stranger's accent, which was eluding him.

"Oh, you are likely curious. My, yes, manners. Apologies. I am known by many names, but you can call me Solon. As for my station, I have, these years past, found that I wish only to be left alone on my estate with my women, and the leisure to sift through the reminders— trophies, that is—of my destructive but otherwise fulfilling life. However, to achieve that life, I am bidden to take yours. Alas."

The man paused a moment to survey the campsite not far off.

"Everyone still abed? Good. Anyway, as I was saying—alas. You seem like a good fellow. At least that is my opinion from having followed you over this time. By the way, congratulations again on having such powerful and resourceful friends. Sorcerers, skilled warriors, subtle *Aelvae*— and all at your age. Impressive."

Thaddeus was thinking furiously. Gymnastics did not work. Hopefully, this Solon would keep talking, and soon Master Silvestrus or the *Aelvae* would somehow intuit his distress and come to his aid.

"You know, in addition to having powerful friends, you must yourself be somehow important. By that, I mean, look at me, a Cinnian, here in this strange land, set to assassinate a stripling lad—and possibly his companions if I can get to them—for no other reason than that you are the subject of a commission. But what a commission! Whoever receives a commission like this?"

The limping man chuckled to himself, then continued. "Of course, truth be known, it was not a commission as much as it was a set of orders —a commandment, really, and personal. 'Locate four boys traveling with a Master Sorcerer and kill them, especially their leader.' That was what I had been charged to do. Pretty thin soup, yes? But there was no declining this one. It was from the Emperor—I mean to say the *future* Emperor—himself. And he intimated it had been passed down to him from 'on high.' Now, I would give a Din or two to know what is 'on high' to a Cinnian Emperor."

Cinnian! Then the Master was right! But Thaddeus began to think it would not make a difference. His head was starting to swim, and things were growing dark.

"Well, much as I hate to, time to get to work. Hmm. 'On high.' Wonder if he means the *Daemon*? Oh, well."

The limping assassin began to advance on Thaddeus. He pulled out what looked like an exceedingly sharp butcher's knife and continued speaking conversationally.

"I don't know why it's so, but they insist they have to have the head. I even had to purchase a leather bucket, myself, and bring it along with me, for this purpose."

As he bent over to pick up the bucket from off the ground near his feet, an amulet on a thong slipped out from his tunic and dangled in front of his chest. He straightened and, with his free hand, turned it so he could look at it.

"Now, here is a treasure, certainly. After conferring this commission, his Majesty sent me to get this from an old witching woman—Madrin, her name was. She told me many fancy—and, truth be told—unimaginable things. One of those things being that this amulet would guard me and keep me unseen from all enemies—Sorcerers and even the *Aelvae*—so that none could detect me. Well, it's worked so far, I must say, though not so much for those who came with me. I suppose you've already heard that the *Aelvae* got to them—and not so long ago—forcing me to have to get to *them*. What a waste. But, oh, well. Now, down now, down to business."

Thaddeus, his neck aching from looking up at his captor, contorted himself, and with one last glance searched the patch of ground near his head. He could touch it if he wanted to. And right there, a strange sight—a strange sight indeed.

His greenstone was pulsing in regular bright green bursts, like the beating of a heart.

"What is that, Marsia? Why is your greenstone glowing like that?"

"I—I do not know, Nannsi. It just started doing that. But I fear that it means something—something is happening to Thaddeus," she exclaimed as she gazed at the throbbing stone in her hand.

"Well, now, that is not to be, dear girl. My mother always told me when you have something that you share with the one you love, grasp it tightly and never let go. Here. Close your fist and don't let go."

The tall girl complied.

"Now, mayhap it will work best if we all try together. Sonnia! Come over here quickly and clasp Marsia's and my hands. That's it! Now all of us, think on Thaddeus and think hard!"

The stone's light abruptly stopped its pulsating, and its brightness grew in intensity till it filled the room. It was almost blinding.

Thaddeus saw the stone become bright and then brighter still. Straining with all his might, he reached out and grabbed ahold of it. The light flared through his fingers.

Solon stopped, then backed a step. "Is that your stone? I can hardly bear to look at it. Why is this happening now?" he asked the green-tinted air.

Thaddeus began to feel strength return to his limbs, to his entire body. He swung up in one smooth move, and, with a strength he didn't know he possessed, he snapped the cord that held him, falling to the ground and kicking his leg free of the length of restraint still attached. He rolled to his feet and faced his opponent—the man sent to kill him, his friends, and his Master.

"So, boy, you're on your feet now. Well and good. Cin's truth, killing your mark in battle is better than in cold blood, though I suppose in the end it's all the same." He took a step forward.

Thaddeus had always found Rolland's many antics amusing, but he knew the redhead had his serious side. This had been manifested in two things the street thief had taught him since they had begun their adventure together.

The first thing Rolland had taught him was *because you never know when you're going to lose your knife, always carry one in your shoe.*

Thaddeus reached down and withdrew a blade from his boot.

"Oh, now it's to be a fight, is it? Well, so much the better. I've needed a little practice. It does no one good to get rusty, but I think the outcome's to be the same. You see, I'm a trained assassin, boy, and you, why you're just backcountry fish bait." Solon shrugged off his hooded robe, letting it fall to the ground.

The second thing Rolland told him was *once you had your knife in your hand, you should have an idea of what to do with it*, especially if you were a thief…and especially if you fought dirty.

Thaddeus put himself into a practiced crouch while the assassin moved in confidently. The man faced the boy with his bad leg behind him. Perhaps that would be an opening.

Thaddeus remembered Rolland's peppered instruction. *No, go for the torso or the neck. If nothing else, he'll bleed out before long.*

Suddenly, Solon threw back his arm, then whipped it forward. Thaddeus acted with lightning speed but still felt the blade brush his side as it flew by him. Thaddeus winced, but as the limping man reached for another dagger, Thaddeus rushed forward.

Solon stepped back, and now a new knife—Thaddeus' own—appeared in his hand. He smiled.

The smile, however, turned to a puzzled frown as his game foot trod on the uncoiled rope that had, earlier, bound Thaddeus' leg. Upon that hesitation, Thaddeus completed his rush and came up hard against his older opponent.

With all his strength, he thrust his blade forward, feeling it pierce, then sink solidly into Solon's flesh. The assassin grunted, then gave a sigh.

Thaddeus stepped back as his attacker slid to the ground on his knees, the dagger falling from his hand.

The wounded assassin clumsily reached to his side, blood gushing out over his fingers, unstoppered. He looked down in amazement, then up to the boy standing near him.

"Well, what do you know? You must have powerful friends indeed, boy. Powerful friends. I—I—" Solon fell silent, toppled over, and never spoke again.

Thaddeus stood dumbfounded. He could hardly believe what had happened. The rush of feelings coursing through him all at once was overwhelming.

How could this be?

"Thaddeus," a gentle voice came from behind.

The tall boy whirled around to behold his master, framed in the moonlight, regarding him.

"Oh, Master, I have…I've just killed a man!" his quavering voice responded.

"Ah, well, so it seems, lad. Here, best to sit down a moment—let things settle a bit, you know. I will have a look."

Thaddeus sank to the ground, his mind numb with what had happened, while his master made his way over to the fallen Cinnian and began to examine the newly-dead corpse.

Silvestrus was methodical and thorough.

He's done this before, thought Thaddeus.

After several minutes, the Sorcerer rose and walked to where the Cinnian's cloak lay and examined it as well. The old man gazed for a moment at the leather bucket, then came to where Thaddeus sat in shock and sat down in front of him.

"Well, Thaddeus, I think this clears up some things." He proffered a rolled-up piece of parchment. "This is an official Imperial Cinnian document—a 'commission' it says, for one Solon of Tobruk, authorizing 'the assassinations of said persons traveling in the Farther Westlands.' Hmm. That is not very specific, now, is it? Ah, I see, we are all mentioned —at least by description. Hmm. How in the world did they come to know so much about us?"

Silvestrus read the document, then rerolled it and put it aside. "Now, here, look at this; a heavy purse, and it is full of golden Centi-Dins. Well, that solves that problem. And, finally, observe this very interesting amulet. I think it must be a Medallion of Non-Detection, or Metamorphosis. Interesting.

"So, we know who sent our assassin, how he had the means to support his mission, and how he avoided our eyes—not to mention those of the *Aelvae*. What we don't know is *why*? But I think I may have an idea about that."

"Why, then, did he do it, Master? Why did he try to kill me—to kill us?" Thaddeus found that he had begun to tremble.

"A good question, lad." The Master took stock of his overwrought Apprentice. "But perhaps a good question for another time."

"But, Master… I killed a man!" Thaddeus repeated, shaking harder.

"Yes, you did, Thaddeus, and well so. He was certainly going to kill you and take your head in the bargain. But the hour is late, and you have had more than your fill of adventure tonight. I believe I will, um, clean up the area. If you had not been so efficient, Charles could have helped us with the death and details, but not this night.

"You, on the other hand, need your rest. But I think sleep will not come so easily to you with all these recent, discordant memories. So, Thaddeus… *Obliviscatur eum!*"

Thaddeus shook his head.

What was it?

Then, thinking there was really nothing more to do, Thaddeus returned to his tent. His two best friends were sleeping where he had left them. And though his heart had stopped racing, his mind had not.

Aelvae. All his life, he had heard of the *Aelvae* and now to meet not one, but three—quite remarkable. Of course, he'd not put his best foot forward.

In the midst of these thoughts, came another thought—an intrusive one that seemed less his own, and more, somehow…from outside, as it were. If he had to give a direction to the thought, it would seem to be coming from…the East.

And there were feelings associated with the uninvited thought: anger and frustration—as if something greatly desired had slipped away. Accompanying this gnashing of teeth, as it were, was a further feeling of great urgency as if he had been given a warning: *We are not done with this yet.*

Thaddeus had no idea what these musings meant, but he somehow understood that they were, one: definitely not his own thoughts; two: he'd never experienced such as these before; and three: that they were very disturbing.

These concerns plagued his mind, convincing him that he would surely be wakeful for the remainder of the night. In this, however, he was mistaken.

After hardly any time at all, he had drifted off to sleep.

35

To the College
Ad Collegium

haddeus awoke with a start.

"Anders," he fairly shouted, shaking the shorter boy's shoulder. "Anders, get up! I saw *Aelvae!* They were right outside our tent. They spoke to me!"

Anders yawned. "That's nice, um, Thaddeus. Was Nannsi with them? I think that is… All right now," he added before drifting back off to sleep.

Hissing in frustration, Thaddeus turned to knee the redheaded thief in the ribs.

"Rolland! Wake up!"

"Bloody Hells! What are you on about, attacking me! Leave it off, Bee-Head!" He turned over to his other side, stringing a series of profanities together.

Grumbling to himself, Thaddeus slouched out of the tent and sought his Master to report the amazing events of the night. He found Silvestrus sitting on a log with his morning tea. The old man motioned Thaddeus to join him. "I believe we may have had visitors late last night, eh, my boy?"

"Yes, Master, but how did you—?"

"Why not tell me all about it?" Silvestrus smiled encouragingly at his Apprentice and bade him draw closer.

Thaddeus shook himself. "Oh, yes, of course. Well, Master, it began with a noise I heard just outside the

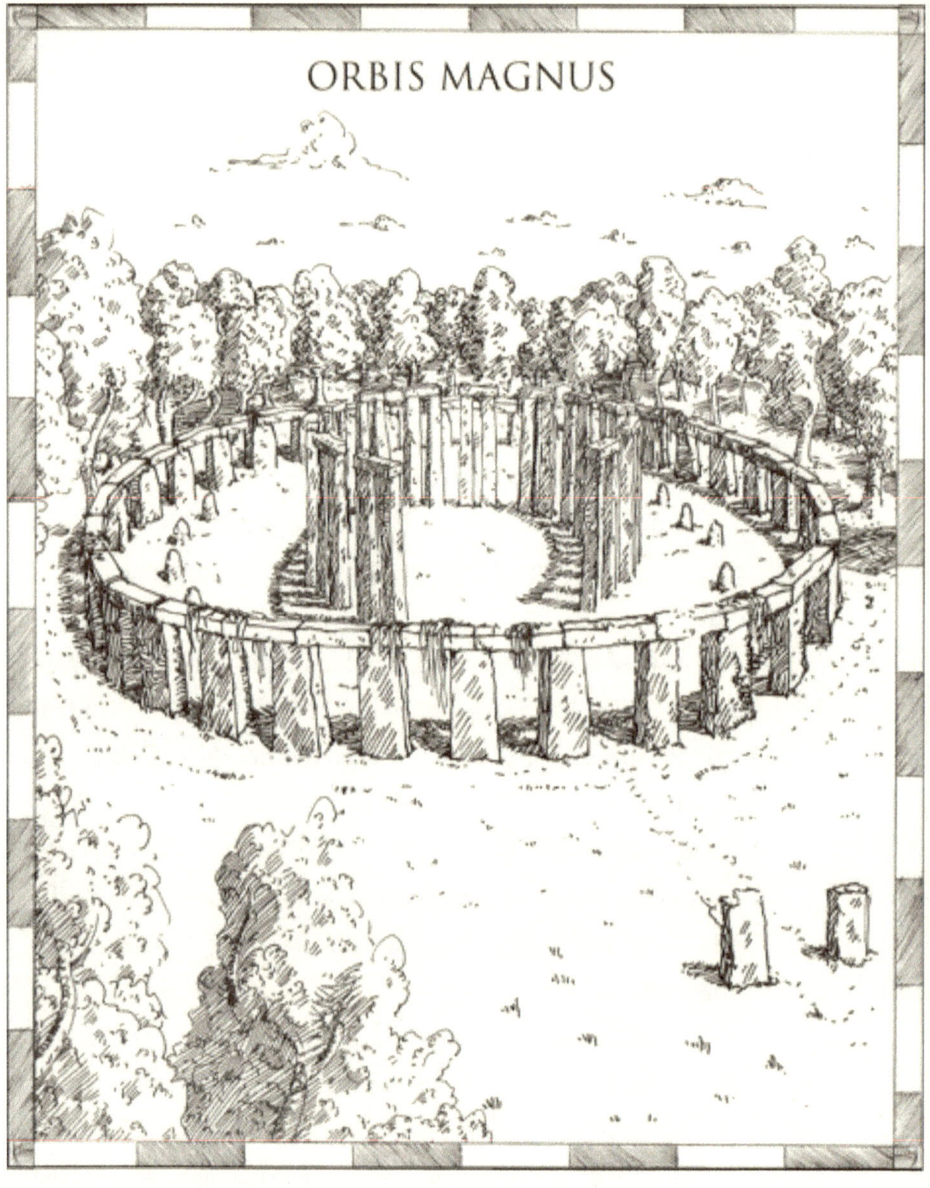

ORBIS MAGNUS

tent. After a moment, I could tell there were voices. I thought it might be those who were following us to do harm. I feared we might be in danger of some kind, so I…"

Glad, at last, to have an appreciative audience, Thaddeus quickly warmed to his subject and related the entire incident concerning the *Aelvae.*

Silvestrus took out his pipe and lit it as the recitation ended. "Ah, well, that is good news, at least. We will all travel with lighter hearts for the knowledge that the *Aelvae* watch over us so closely."

Thaddeus nodded in understanding, then decided to hazard a question. "Master, I have not met any of the *Aelvae* before. Do you see them often in this wood?"

"Generally speaking, Thaddeus, you do not see the *Aelvae* at all unless they wish it—and that only rarely. That you—a novice in this forest—surprised them, in addition, is unheard of. They are, no doubt, right now considering how to work through their shame at this lapse in concentration and considering how much of it they will be obliged to reveal to their fellows." Silvestrus laughed, shaking his head, then continued.

"I may decide not to be so charitable in regards to their sensibilities, however, in holding back that one of my fledgling Apprentices so easily took them unawares. Ha! They have had the better of me on occasion—and crowed about it after, that is certain enough." He chuckled to himself as if remembering something. His expression of delight lasted a goodly while before he spoke again.

"Now, to the subject of your question. There are, of course, different types of *Aelvae.* Those who live here in the forest are the Greensward *Aelvae.* They are organized into small bands of several families each, joined together in a loose tribal confederation. None excel them in woods lore. In general, we at the *Collegium* always strive to maintain good relations with them. They have proven to be staunch allies over time, though they have their own purposes and preferences. It is usually best not to intrude nor presume upon them. But it would be better for us to turn our attention to other matters now. If I were to go on regarding the *Aelvae*, we would be days late in reaching the College—not a choice you would favor, I think."

Thaddeus nodded. Then, gazing around the camp, he at once became alarmed. Something was different here. He was not one to boast about the grade of his forest craft, but he was confident in recognizing when something was not right.

"Master, something has altered. This is not the same forest we entered last evening. It's transformed."

"Yes. Applause to you on your powers of observation. Know that in this wood, one never finds the same path twice. I, myself, have wondered from time to time whether, perhaps, it is a ploy to bewilder intruders and potential enemies. But I think, more likely, it is the Fey simply being the Fey. It is their woods, after all, and of all things for which they show disdain, straight lines have the least competition. Never fear, though. The way toward it may change, but the destination does not."

Thaddeus nodded again, even though he did not quite understand. "Master, just one last question. The *Aelvae* mentioned the *Orbis Magnus*. I would think they meant to say the Great Ring, but I have not heard of it before. What is it, Master?"

"It is a construction, Thaddeus, located a bit north of here. It is said to have been built by the First."

"The First, Master?"

"The First were a people so designated because they are thought to be the original inhabitants of this land. A short, slender race—human, not Fey—and light brown in color with blue eyes, it is said. Timid they were, but with significant skills in stoneworking and cooperative engineering. Little else is known concerning them. It is believed that the *Orbis Magnus* represents the culmination of their collective cultural energies, the apex of their achievement, though its true purpose remains unknown." Silvestrus paused to sip his tea and exhaled slowly.

The tent flap fluttered, and Anders stumbled out and moved to join the group.

"Could it be a temple, Master?" Thaddeus asked.

"A temple? There is nothing in the literature nor the remains that exist to suggest a religious interpretation," Silvestrus replied.

"Then, Master, what could be its purpose?" Thaddeus queried.

"That is an excellent question. I will tell you what I know. It is believed to have been built over a period of approximately fifteen hundred years in three distinct stages. Its physical structure is that of a giant outer ring of thirty-six huge upright stones. There is a horseshoe arrangement of even larger interior stones —twelve pairs in number—with a capstone connecting each pair at the top. Each pair of stones with a top stone is separate from the other trios. At special places in the structure, one can, by sighting along certain grooves in specific stand-alone stones, predict the sun's position on the four Cardinal days—both *Aequinoctia*, Vernal and Autumnal, and the two *Solsti*, Winter and Summer."

"So, it is a calendar, Master?" Anders asked, glancing back over his shoulder as Rolland emerged from their tent.

"Yes, but more of a chronologue--a timepiece of a sort—none know for certain.

"Well, now that you are all up, let us see to our morning's repast so we can begin the final portion of our trek. I will speak with Asullus."

"Well, Master," Rolland said with growing anticipation. "What is it we shall have for break-fast, then?" he asked, smiling.

"Well, Apprentice," Silvestrus returned, "I imagine it shall be what-ever it is you decide to prepare." With that, the Master Sorcerer turned on his heel and began his brief journey over to the old mule's line.

Rolland's smile slipped from his face in bits and increments.

Dabbing a tat of porridge from his chin with a linen his mother had sent along, Anders looked curiously at the forest surrounding their camp. He paused a moment, then touched Thaddeus' arm.

"Thaddeus, look there. Wasn't that path there, on the right, over on the left yesterday?"

"Yes. You're right, Anders. I noticed that myself and mentioned it to Master Silvestrus. He says the *Aelvae* change things around each night to fool enemies."

The thief scoffed. "Well, whatever is the point in that? Can't trust them, I say. How would it be if someone changed the streets in Fountaindale each night? How could anyone find a mark to lift his wallet? Besides, what do they do, move all these trees? It's just tricksters, plain and simple."

"Rolland, you might want to wait till we're *out* of the woods before you criticize something *about* the woods, you know," Anders admonished.

While the three finished their break-fast, Thaddeus told his friends of the encounter with the *Aelvae*—the Silver Folk. As he spoke, he absently stroked his left side, then flinched. After a second attempt with a similar reaction, he lifted his tunic to reveal what looked to be a deep scratch, already healing.

"Thaddeus," Rolland said with concern, "that's a knife wound. How did you come by that?"

Thaddeus looked bewildered, then became composed and said, "That's not possible. I haven't been in any knife fight."

The thoughts tumbled through his head. *Why would Rolland make such an odd query? Knife fight? Should he be worried about the redhead's current state? Was he subject to some sort of humors?*

He quickly resumed his recital, ending with a question.

"Anders," he said, "do you think the way the forest paths change has something to do with the *Orbis Magnus?*"

Anders frowned with concentration. "You know, that's a good question. I don't know."

"Something he doesn't know?" Imagine that…" Rolland said, just loud enough to be heard.

Anders' head whipped around to the thief, but the redhead's attention seemed to be focused on a small stain on his tunic, which he began working with a fingernail as if he had no idea of who made such a comment.

Thaddeus began again. "I have to say, all these new things make my head spin. I don't understand any of it."

"It's possible we are not intended to, Thaddeus," Anders offered. "It could be part of the reason we're to go to the *Collegium*—to discover answers to these things. You know, if we already knew it all, there'd be no reason for such a school."

Thaddeus nodded in appreciation while Rolland snorted. "How do you know it's all real, in any case? Perhaps it's just a show to get us to believe in fantastic things that truly have no real basis," he said with a knowing look.

"I see," Anders said. "And what would be the reason that a group of adults would want to fool three lads like us into believing something is supernatural?"

"Why to…that is…uh, it could be…" Rolland cocked his head to one side as his voice drifted off.

"Exactly," Anders replied.

When they broke the campsite at last, the party set out with more trepidation than usual.

Today they would arrive at the *Collegium*.

On this day, Silvestrus did not take his usual nap in the cart but sat alert, reins in one hand, pipe in the other. As they walked, the boys clustered around the old gray mule, nervousness heightening each step that propelled them closer to their goal.

To relieve the anxiety, the Apprentices began to pepper the faithful beast with questions, Thaddeus being the first to ask.

"Asullus, what does the *Collegium* look like?

"'Tis a big hollow stone square set in a large meadow," the mule responded.

"What will our lives be like there?" Rolland wondered.

"Like any new experience—hard at first, easier as ye learn it up an' goes along."

"What are the Masters like?" Anders ventured.

"Mostly the same, though each be different."

"And how many Masters are there, Asullus?" Thaddeus asked.

"They tends, always, to have thirty-three, each wi' a different color, an' each wi' a different callin'."

"Really?" Anders said. "Why would that be?"

Asullus turned to look at the young scholar. He paused a moment as if deciding between accommodation and prudence. Then he spoke. "Because."

The three exchanged glances. It was clear they were not going to learn any more concerning that topic from Asullus this day.

After a moment, Rolland spoke up. "What about the other Apprentices?"

"Much as yourselves."

"How many are there?" Thaddeus asked, interested.

"Varies from year to year, it does. Ne'er seen less than four in a class. Ne'er seen more than twenty-four. Altogether, mayhap around fifty."

Anders, who had been staring at the giant redwoods as they passed, asked, "What will we do there?"

"A big servin' o' hard work—chores at the crack o' dawn, break-fast, chores, classes, mid-day, chores, classes, e'en-tide, chores, study, repose, an' then it begins all over again the next day."

"It's like that every day?" Rolland complained.

"Nay. Ye get some smidge o' time to yerselves on Saturn's Day an' Sun's Day. More, as ye advance."

"Will we all be together in our classes?" Thaddeus wondered, anxious to keep their camaraderie.

"More so at the beginnin'. 'Tis not unheard of o'er the years, though, fer each o' ye to be seekin' out this Master or that, fer further study in some special area as ha' captured yer fancy, or fer some topic as to which ye ha' shown a special knack."

"How long will we be at the College, I mean, the *Collegium*?" Rolland asked, now with a skeptical tone.

"Varies, though wi' most, 'tis four years. Some stay, some go… sometimes."

As Asullus padded along the soft forest floor path pulling the creaking wagon behind him, Anders, pacing by the old mule's rear quarters, reached over to pull out a stray twig from the old gray's tail. Then he asked thoughtfully, "What are the older Apprentices like?"

"All different, one from the other, as ye might imagine. Some'll treat ye kindly; some'll gi' ye a hard way to go. Most'll ignore ye, 'less ye do somethin' as to trouble 'em, whether a-purpose or by mischance. Then they'll make ye wish ye had no."

"And how about the Masters? How will they treat us?" Thaddeus wanted to know.

"More or less the same. Ye'll wish to be on yer best behavior wi' them, however. Their way o' dealin' wi' those as irritate them can run to the harsh, don' ye know. An' yer knowin' Master Silvestrus here'll be no protection fer ye. Should ye transgress badly, ye'll be sent back to yer home wi' ne'er another chance to try again."

Asullus grew silent for a moment before continuing. "There be one o' the faculty—a younger fellow—ye'd best be 'specially wary o', however. Him, 'tis worth avoidin', as ye can. An' ne'er gi' him an excuse to be at ye."

Anders strode up till he was even with Asullus' bridle. His look was intent. "Who is it, Asullus? Can you tell us his name?"

"Nay, I canno', 'tis forbidden, I am, to mention a Master by name in that way. But ye'll find out fer yerselves soon enou'."

"Well, is it hard work like that all year for us?" Rolland asked.

"Nay, 'tis different o'er the warm months. Then, ye may ha' more time to yerselves or to visit yer home, if ye're allowed, or to be sent on a quest."

"A quest? What is a quest?" Thaddeus was unfamiliar with the word. No one in Beewicke had ever spoken of a quest.

"This here *Collegium* was built to educate the young as has certain talents. These talents are supposed to be used in the service o' the public weal. So, from time to time, folks here an' aboot as have trouble wi' one thing an' another will write or e'en come in person to the *Collegium* to petition the Masters to help them wi' this or that problem. If 'tis a serious matter, a Master'll go. But if 'tis no' so bad, a likely lad'll often be sent to see what he can do. 'Tis a bit o' an honor to be selected fer such a task, as they say. I meself ha' ne'er heard o' them sendin' a *Tironis* on such a mission, though I suppose 'tis possible."

"How do they fare?" Thaddeus wondered.

"Mostly fair enou'. Though on occasion, one'll no' come back."

Here, a silence fell as the boys gave each other looks full of doubt and began to fidget.

"What did you say? Sometimes an Apprentice does not come back? I mean, does an Apprentice die? I mean, how is that possible?" Anders asked, visibly shaken.

"Aye. There be reasons why one o' ye may no' return. Sometimes one may no' care fer the quest he's on, an' decides it's past time to go on home. Sometimes one'll decide to run away—or, p'haps, get himself distracted, don' ye know.

"But, sometimes, it'll happen that the quest'll get the better o' the Apprentice, an' we'll be holdin' a service fer the lost one. Thanks be, 'tis no' so often, but I ha' been to two or three such. Sorcery is no' so much a life free o' risks, lads. Ye'll need to be clear on that, should ye take it in yer minds to continue on wi' this path. 'Tis one o' the reasons yer Masters take the pains they do in teachin' ye yer trade."

"What is it they will teach us?" Anders asked, his voice unsteady.

"Well, now, as ye might expect, all manner o' useful things. How to develop an' use yer powers fer the best. How to think. Mostly how to be a credit to yerselves while helpin' others as is less fortunate."

"There's another piece of it for us, though, isn't there, Asullus?" Thaddeus asked pointedly.

"How mean ye, laddie?"

"Our part in the Prophecy."

Asullus tossed his head, stealing a glance back at Silvestrus. The old man, however, was gazing placidly into the distance.

"Aye, lads, ye've hit on a most sensitive point here. Doubly blessed, ye are—no' only special to be chosen fer ye're being Sorcerous ones, but o' that group, bein' picked to tweak the fate o' all the rest. But heed me words when I tells ye: Take a care wi' yer questions concernin' certain topics now, as we be approachin' the *Collegium*. I canno' help ye in matters such as these once we arrives to the College."

"Will we be able to use our Sorcery right away?" Anders asked anxiously.

"Nay, 'tis strictly forbidden fer the *Tirones* to do such, except fer yer classes where ye're closely supervised. Unallowed Sorcery is dealt wi' mostly in a variety o' unpleasant ways ye'll no' be wantin' to discover. An' do no' be thinkin' ye can test out yer talents down the hall or 'round the corner wi' no one the wiser. They always know when ye do it, an' they always responds to it right at the instant. Now ye be boys like any boys, an' from time to time, ye'll be sorely wantin' to see what yer limits be or to show off yer skills, or ye'll ha' the impulse o' the moment to send a pie out o' thin air into yer friend's face an' such—but *don' ye do it*. There be no levity as will be worth what'll be sure to follow fer ye.

"An' ye mark me well on that, young Master Rolland, in particular. Sportin' a blue nose fer a sum o' some days is as nothin' to what can happen should ye be bendin' the constraints. I ha' been at this fer some time, lads, an' I knows whereo' I speak." Asullus ended his speech with a long stare at the redhead.

Thaddeus suddenly looked at the old mule with interest. "Will we be sharing our studies with the girls?"

"Hah. 'Twas wonderin' when that question'd come up. Nay, lads, ye'll no' be seein' those fair ones in yer daily classes. They ha' their own school, as ye ha' heard. 'Tis called the *Ludia*, an' 'tis in Northfast, I trow, far to the west o' here on the coast."

"Oh," Thaddeus responded, his face falling.

Asullus flicked a glance at the tall Apprentice, gave his head a shake, and turned back to view the forest path once more.

After a moment, Anders spoke. "Do the girls have the same training?"

"I canno' answer fer certain, havin' ne'er been swaggled into their servitude as I ha' been here these many years. 'Tis me understandin', however, that 'tis much the same, though allowin' fer the disimilarities as come from bein' o' an entirely different species altogether, don' ye know. *Haw-haw!*"

"I wonder if they are nervous about starting their first day?" Anders asked, scratching his arm absently while looking up the trunk of a tree they were passing. It was so tall he could barely see the top.

"Mayhap ye mean as nervous as yerselves? Well, 'tis no doubt there, I should say. But perhaps ye'll have an opportunity to ask 'em yerselves."

"How's that, Asullus?" Thaddeus asked, his heart racing at the thought.

"Well, 'tis the tradition fer the young 'uns o' each school to get together every year—or every other year, dependin' on certain happenings, o'er the summers, usually—fer a holiday. Principally, I think, as the ones in charge wish ye to get all matched up."

"What? Why?" Rolland demanded to know.

"So as to ha' the best chances o' there being more little Sorcerers an' Sorceresses o'er time, o' course. Would ha' thought that'd be obvious."

"Oh," Anders said as a slow flush spread over his face. After a moment, he swallowed, then spoke. "Well, if Nannsi would wish to consider spending some of her future with me, I would not mind, I think."

"Now, there is a noble sentiment, if e'er I did hear one," Asullus said earnestly.

Thaddeus said nothing, but his thoughts were again filled—as they often were these days—with visions of a tall girl with long, honey-blonde hair, green eyes, and a tender, quiet way, who, at special times, might touch the side of his face as if she really liked him.

"But, Asullus…" Rolland began.

"Lads, I ha' answered all yer thoughts all this mornin', an' enou' be enou'. Some o' what's to come ye'll just ha' to see on yer own. There's no good to be had in spoilin' it all for ye now, is there?" With that, Asullus proved impervious to any further entreaties for information.

Nearing mid-day, Master Silvestrus bade Asullus stop the cart. "Boys, make a camp and prepare some food. I must confer for a moment. Remain here and do not wander off."

The old Sorcerer climbed down from the cart and made his way, soon disappearing into the old forest growth.

"Now, where has he gone?" Rolland asked while helping his brothers unpack the mid-day meal supplied from the back of the wagon.

Curious, Thaddeus followed the old man's track till he was lost to sight. He had just started to turn his head back to the cart when he thought he saw a brief flash of purple. He looked back quickly but saw nothing untoward.

It was several moments before Master Silvestrus joined them again.

As the boys cleared the site following their meal, Silvestrus put down the pipe he'd been smoking while sitting at the fire and addressed the group.

"Well, boys, another bit of traveling, and we will arrive at our destination. You should think to prepare yourselves for sights, sounds, and experiences few of your fellow beings ever have had the opportunity to witness. You stand at the doorstep of a very different existence, of which this little journey of ours has been but the first part. So far, you have done well.

"Above all else, remember: Belief is the key—always the key. Please, let us move on."

With that, the old man stood, walked to the wagon, and regained his seat, taking up Asullus' reins once again. The boys grabbed their staffs and took up their accustomed marching order, clustered around the mule.

Nearing even-tide, Thaddeus, hiking in front, observed how the shifting sunlight was caused by the wind stirring the high canopy of leaves back and forth. The old mule interrupted his reverie.

"*Ssst,* laddie. Look before you!"

The party suddenly emerged from the forest to behold a bright green meadow laid out before them, bedecked with innumerable ground flowers and an equally incalculable number of butterflies flitting amongst them.

A short distance away stood a great stone building like nothing any of them had ever seen before. Towering just beyond the structure was a soaring white cliff running from one side of the horizon to the other. It looked to be made of solid ice.

"Do you see what I see?" Rolland asked in awe.

"It's amazing," Thaddeus said.

"Now it begins," Anders offered.

Behind them boomed the voice of the old Sorcerer. "Behold, lads, the *Collegium Sorcerorum*! You have now come home."

Epilogue

urious, the young Master Sorcerer stormed across the Gray Quadrangle's courtyard, making his way up to his apartment suite in the *Collegium Sorcerorum*'s Staff Quarters. How dare they suggest reducing his stipend purse for the upcoming year? He should turn them all into toadstools.

But then, who would be able to tell the difference?

These meetings with the Masters of Accounts always left him fuming. How could all those old men not understand the paramount importance of his studies? He had told them—he had even stooped to explain the whys and wherefores of his Great Work. Yet still, they acted with such ignorance.

"*Pfah!*" Perditus muttered to himself as he strode down the hall. Reaching the entrance to his rooms, he withdrew from his robes the large iron key supported by the chain around his neck and inserted it into the oaken door's lock. Following a rusty click, he pushed against the stubborn massive portal until it grudgingly swung open, allowing him entry.

Doffing, then flinging his threadbare and patched coarse black cloak onto the peg by the door, he trod

THE GREAT ICE WALL
THE TOWER OF THE EAST
DUN MEADOW
THE COLLEGE OF SORCERERS
(COLLEGIUM SORCERORUM)
THE FOREST SURROUND
THE SOUTHWEST CAVES
ARX MONTIUM (MOUNTAINGAARD)

across the cold stone floor to the interior wall's only window. He needed air. In passing, he tapped the top of the collecting bottle he kept on his desk, then sighed.

Would this be yet another summer of sticking pins in blue butterflies? Seven years of summer seasons come and gone so far, and what to show for it? All those promises made that time ago by that ridiculous old man, Silvestrus, and his equally ridiculous old gray mule, Asullus.

My genius is being wasted, completely wasted!

Even the ancient Master Beatus, *Princeps Academiae*, had acknowledged his intellectual gifts. Yet, here he was, sticking pins in butterflies and dragging dullard Apprentices through the most basic and tedious levels of their first-year lessons. And to what purpose? So, they could go out, say magic words, help crops to flourish, and generate yet another generation of dullard Apprentices?

"*Pfah!*"

I am wasting my time. If only there were more to this world … More to capture my imagination, my sense of discovery, new keys to the opening of greater powers. If only there were more…

After an hour of staring into space, his hot rage gradually became cold disdain. He withdrew from the window, took up his cloak again, and made his way back down the rear stairwell to the faculty gate and out onto the Commons.

Throwing up his cowl and closeting his hands, Perditus wove his way around various knots of his alleged colleagues—*alleged colleagues*, he thought angrily—and headed toward the Tower of the East. He acknowledged but a few of the others.

Oh, they were all polite, nodding just enough not to give outright offense, but it was clear by this time that they did not favor him—not like they did that dolt, Sir Eques, for example. All brawn, fit for shield-denting only, and little else.

The two had taken a rather immediate dislike of each other from the beginning. What idiocy to require that all Apprentices bear arms. Any clod-shoed peasant could lift a sword and wave it about him in the air before cutting off someone's ear. What was the utility in demanding someone of his stock to learn how to poke a fellow in the liver? The answer to that was *none!*

That one instance, though, he had to smile to himself. Yes, that one time he had smote Eques on the head—the back of the head, that is—with his morningstar during combat training. That had caused the fellow to fall to a swoon, had it not?

And what a fuss he raised, just because I gave him a bit of a trip as he went lunging by. Served him right, though.

And, he had to admit, the blow had produced a moment of feeling true power, which was, in itself, rather intoxicating. Yes, *power.* Power over situations or, better yet, over people…especially people one despised.

That was good.

But procuring such power? How did that happen? And at what cost?

These were questions for another day, he told himself as he crossed the threshold of the ancient Tower of the East. The structure was, in his estimation, the ugliest of the world's ugly buildings—not aesthetically pleasing in any detail. And few would come into its presence, let alone ascend to its topmost height to consider the world, as he regularly did.

Yet he regarded it as a retreat, a refuge of sorts. Here he would not be bothered by all the transient smallness of mind that the other instructors seemed always to wish to inflict upon him. Here, he could think great thoughts and wrestle with weighty matters of high import. Here he could be alone—truly alone.

It was, in its way…*delicious.*

After his long climb up the cold stone stairs, he reached the Tower's brim. He passed through the interior section, past some of the mirrors and sighting devices he had brought there, back when he had begun his studies here—the larger resting on the floor, the smaller on the rickety old oaken table he had set up during his first year of teaching at the College.

Walking under the archway took him to the outer balcony, where he once again faced the ice shelf towering above the school. He always thought it clever how the College managed to be so temperate even though it was so close to such an immense field of cold.

Now there *was power well spent.*

He strolled around the turret, taking in the campus—there, the Forest Surround, and there, the buildings of the school itself. Ah, seven years of so much potential…and so little result. For all the good he had done here, or, rather, for all the good done for him, he might as well have jumped off the edge of this old tiled roof years ago.

And yet, at the back of his mind was the feeling that something— something of greatness awaited him. He had just yet to achieve it.

How much longer must I wait…

He sighed and turned away from the wall's precipice. No new insights were to be achieved this day. It was time to make his way back down and out of the obscenely colored yellow Tower with a blood-red spire.

He sighed again as he passed by the table and mirrors. If only he had some hint as to what lay in store for him: some sign; something. For seven years, he had made the same wish. It was a cruel but real lesson in what the usual results of making wishes amounted to.

Then, off to his left, he heard a sound—a low rumble. But it did not sound mechanical—no creaking of stone or boards expanding in the summer's heat. He had never heard such a sound before.

It sounded…*alive.*

"Wha—what is it?" he demanded aloud.

His head whipped around, his vision washing quickly over every foot's-length of the Tower interior. Nothing. He had been mistaken, which was odd, because that almost never happened.

Whatever it was, it was not repeating itself. Well and good. He'd best be about leaving. He was a busy man with work to do, and had no time to be troubled by fancies.

He took a step forward, only to be interrupted by a second sound.

"*Sorcerer,*" came a deep, rasping whisper.

The hairs on the back of Perditus' neck stood erect as a chill ran down to his gut, and sweat popped out on his brow.

"Who are you?" he asked timidly. Then he spoke out more forcefully. "Identify yourself!" The Sorcerer began to be aware of the smell of sulfur in the room.

A pause followed again by the strangely rasping speech.

"*Perditus.*"

Thaddeus and the Master

Prologue
In the Halls of the Inferna

"And so, son, as you know, we have spoken often of these days—the days when we would once more establish contact with the strangers. And, I have had the feeling lately that those days have come once again. It is a thing that has been building in my breast for some time now, and this day I have felt the first real stirrings—the first tuggings at my heart."

"What are we to expect, then, Father? Will there be danger for us?"

"Momentous events that provide such opportunities as these always present dangers, son. But that does not mean we shirk them. No, rather, we strive to embrace them. Think of the possibilities; think of the resources this might provide. It staggers the imagination."

"How do you believe this will be achieved, Father?"

"I will stand ready to be the first to make contact. Obviously, the strangers will put forward one of their wisest, and I will need to convince them of our good intent." Here the older of the twain smiled. "Then each of us will work toward a more perfect union. I see no reason, now, why that cannot be established. I must say, however, though the feelings are definite, oddly, they seem to have shifted somewhat from where we originally met. But no matter. One place is as good as another for that which we will work together to accomplish.

"The most important thing, though, is to define the benefits we can offer and our suggestions for their equitable distribution."

"You sound as if you were giving a lesson in rhetoric, Father," the younger one said.

"Well, rightly enough, I suppose, my son. In any case, I know this will come off well for us, and I know I will be successful in the making of it."

"Hmm. Then I wish you the best of fortune, Father. And if you are as successful in this as you propose to be, then I will offer you my heartiest congratulations."

"I see. And if, by chance, I am not?"

"Then, Father," the leaner, gray, warty-skinned figure said, licking bubbling spittle from his chest, "I shall pick your bones with my teeth."

With that, the young Daemon rose, turned, and strode away, burning orange-red flames leaping up to his knees at every step.

The Fourth
Quartus

The *Collegium* was, indeed, as Asullus had described it, an imposing square—or quadrangle, as Anders called it—set on the bias in a back corner of a giant meadow. At some distance, it was surrounded on two sides by impossibly high walls of ice—the Great Northern Shelf. Yet the sun shone down warmly on the party, and only a gentle breeze stirred. The open fourth side of the College faced the meadow to the southwest.

The four-storied structure was built of gray granite blocks with turrets at each corner. Between the northwest wall and the ice shelf rose a tall, slender, freestanding yellow rod of a tower topped by a bulbous red cap, hideous in appearance.

The Tower. Thaddeus knew it immediately. No flames or flashes of lightning emanated from the Tower this day, however.

As the party approached the *Collegium* over a bricked road, Thaddeus noted rows of windows marking each floor, staring out from the ivy-covered walls like watching eyes.

Anders said Silvestrus had told him the outer ring of rooms were protected by thick walls—walls deep enough to withstand a determined siege. Windows of an inner circle of rooms reportedly overlooked a large courtyard, or Commons, where worn paths wound their way among statuary, fountains, and ancient shade trees.

On impulse, Thaddeus looked over his shoulder to see numerous trails that led from the College into the forest, entering the wood in a random pattern every dozen paces or so. His gaze shifted back to the grounds. Tall trees dotted the meadow with a large grouping of them—an orchard of some kind—standing midway by a stream that meandered down from the ice wall to the northeast, eventually passing close by the brick path.

He turned again to mark the stream's entrance into the surrounding wood—and started in surprise. The paths suddenly seemed different—subtly perhaps, but definitely different.

A series of low buildings stood to the left—evidently sheds, work-rooms, and stables. A figure standing near one of the sheds drew his attention immediately. It was a man-horse wielding a rake. He was policing the area around the stable. The other boys gasped as they, too, noticed him.

"Asullus," Thaddeus whispered, "who is that, um, fellow over there by the stables?"

"Aye? Oh, that be Chiron. He's one o' the Arms Masters. Ye'll be meeting him later. In the off-season, he works as the chief groundskeeper. A gruff lot, but steadfast. Pay attention to what he says, an' ye'll learn more than a plateful."

Of a sudden, the Centaur looked toward the group, shading his eyes as Asullus brayed out a greeting. The creature carefully leaned his rake against a shed, then galloped full-out toward the party.

Thaddeus was anxious, not knowing what to expect, but as Master Silvestrus and Asullus paid no particular heed to the Centaur making for them at a good speed, he tried to mark it as an everyday occurrence. Behind him, Thaddeus heard Anders and Rolland stop moving.

The man-horse pounded to an abrupt halt in front of the group. The creature gave a brief bow to Silvestrus and a nod to Asullus. "Master Silvestrus, greetings! I welcome you back. I see you were successful in your journey."

"That I was, Master Chiron. That I was. How fare things with you and the College altogether this warm season?"

"As you might expect, Master Silvestrus. A quiet summer—except, of course, Midsummer's Eve." The Centaur and the Sorcerer exchanged meaningful glances. "But our new charges have begun to arrive. The usual lot, which we will attend to soon enough. Peace to you, Asullus. How was your burden?"

"Fair an' away, old friend. Now tell me true, is the straw fresh an' the bag an' trough full?"

"Of course. It is I who have been on duty, is it not?"

The Centaur's craggy visage shifted suddenly to Thaddeus, and he spoke without preamble. "Have you a son?"

The question jolted Thaddeus. "What? I, I mean, excuse me, Master. How mean you?" As the horseman's aspect was serious, the boy realized he was posing no jest. However, the fact that he was singled out for such attention, coupled with the bizarre nature of the question, totally confused and tongue-tied the tall Apprentice.

"I will repeat my question. Have you a son?"

Thaddeus, by this time more than uncomfortable, glanced at his Master, whose own expression was not alarmed but merely thoughtful. The Old Man nodded once in reassurance.

"Um, no, Master. No, I don't. I'm not even married."

The Centaur nodded once but appeared to be disappointed. He turned back to the old Sorcerer. "I have more tasks yet to complete this day, so I will leave off our conversation for now. Again, welcome back, Master Silvestrus. Asullus." With that, he turned abruptly and trotted back the way he had come.

"Aye!" Rolland let out explosively. "What in the Hells was that all about?"

"I don't know. I haven't any idea at all. Master?"

To Thaddeus' frustration, Silvestrus only shrugged, though he could have sworn a smile stole briefly across the old man's lips. "Let us follow the Centaur to the stables and see to our faithful mule's needs. Then I will take you over to the quadrangle, and Lilyput can take charge of you."

"Lilyput?" Rolland mouthed to Anders, but the young scholar only shook his head and shrugged.

At the stables, they unhitched and stored the cart, hung the tack, and groomed Asullus.

"I can see to meself from this point, young Apprentices. Now go on an' be aboot yer trainin'. Be respectful o' yer Masters, take yer studies seriously an', most o' all, donno' embarrass the family."

Of a sudden, the boys realized that the close comradeship they'd come to take for granted was being sundered.

"Take best care, old mule, and thank you for your loyal service. We'll come to see you as often as we may," Anders said, his voice thick with emotion.

"There's no kitchen pantry in the world that's safe from me when I have the chance to borrow an apple or three for a good friend," Rolland promised, attempting to project a jaunty tone while stroking the mule fondly behind the ears.

Thaddeus found he didn't trust himself to speak but threw his arms around the old gray mule's neck, giving him a fierce hug.

"Aye, laddie," Asullus said softly, "'tis all right now. I'll be fine here in me own home. An' as our short friend ha' said, ye'll come to see me as ye may. Go on now wi' yer Brothers. It'll do no one any good to start wi' any snifflin' an' such. 'Tis here I'll be when opportunity an' inclination allow."

Thaddeus nodded, took a deep breath, and stood away. As a group, the boys signaled farewell, then turned and walked out of the dimly lit stable. Last to leave, Thaddeus gave a final wave before joining the others to walk behind their Master, who was waiting patiently for them in the cheerful sunlight.

The boys hefted their travel packs and followed their Master up the well-worn limestone path traversing the slight incline of the meadow toward the main building. Rounding the corner, they reached the front of the structure. Silvestrus brought the group to a halt at the bottom of a thirteen-step stairway up to the College entrance.

Two statues, one on either side, stood at the bottom of the stairs, as if guarding the entrance. The black marble figures made an odd pair— the one on the left represented some beatific figure in long, flowing robes, her innocent face turned toward the Heavens.

The other figure, however, was quite different. It squatted, elbows on knees, chin in hands and a long, forked tongue protruding from a lipless slit of a mouth. A pair of short, curved horns rose from the brows of its hairless head. Stubby, bat-like wings grew from below its shoulder blades, and a spiked tail rose in a curl. It was also definitely male. Definitely.

"You lads wait here. I will return shortly."

The boys watched the old Sorcerer make his way up the steps, through the *Portus,* and vanish into the interior of the building.

Rolland waved a hand derisively. "So this is the College of Sorcerers. Well, it doesn't look so overpowering now, does it?"

"We're not even inside yet," Anders rejoined. "Just wait."

Thaddeus, distracted by a low murmuring, listened closely, focusing his attention. Voices were speaking. And nearby.

"…all ugly, just like you. And they're not impressive. I think the Old Man has finally gone senile if he thinks to bring these pitiful specimens here and try to pass them off as some key part of the Pro…"

"Forbearance, Alistair, forbearance. The Master knows what he is about with the lads, even better than you. I would venture that there is great virtue here if we but look for it. In fact, I am reminded of the time when you thought…"

"Oh, stuff your snot-rag in it, Thra-gora, you hopeless priss. You wouldn't know a virtue—if there is such a thing—if it came up and bit you on the ass. Speaking of which, if you're not busy this Saturn's Day night…"

"Anders! Rolland! Do you hear that? Why, it's—it's the statues." Astonishment was writ large on the tall boy's face. "They're talking to each other!"

"What do you mean?" Anders asked. "Only Rolland and I were talking. Besides, really, you know masonry cannot speak."

"Thaddeus, I've heard nothing," Rolland responded with a sideways glance. "At least nothing of importance."

Thaddeus was about to reply when a shrill whistle coming from above distracted him.

"Boys! Up here. To me!" the Master called.

The Apprentices re-shouldered their packs and climbed the wide, marble steps. It was an easy journey as the risers were only a hands-width high.

As they neared the top, they found the old Sorcerer was not alone.

Lounging in a spacious niche in the wall by the entranceway next to a great urn was a boy who appeared to be of an age with them. He had some sort of stringed instrument in his lap, which hung from a tooled leather strap around his neck. The tooling looked to be gold. The young man strummed diverse chords from time to time as he talked with Master Silvestrus.

His garish yellow and orange silk attire most riveted Thaddeus' attention—gaudy as a parrot with matching, curved, pointy-toed slippers. The youth wore several golden rings on his fingers and had even more attached to his ears. A large, brilliant yellow jewel was centered on a white satin sash encircling his head, its tails hanging down his back. The boy's large brown eyes matched his skin and seemed to miss nothing. His mouth was curled into a slight smile. Thaddeus wondered, however, whether the smile denoted amusement or contempt.

"Lads, come meet a fellow in the year just ahead of you. Thaddeus, Anders, Rolland—meet Zoarr of Mauretesia, Prince of the House of Abdomoolano. Prince Zoarr, allow me to present Thaddeus of Beewicke, Anders of Brightfield, and Rolland of Fountaindale, all from the Westlands. Boys, it is not polite to stare. Come now, say your greetings!"

With a great deal of reluctance, the three country lads shook the Prince's proffered hand perfunctorily, mumbling their hellos. Anders even managed a short bow, which earned him a sharp stare from the redheaded thief.

The dark young man gave each of them a penetrating gaze, then remarked to the old Sorcerer over his shoulder. "Ah, Master Silvestrus, I see we have *Septentrio, Occidus,* and *Oriens.* The verse is now complete, is it not?"

"That remains to be seen, Zoarr. And it may be none of your concern."

"To the contrary, Master, I believe it is very much my concern."

Startled by the youth's assertive attitude, Thaddeus felt Rolland stiffen beside him. Knowing his friend well by now, Thaddeus tried to think of a polite way to move them on quickly so as to prevent unfortunate bloodshed.

The Sorcerer cleared his throat meaningfully. "Yes, well, be that as it may. I believe the four of you will be spending some time together in the future, so do try to get on. Another time, Prince. This way in, lads."

"*Ave,*" intoned the swarthy lad and returned to his strumming as the three country boys entered the dark, cool interior of the *Collegium.*

Imperial
Cinnian Family Tree

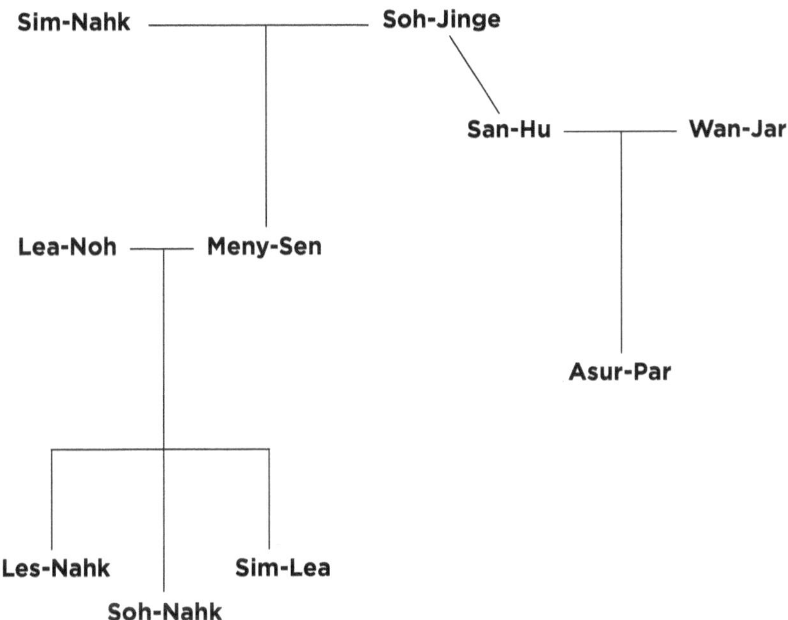

Character Log

A

A The first and greatest Daemon. Said to be creator, by will alone, of all. The Wise consider that it is the character of the Daemon, unavoidably suffusing its creation with its own essence, that accounts for the imperfections observed everywhere in the Universe and in Man, himself.

Adjurford A Sorcerer at the *Collegium Sorcerorum*. Second in command to **Portoman** during the Sorcerous raid on the capital of the Cin in the time of the Eastern invasion, occasioned by the greed of the last Emperor of the Westlands, **Tyrannus Superbus.** Their original mission was to destroy the Tower of the Cin. However, following **Portoman's** descent into madness, **Adjurford** assumed leadership of the small band of Sorcerers and succeeded in making away with the Tower instead. He was able to return to the *Collegium Sorcerorum* with all his men, including the severely compromised **Portoman.** Speculation later arose that a young **Silvestrus** of Somerset was a member of that party.

Aldo Male servant employed by **Oliffe**, Innkeeper of The Sword in the Scone, a Fountaindale hospitality establishment.

Al-Donn Aelvae. Lieutenant to **Non-Dar**, Lord of the Greensward Aelvae. Favors acorn soup.

Anders of Brightfield Manor Only child of **Astonius** and **Sophia**, successful distillers near Meadsville. Intelligent, clever, and well-tutored by his teachers. Subsequently apprenticed to **Silvestrus** of the *Collegium Sorcerorum*. First of the three Brothers to **Thaddeus** of Beewicke. He is identified with the cardinal point Occidus (west)—of the *Octipes Circuitus Magnus,* the Great Compass.

Annis Male servant to **Ormerod**, master vintner of Figberry.

Apiarius Magister Chief Beekeeper of the Hives in Beewicke, having inherited the position from his father.

Ardens Sister. Septuagenarian member of women's religious order of nurses *(Sorores Silentii),* residing at the Convent of the Silent Sisters. Impulsively sought to disavow Holy Orders following the advent of **Rolland** of Fountaindale and his fellow Apprentices at the Convent.

Argus Loyal hound, eager companion, and early protector of **Thaddeus** of Beewicke.

Argutia Intellect. One of the four daughters—the *Intelligentiae*—of *Mater Naturae,* who together are tasked with preventing the Daemons at the Earth's core from breaking through to the surface via the Tower of the Cin to ravage her planet.

Astonius Master distiller and astute businessman at Brightfield Manor, he is husband to **Sophia** and father of **Anders**.

Asullus Sentient mule, born in Cobbly Knob in the year of the Great Comet, and chattel of the witch woman, **Lilith**. Achieved capacity of speech and other gifts through his Mistress' Magicks and has not been silent since.

Attacondros King of Red Dragons. Passionate suitor for the favors of **Mari** the Green, Queen of Sea Dragons (*Regina Draconum Marinarum*). Frustrated by the failure of his suit, he pronounces a terrible curse upon the Green Queen.

Auricia Maternal aunt to **Thaddeus** of Beewicke. Developed intestinal tumor and went to live with her sister until her death.

B

Babaiaga By chance, only female Daemon to come to Earth. Much sought-after by her own kind. Developed strong interest in **Groton** the Black I, whose attributes lured her to the surface where their relationship resulted in **Lilith**. Following this, entombed by her peers in a granite cell under Seyzoa River. With time and isolation, became unbalanced, but retained sufficient power to influence the occasional sensitive and susceptible witch, of which ilk, **Madrin** of Cinoton, is the most current example.

Barnabas Cleric and Brother of the Order. One of only a small number of members of the Holy Orders allowed by the Council to study and teach at the *Collegium Sorcerorum.* He has a passion for the study of law and serves as an administrator of the College.

Bartsome Innkeeper of The Friend in Mead, Bostle's premier—albeit only— inn. He keeps a good and generous table known as "**Bartsome's** Best."

Beatus Master Sorcerer and current *Princeps Academiae* at the *Collegium Sorcerorum.* Benign shepherd to his flock. Many believe that upon his retirement he is likely to be succeeded in that position by **Silvestrus** of Somerset.

Bede Venerable Master Sorcerer and early *Princeps Academiae, Collegium Sorcerorum,* to whom **Silvestrus** of Somerset was apprenticed.

Bellis Golden hunting dog rescued by the three Apprentices from a beating by **Corrigan** the Mad. She decides to travel with the Apprentices on their journey. She is thought to be associated with **Luperca**, the alpha female of all wolves, who also can appear as a tawny-haired woman or as a young girl.

Bernardus Soldier of the cursed and ghostly 101st Leopard Legion —the Deserter's Legion—encamped on the City on the Plain, Terminus, a city said to be visible only on nights of the full moon.

C

Caerulea *Regina Papilionium,* blue Queen of Butterflies. Life mate to My Lord **Spadix**, *Rex Blattarum,* King of Moths, who is widely known to be both unfaithful to, yet jealous of, his Queen. Rumored by some to have history of assignation with **Thaddeus** of Beewicke.

Carlus (aka **Charles**) Minor Brown Daemon of the Lower Vale, whose existence was spared long ago by **Silvestrus** of Somerset following the loss of a mortal wager. Per agreement, **Silvestrus** can summon **Carlus** to perform tasks—typically involving combat—with the proviso that the spoils of such contests are given to the Daemon to do with as he pleases.

Carolle Former Governess to **Anders** of Brightfield at Brightfield Manor, whose niece, **Nyree**, took a fancy to her aunt's young charge.

Cedric Assistant to *Apiarius Magister,* Keeper of the Hives at Beewicke. Married to **Hycynthya**, the old miller's daughter and father of **Thaddeus** of Beewicke.

Celsius Skilled Physician, Master of the Healing Arts at the *Collegium Sorcerorum.* Enjoys drama and attention, typically arrives in a cloud of green smoke. He is eternally anxious concerning compensation for his services.

Charles (aka **Carlus**) Minor Brown Daemon of the Lower Vale, whose existence was spared long ago by **Silvestrus** of Somerset following the loss of a mortal wager. Per agreement, Silvestrus can summon **Charles** to perform tasks—typically involving combat—with the proviso that the spoils of such contests are given to the Daemon to do with as he pleases.

Cin the Cautious Legendary founder of the land bearing his name who, after leading his followers to an area, as if under a compulsion, discovers a starkly ugly yellow tower with a red Top erected in the middle of the landscape.

Corrigan the Mad Alcoholic and bipolar stepson of **Mattom**, Arch Druid of River's Wood community. From childhood, he was a darkly moody youth who jealously harbored suspicions regarding his playmate **Luperca**, with whom he shared his stepbrother, **Madigan**.

Cynthia Early roommate and confidant of **Ethne** of Tarandon following the latter's arrival at the House of the Lilies in Fountaindale.

E

En-Jannen Cinnian Emperor at the time of the Westlands invasion 1000 years in the past. With the help of Daemon-assisted Ancient Ones, his forces were able to overcome the invading legions, taking Westlands Emperor, **Tyrannus Superbus,** and his son, **Publius**, prisoner. Shortly thereafter, at a time calculated to exactly coincide with the purloining of the Tower of the East, the Emperor's relatively enlightened reign changed significantly and he became more feared than adored. In later ceremony, for example, he had his enemy's son slain in a horrific manner and the Westlands Emperor encased in an enchanted and impervious crystal dome in the great hall of the Imperial Palace.

Eques Sir Knight-Master and leader of the Battle-Masters of the *Collegium Sorcerorum*. He is the most knowledgeable and skilled of the Combat Masters in the use of edged weapons and armor. Bears distinct dislike and disdain for his colleague, **Perditus** of Skara Brae.

Equus God of those who are four-footed, and frequent mount-in-service to *Mater Naturae*.

Ethne of Tarandon Lady of the Flowers of Sorrow *(Domina Dolorosa Florum)*. Mistress of vintner **Ormerod** of Figberry. Provides initial instruction to **Thaddeus** of Beewicke regarding the niceties of life and other subjects. Forms significant relationship with her charge.

F

Fabia One of twin girls born to the union of **Silvestrus** of Somerset and **Merriwhiddle** of Maritanius, who is believed to have been sacrificed by her mother to the evil sentient tree, **Garrungroot**, in return for power, immortality, and invulnerability.

Fabrica One of twin girls born to the union of **Silvestrus** of Somerset and **Merriwhiddle** of Maritanius, who is believed to have been sacrificed by her mother to the evil sentient tree, **Garrungroot**, in return for power, immortality, and invulnerability.

Faran of Fountaindale Redheaded leader of **Faran's** Falcons, Young Thieves' Guild. Unrecognized relationship to **Melaphen**, mother of **Rolland** of Fountaindale.

Floria of Copperville Jilted fiancée of a Thieves' Guild member, who exacted a dramatic revenge on her unfaithful espoused.

Franciscus Soldier of the cursed and ghostly 101st Leopard Legion—the Deserter's Legion—encamped on the City on the Plain, Terminus.

G

Garrungroot Evil, sentient tree with whom failed Sorceress, **Merriwhiddle** of Maritanius, strikes a deadly bargain. He has knowledge of all that trees know and observe and, with sufficient incentive, is able to become mobile.

Geanninia of Glascoton Imposing Sorceress, Professor and Headmistress at the *Ludia*. She has been romantically linked with **Silvestrus** of Somerset in excess of a lifetime.

Geoffrey of the Broom Lord, skilled warrior, and commanding officer of the Iron Company of the *Arx Montium,* Mountain Guard, Defenders of the *Collegium Sorcerorum*. He has a long-held desire to retire to the South, marry well, and initiate a dynasty.

Gertie Female servant employed by **Oliffe**, innkeeper of The Sword in the Scone, a Fountaindale inn.

Gethin Male servant to **Ormerod**, vintner of Figberry.

Gladitorius Unpleasant youth and member of **Faran's** Falcons of the Young Thieves' Guild of Fountaindale. Considered a bully, he worked under the direction of **Sagar, Rolland** of Fountaindale's former colleague and chief competitor in that organization.

Grunius Sergeant and second-in-command of the Iron Company. Stationed at *Arx Montium,* Mountain Guard, he is charged with limiting access to, and defending those in residence at, the *Collegium Sorcerorum*.

H

Hadrout Irascible centaur. Formerly partnered with, and disgruntled employee of, **Silvestrus** of Somerset in the recruitment of likely lads for the *Collegium Sorcerorum*. He resigned from that post following a dispute concerning his lack of willingness to carry either the recruits or the Master Sorcerer on his back, and other complaints.

Hectorus Seaman and lover of **Melaphen** of Fountaindale, a woman of the night working for the Thieves' Guild. He is the biological father of **Rolland** of Fountaindale. Dark-haired, with a sinewy frame, several golden teeth, earrings and tattoos. Good with a knife and horses.

Helveticus *Centurio Prior,* Centurion Major, of the encampment of the City on the Plain, Terminus. He was the leading spirit of the cursed camp of the ten thousand, whose souls had been recruited for the ill-fated Eastern campaign against the Cin. Husband to **Marta** and father of four sons with her.

Horatius Soldier and scholar of the cursed and ghostly 101st Leopard Legion—the Deserter's Legion—encamped on the City on the Plain, Terminus.

Hycynthya Mother of **Thaddeus** of Beewicke by **Cedric**. She is the daughter of Beewicke's old miller and only survivor of a curse placed on her family when she was a child.

I

Ingenia Wisdom. One of the four daughters—the *Intelligentiae*—of *Mater Naturae,* who, together, are tasked with preventing the Daemons at the Earth's core from breaking through to the surface to ravage their Mother's planet.

K

Kenneth of Walworth County He was the childhood sweetheart of **Melior**, the *Mater Amplior* of the *Sorores Silentii,* the Convent of the Silent Sisters. He was left at the altar following a last-minute, gut-wrenching decision by the future Mother Superior.

Ko-Thas Aelvae and Lieutenant to Lord **Non-Dar,** whose tribe abides in the forest surrounding the *Collegium Sorcerorum.* He enjoys willow bark and legumes.

L

Lallie Daughter to **Morella** and, with her, house-servant to **Ormerod**, the Vintner of Figberry.

Les-Nahk Most Favored First Son of **Meny-Sen,** Imperial Heir-apparent, and **Lea-Noh.** Following the loss of his parents at the hands of the Imperial Step Great-Mother, **San-Hu,** his life turned to one of exclusive appetite gratification, wherein the demands of his imbibing were exceeded only by those of his libido.

Lea-Noh Beautiful niece of Cinnian Imperial High Chamberlain, who married the Imperial Heir-apparent, **Meny-Sen,** in a true love match and bore him three children (**Les-Nahk, Soh-Nahk** and **Sim-Lea**). Believing her step-mother-in-law, **San-Hu,** responsible for the death of her mother-in-law, **Sim-Nahk,** and also that the woman threatened her three children, she arranged for the death of that Lady's son, **Asur-Par,** by agents of the Janeh-Keene assassins. She was believed to be in the midst of planning to do the same with **San-Hu,** herself, when the Emperor's second wife arranged her death—along with that of her husband, Heir-apparent **Meny-Sen**—in a "hunting lodge accident," allegedly without the Emperor's knowledge.

Lilith Witch-woman of Cobbly Knob, and third cousin to **Silvestrus** of Somerset. She is an animal trainer, and owner of the mule, **Asullus**. At the request of her cousin, she imbued **Asullus** with the ability to speak, an act generative of peculiar and unintended consequences. Rival with girlfriend **Eve** for the affection of her man.

Luperca Ancient, minor goddess, usually found in the company of wolves. She is said to be able to take the form of a tawny-haired woman, but is also apparently associated with a small girl, as well as a golden hunting dog named **Bellis**.

M

Madigan Arch Druid and Sachem, son of **Mattom**, Arch Druid before him, and stepbrother to **Corrigan** the Mad. He officiates from the Holy Grove in River's Wood. He is a childhood friend of the current avatar of **Luperca** of the wolves. He is the custodian of the predictive power of the Great Wheel of the Ancient Oak.

Madrin Elderly Cinnian woman with certain powers—among them soothsaying—which manifest mainly during times of suffering fits when she, due to her various sensitivities, may serve as a conduit for the **Daemon Babaiaga.** Supports herself with small crafts of Magicks items that, actually, have significant potency. Is compelled to seek out **Soh-Nahk** for a task involving murder.

Marcellus Leader of patrol of Legionnaires of the 101st Leopard Legion—the Deserter's Legion—marking the perimeter of the cursed encampment of the City on the Plain, Terminus.

Mari the Green *Regina Draconum Marinarum,* Queen of Sea Dragons. Has earned wrath of **Attacondros**, King of Red Dragons, after spurning his advances and, as a consequence, is cursed.

Marsia of Dorset Downs, Northfast A tall girl, with hip-length honey-gold hair and emerald eyes, she carries a pair of greenstones, split from a single source and given to her by her Great-Mother, each greenstone having special properties. She was recruited to the *Ludia* by Mistress **Geanninia** and travels with her, later joined by **Nannsi** of Zorbas and **Sonnia** of Frantilla.

Marta Wife to **Helveticus**, *Centurio Prior,* stationed with the 101st Leopard Legion, City on the Plain at Terminus.

Mater Naturae Mother Nature. Important figure of prehistoric times, enraged at the violation of her Earth avatar by Daemons from **Bellona**. In response, she has charged her four daughters, the *Intellegentiae* (the products of the violation), with the task of thwarting any attempt by those same Daemons to win their freedom from the Earth's core—into which they were cast and entrapped—and making sure they are never able to escape to the planet's surface.

Mattom Former Chief, or Arch Druid and Sachem, at River's Wood. Father to **Madigan**, current Arch Druid at River's Wood and stepfather to **Corrigan** the Mad. Able to persuade **Luperca**, an ancient goddess, to bring to fruition her part of the Ring's Plan, by assuming her alternate forms for various periods of time so she and **Madigan** could be raised as childhood friends. Before his death, **Mattom** was able to pass on this knowledge to his son, the subsequent Chief Druid, **Madigan.**

Melaphen Fiery, redheaded prostitute and mother, by **Hectorus** the sailor, of **Rolland** of Fountaindale. Following the loss of her seaman before the birth of their child, she strove to devote her remaining time and energy to raising her baby. She was later slain by a drunken customer during the boy's infancy, and the responsibility for his care passed to Faran of Fountaindale. Cautious rumors hinted at some manner of special relationship between **Melaphen** and **Faran**. Some few considered her demeanor, at times, otherworldly.

Melior *Mater Amplior.* Abbess of the Convent of the *Sorores Silentii.* Early, she was betrothed to **Kenneth** of Walworth County, but following a soul-searching weekend retreat, gave up the prospect of a husband and family to enter a religious order of nurses. Though an excellent and highly skilled healer, she always struggled between embracing human relationships versus pursuing what she considered to be the higher good.

Meny-Sen Wildly popular Heir-apparent to the Cinnian throne, he married his true love, **Lea-Noh,** who bore him three children (**Les-Nahk, Soh-Nahk** and **Sim-Lea**). Unaware of his wife's activities on his behalf, he met his doom—along with that of his wife—in a "hunting lodge accident" at the hands of his step-mother, **San-Hu.**

Merriwhiddle of Maritanius Failed student of Sorcery, and competitor with **Geanninia** of Glascoton for the affections of **Silvestrus** of Somerset. Convinced by that Sorcerer to allow him to accompany her to her homeland, she left the *Ludia* in her fourth year, unfulfilled. **Silvestrus** then abandoned her after she became pregnant with twin girls **Fabia** and **Fabrica**. In a rage, she formed a compact with the evil Tree Spirit, **Garrungroot**, who promised her power, knowledge, invulnerability, and immortality in return for lifelong servitude and the lives of two others.

Morag Arch-Daemon, who has long cultivated a connection with the Cinnian Tower, placed by his kind in the land of the peoples who would come to be known as the Cin. However, he abruptly lost power when a ragtag band of Western Sorcerers, in a surprise maneuver at the height of battle, purloined the Tower of the East, eventually lodging it on the grounds of the *Collegium Sorcerorum.*

Morphia Purple-winged and often somnific representative of *Spritae* family of the *Faerrae.* Such Fey are often sought after for accomplishing tasks and fetching items. Some are said to be exquisitely sensitive to the addictive powers of *Pixae* honey, most especially the strain extant in Beewicke.

Myrtelee of Tarandon Mother to **Ethne** of Tarandon. Peasant woman to whom, at the height of a harsh winter, four women appeared, initially identifying themselves as faggot peddlers. This pretext was rather quickly abandoned, however, and the four visited upon the unsuspecting woman an annunciation that her daughter, at a certain time, would be given the choice of everlasting fame or long life. She was instructed to ensure that her daughter learned the text of this pronouncement by heart.

N

Nannsi of Zorbas, Graecolia Daughter of a successful merchant. She is the only short and dark member of her sib line, resembling none of her brothers and sisters. Attentive to details, she objects to much that she calls "frivolous" in life and searches for an understanding soul mate.

Non-Dar Lord of the Greensward *Aelvae* dwelling in the forest surrounding the *Collegium Sorcerorum.* He is traditionally the ally of the Sorcerers and a blood enemy of all Goblin kind. He is often a bit stuffy and full of himself, but is considered steadfast and handy to have around in any altercation.

Nyree Niece to **Carolle**, former Governess to **Anders** of Brightfield Manor. She was a frequent visitor at Brightfield over the summer months during which times she is alleged to have struck up an improper relationship with **Anders**.

O

Oliffe Innkeeper of well-appointed Fountaindale inn, The Sword in the Scone, standing between a smithy and a bakery. He suffers regularly from visitations by **Faran's** Falcons of the Young Thieves' Guild.

Orbis Sister. Chief Librarian at the Convent of the Silent Sisters, who, through her research, was able to divine the existence and purpose of Stones of Resonance.

Ormerod Well-regarded vintner of Figberry, whose purberry wine vintages are famous in the region. Long-time acquaintance of **Silvestrus** of Somerset. He has taken as mistress, **Ethne** of Fountaindale—a former lady of the evening working there—however, saying only that she is his niece. He eventually succumbs to a type of pulmonary consumption not uncommon to that city at that time.

P

Perditus of Skara Brae The youngest Master to sit on the Governing Council of the *Collegium Sorcerorum.* Unpopular and antisocial, yet brilliant and ambitious, he is a dedicated student of Eastern Magicks, especially their rumored links to otherworldly powers. He has made a life study of the Tower of the Cin, the only known artifact extant in the Westlands to date from before the time of the great Invasion of the East. Some consider that his confidence in his ability to control events may be overdetermined.

Phoebe Friendly dapple mare recruited by **Silvestrus** of Somerset to distract **Asullus** the mule from his preoccupation with the imminent drudgery of towing a Sorcerer-laden barge up the Greater Flatstone River to the town of River's Wood.

Pisca Mermaid and seer to the court of **Mari** the Green, *Regina Draconum Marinarum*. She brought the Sea Dragon Queen's attention to patterns in the stars foretelling the advent of a young human male of great importance to her mistress. The sea creature met her doom at the claws of **Attacondros** the Red, a frustrated suitor of this same mistress.

Portoman Master Sorcerer, *Collegium Sorcerorum*. One of a company of Sorcerers volunteering to serve the Empire during the invasion of the lands of the Cin. It was **Portoman**, who, informed of such by a junior member of the party, declared that the Cin's unanticipated success in first repelling and then slaughtering the Imperial Legions was related to a magical concentration of dark spirit emanating from the Tower of the Cin, lodged in the enemy's capital city, Cinoton. He and his companions, therefore, contrived to steal away the Tower—but at great cost to **Portoman's** sanity. He was eventually brought safely back to the College along with the mysterious Tower. His broken mind, however, never healed, despite best efforts, and he did not long survive his return.

Primus First of three tutors engaged by **Sophia** and **Astonius** of Brightfield Manor to educate their only child, **Anders**. He is bilious in nature.

Providentia Foresight. One of the four daughters—the *Intelligentiae*—of *Mater Naturae*, who together are tasked with preventing the Daemons at the Earth's core from breaking through to the surface to ravage her planet.

R

Raugauld Cook to the Iron Company, *Arx Montium*, at Mountain Guard. Makes passable bear stew.

Rolland of Fountaindale Only surviving child of **Hectorus**, seaman, and **Melaphen**, redheaded prostitute. He is a street thief, Excelsior class, junior Thieves' Guild, **Faran's** Falcons. He is rumored to have some special relationship with the very same **Faran**. Later, he is apprenticed to **Silvestrus** of the *Collegium Sorcerorum*. He is the second of the three Brothers to **Thaddeus** of Beewicke. He is said to favor **Sonnia** of Frantilla. He is a Cardinal Point—Orientem (East)—of the Great Compass.

S

Sagar Young lieutenant to **Faran**, leader of **Faran's** Falcons, Young Thieves' Guild, Fountaindale. He is an early, close colleague of **Rolland** the Red, later employed by **Solon** to bring about his friend's capture.

Sapientia Wit. One of the four daughters—the *Intelligentia* —of *Mater Naturae*, who together are tasked with preventing the Daemons at the Earth's core from breaking through to the surface to ravage her planet.

Secundus Second of three tutors engaged by **Sophia** and **Astonius** of Brightfield Manor for the instruction of their son, **Anders**. He is phlegmatic in character.

Shire Reeve Chief officer of law enforcement in Fountaindale and surrounding communities.

Silvestrus of Somerset Master Sorcerer and Professor at *Collegium Sorcerorum*. Over time, he was recruited as a Disciple by the Lady, *Mater Naturae*, serving her will through the Four *Intelligentiae*. He is the father of twin girls by failed Sorceress Apprenticiatrix, **Merriwhiddle** of Maritanius. He is currently affianced to **Geanninia** of Glascoton, Headmistress of the *Ludia*. He sometimes bears the moniker "the Wooden One," given his name and customary demeanor.

Silvie Aunt to **Anders** of Brightfield Manor, who tended to shower family with useful adages such as noting that a regular diet of red meat is not good for you.

Sin-Dol *Aelvae* He is a member of the tribe led by Lord **Non-Dar,** who dwell in the forest surrounding the *Collegium Sorcerorum*. He has studied the procurement of the rare and elusive substance, ambrosia.

Soh-Nahk Most Favored Second Son of **Meny-Sen,** Cinnian Imperial heir apparent, and **Lea-Noh.** Following the loss of his parents at the hands of the Imperial Step-Great-Mother, **San-Hu,** he develops a hunger for the throne. After a diligent search, he uncovers the Cinnian Imperial Family Journals, which hint at the role his Imperial Step-Great-Mother played in the deaths of his Imperial Great-Mother, **Sim-Nahk,** and his parents. Believing that these deaths would be unlikely without, at least, passive Imperial consent, and blessed with a towering intellect bereft of the burden of any moral imperatives, he contrives to reach his goal through a series of assassinations, including that of the Cinnian Emperor, **Soh-Jinge.**

Solon Grizzled old man, often appearing both irritated and wary. Once employed as a Spy Master and assassin by the Old Cinnian Emperor, now retired and living some distance from Cinoton, at Tobruk. Receives secret commission from **Soh-Nahk** to eliminate four boys from the Farther Westlands on the urging of an elderly Soothsayer, **Madrin**—a crafter of powerful amulets. He fancies the challenge of slipping past both *Aelvae* and Sorcerers in order to score his quarry.

Sonnia of Frantillia Second child and only daughter of a successful merchant; outrageously spoiled. Sea life was her major interest until she was recruited to become a Sorceress at the *Ludia*. She is of average height and typically wears her waist-length brown hair in a braid, but her brilliant smile is judged her best feature. If she has any faults, it may be her ambition and undue attention to classist positions. Against all reason, she may favor **Rolland** of Fountaindale.

Sophia Mistress of Brightfield Manor, wife to **Astonius** and mother of **Anders**, her only child. She is known for her superb business acumen.

Spadix *Rex Blattarum,* King of Moths, life-mate of **Caerulea**, *Regina Papilionum,* Queen of Butterflies. A Great Brown Moth, he is always addressed as "My Lord **Spadix**." He is particularly jealous of his wife's interest in others. His moth dust is said to have certain special properties.

Stooks Pimple-afflicted adolescent member of **Faran's** Falcons of the Young Thieves' Guild, Fountaindale, under the leadership of **Faran's** lieutenant, **Sagar**. Recently recruited by **Solon** to accost fellow thief, **Rolland**, and companions.

T

Tertius Third of three tutors engaged by **Sophia** and **Astonius** of Brightfield Manor to educate their only child, **Anders**. Later dismissed following a reputed difficulty with the cook. He is sanguine in nature.

Thaddeus of Beewicke Only child of **Cedric** and **Hycynthya**. He is apprenticed to **Silvestrus** of the *Collegium Sorcerorum*. He is identified with the cardinal point *Septentrio*—(North)—of the Great Compass. Rumors abound regarding possible relationships with **Ethne** of Tarandon, **Caerulea**, *Regina Papilionium*, **Mari**, *Regina Draconum Marinarum*, and **Luperca**, Minor Canine Diety. However, may favor **Marsia** of Dorset Downs.

Tyrannus Superbus *Imperator Ultimus,* the last Emperor of the Westlands, reigning from the imperial capital at Fornia, who, one thousand years in the past, led a million-man army consisting of ninety-nine Imperial Legions at full strength in the Invasion of the Cin of the East. The campaign, however, proved a disaster, ending in the total annihilation of the invading force by the Cin's employment of their Ancient Ones—skilled users of Magicks—thought to have been aided and abetted by Daemon-kind. Two of the very few survivors of the entire campaign later vouchsafed under oath that at the conclusion of the final battle, they witnessed the still-living Emperor and his son being led off by the enemy.

W

Wy-Jinge Cinnian Ancient One, contemporaneous with **Silvestrus** of Somerset. Six years prior to the advent of **Thaddeus** of Beewicke at the *Collegium Sorcerorum,* he announced he, from some source, had been sent a compelling dream in which four ladies (who some suggest were the *Intelligentiae*) indicated that he and his apprentice, **Tai-Pown,** must travel west —an unheard-of quest for the Cin. Skeptics in the Cinnian Court suggest that his quest was, in actuality, a spy mission mandated by His Imperial Majesty for his own, unrevealed, purposes.

Z

Zoarr of Mauretesia, seventh, and only surviving, son of **Zauda**, House of Abdomoolano, King of Mauretesia. He is apprenticed to Master **Silvestrus** of the *Collegium Sorcerorum,* recruited one year earlier than the typical age as a result of regional political considerations. He is the third of the three Brothers to **Thaddeus** of Beewicke. He is the cardinal point—*Meridies* (South)—of the Great Compass. May favor **Molly-O-the-Willows**.

Glossary
Lingua Imperatoria

A

Ab – from

Abitus – departure; of a departure

Academiae – of the school, of the institution

Acini – of a grape

Ad – coming to; arriving at

Administer – manager

Adrogantia – hubris; nerve; chutzpah

Advenae – newcomers; those just beginning study

Advenarum – of, or pertaining to, those beginning the year

Adversa – bad; unfortunate; adverse

Aelvae – largest of the *Faerrae*; bold warriors, archers, without peer, excellent in sport

Aequinoctia – either of the two points on the celestial sphere where the celestial equator intersects the ecliptic; or either of the two times each year (as about March 21 and September 23) when the sun crosses the equator and day and night are everywhere on earth of approximately equal length.

Aequinoctium – equinox

Aestate – summer; in summer

Alvis – from the bowels

Amazones – female warriors

Amici – friends

Amicus – male friend

Amores – affairs of the heart

Amplior – superior, larger

Anicula – old woman

Anima – breath

Anni – of the year

Anno – in the year of

Antiqua – old

Apiarius – beekeeper

Aprilis – fourth month of the year

Aquila – eagle

Aquilo – North wind

Arbiter – referee, judge

Arbor – tree

Arborea – pertaining to a tree

Arcanum – secret

Argutiae – wit

Arx – arc; range

Ascende – ascend; rise

Atrium – hall

Auferre – take away

Auster – South wind

Autumnale – autumnal; pertaining to the fall

Ave – hello; goodbye; hail

B

Balustradae – siege engines, hurtling large arrows as a ballista.

Bellis – pretty

Bellona – Sister to Mars the God of War. Also, Mars-sized body striking Earth early in its history leading to the formation of the Moon (*Luna*)

Blattarum – of the moths

Brevis – short

Bruma – winter solstice

C

Caeca – blind

Caelum – heaven

Caeruleus – blue

Calcitra – kick

Caninum – pertaining to dogs

Canis – dog

Cantare – singing

Canum – of dogs

Caput – head

Cardines – cardinal, or major points of the compass (NESW)

Cardinis – cardinal, or major point of the compass (NESW)

Castra – encampment; camp

Castratus – castrated one

Caupona – inn

Centurio – centurion; a position in the Imperial army during classical antiquity; nominally the commander of a century (a military unit of 100 legionaries). In an Imperial legion, ten centuries were grouped into a cohort, with ten cohorts making up the Legion. The prestigious first cohort was led by the *Primus Pilus,* a senior centurion, while all centurions were led, in turn, by the *Centurio Prior,* the most senior centurion of the Legion.

Cerealis – eighth month of year

Cibus – food

Cincinni – curls

Circuitus – circular instrument as a compass; a compass

Circulus – of a circle; circular

Cogitatio – cognition; thinking process

Collegii – of a college

Collegio – college

Collegium – institution of higher learning for boys

Cometae – comet; of the comet

Commercium – commerce

Commuta – transform

Concidit – give up; surrender; deny

Condicio – proposal

Conloqui – talking; speaking

Conloquium – negotiation

Contrahe – shrink in size

Conventus – convent

Convivium – feast

Coquere – cooking

Coronifer – slave holding wreath over the head of the Triumphant, while repeating a formulaic warning against over-weaning pride and the transience of glory in her/his ear

Cortina – cauldron

Creationis – of creation

Cultri – knives; cutlery

Cum – with

Custos – gatekeeper; guard

D

Daemon – Daemon

Daemonis – of a Daemon

Debellatum – concluded war, contest

Decem – ten; tens

Defundat – may it pour forth

Destrue – destroy!

Dicit – speaks

Diem – day

Dies – day

Discere – learning to

Dissimulator – camouflage artist

Dolorosa – of sorrow

Dolorosus – pain

Domina – lady; house-mistress

Dominus – head man; boss

Domo – going away from, or leaving home

Dormi – sleep

Draco – dragon

Dracones – dragons

Draconis – of dragon or dragons

Duodecem – dozen

Duri – hard

E

Epulae – foods

Erroris – of error

Est – it, she or he is; it occurs, happens

Et – and

Eum – it; him

Eurus – East wind

Ex – from

Extende – expand in size

Extincte – extinct

Exitus – consequence

F

Facere – making

Facite – make; restore

Factum – making; rendering

Faerrae – one of the major orders of Fey. The *Faerrae* are divided into *Pixae, Spritae,* and *Aelvae* by among other things, increasing size

Faerrarum – of the *Faerrae*

Fatuus – fool

Faunus – non-human sentient animal, often caprine in form; faun

Februarius – second month of the year

Ferias – holidays

Festivus – festival

Fiat – let it become; make it so; let there be

Fides – a belief; faith

Florum – of flowers

Forfices – scissors

Fortuna – luck; fortune

Fur – thief

Furiae – the Furies

Furis – of the thief

Furum – of thieves

G

Gens – nation; kind; grouping

Globi – balls

Globulus – globe; sphere

H

Heus – hark! listen!

Homo – man

Hominum – of men

I

Ianuam – doorway

Ianuario – of January

Ianuarius – first month of year

Igenium – genius

Ignave – coward

Ignesce – ignite

Ignis – fire

Illos – them

Imitatrix – mimic

Impeditus – thwarted; thwarted one

Imperator – emperor

Imperatoria – Imperial

Imperatus – of those commanded, of the Empire

Imperii – of the Empire

Imperium – Empire

Impetus – attack

In – in; at

Incendat – let it catch fire

Incipe – start; begin

Incipere – starting

Indigenae – those already present at their study; those of the second, third or fourth years at a school

Inferni – inhabitants of an infernal region

Inflationis – flatus

Inflatus – inflated

Ingenia – cleverness

Ingenium – spirit of

Initio – the beginning

Initium – the beginning

Inquisitio – quest

Insanus – insane; mad

Insignia – insignia

Intelligentiae – mindful ones

Intellegis – do you understand?

Inter-Imperium – period between Empires; interregnum

Inverte – turn inside out

Invicti – victorious

Invictus – invincible

Iovis – Jove, King of Gods

Iovius – seventh month of the year

Iter – journey

Iudcare – to judge

Iudex – judge

Iudicare – to judge the status of

Iudicium – judgment

Iunii – of the sixth month

Iunio – in the sixth month

Iunius – sixth month of the year

Iusti – high; just

L

Lapidum – of the stones

Lapis – stone

Latrina – toilet

Lavatio – washing

Leavus – left-handed

Legatum – bequest; legacy

Legere – read

Leges – law

Legio – legion

Leopardinus – of the leopard

Lepidopterae – members of an order of insects that includes both butter-flies and moths

Lex – law

Liberate – be free of bonds; restraint

Librum – book

Ligate – bind

Limine – threshold

Lingua – language

Litterae – letters

Litterati – literate ones

Locus – place; place of

Luctator – fighter using no weapons other than hands and feet

Ludere – play

Ludi – game

Ludia – institution of higher learning for girls

Ludos – classes

Luna – the moon

Lunares – men of the moon

Lunaris – man of the moon

Luporum – of wolves

Lyceum – oldest, most traditional and prestigious preparatory academy in Fornia

M

Magister – master; expert; head person

Magna – great

Magni – great

Magnus – great

Maio – of May

Maius – fifth month of the year

Manes – ghost; undead

Maritima – of the sea; marine

Martius – third month of the year

Mater – mother

Materna – mother's

Mathematicarum – of mathematics; mathematical

Matris – of the mother

Maximi – greatest ones

Mea – my

Media – mid

Medice – physician

Medici – of the physician

Mehercle – exclamation: 'By Hercules!'

Mel – honey

Mellum – honey

Membrum – member

Memento – remember

Mense – in the month

Meridianus – meridian

Meretrix – female pleasure worker

Meridies – South

Mille – thousand

Millibus – distant by a thousand paces

Minimi – least ones

Minor – minor

Mitra – religious headwear

Monumentum – monument

Montium – of mountains

Mores – morals

Mori – to die; to be mortal

Mortui – dead

Mundana – world

N

Nasus – nose

Naturae – of nature

Neglegere – breaking

Neptunius – tenth month of the year

Nivei – snow

Nihil – nothing

Nova – new

Nox – night; night's eve

Numeri – of number; numbers

Nuptiae – of marriage

O

Obliviscatur – forget

Occasus – downfall

Occidus – the west

Octipes – eight-footed; eight-pointed

Omnino – wholly; entirely

Oratio – speech

Orbis – ring

Ordines – ordinal, minor points on the compass (NE, NW, SE, SW)

Ordinis – ordinal, or minor point of the compass (NE, NW, SE, SW)

Oriens – east

Orientalis – eastern

Orientalium – of Easterners

Orientem – of, or pertaining to the East

P

Palla – religious mantle, robe; official outerwear

Papiliones – butterflies

Papilionum – of the butterflies

Papyrus – paper

Parare – to prepare; preparing

Parthorum – of the Parthians

Passus – of paces

Patefacta – yielded up; given up; surrendered

Pax – peace

Pendentium – of those hanging

Per – through

Perditi – lost; perished

Peregrinus – foreign; stranger

Perennis – everlasting

Philologe – Scholar

Physica – female scientist; biologist

Pila – ball

Pilae – balls

Piscatorum – of the fish

Pistoris – of a baker

Pixae – smallest of the *Faerrae*; frequent pollinators, fond of gyre and gimble

Plutonius – eleventh month of the year

Populusque – of the people

Potestatem – power

Praeceptor – preceptor; teacher, instructor

Prave – depraved one

Prima – main; primary

Primus – primary

Princeps – leader, chief, dean

Prior – first, chief, highest

Procax – bully

Prodi – go; get going; giddy-up

Prolatus – offer

Protervus – imp

Providentia – foresight

Prudens – rational

Puella – girl

Puellae – girls; dolls

Pueri – boys

Pueros – children

Pugil – boxer

Pugna – fighting

Pugnare – fighting

Pulchella – pretty; beautiful

Pulicium – of fleas

Pumilus – dwarf

Purgata – cleansing

Pustula – pimple

Q

Qua – which; that

Quaesitor – inquisitor

Quaestor – official

Quartus – fourth one

Quercus – oak

R

Recludite – open

Regina – Queen

Regulos – rules

Rerum – of matters

Residuae – those things left over after some occurrence or procedure

Respica – look behind

Restitutum – restoration; restored

Reverte – return to previous state

Rex – king

Ruber – red

Rumpite – swell to bursting

S

Saccularii – of the pickpockets

Sacra – holy

Sacrum – holy

Sana – sane

Sanguis – blood

Sanum – healthy

Sapientia – wisdom

Sapo – soap

Saturnalia – annual farewell old year; welcome new year festival

Saturnius – twelfth month of the year

Saxum – rock

Secundi – those in the second year of study

Semper – always

Senatus – the Senate; governmental ruling body

Senex – old; old man

Septentrio – morth

Septentrionum – of, or pertaining to north

Sepulchri – tombstone

Sepultura – burial

Sidera – planets

Silentii – of silence

Sine – without

Sint – let there be

Sis – may you be

Sit – let it be

Solares – men of the sun

Solaris – man of the sun

Solitarius – hermit

Solsti – the two occasions in a year when the Sun appears to reach its most northerly or southerly excursion relative to the celestial equator on the celestial sphere.

Solstitum – summer solstice

Somnia – dreams

Sorcerorum – of, or pertaining to sorcerers

Sordida – outdoor; trail; rough; common

Sorores – sisters

Spadix – brown

Speculum – mirror

Specus – cave

Sphaerae – balls; spheres

Spiritus – spirit

Spritae – midsized *Faerrae*; sought to accomplish tasks, fetch items

Spumo – foam at the mouth, as with soap

Stadia – multiple units of measurement of 125 paces in length

Statim – immediately

Statius – statues

Stercus – feces

Stola – woman's gown

Sub – under; preceding

Subtercollem – under hill

Sudarium – traditionally, a small cloth of fine material, often scented, secreted by a lady in her bodice for various purposes

Supremi – those in the fourth, final year of study; the most advanced of a group

Supremorum – of those in the last year of study

Supremus – one in the fourth or final year of study

T

Tace – silence; be silent

Tauri – of the bull

Te – you

Terra – land

Tertii – those in the third year
of study

Tertius – third one

Tirones – recruits; those in the first
year of study

Tironis – recruit; in the first year of
study

Tres – three

Turre – tower

Turris – tower

U

Ultimus – last; final

Uranius – ninth month of
the year

V

Vale – salutation and valediction;
hale and farewell; hello, goodbye

Vanitas – vanity

Veni – (to one person) come

Venite – (to more than one) come

Venereus – of Venus; love

Vermes – worms

Vernum – spring

Vesanus – madman

Vesica – bladder

Vespertiliolis – little bat

Vestimenta – clothes

Via – road

Vicerunt – they have won

Vigilanti – vigilance

Vinarii – of the vintner

Vincite – entangle

Vires – power

Virgines – virgins

Viridis – green

Vites – vines

Volans – flying one

Z

Zephyrus – west wind

Discussion Questions for
Book 1: Thaddeus of Beewicke

Book Club Leaders ... contact Louis to participate in a special meeting to discuss the book; the concepts; and the evolution of the series. In-person gatherings are possible if you are in the Midwest and Louis is available. Otherwise, Zoom is always an option.

1. The Master Magician, Silvestrus, contacts Thaddeus' family to procure its support in allowing him to take Thaddeus to The College of Sorcerers. When the family resists, he employs sorcerous powers to get his way. What are the ethics of Silvestrus' enchanting the family so that he may take Thaddeus with him?

2. Marriage commonly occurs in the early teens in this alternate 10th century world. Even so, what ethical Prophecy would enlist young teens as a means of its fulfillment? Is it abuse? Is saving the world a justifiable excuse?

3. As Thaddeus comes into his own, what traits and behaviors must he acquire to successfully challenge his elders? What of the risks?

4. The key to Sorcery is the power of Belief. In what ways can this Belief" be reinforced or supported?

5. Asullus, the mule, is both sentient and verbal. Mules are invariably infertile. How, then, is he able to successfully romance the unsuspecting? How does this compare to his Master's behavior?

6. Thaddeus is an unsophisticated, backwoods boy when recruited. His new friends, however, come from vastly different backgrounds, yet over time they become Brothers. How do the challenges they face together create the bonds that are formed between them?

7. From his early years onward, Thaddeus has always yearned for a deep and lasting lifetime relationship. It seems that the Prophecy coldly dictates his seduction. How can his desire find fulfillment in the face of the Prophecy's demands?

8. A twisted Tree Demon offers a spurned Sorcerous invincibility and immortality in exchange for the lives of her children. Does the cost justify the price?

9. The Chief of Cinnian Assassins has vowed to his Emperor that Thaddeus and his Brothers will never reach the College alive. With their Master absent, how can mere Apprentices hope to survive such an attack?

10. How much must Thaddeus sacrifice to achieve what his Master implies is his Destiny? If he had refused the Old Sorcerer's proposition, would Thaddeus' life have been better? Happier? Longer?

Contact Louis for Book Clubs, Author visits,
or with general questions at:
414-248-0427
AuthorLouisSauvain@gmail.com
Protinus Press
Mailbox 225
3900 W Brown Deer Road – Suite A
Milwaukee, WI 53209

Meet Louis Sauvain

sing my background in health care, I have always been interested in how people employ fantasy to escape their current circumstances; and sometimes, their pain. Before turning to writing full-time, I knew that such a distraction could help create an ability to tolerate what might be momentarily unbearable.

As retirement loomed, there was finally time available to free creative juices that allowed my fingers to flow, creating characters and scenes unfolding what I hoped would become epic stories. And as they flowed, the characters spoke up, guiding how they would respond when scenarios were created. The muse on my shoulder took the form of my high school English teacher who pushed me with her trusty red pencil and supported my creativity and love of words.

Now, writing epic fantasy, my books have become an allaying salve for pain, relief and escapism to abandon, for the moment, this world and embrace, for a time, another. Sometimes it's for myself…and always for those who are just looking for a worthwhile read.

Born and bred in the Midwest, I call Wisconsin home. My reveal: Most of my ideas come in the shower when I ask my characters, "Okay, where are you going to take me today?"

My challenge becomes…how to bring YOU…my readers…along so that you, too, can enjoy my path to completing each book's storyline. To me, that's gold.

—Louis Sauvain

How to Work with Louis Sauvain

Author Louis Sauvain is not only a gifted storyteller, but also a witty and fun speaker. Bring him to your organization either in-person or Zoom.

For Book Clubs, use his Discussion Questions as a starting point found within the Book tab on his website: www.AuthorLouisSauvain. com. Or, query your members and let them do the asking, sending him the questions their inquiring minds want answers to.

For Libraries, with over 80% of the population believing that they have a book in them, Louis would be delighted to lead a discussion on any of his books—their creation: the storyline; and his unique writing process; the process of creating a multiple book series; writing fantasy —either general or epic; and how to create a fantasy world.

For Authors and Writers, Louis would be available to lead a discussion on writing fantasy—either general or epic; how to make a "mark" for the world of book marketing strategy; and when to use a PEN name.

To check his availability, contact him through his website or directly:

414-248-0427

AuthorLouisSauvain@gmail.com

Protinus Press

Mailbox 225

3900 W Brown Deer Road – Suite A

Milwaukee, WI 53209

Follow him on:

 @LouisSauvain

 Instagram.com/LouisSauvain

Facebook.comn/LouisSauvain

THADDEUS AND THE MASTER – BOOK TWO
AVAILABLE WINTER 2022

Coming to the College of Sorcery following a harrowing escape, Silvestrus of Somerset's first apprentice Thaddeus must now bond with his Brothers to discover an evil Master's treachery before the traitor and his Daemon mentor can destroy the world they know.

Will he succeed in securing the Scholar, the Thief and the Prince to his cause despite their mutual distrust of each other?

Will the women of the Ludia choose to side with the young Sorcerers in their moment of dire peril?

Will the Golden Pack Leader reveal her true identity in time to thwart the approaching Goblin Horde?

Thaddeus and the Daemon – book three

available Summer 2023

Can a Sorcerer break his Oath-bond to his Brotherhood and shed the very dominance that made him the First in Strength? If he surrenders his Power will he then become vulnerable to that same Power?

Thaddeus must now face the wrath of the twisted Master and the Daemon Morag with only the help of a long-dead Spirit to aid him in his struggle.

Will he succeed in summoning his Brothers and Sisters before all are turned to stone?

Will the warnings of his Master and Asullus the Mule come in time to divert this great tragedy?

Will he seek rebirth from the Ancient Ones of the East? And, at what price?

Next from Louis Sauvain …

Collegium Sorcerorum 2nd Trilogy

Volume IV: Thaddeus and the Ancient One

Volume V: Thaddeus and the Emperor

Volume VI: Thaddeus the Faithless

available winter 2024